ARC OF A DIVER

a biographical novel

Mark Woytowich

ISBN 979-8-218-43015-3

Cover design by: Linda Woytowich
Library of Congress Control Number: 2018675309
Printed in the United States of America

To all among us who have seriously considered taking their own lives and to those leaving this life by their own hand, may this humble offering bring grace.

ARC OF A DIVER

By
Mark Woytowich

PART ONE

THE LONG WAY OUT

The greatest discovery in our generation is that human beings, by changing the inner attitudes of their minds can change the outer aspects of their lives.

WILLIAM JAMES

As he thinketh in his heart, so is he.

PROVERBS 23:7

If the summer changed to winter, yours is no disgrace

THE YES ALBUM

PROLOGUE

A tour of sound:

The billiard balls when they're dumped on the table. The smack! when someone breaks the rack. The rolling, whizzing sound as a hard-hit ball spirals down a leather pocket.

The steady clacking of a ping pong game, precise as a metronome.

TV voices trailing from the lounge, twisting through the halls, garbling, echoing so that by the time they reach your ears they're saying something different. Saying something you don't want to hear.

The showers hissing at night. Voices echoing off the tiles. Someone's flip flops slapping against the bottom of his feet.

A toilet flushes like a monster clearing its throat. The shuddering sound when someone hops on the scale in the examining room. The sound of the weight being slid on the bar.

The rumble of the clothes dryer in the utility room. The bell for meals. Chairs sliding in the cafeteria. Hands stirring the silverware in the colanders. The ice machine spitting cubes into a glass.

The sound of a nurse snapping shut her charts. The Christmas-like jingle of the medication keys. The electric door locks buzzing like the wrong answer on a game show. The pay phone slamming. A checker game being turned over. Someone shouting. Someone punching the wall. Someone screaming in the quiet room, bashing against the door.

There's only one sound I don't like and that's the broken piano. Almost all the keys are dead and what notes it still plays are stilted and warped, like music from bones.

There's something about a new patient arriving on the ward, especially when they're committed here. They wear that fragile, protective look on their faces. At first they act oblivious to their surroundings, dressed up as though on their way to church. They won't admit it yet that this is their new home. To postpone the shock of that realization, they see the piano and think, "Great. Here's a place where I can ignore all this stuff. As long as I can play I can keep dreaming."

Poor losers. The dream crashes the moment they strike those first mutant keys. The piano becomes an instant reflection, a broken reminder of how badly things must have gone in order for them to be here. It's instant therapy. Hell, most people cry right on the spot.

CHAPTER 1

As I recall, the living room couch was perfect for dying. Simply perfect. It was the best piece of furniture in her house, firm yet cushy, and offered a commanding view of the different people scuttling to and from the other rooms: Joni, my bullet-headed sister, Courtney and Jennifer, her two frightened little girls, and Rowena, the Thursday housekeeper who was getting dismissed early because I was engaging her mercilessly in a discussion of Jehovah's Witnesses.

"So, are you one of the chosen, Rowena?" I called out as she walked through the arched doorway. "Don't answer if you don't want to," I said. "I wouldn't want you losing your place in heaven's line simply because you gave away the big secret to a pagan like me."

Rowena, a tall, dark-skinned woman who always managed to look immaculate in a freshly pressed cotton dress as she swept and scrubbed from room to room, sighed before looking in my direction.

"There's no 'big secret' out there, Mr. Wolyczin. God knows everything and is gonna reveal everything in His own good time."

Rowena's hands traveled down the collar of her blue dress, crossing over her heart, where they rested. She sighed again, picking up her purse from the table.

"If God knows everything," I said, "then God knows all about those Mormons and that nasty wife swapping. Nasty stuff. Or lucky bastards, depending on your point of view.

Either way I suppose it beats gambling and drinking soda with caffeine." I adjusted the pillow behind my back. "In fact," I said, "the big secret is that, when the kingdom comes, God is going to put you Witnesses in charge of the whole fucking planet. Won't that be something? It certainly would make *me* want to join. In fact, I have it from the holy ghost himself that after Armageddon's done and over, the Mormons will come in to clean up *your* houses."

Rowena leveled a smoldering glance in my direction. "I'm gonna pray for you," she said, opening her purse and pulling out a rigid, white paper tissue.

"You do that," I said. "You go on and pray. But I want to know something first. Exactly how many of you are going to heaven? How many are getting through the tribulation? A hundred and forty-four thousand, isn't it? Something like that. Boy, talk about being on your best behavior."

Rowena said nothing and turned away.

"Pray for me real hard, Rowena," I called out. "Pray I see the light and join the one-forty-four club. Then I can hand over my ten percent so maybe your missionaries will wear yellow ties once in a while. A damn good cause if there ever was one."

Rowena stepped out of sight into the hallway. I heard the snap of her purse and her thanking my sister for something, then my sister apologizing once again for the miserable afternoon it had become.

"It hasn't been so bad for me," Rowena said. "It's someone else's trouble now. Lord have mercy on you both."

"Thank you," Joni said. "You've been most helpful."

"I'll call tomorrow to see how he is."

"Don't bother," I yelled, raising on one elbow. "Dial 6-6-6, Rowena. That's the devil's hotline. You get time, temperature, and days left to the end of the world."

Courtney, my younger niece, started crying again in the bedroom. Hurriedly Joni said goodbye to Rowena, excusing herself to shut the bedroom door. Rowena passed by once more, and I heard the hydraulic whine of the screen door opening and her heels clacking up the steps to the street. I had a good mind to turn around so I could catch a street-level glimpse of whatever thighs Rowena sported under her loose summer dress. But no sooner had I adjusted myself for a beaver broadside than my sister came in, walking slowly, wiping flour off her hands with a damp dish towel. She cocked her head as she looked down at me, a wry smile stitched across her lips. Her big blond curls, sagging from the humid weather, dangled off to one side.

"You know," she said, drying her hands on the red apron around her waist, "no one dies from getting too much help, Mark."

For the past two hours we had been talking about help. Help for the poor, help for the needy, help for the mentally deranged. It all started with Joni wanting to help me. That very morning she had called and talked me into stepping outside of my apartment in Manhattan for the first time in four days. She knew I was out of food and not sleeping again. Plus I was driving my neighbors nuts by singing and chanting all night long. The guy downstairs was probably sweeping up plaster from poking his broom against the ceiling and yelling all night for me to shut the fuck up. He swore to break my jaw if he ever caught me in the elevator. But I had three locks on my door and a sawed-off baseball bat with two dozen nails sticking out of the end. Nevertheless, Joni convinced me not to hold up in a fortress, waiting for the rescue squad, but to get out among friends as soon as possible. Over the phone she persuaded me to pack a few things in a small suitcase and take the subway to her place in Brooklyn Heights.

I snuck down the stairs from my apartment, hopped an A train, and soon found myself on the street outside her home. Near the black iron gate above the basement steps lay a crumpled figure on his side, a man we called Wilkie. Oliver Wilkins was an old, toothless, piss-stained drunk who was as much a part of the neighborhood a shoe-flat dog shit and the nightly wail of BMW alarms. Basically, he was a pile of rags that rolled up and down Willow Street, often plopping next door to my sister's place where he would cough and ramble his verses and curses—a slurry monotone that everyone in the neighborhood learned to ignore, like a radio news program turned way down. His smell, though, was much more intrusive, perfuming the area like garbage ripening from a five-week strike. The most interesting thing about this man— beside the fact that, like a migrating bird, he disappeared every year during the cold winter months—was that he supposedly was heir to the Wilkins Razor fortune. However, the money reportedly got into the hands of his evil twin sister, who gave it all to the Jehovah Witnesses.

As anyone who knows anything about Brooklyn Heights can tell you, the World Center for the Jehovah Witnesses sprawls throughout this upper-class neighborhood like brushfire smoke curls through trees. The Witnesses have been gobbling up the Heights, year after year, block after block. You can see the giant clock of the Watchtower Building from most any point on lower Manhattan. Next door to my sister's brownstone rose one of their dormitory and office complexes, this one seven stories high, the windows of which look down into her backyard garden. On the seventh floor the lights stay on all night, and sometimes you can see shadows moving against the curtains. I always imagined that that was where the magazines *Awake!* and *Watchtower* were concocted, where scripture was reviewed and reinterpreted, then set into type —every story providing one more reason for why the world was ending soon. I imagined that no more than a few feet of concrete wall separated my sister and her family from the place where Truth itself was manufactured, where God's Own Word was embellished with illustrations of Him, mighty Jehovah, drawn with the exactitude of a child's coloring book.

Concerning old man Wilkie, however, and how he, I, and the Jehovah Witnesses all intersected one summer afternoon, it was Wilkie's penchant to sleep on the sidewalk in front of the dorms next door, where he'd taunt the Witnesses every morning as they stepped over him on their way to work. Every morning they streamed out like ants. And every morning Wilkie played the ant eater, doubled up on his side, taking swipes at them, pawing the air, cursing and reeking and wetting his pants.

He was next door when I arrived around noon, my hand-me-down suitcase stuffed with clothes, I thought, for a weekend in the Hamptons. Wilkie half-sat against the wall, and I noticed his khaki green pant legs rolled up to mid-calf where his ankles, purple and swollen, looked like bloated beets above his newspaper-stuffed shoes. The skin above his ankles was scaly and reminded me of whittled wood or alligator hide. As I walked past, he swiped his hand at a phantom insect and mumbled some guttural reference to his family and how they left poor Wilkie out in the cold.

"What are you talking about?" I said, setting my suitcase on the sidewalk by his feet. "It's the middle of July, asshole. No one's going cold around here."

Wilkie sat up and looked at me, his hand shading his eyes and his eyes trying to scrutinize my features through their alcoholic glaze. His gray hair was a gnarly nest containing bits of paper, twigs, and seeds blown off of trees. It split off into a thousand directions, stiff little spikes that looked as though they had been dipped in spit and dried. Sticking out of the crown of his head was either a furry caterpillar or a cigarette filter with the paper torn off. His eyes were set deep in their sockets, and his face was the color of battleship gray. His beard, though not as long or thick as Abraham Lincoln's, had that uneven, flecked appearance, another shaggy, gray nest with peppercorns or God knows what other tiny black creatures tangled in there. His whiskers reminded me of the waste basket in my mother's laundry room, where she'd drop the lint trimmings from the dryer. Dried purple wine or maybe vomit streaked the port side of his beard.

I dared to poke the toe of my shoe against the worn-out sole of his.

"Who's that?" he asked, shielding his eyes.

"I've got a million dollars that says you can't whistle dixie, old man. I bet you can't whistle or piss standing up."

"Whose side are *you* on?" he asked.

"To be honest with you, I don't know these days," I said. "It changes every five minutes. Just when I think I've got the license number, the goddam car speeds away."

I looked up at the dormitory and felt something like a spring tightening in my belly; a storm had been brewing, an incredible conflict stirring inside me for years. Like Wilkie, I hated the Witnesses, hated Catholics, Mormons, Moonies— anyone who demanded obedience as a condition for heaven. I hated them all. They had all the right answers, of course, because they needed to keep the show going.

No doubt that somewhere in the honeycombs of Jehovah Witness Land, perhaps in the very building I was looking at, lay a pamphlet entitled, "Confusion: The Answers You Need," and it would contain the exact scriptural passages required to deliver me from my madness, from the sense that I was at odds with what everyone else in the world was willing to settle for. On the cover of the pamphlet there'd be a wondrous ink illustration of a confused man climbing a staircase to heaven, above him rays of light breaking from the clouds like a WWII Japanese flag. Old Father God would be up there like Santa in His nightshirt, His ribbon of a beard and His great, guiding Hand.

I wanted a savior so badly, but I didn't want a savior who collected membership dues.

In fact, as I stood before Wilkie and pondered his question as to whose side I was on, I recognized my need for the Sacrament of Confession. Raised a Catholic and away from mass for years, I felt a terrible urge—a panic almost—to get my slate wiped clean, to find a balance between all the good and bad in me, especially with the strange feelings I had been having lately. I felt as though the middle ground—all the gray —had been sucked out of the world and that things were going to go only one of two ways: towards Apocalypse or salvation. It seemed as though the world's destiny was being played out in my mind like a chessboard, the primal forces of good and evil battling inside of me. At times I felt allied with evil. But five minutes later I'd be Christ on His cross. I needed Confession because Confession would prepare me for the ultimate end, no matter which end it was.

I stooped down in front of Wilkie, resting my haunches on my heels. I ignored his outhouse odor and extended my hand for him to shake. "You think they're ready for the antichrist?" I said, nodding in the direction of the dorms.

"Antichrist, hell," he said, "they couldn't've made it this far without stealing ol' Wilkie's money. Bunch of antichrists themselves. C'mon, fella, help me out, won't ya?"

Wilkie snatched my hand in a surprisingly firm grip and pulled me toward his face. The vomit smell was like buttermilk and dead fish.

"Help me out," he said. "All I need's a quarter."

Repulsed by his smell, I recoiled as though receiving a shock from an electrical appliance. I regained my balance and pulled free from his grip.

"You're a sorry thing," I said, brushing off my hands and snatching up my suitcase.

Suddenly, as I stepped back from the building, wondering again what kind of lies were printed on Jehovah Witness paper stock—suddenly I flushed with the urge to . . . well, dance. Dance. Click my heels with joy as the idea of paying a visit to my local Kingdom Hall shot through my brain. It would be delightful, I thought, to get in a little Confession before I stopped by my sister's. It wouldn't be Catholic, of course. No darkness and whispers and first names only. But that would make it better still, make it something to remember. I walked down Willow Street and into the Kingdom Hall building. Setting my suitcase by the door I entered a large, dark marble and oak lobby and interrupted a cluster of heavyset men in gray suits with black Bibles in their hands. There were five of them, each with a navy blue tie that cascaded over a tight white shirt hugging their plump bellies. Thinking nothing of how I looked or what I was doing (I hadn't showered, shaved, or changed clothing in four days, though I reasoned this didn't matter because Jehovah Witnesses barged into homes all across the country) I picked out a young man with very short, blond hair and asked him if he were ready to witness to me.

Just like that, I said it. "I need you to witness to me," I said.

The group fell hushed, each of the other men stepping back from the one I had selected until he and I were in a little group of our own. His face showed surprise, discomfort, dismay. His eyes focused on everything but mine, roving among the expressions of his backpedaling friends, a silent plea, I believe, for one of them to volunteer in his place.

"You *are* a Jehovah Witness, aren't you?" I said. I was now aware of many people holding still, watching us. Whereas before there had been that rumble of voices so appropriate to marble lobbies, suddenly the din evaporated as though above us someone had popped off an airtight lid. An elevator went ding! and its doors whooshed open. Two women stepped out and held instinctually still.

"Can't I get a Witness? What's wrong with you?" I said. "Don't you see how important this is?"

The man nodded reluctantly, his face forcing a smile as he loosened the knot in his tie. Again he looked to his companions for assurance. A tiny bead of sweat appeared at his left sideburn and slowly trickled down the side of his face.

"I might be able to help you," the man said. "My name's Bill."

"Good," I said. "I want to talk to you, Bill. I have some important information about the end of the world." I put out my hand for him to shake. "My name's Mark. I live right next door." I gave him the number on Willow. "Come on over as soon as you can," I said, grinning. "Hell, you guys can practically tunnel through the wall."

As a matter of fact, I had heard them often on the other

side of the wall. In the subbasement. It was the machinery of Truth. It whirred and groaned and clanked like something part-Panzer tank, part-food blender, part-chains, part-keys. I was afraid the thing, whatever it was, would come loose from its bolts and moldings and break down our wall.

Bill agreed to see me in an hour.

"Hurry up," I said. "The end is coming sooner than you think."

Finished, I turned and left the Kingdom Hall for my sister's, completely unprepared for what Wilkie had in store. I was surprised as hell just to see him stand. But stand he did, and quickly, too, not giving me any clue that he was fixing to take a punch at me. He swung and missed, but his motion carried him forward in an awkward lunge, his arms finding me and pulling me to the pavement. Concrete greeting! I whacked my head on unyielding stone. My torso landed on its left side, my ribs sandwiching my suitcase against the pavement and the shock transferring straight through. The latches sprung open. My ears rang with a pain that forced my eyes to squint, tears pumping from behind them. With one lopsided tackle, old wino Wilkie had knocked the wind out of me.

I pushed back on his arms but they were locked tightly around my waist. He began crawling on top of me, wiggling, climbing me like a bull seal mounting one of his harem, his hideous face exhaling his poisons, flecks of dirt and vomit falling from his beard to my chest. The top of his head was grinding toward my chin.

I couldn't think of what to do so I called for my sister. I didn't want to strike the old man because he might be an agent of Jehovah, someone chosen by God to draw my attention.

"Joni!" I yelled. Twice I called her name.

Joni came out and helped pull Wilkie off me. "Don't hit him," she said, breathing hard and dodging his wayward punches. "He doesn't know what he's doing." She grabbed his jacket from behind his neck and pulled him along the sidewalk like a heavy sack of mail.

I kicked free and rolled the other way. A large crowd was standing around, Witnesses in the truest sense of the word, most of them with polite, sympathetic expressions. I thought I recognized a few of them from the Kingdom Hall lobby.

My sister grabbed my suitcase, stuffing my clothes back in, and steered me inside her front door. I went downstairs and lay on the couch and let her take my shoes off—and that's where I remained for the next couple of hours, taunting Rowena until she asked to be dismissed.

During the time I was being so nasty with her housekeeper, Joni decided it would be an excellent opportunity for baking cookies. Several times she came in the living room and asked me if I wanted to join her. "No thanks," I said, quite content with her couch being my confessional, and perhaps my deathbed as well. I was sure once Bill arrived that he would hear me out, pass on some advice, and then let me know one way or the other if my name was written in the Book of Life. I doubted that it was. Being tired of all the running and barricading and fighting I had been doing lately, I was working up the spiritual surrender necessary for the Angel of Death to come and claim me right there and then on the couch.

What I wasn't aware of, though, was that my sister baking cookies was merely her way of dealing with all the stress I was causing. During this time she was also using the kitchen phone for a flurry of phone calls—doctors, counselors, and experts in psychosis. She had come home from work specifically to deal with me, sending home the babysitter, dismissing Rowena, plus keeping the kids insulated in the other room with coloring books and the TV up loud.

When I mentioned that Joni was bullet headed it didn't have anything to do with the shape of her head as much as it did with the kinds of thoughts she kept up there. She was very one-directional once she made up her mind. Like an arrow. I knew her well enough to realize that while ostensibly "we" were discussing types of help available, she had undoubtedly drawn up a very clear battle plan and was maneuvering me into her scheme of things whether I went quietly or not. It was her game to make me think I had a choice or two. Joni was seven years older than me—though often it seemed a lot more —and back there on that sweltering day in Brooklyn Heights, I was still responding to the big sister who used to cajole, bribe, and threaten me into doing the dishes with her when we were kids in Ohio. Even though I was now twenty-seven and she, thirty-four, as far as the pattern of our relationship was concerned, I still viewed the wet dish towel in her hand as a deadly weapon, a scorpion's tail ready to sting me into submission. I was on guard. I was in trouble once again.

CHAPTER 2

"I'm sure there have been times in your own life, Mark, when you've been glad to help someone," Joni said. With the back of her flour-caked hand she nudged the curls off a forehead glistening with sweat. "Doesn't helping another give you a good feeling?"

"What's your point, Joni?"

"My point is that for many years now you've been in a position to help others. It's just that now, maybe, it's time you let someone else help you."

"And who could that be?" I said, rolling on my back and looking up at the ceiling. "Let's see, let me guess. Could it be my darling sister, who just happens to be a psychiatric nurse?"

"*Was* a psychiatric nurse," she said, winding the towel like an ace bandage around her wrist. "Besides, that has nothing to do with it. I want to help you because I care."

"I don't mind that a bit, dear sister. But where I have a problem is when you turn me over to sixteen gorillas in a state institution. I'm not so sure those people really care, other than to zonk me out so badly that the kind of 'care' I get is equivalent to what most people give a houseplant. No thanks."

"Mark, you have nothing to be afraid of," Joni said. "This wouldn't be like the other hospitals."

"Oh, I see it comes highly recommended," I said. "Well, that's comforting. I suppose you have a color brochure."

"You have my word, that's what you have."

Though my glance was at the ceiling I sensed Joni stepping

toward me. She stopped when I shifted my eyes. "Tell me, Joni, do we get to pass notes to each other under the chicken wire, or do we have to talk through the hole where they slip me my food?"

"Cut it out, brother."

"Why can't I stay here?" I asked. "You've got training. You can monitor me. And I promise I won't leave the yard."

"I'd like you to stay," she said, "but you're slightly unpredictable right now. Plus you've frightened the girls."

That was true. Upon entering the apartment that day, still flushed from my scrap with Wilkie, my mind had dwelled on the possibility of the old wino being some type of kindred spirit. I believe the actual thought was that Wilkie represented my future karma, and that, thirty years from now, I too would be sleeping on the street, getting harassed by misguided young men.

But no, the voice of reason said, no way because you're the fucking antichrist, remember? You're going to be killed by a Jehovah Witness hit squad. You'll never even live long enough to end up like Wilkie.

After my sister had taken my shoes off and left the room to go make her phone calls, poor little Jennifer and Courtney scuttled in, only to interrupt me in my most morbid thoughts. (Jennifer was nine; Courtney five at the time.) I believed I was a condemned man, and it showed on my face. It was a withering look, a look that killed. It was harsh, naked, and so unlike their Uncle Mark that they reeled back as though hitting an invisible wall, and fled in terror. To them, I imagine it was like walking into a room where a murder—a bloody, brutal murder—had just taken place. They were to dream about the incident for months to come.

Joni took my hand and tugged on it for me to sit up. "You can help me finish my cookies," she said. "We'll see how you do with that, okay?"

"Great," I said, happy to have a purpose. If I could show her that I could be trusted with her cookie dough, I thought, maybe things would work out after all.

Joni walked me to the bathroom. "Wash up first," she said.

"God, it's hot back here," I said, eyeing her kitchen counter where a cookie sheet lay adorned with dough balls spaced in rows like little trees on a Christmas tree farm. "Whose idea was it to bake cookies in the first place?" I said. "It must be ninety degrees outside."

"Eighty-two," she said. "And I think cookies are the thing to do right now. So hurry up and get washed, will you."

I turned on the faucets and bent down to scrub my hands. "I get it," I said, "this is just to get me clean for the hospital, right? I know how you operate, Joni."

I looked up from the sink and saw Joni's face behind mine in the mirror.

"Wrong, little brother. You stink from your fight with Mr. Wilkins. You're not touching food in my kitchen until you get clean."

Joni leaned forward so that her face crowded mine out of the mirror, then licked her finger, moistening her eyebrows. She had always been a beautiful woman. Sharp, brown eyes, firm chin, and a well proportioned, triangular nose. Her face had what I would call a regal affect—a head that belonged in an early Victorian photo, chin up and over a stiff, high collar and a parasol over her shoulder. Her eyes bored into you with a mixture of sensuality, self-discipline, and pain. Unfortunately, Joni suffered from too much facial hair. Her eyebrows needed constant plucking. And along both sides of her jaw she sprouted fine white hairs that swirled in circular patterns—like twin hurricanes on a weather map—the fuzz sweeping counterclockwise on her cheeks beside each earlobe. It was something you never noticed until the light struck a certain way.

An automobile horn honked twice outside. Joni and I looked at each other in the mirror.

"So much for cookies," she said.

The room filled with silence. Upstairs I could hear the

television, very faint, and an image popped in my mind of a big watering can that was also a television and it had legs and it bent over and watered my two nieces who were sitting in front of it, transfixed.

The horn sounded again.

"That's Richard, isn't it?" I said, referring to her husband.

She nodded. "Come on," she said. "This won't be so bad."

"I don't want to go," I said. "I thought you said I could stay here with you."

"It's a really nice place," Joni said, putting her arms around me and squeezing tight. "You'll be fine. Richard and Susan will be with you all the way."

Susan Sloan was my girlfriend. A true New Yorker, I had known her half a year but was only now getting used to the idea that she represented someone who really wanted to do things with me, who expected me to call her now and then, and who, when talking about the future, used the pronoun "we" in her sentences. Susan was beautiful, outspoken, and strong-willed. She was also actively shaping our relationship into a decent romance novel, the kind where the hero suffers from temporary blindness and the woman volunteers to navigate until he gets better. In contrast, I approached romance more like a spectator sport, browsing over memories, over moments we had shared together in much the same manner as I might flip through a travel brochure, uncertain if Susan was my final destination.

Joni took me by the hand and walked with me down the hall. "Here," she said, "don't forget your suitcase."

"Wait a minute," I said. "What about Bill?"

"Bill?"

"The Jehovah Witness. I talked to him earlier—"

"I met Bill," Joni said, untying her apron. "I asked him to come back later."

"Dammit. Why'd you do that?" I said. "They get upset when you lead them on."

Joni tossed her apron on the steam radiator by the door.

"Actually, he looked rather relieved," she said. "You'll have to tell me how you two met sometime."

"I went into the—"

"Save it for later," she said. "Let's go, Richard's waiting."

Joni opened the door, and I stepped out into a stale, scorching July afternoon. The sky was cloudless and the sun glared on the windshield of Richard Kerrigan's car. Susan hopped out and met me at the iron gate. Our eyes met and I looked away, overcome by the strangest thought: I was concerned that old man Wilkie was watching me and knew where I was going. It was as though he and I were changing places once again. This time it was my turn to fall and his turn to taunt me. I looked up and down the block. But I couldn't see him anywhere.

Susan reached up and wrapped her arms around my neck, planting a kiss on my lips that was warm, firm, but unfortunately artificial, mostly on account of her too-red lipstick, which was bitter and plastic to the taste. Still, she was stunning to behold: five-foot-nine, curvaceous and slender as a swan's neck, with a full mane of dark brown hair permed into hundreds of tight little curls, each jouncing off her shoulders like a stretched-out telephone cord after you hang it up.

I let go of my suitcase and squeezed her in my arms, releasing a great deal of tension from which we both went limp. I had the strangest feeling that our embrace was both a greeting and a parting. But just then Joni dashed up the steps and hugged me one more time, clasping Susan and I together in her arms, giving me one last kiss on the cheek and shepherding us toward the car. Susan opened the front door of the white Lincoln, and I slid in beside Richard. Then she picked up the suitcase and climbed in the back. With a final honk we waved back at my sister, pulling away from her slowly as we headed down Willow Street.

"You're really gonna like this place," Richard said. "It's up in the Catskills, which is a helluva lot nicer than New York this time of year. Christ, you can fry bacon on the sidewalk today.

The whole bloody town heats up like a giant brick. No wonder the natives get restless."

Richard was a Brooklyn-born Irishman, a short, strong, and wiry fellow with pumpkin-orange hair and a rugged face shaped by an unbeaten Golden Gloves career and many years of sailing. At fifty-one years of age he was the sole owner of a Jersey City shipyard that specialized in hull repair on oil tankers and freighters, and had his own boat moored in Oyster Bay, a forty-two-foot Bristol that had taken us all to Montauk for two weeks last summer. He had met and married my sister four years earlier, when her youngest daughter was around two years old.

"Yep, it's gonna be nice to get out of the city," he said, " 'cept traffic's starting to thicken up a bit. Shouldn't be too bad once we cross the G-W."

The Lincoln's air conditioning fanned the hairs on my arms, the coolness inspiring me to close my eyes, relax, and imagine a quiet place far from Manhattan. This place they were taking me, what would it be like? Maybe there'd be a lake, I thought, a freshwater lake with fish rippling below the surface and cool, flat stones under my feet, a place with shade trees and soft, cool grass where I could sit and do nothing until the world slowed down.

"Mark?" Susan reached forward and stroked the back of my neck. "Mark, can you tell me what happened back there in Pennsylvania? You said something about a river and going down some rapids, but I never understood what you were talking about."

"Yes, the rafting trip," I said, my eyes still closed. "There was a party, then a rafting trip. And the next thing I knew, I was getting on a plane and flying back to Manhattan."

"Maybe Mark doesn't want to think about that now," Richard said. I opened my eyes and saw him looking at Susan in the mirror. He swung the car through Cadman Plaza and onto the rampway for the Brooklyn Bridge.

Richard was right, I didn't want to think about last

weekend. But at the same time, the seriousness in his voice upset me. He was scared *for* me. I could tell. But I didn't want to go to another hospital, either. This hospital or any other hospital. I didn't care how nice it was. They always kept you too long. All my bills would go unpaid. I had rent and tuition. Plus I'd probably lose my job.

I turned around and looked into the deep, dark eyes of the only friend I had had for the past six months. There was a lot I could lose by going to the hospital.

Susan smiled and raised her hand for me to hold. "Don't worry about Pennsylvania," she said. "And don't worry about work, either. I'll explain everything. They understand about things like this."

Delusions are funny. Whenever someone else has them, it boggles the rest of us folks because their delusions persist no matter what kind of evidence we show them to the contrary. Like the fear of elevators. Or crowded places. We can't understand how the mind, 99.9 percent predictable, suddenly rejects reason for some whimsical spark, some strain of fantasy that, to this day, the world's best doctors and scientists can't isolate, photograph, or place inside some sterile tube. There's no logic at all. Is it that some of us insist on being stupid? Or self-destructive? Why is it that some trains seem to like to jump the tracks?

For myself, right up to the very moment that Susan mentioned explaining my situation at work, I, too, lived under a delusion. My delusion was that there was nothing wrong with me. Certainly nothing that required hospitalization, even though I had admitted to my sister on the phone that morning that I had been hearing voices in my head. Even though I had left work suddenly one night, ran across Central Park at two a.m., and barred myself in my apartment, even though I believed that people were reading my thoughts, that "Crazy Eddie" was me, that the Jehovah Witnesses needed my testimony to seal the Final Days—even though I hadn't eaten or bathed in five days, I believed I was still alright. I had delusions, all right. But the biggest delusion was that I had no delusions. In fact, I believed that whatever had gotten into me would just as easily go away. Like a headache. This riding around in Richard's car was all a game. My brother-in-law was merely goofing off with Susan and me while I cooled down and learned a little respect for people like Wilkie and Rowena. We were joy riding, that's all. In a little while the crisis would be over. Maybe we'd go for a picnic. Then we could joke about it all and get on with the rest of our lives.

But the look on Susan's face said we weren't joking at all. Beside her was my suitcase. Richard's face grew more solemn by the second, his jaw setting and his lips stretching tight. The delusion dissolved. It was obvious that I was going to a hospital. We were on the bridge now. Traffic was thick and streaming to Manhattan.

My mind searched ahead, anxiously filling with pictures of what the next days would hold. At the admission desk they'd do a body search and put my belongings in a wire basket. Watch, keys, and coins would go in a little brown envelope. I'd have to stand in my shorts, my bare feet on the cold floor. If I protested, even mildly, I'd be locked in a padded room. I'd be assigned an Indian doctor and neither one of us would ever be able to pronounce the other's name. He'd give me drugs to make my tongue go dry, make my vision blurry and my feet feel like they belonged to someone else. If I fought against them they'd tie me up in bed, locking straps around my wrists and ankles. I'd be spread out like a giant "X". Even after they let me loose, I'd have to spend the next six weeks in threadbare hospital pajamas and foam slippers, shuffling up and down the same hall on a locked unit, my head throbbing and bowed low from all the medicine and my ears ringing with my own voices mixed in with the other patients talking to themselves.

I looked out the window and saw Manhattan growing closer as we crested the center of the Brooklyn Bridge. Sunlight shown on the silver cables webbing out like harp strings from the giant stone tower on the Manhattan side.

"Stop the car!" I yelled. I grabbed Peter's wrist and pulled his hand from the wheel. Frightened, he braked, pushing me back with his right arm. I lunged at him again, and again he repulsed me. I fell back the other way and threw my weight against the door, popping the lock and swinging it open. Hot wind shot into the car. I could smell the road and the auto exhaust. I leaned out, my eyes transfixed on the pavement whizzing below. Holding the armrest, I jumped out of the car, my feet hitting the pavement and rebounding back up. We were still doing twenty-five miles an hour.

"Stop, goddammit!" I glared at Richard's panic-stricken face. He slowed some more and my feet hit the road again, spinning on the treadmill, going out from under me as I tried to keep up with the car. He reached out to grab me. Suddenly I let go and barrel rolled out of the Lincoln, tumbling to the right. I bounced off an iron railing, landing on my stomach and curling in a ball, the car behind me swerving as it passed within inches. Road gravel tore into my elbows and knees.

I stood up, ignoring the pain, and ran across several lanes of traffic, dodging cars as though they didn't exist. I hopped the other rail and landed on the wooden walkway, frightening a middle-aged couple strolling on a sunny afternoon. Protectively, the man pulled the woman behind him. Over his shoulder I saw something that brought a smile to my lips: Susan running across traffic and heaving herself over the rail. She raced toward me waving, calling out my name.

"Just like Romeo and Juliet," I yelled at the couple. They backed against the outer rail.

Meanwhile, Susan was making quite the impression as she ran toward me in her white blouse and white linen skirt—with just a touch of red in her shoes and sash around her waist. I ran to meet her, and she held out her hand. I grabbed it. She was frightened, breathless, and didn't resist when I pulled her forward.

"C'mon, baby, we'll be late for the show."

"Mark," she cried, "where are we going?"

I locked my fingers around her wrist and pulled her with me. Together we raced up the walkway. Beams, cars, and cables all went whooshing by. People of all ages, their faces blank and wide eyed with shock, cleared out in front of us, stepping back while shielding themselves as though they were facing the bulls at Pamplona. Up ahead a cluster of Japanese tourists blocked our way. We went through them like a bowling ball striking its pins—as we did, one brave man leaned forward and snapped our photo as we broke through the crowd.

Susan pleaded for me to stop. Her legs ripped the slit in her tight linen skirt. "My shoes," she said. "I can't run in these!"

I stopped and she pulled her red shoes off, putting her hands on her knees to catch her breath.

"No," I said, "we're not stopping!"

Regaining my lock on her wrist, I jerked her up. I began running again, Susan lurching forward, still clutching her shoes in her hand. Her pantyhose split beneath her heels and huge holes traveled up the backs of her legs. "My feet are burning!" she yelled. But I kept yanking her forward until we had reached the highest point on the bridge.

"Let's go," I said, panting. I released her and hoisted myself onto an I-beam. A few feet out the beam was crossed by a half dozen electrical wires spaced about twelve inches apart, each of them threaded above the beam like strings on a guitar, only running the other direction. Beyond the wires the beam jutted another fifteen feet out over the side of the bridge. Beyond that was nothing. Just a yawning space with the East River rumbling below. Above, only sky. Perched on the horizon—like a figurine on a wedding cake—stood the Statue of Liberty at the mouth of New York Harbor.

I rose and balanced myself on the narrow beam. I looked down at Susan, her hair wet at the sides of her face. I could see her heart pounding in the hollow of her throat. Smiling, I bent down and reached for her hand, but this time she did not give it to me.

"Aren't you coming?" I said.

Susan stepped back. Her hand went to her chest.

"Susan, this is it!" I yelled. I got down on my knees and leaned over, waving my hand for her to grab. She stood back, shoulders straightening, her eyes fixed and cold. Slowly, mechanically, she shook her head, her lips forming the word, "No."

"Susan!" I looked up. Men in blue uniforms were galloping toward us, their nightsticks, guns, and walkie-talkies jiggling.

"You must join me, my love. You'll never get another chance."

Susan's eyes appeared hollow and far away. The police were closing in from both directions.

"Susan? Susan? Aw . . . fuck you!" I yelled. I rose and turned away. As though balancing on a curb, I crossed the I-beam, stepping easily between the wires, laughing at my effort to avoid electrocution. Fucking absurd.

I cleared the wires and eyeballed the final few feet. Taking one last breath, I dashed off at full speed, diving from the edge as though it were nothing more than a spring board at a public pool. I never looked down, never aimed or calculated what I was doing. Instead, I threw myself into the air and let gravity do the rest.

My body wrenched from the force of the speed of my fall. I felt myself pinned like a butterfly to a sinking piece of sky. The East River rose to meet me like a broad, flat plain, spinning, spiraling, turning upside down. Air whistled by my ears, and I felt both me and the world squeezing through a narrow tube. The skin on my face stretched back as though being peeled by gravity. I feared my face would rip apart.

Faster and faster I hurtled toward the river. My heart was shaken loose like on the first hill of a roller coaster, only this hill had no bottom, no place for the shaking to stop. The water raced up to meet me like a solid brown wall. At the moment I hit, my neck bent forward and I broke the water with the top of my shoulders. I felt like a two-by-four had been cracked across my back. The air blasted from my lungs. I turned under water and floated downwards on my back, my limbs twitching from the impact, my lungs emptied for the very last time. I watched the bubbles trail away, rising like pearls to the surface. I felt life—anxiety, urging, action, willpower, whatever you call it—draining from me. All hope gone, gone, gone. All my future, all my plans. Gone. Peace closed in around me; I was cupped in warm, watery hands, a silver dollar slipping to the blackness below.

Yet awareness never left me. Never once did the lights wink out. In fact, I was acutely aware. Aware in a way that amazed me. Damn if the water wasn't blue. And damn if I wasn't amazed to see not one but *two* suns shining in the sky above me.

CHAPTER 3

A tour of my face:

It is as good a time as any to talk about my appearance since right now I am temporarily blind. The blindness occurred last night while I lay on my mattress on the floor. Light shone through the crack of the door at the bottom, and whenever someone walked by, nurse, doctor, patient, whatever, the light broke and followed their footsteps, moving side to side. It was like a shadow dodging, rolling from side to side.

I sort of hypnotized myself, I guess, because I couldn't take my eyes from the bottom of the door, and pretty soon all that existed in the world was that narrow strip of light. I prayed to it. I wanted it to grow and deliver me. I watched it with such concentration that when the evening shift was over and the hall lights went out, so did my faith. And my sense of being alive. There was still a floor light or something faint on the other side but eventually that faded, too, until finally it was no more than a pinpoint, and I myself felt shrunken to almost nothingness. I needed that light and it was totally black in my room. I felt the fingers of death wrapping around me like cold, constricting worms. It was as though I were sinking into the earth, becoming covered with dirt, turning to soil myself. This was extinction, said a voice in my head. I prepared my mind for a long, dark sleep. It was death with awareness.

But now I know different. I am being taken care of by the nursing staff. It is daylight again. They have me sitting on the edge of my mattress and they are washing my eyes with some kind of solution in warm water. I still can't open them yet. Apparently I've sealed my lids together, welding them shut with the crusty stuff I often find upon waking. There is a nurse on my left, a young one by the sound of her voice, and she smells fresh and pretty as chamomile tea. A strong man with a Jamaican accent, Charley, I believe his name is, is holding my arm to keep me steady.

I have not seen my face in many days, long before I went blind. When I got here it was September 1, and I suspect two or three days have passed since then. I have not been in control of my emotions and only since this morning have allowed others to touch me.

"Mark, do your eyes hurt as we're doing that?"

It's a woman's voice, not the nurse's, but someone a little further away, near the door.

"A little," I say, "but the warm stuff feels good."

I try to raise my lids and can now see through a tiny hole in my right eye. I do not suppose that this has happened to many of you, but if you are among the few to ever pass through a long ordeal, like being held hostage or lost for days at sea, a moment comes when the ordeal is finally behind you and, perhaps in a hospital like me, you take that first look at yourself in a mirror. It is shocking. There is a sense that you must be looking at someone else, at some remnant or shell that your spirit must have fled while you suffered your ordeal. Flesh is seen for what it is—fragile, impermanent, subject to decay. It is like climbing out of a terrible accident, unscratched, and viewing the twisted remains of what was once your car.

My hair, what is left of it, is blond. My nose is unremarkable, except for the fact that it's not broken. The eyes are hazel. And my chin, which takes up most of my face, is that lantern variety that stands out more and more as I grow thinner. My last dentist, the one in Manhattan, says I grind my teeth at night. That's why the enormous jaw. It's also why my teeth are chipped, the two upper ones in front angled away from each other like the starched flaps of a banker's shirt collar. Trying his best to be polite and matter-of-fact, my dentist suggested a psychological source for my problem, hinting that perhaps I held my emotions in and needed help in expressing myself. His friend in the office upstairs was a therapist, he said. A good one.

His suggestion of therapy, five months ago, amuses me now.

"How's it coming?" the woman's voice says. She sounds older and seems to hold some authority.

"Almost done," the nurse says.

A few more minutes and I can finally see. I am in a square room without any furniture. There is only one window and that is a small one in the middle of a door, not the door connecting to the hallway, where I watched the light, but the door to the nurses' station. It has unbreakable glass and, just in case, there is chicken wire laced through it in a hexagon pattern. There is also a brown smear on the door, something I am ashamed of.

Charley stands up, crossing his arms as he looks down at me. His dark skin contrasts with his white uniform top, which is zipped down in a narrow V. The nurse, a pretty brunette wearing a plaid top over white pants, gathers up the metal wash basin and goes out the door. Charley steps aside, and I see the owner of the other voice, a strikingly attractive woman in her early forties, black hair with a hint of brown to it, and dark eyes that look at me directly, revealing no emotion whatsoever. She wears a burgundy blazer over a cream-colored blouse that has ruffles down the middle. It is a very expensive, sharply tailored coat, and the matching slacks have such a sharp crease on them, either leg could serve as the bow of an arctic ice breaker.

"Can you see now?" she says.

"Yes."

"Good. Allow me to welcome you to your new home," she says, coming closer and extending her hand. "I'm Barbara Bowman, your physician. I will be working with you as long as you're here."

I take her hand and feel her tugging, so I oblige by standing up. She is almost as tall as I am.

"You're going to be my doctor?" I say.

"Yes. Do you have a problem with that?" She motions for Charley to leave.

"In a way I do," I say, feeling unsteady on my feet. I brace my arm against the wall and rub my other hand over my face, feeling beard stubble as coarse as a green scouring pad.

My voice feels scratchy. My lips are dried and cracked. "I don't think this will work out," I say, clearing my throat.

"And why is that?" Bowman says, crossing her arms.

"I'm not so sure I want to spill my guts to a woman."

"That's interesting," she says. She nods as if pondering an unfathomable mystery. "Do you think you'd be able to tell me why?"

***

My parents (who recently celebrated their fiftieth wedding anniversary) still live in the same house in Youngstown, Ohio, where I grew up as a child. 2029 Dogwood. There's a big coat closet on the right as you come in the front door, and that's where they keep their photo albums, stacked on the shelf next to the hats and gloves and scarves and umbrellas. Among the many acetate binders is a collection of photos from the Island of Guam, a parrot-green album with a gold plastic emblem in the shape of the island glued to the front. It's the Guam photo album.

In it you'll find some photos of me high diving from the top of a waterfall, my body a white blur against the jungle foliage. There's another of me diving into the ocean from jagged volcanic cliffs. They were taken in 1971 when I was fifteen.

I had a lot of my "firsts" when I was fifteen. I flew on my first jet, the Boeing 747 that took me to Hawaii on my way to Guam. It was my first time away from home, a long-term separation designed to put a little distance between my mother and me. We had been fighting for the past several years, mostly on account of my refusal to grow into the mold she had made for me. She knew what a good boy I could be and dammit if that didn't take all the fun out of it. I was a smart youngster, plenty smart, and believe me there were times when an "A" at school was not only an easy thing to secure, but getting anything else was positively hard work—yet I chose to knock over the A-is-for-Apple cart simply because defying her strengthened my own sense of self. I would never be good— not as long as it was expected of me. That wasn't love. That was extortion.

On Guam I had my first legal guardian, my oldest brother Dale. He was the first of six children, and with an aggressive younger brother, Scott, and my sister, Joni, right behind him, he snatched up a teaching degree and took it with him to the Pacific island, where he found work instructing fourth graders in the southern village of Umatac. Twelve years older than me, he had already taken me to places like Canada and Mexico when I was only ten. The last time we had gone traveling together he had caught me buying cigarettes on our camping trip to Canada. He caught me again on our trip to North Carolina. For punishment, he made me smoke one of those giant tourist cigars, the ones as big as highway flares and packed with pencil shavings. Now it was five years later and I was worried that I might repeat another slip-up and force him to put me on some kind of restrictions. He knew me better than my parents and knew the kinds of things I liked— in that way he could always punish me more effectively than they ever did. But I had nothing to worry about. We got along pretty well, despite the fact that I got drunk at my "Welcome to Guam" party on the first night I was there, threw up in front of the mayor, and ended up sleeping in the bathroom on the floor. Another first.

In the long run Dale gave me more freedom as a fifteen-year-old than most people find in their entire lives. I got to drive my first car, Dale's bright yellow Datsun 240Z. He let me take it over the mountain passes when we went north to do laundry or south to get the mail. From Guam I visited the Orient for the first time in my life: Hong Kong, Taiwan, Japan, and the Philippines. On Guam I also smoked my first marijuana cigarette and kissed my first girl. The marijuana did nothing. The girl, however, sucked my tongue down her throat and held it hostage for about fifteen minutes. I knew nothing about French kissing so I never suspected that the idea was to move each others 'tongues in and out and swish them around a little. She was a few years older and obviously more experienced, so out of politeness I surrendered my tongue to her, figuring she'd change the pace as soon as the time was right. She sucked it until she broke all my blood vessels. If you've ever been a kid and sucked a cup on your chin, turning it purple, then you have some idea of what happened to my tongue. It swelled about three times in size and felt like it had been used to paint a Mail Pouch ad on the side of a barn. I couldn't talk for several days. Once my brother found out how it happened, I had to sit there in silent embarrassment while he explained to his friends how I had gotten my first lesson in lip smacking with a Guamanian girl.

On my trip to the Orient I also had my first sexual experience with a prostitute I picked up in a bar in Taipei, Taiwan. I was traveling with my brother and our cousin Nola, a half cousin, actually, from our father's side. She impressed me as a very bookish woman, slightly obsessed with departure times, dinner prices, and things like that. They were both much older than me, and one night they wanted to ditch me so they could go dancing and dining without worrying about someone underage. (As if Taiwan in 1971, during the height of the Vietnam War and a top military R&R playground, recognized the concept of underage.) As a matter of fact, the night before we had stuck our heads into one of the many crowded bars that specialized in providing affectionate females for American GIs—a dark, tawdry establishment with topless Oriental girls lethargically grinding to jukebox music on a smoky, plywood stage. I not only walked past the bouncer but was immediately offered a drink by the man behind the bar.

As a way to take my mind off my disappointment for not being invited out with them, Dale suggested, half jokingly, that I try my luck there instead.

"You mean back at that bar?" I said.

"Why not?" he laughed.

Dale and Nola got dressed and went out.

Curious, but more scared than curious, I dressed and retraced the route back to the bar. The entrance was off a narrow alley that smelled of piss and rotting garbage. I pushed open the door, and an old, stooped-over, spectacled Chinese man showed me to a stool. He was thin and wore a white sleeveless T-shirt that revealed a pair of lightning streaks, crossed like swords, tattooed on one arm. He went behind the bar and started wiping the surface in front of me with a damp white rag. He wheezed from a non-filter cigarette dangling from his lips and spoke in sing-song, garbled English.

"You here for pretty babe?" he said.

I smiled, embarrassed.

"You want it, we got it. You right fine mister. Best man, good fella, eh?"

It was like American culture had been shoved in one of his drink blenders, spun on high, then strained through the words coming out of his mouth. He kept talking about the MPs, calling them "clocksuckers," and I kept looking at my watch, wondering if he was warning me about an impending raid. I finally realized he was calling them cocksuckers, and just shooting the breeze with me in the way two strangers talk about the weather. Embarrassed for him, I found myself agreeing with everything he said because it was less painful than asking him to repeat it.

It was about eight p.m. and the place was pretty empty. The dancing lights were off and the music was much quieter than the night before. I bought a drink—bourbon on ice—and the bartender introduced me to a dark-haired Chinese girl who had just taken the stool beside me.

"Lees is Lilly. Lilly good girl. Make you plenty happy."

Lilly did nothing. She didn't even look my way. She had a deck of cards in front of her and appeared to be playing solitaire, although I noticed right away that she topped red kings on black tens and turned cards out of order. I suddenly realized that Lilly was making up the card game, which made me feel like I was in some poorly cast Western movie, the Youngstown Kid about to lose his cherry in a sawdust saloon. It was very unreal, an imitation of life. The Chinese man watched us both for a few minutes and then said something else I didn't understand. Again I smiled and nodded. Trying not to be obvious about it, I appraised the thing on the stool beside me. Long, dark, shiny hair that plummeted straight to her waistline. Tiny breasts beneath a low-cut blue silk dress. Open-toed, blue, high-heeled shoes with red painted toes winking inside. A flat but attractive face and long, long fingernails. Incredibly long fingernails. With those she'd never need chopsticks. They were so long and curved they reminded me of dugout canoes.

I didn't know it, but by nodding to the bartender I had just bought Lilly a drink. Now she turned and faced me, smiling as she took my hand. It was so elemental: buying her a drink was like hitting a switch marked ON.

I bought her a second drink and her hand traveled elsewhere. Who needs English, I thought. "I get it now," I said, sitting up, pleased with myself.

"You want now?" the bartender said, leaning over. "Very

good. Lees is best way. Go now. Go all night."

He swept aside the drinks and brought out a pad of paper. The next thing I knew I was signing a contract and handing over fifteen dollars.

"Tiger boy is big, strong fella," he said, winking. He revealed devastated teeth with his smile, tearing off and handing me the bottom pink copy as my receipt.

My head swimming as though I had just returned from another planet, I escorted Lilly through the streets of Taipei, missing our hotel twice but getting a strange pleasure from the blind leading the blind—Lilly couldn't speak English and had no choice but to follow me. But part of me didn't want to find the place anyway. I regretted going to that bar and felt that I had been coerced into signing the contract. To tell the truth, I didn't know if I was going to go through with it or not.

Eventually we made it back to the hotel where, upon requesting my key, the desk clerk handed me a telegram that was meant for someone else. I remember opening and glancing at it, taking it with us into the elevator, though nothing registered because my brain was numb with terror. Lilly, however, showed a keen interest in the message, which was in Chinese, and read it over my shoulder as we rode up to our room. She kept looking from the paper to me, her face, if I had only been aware of it at the time, probably wearing the same expression mine did when I discovered she was faking her solitaire.

Inside the room I set the message on the dresser. When I turned on the lights I was overcome by how incredibly bright they seemed. I looked on the wall for a dimmer switch but couldn't find any, the room striking me as being too boxy, with nothing much in it except two queen size beds. They looked like two pieces of bread. The thought occurred to me that, in fifteen minutes, we'd be the meat in a hot sex sandwich.

I pointed toward the window to indicate which bed was ours. Lilly sat on the edge of it, watching my expression to be sure it was okay. She folded her hands on top of the white purse in her lap, and I went to the window and closed the venetian blinds.

"Well," I said, gesturing. "How do you like the room?" Lilly sat up straight, watching me with a half smile. Then she glanced at the nightstand between the beds, eyeing a half-empty bottle of Dubonet beside two dirty glasses. Both beds, I suddenly realized, showed signs of being slept in.

"My brother's with me," I said. "He's out dancing. You understand 'dance'?"

I shuffled my feet.

"Ah, dahnce!" she said, nodding.

"You understand 'brother'?" Lilly made no response.

"Yeah, well, uh, he's a pretty good guy. Here he is here," I said, going to the dresser and knocking over a pile of Polaroids we had taken in Hong Kong. I showed her one of him leaning against a railing on a ferry.

I pointed, she nodded.

"Well, maybe we should undress. You know 'undr—Aw, forget it," I said. I tugged gingerly on her sleeve. She smiled, looking up at me. "Like this," I said, kicking off my shoes.

From that point on my senses absorbed a flood of information, assembling it on the run, so to speak. I had so much to think about, and so little time. Unfortunately, most of the data did not correspond to what *Playboy* had taught me. Instead of holding still like the pictures with the staples in them, Lilly had me follow her into the bathroom where she soaped up my groin. Bad move. My penis shriveled up like styrofoam on fire. And instead of me mounting her and thrusting her with bold, savage strokes, we had to stop several times while she fingered the top of her labia, the reason for which completely escaped me.

When I finally did climb on top, spastic with nervousness, it was more like trying to dock a space capsule than joining the fruits of love. With our faces only inches apart we mirrored each other's concern as I fumbled with plug and socket, skipping foreplay entirely. I wanted to get it over with. Besides, I wouldn't have enjoyed foreplay anyway because a voice in my head—whom I shall call the "Erogenous Coach"—was driving me nuts, telling me to kiss her here, kiss her there, squeeze her butt, check your erection, don't forget the nipples, etc. It was like an airline pilot doing his preflight safety check.

Finally Lilly reached down and WHAM! I plunged inside. Before I could register the sensation, she immediately began sweeping her pelvis, tugging me with something soft, yet tight as a beak. Before I could think Vaseline or candle in a blender, before the Coach could even say, "Fuckin' A!" I went off—not like a rocket on Fourth of July, not like a cannon—but more like a firecracker muffled under a pillow. A good shot, but not one heard round the world.

I looked at my watch. It said 10:15. What'll we do now, I thought.

A few hours later my brother returned. I was never so happy to see him. But Dale scowled. Where did you get her, he wanted to know, lifting her dress off the back of the chair.

"The place you told me to go," I said. I sat up in bed but Lilly slid down, tucking her head against me and pulling the covers to her chin.

"You weren't supposed to listen to me," Dale said. He hung her dress up, then took off his tie and tossed it on the dresser. Then he dumped some things out of a small paper bag. "I wanted to write postcards tonight," he said. "How am I supposed to tell Mom what a good time we're having?"

"Just don't tell her, 'Wish you were here.'"

Apparently Lilly understood that phrase and giggled beneath the sheets. My brother rolled his eyes upward and let loose a long, low whistle, the sound he always made when doing damage assessment, like the time he walked around the Datsun after I jumped a curb. He unbuttoned his shirt and pulled the tail out of his trousers, shaking his head at me in the dresser mirror. Suddenly Lilly bolted up and, still clutching the sheets to her, leaned over and grabbed her purse. "No, no. No can do," she said, pulling out her copy of the contract.

"Oh, Jesus," Dale said, going into the bathroom. "Please tell your friend I'm not part of the act."

He stayed in the bathroom for almost an hour. But when he came back he warmed up considerably, and after taking both our wallets downstairs to be locked in the hotel safe, he returned with a bottle of brandy and proceeded to write postcards to friends and family. As Lilly and I cooed beneath the sheets, Dale smiled in the mirror and read the postcards aloud, the two of us laughing when he used such phrases as "exploring the Orient" and "Mark's education."

Lilly laughed too, which I found fascinating because she couldn't understand a word we were saying. Yet I was certain her laughter was genuine, which threw into sharp contrast the dry, mechanical aspect of our sex. I felt cheated. Later, when I awoke in the dark to the rich discovery of the soft, sweet-smelling woman so warm beside me, I again felt something wrong. The feeling of closeness was an entirely different world than my fumbling and uneventful first penetration.

The next morning Dale got up early and went for a walk. "I'm going to get Nola before she stops over," he said. He hiked his thumb in Lilly's direction. "See that she's gone before we get back."

Lilly and I took a shower together. I began feeling sorry for myself, as though my virginity had been asked to audition, had come out on stage, but then bowed and walked off without saying a word. It was empty. A waste. I didn't have anything to show for it at all. In fact, as I toweled off and poked through the blinds to see what kind of day it was, I began reinventing the whole night over, skipping the embarrassing parts and making others seem better. Then I got an idea. As Lilly was slipping her dress on, I told her to wait while I grabbed Dale's Polaroid camera.

"Here," I said, bringing her the chair and motioning for her to put a leg up. She did so, but at the same time, did not hide her displeasure. She pointed at her wet hair. "Don't worry about that," I said. "Here, just a little more." I hiked up her hem. Pop! went the flash. "Take off your panties," I said. Pop! and Pop! again.

Needless to say, none of those photos ever made it in the Guam family album.

CHAPTER 4

Susan showed me photos of herself one day. She was modeling a one-piece red bathing suit in somebody's backyard, standing in front of a tall, bushy, flat-topped hedge that ran beside a large, white house. To her left was a big, boxy air conditioner, the kind that sit on the ground with a propeller on top and are always dripping water out of a small black tube. The air conditioner was in every photo, and though the camera angle favored Susan, the sheer size of the apparatus seemed to upstage her, or more precisely, gave the air conditioner the appearance that it was competing with her, trying to draw the eye's attention.

Susan's expression was one of annoyance. There were six photos of the same basic pose, and while sorting through them, I became aware of the subtle eclipse at the corners of her mouth—a smile, a very unnatural smile, had either been coaxed by the photographer or had slowly faded throughout the ordeal. I was curious as to which order it had been but I didn't ask her because I didn't want to hear her discussing the situation—in particular, I didn't want to hear the name of the photographer.

Susan could have easily been a model. She had a pretty face with a clear complexion highlighted by natural pink blush on her magnificent, Katherine Hepburn cheekbones. Below them, her face narrowed like the bottom of an oval, tapering down to a little knobby chin that, in our languid, bedroom hours, I had lately taken to sucking in foreplay. I was still working on a pet name for it. Her eyes were large and almond shaped, reminding me of the perfect eyes of a Hindu goddess. Incredibly dark, they were like two roasted coffee beans.

Susan glided on long legs with just the right amount of musculature in her calves so that they flexed sensually like pistons. For a short time she worked as a hand model and told me that while she was in college her hands were insured for a hundred thousand dollars—fifty thousand apiece. But Susan never took modeling seriously, choosing instead to become a nurse.

I was twenty-six when I came into her life; she was three years older. I was working full time nights, carrying a full credit load at New York University. I was going to be a playwright. In the summer of 1983, just before I leaped off the Brooklyn Bridge, Susan and I spent a great deal of time together. Here is some of what she taught me:

· Never make conversation with a cabbie; it's a tip-off that you're a visitor, green behind the ears, or too damn lonely for your own good.

· Never step into a subway car that isn't well lit.

· Don't feel sorry for the waiter if the food is no good.

· Young men, even poor playwrights like me, could still dress up and *look* successful.

· Plays about nuns, especially a comedy like mine, were a dime a dozen and doomed from the start.

· Don't call your mother simply because you think you ought to. If it's her birthday, fine, call her, but first write down a few nice things to say about yourself and don't feel bad if you sound like you're bragging. Mothers don't hear it that way. Brag a little and she'll love it, and that'll make you feel better about yourself. Then it'll be easy to say happy birthday and neither one of you will detect any insincerity.

· Everyone needs a cheerleader.

· Never—and I mean never—leave a woman waiting more than ten minutes at a public location.

· Using the same toothbrush is fine, just don't make a habit of it.

Something else Susan taught me, though she never said anything official on the subject, was how to smile politely while verbally chopping up someone like a machine gun. One time we were at a restaurant on the Upper East Side and the food was horrible. The salad greens were bitter and rusty around the edges, inspiring Susan to draw our waiter over with a smile and a wiggle of her finger. He came to the table and she started to whisper, enticing him to bend over. She caught him by the sleeve and said, "We are either going to start all over here—that means new bread, new salads, and a guarantee that the rest of the meal won't be a waste of our time—or we are going to walk out right now. I trust you can find some fresh lettuce back there, or will I have to ask the manager to help you look for it?"

Their noses were about two inches apart, and Susan never lost her smile or the twinkle in her eye. I could sense the waiter's blood rushing to his head, and perhaps his balls, too, scuttling up for cover.

Whispering venom became a classic approach when Susan was angry. The other was to stand there, hands on hips, and fire away, loud and deadly words that, unfortunately, always made sense. She was fond of tight-fitting body dresses; so you can imagine the sexy incongruence of a tall, leggy beauty going after someone like a gunslinger at the O.K. Corral. For added emphasis she'd karate chop the air with her right hand, slicing it into the palm of the other. Or she'd point that same come-here-please wiggle finger, but this time like a gun.

Susan never took an injury without saying something about it. She told me it was healthy to discharge things, and as quickly as possible. She traveled emotionally light.

After I finally got out of the hospital we talked about my suicide attempt and how I tried to pull her up on the I-beam with me. I asked her to forgive me for saying "Fuck you," and she said no problem. She said if I had made her jump then it would have been another matter. After all, the *New York Post* printed "I'm going" as my final words, but then again they had also said I did drugs in the Hamptons when in reality I had gotten wasted in Erie, PA. "They just like to pick on the Hamptons," Susan said. "It sounds better."

That was another photo of mine which never made it in a family album: me staggering out of the East River like the Creature from the Black Lagoon. I made the front page *Post*, both evening and morning editions, plus most of page 4, with more photos and a story featuring words like "bizarre," "crazed," and "mysterious drugs." I also made the Friday paper back in my home town when the news service wired the story to the Youngstown *Vindicator*. My sister hadn't told my mother yet, so you can imagine how the poor lady felt, picking the paper off the porch and getting the news in the same way as 120,000 other Youngstowners.

How do you think she reacted? With anger? Degradation? Shame? With an overpowering sense of guilt that perhaps she was somehow linked to the tragedy, linked by means of ineffective parenting, thus making her at least partly responsible for all the bad wiring in her son's thinking unit?

Believe me, there were many times I *wanted* Margaret Ann Wolyczin to react that way. Whether it was her fault or not.

But why don't you be the judge? Following is my earliest childhood trauma. (My "momma trauma," Susan called it.) I've gotten so many therapy miles out of it that I've got no choice but to turn it into a book, just to break even. Prior to that I've worked it again and again as a short story. Susan saw so many drafts of the bloody thing that she suggested I miniaturize it and make it into an acrylic paperweight.

So here it is, my most recent edit, 539 words, as it went out last March to *Recovering Adult Children of Dysfunctional Families Magazine*, circulation 800,000.

***

A boy is five years old. He climbs the steps to his room. He thinks it would be fun to turn around and slide back down the steps on his rump. Or maybe slide headfirst with his hands raised like Superman.

But his mother calls. It is time for his bath. He can hear the water running in the tub. He enters the bathroom and she helps him undress. His sneakers are dirty and so are his knees, scuffed from playing soldiers in the dirt.

"You've been a dirty boy," his mother says.

She takes the white washcloth, stiff from drying over the side of tub, and soaks it in the warm water as the boy climbs in. She lathers soap against the cloth, then rubs the cloth over her son's neck and shoulders. Suds drip down his chest.

"What have you been doing to get so dirty?" she asks.

"Playing," he says.

"Playing what?" she asks.

The boy looks at the face of his mother, round and smooth with soft, pink cheeks. She could double as the Quaker Oats man.

"Can I ask you something?" the boy says.

She stops scrubbing. "Why, of course," she says. "You can ask me anything."

The boy looks to his lap. "You know my wiener?" he says.

"Your *what*?"

"My wiener. Vernon says I put my wiener inside yours and that's how we make a baby."

His mother's face drains of color. "Vernon told you that?" she says.

"How can I fit a baby inside my wiener?" he says, gazing down at the culprit.

He looks up but his mother is gone. All that remains is the washcloth, suspended in space. It seems to hang there for a long time, then floats down slowly like a leaf in his lap.

From downstairs he can hear his mother talking. She sounds excited. Angry about something. He hears his father say something back. His mother yells. Next, the boy hears his father's feet climbing the stairs, thumping heavy and slow.

The father comes in and kneels by the tub. He rolls up his shirtsleeves. He fishes for the washcloth, finds it, and slaps it full of soap. He scrubs the boy's knees. The father shakes his head back and forth, emitting a sad yet sinister chuckle that is full of opposite meanings and confusing to the child.

"Dad?" the boy asks.

"What, son?"

"Did I say something bad?"

The boy's father stops scrubbing. A speck of soap is in his eye. He rubs his face against the side of his arm.

"No," he says. "You didn't say anything bad."

"Where's Mommy?" the boy asks. "She always gives me my bath."

"Don't worry about your mother," he says. "Here, give me your foot."

The boy's father works the cloth between his toes.

"Ouch," the boys says. "You're rubbing too hard."

From downstairs the boy hears the rotary dial of the telephone. His mother yells again. The boy hears his name. And Vernon's name. He looks up at his father, who looks away. His father grabs the boy's other foot.

"What did you do today?" he asks.

"Play."

The boy's father reaches for the soap. "What did you play to get so dirty?"

The title I finally chose for the story was "Been A Dirty Boy." It's been rejected seventeen times.

***

September 5, 1983
Lunch hour

The silverware in the colanders makes a sword-fight sound when the dietary workers dump fresh knives and forks into them. I am standing in the cafeteria line with my hand deep into the knife colander, feeling the warmth of the freshly steamed handles. I grab them like a fistful of straws. (Back in first grade, when we stuck our hands in those "feely boxes," the shoeboxes with the strange objects inside, just once I wanted to feel something like hot cafeteria silverware.) I hold up the line and must tell the other patients to go past me because the warmth is heavenly and I do not want to let go just yet.

This is my first time out with the other patients. Doctor Bowman thought it was a nice idea that I get cleaned up and put some food into my belly before we have our first talk.

Charley is to be at my side all day. He is standing down by the desserts, looking at me and probably wondering what I am doing with my hand in the knives. I select a particularly toasty one from the middle and put in on my tray, pushing the tray along as I look through the glass at the steaming bins of corn on the cob and hamburger patties with white cheese squares melted on top.

I am in clean hospital pajamas with a blue pinstriped robe that has no tie at the waist. I only have one slipper, an orange foam slipper, because two nights ago when I was hallucinating I filled the other one with excrement and hurtled it at the door.

I eat in silence. The old man next to me is a hummer. I hate people who hum when they're eating.

At the end of my meal Bowman comes by and asks me to follow her up the hall. My hair is still wet from my shower. She walks ahead of me, the crisp creases in her burgundy pants cutting the air like shark's fins. She walks with straight spine and shoulders squared, precision with every step. I am guessing her sport to be tennis, and in the winter, skiing—though I wouldn't be surprised if she swam a mile a day. I can't wait to ask her, to find out for myself.

Near the ping pong table she puts a key into a lock and opens a door on the right.

"Come on in," she says.

I step into a cubbyhole of an office. There is an antique wooden coat tree, an old oak desk with an antique swivel chair behind it, plus two other wooden chairs facing the desk. That is all. It is a drab little cube. There is one picture on the left wall —tilted of course—a smeary impressionist doing Paris in rain.

"This is your office?" I say, unable to resolve the conflict between it and her wardrobe.

"No. That's upstairs. We use this room for consultations. Of course, as we progress, we'll have the opportunity to meet elsewhere."

"I'd like to talk about that," I say. "This progressing business. Exactly why am I here and what are you supposed to do for me?"

Bowman sat behind the desk and motioned for me to take a seat. "I imagine you have a lot of questions at the present time, and we'll try our best to address all of them. But I too have some questions for you, the most important one dealing with why you may not be able to work with me. Do you recall our conversation earlier?"

"Yes," I say. "But if you could bear with me, before I answer any questions I'd still like to know what I've been charged with."

"We'll get to that momentarily, Mister, ah, how do you pronounce this?"

"Wolyczin," I say. "Wool-ish-en. And I want you to know I pick up on that 'we'll' stuff."

"Beg your pardon?" Bowman looks up from my chart, where she had been glancing at my admission papers.

"All this 'we'll' jargon. Like we'll do this or we'll do that. Or *our* therapy. *Our* medication. Bullshit. It's my therapy. And it's your medication. There's no *we'll* involved at all. So don't try to mesmerize me into thinking there's any kind of cooperation going on. I know how to play the game. It's your will against mine. No 'ours' here, baby."

Bowman fixes me with a long, steady look, her elbow on the desk and her hand up so that one finger covers her mouth. Her nails are long, rounded daggers, also the color of burgundy wine.

"Hmmm," she says, "I see. I wasn't aware of anything going on other than my using them as figures of speech. I'm grateful you've pointed that out to me, Mark." She stands and extends her hand. "I apologize," she says.

"I don't believe you," I say, crossing my arms.

"Well, it's the truth," she says "If I said it I meant it. Now, please, accept my apology. I honestly didn't realize how my words must have sounded. And you're right. It's your therapy. Your life. Please . . . forgive me?"

I rise slowly, cautiously, and take her hand, feeling the same warmth as with the knives in the cafeteria. She smiles and I do too. We both sit down.

"Okay," she says, "your stand is noted. Now, you want to know why you're here. So do I. At least from your perspective. We have a lot to exchange in that regard. But I also want to know if it will be possible for us to work together. And that's only because of what *you* said earlier. The way I look at it, Mr. Wolyczin, is why should I waste both our time if I'm only going to have to turn you over to another doctor? He— or she—can explain just as well why you're here and tell you what's expected of you. That's not the issue. But before we do anything, *we* need to explore your reasons for not wanting to work with me. Fair enough?"

I sit back, conscious of tension knotting my shoulders. It occurs to me that talking might do me some good.

"Do you want a pillow for your rump?" Bowman says. "That chair looks awfully hard."

"No, no thanks," I say. She looks back at me, her hard-edged face softening, her lips relaxing in a crescent smile.

"It may be difficult to talk to me," she says, "and I understand. If you just want to sit here and say nothing, that's okay, too. Sometimes silence is a good thing when it's shared."

At the moment she says that, as if to make her point, the clop-clop of a ping pong ball calls from beyond the door. We listen for a moment before I speak.

"No, I guess what I was thinking of saying was that I apologize for what I said earlier. I have nothing against you personally. Hell, it was my first day talking to anyone. I guess I overreacted. You know how you get to thinking things are going to be a certain way. And then when they don't turn out, you get pissed sometimes."

"You were expecting a male doctor?" she says.

"The last one was. Sorry, no offense intended."

"And none taken," she says. "Go on."

"Well, it just seems as if I've been having one bad relationship after another with women, starting with my mother."

"Nothing too unusual there," she says, smiling, leaning back.

"Actually, I communicate pretty well with women. It's just that I don't know what the hell they want. It seems that once they get to know me, they use that information, you know, turning it on me."

"What about men?" she asks.

"It's not as complicated. I always know where I stand with men. Either above or below them." I laugh. "Besides, I don't tell them nearly the stuff I tell women."

"Why's that?"

"I don't trust them."

"But I hear you saying that you don't trust women, either."

"No, I didn't say that. In fact, I always end up trusting them too much. I wish they didn't matter to me. At least not as much."

CHAPTER 5

The exact date of my Brooklyn Bridge jump was Thursday July 28, 1983. The papers said I fell 135 feet ("the height of a ten-story building") and hit the water at 75 miles an hour. They said I survived the fall with only minor bruises and that, at one point, I was observed by hundreds of onlookers to be "lazily" swimming the East River. I quote Officer Larry Wiltbank as he spoke to the *Post*: "He looked fine. He looked like he was trying to swim the East River twice over."

That was true. I couldn't make my mind up between Brooklyn and Manhattan. There were pros and cons to washing up on either shore.

But going back to the moment I hit the water, immediately thereafter I realized my primary decision—to die—was no longer mine to make. It wasn't happening. All my air was gone. My fight was gone. I didn't kick or paddle or try to rise. I kept slipping further and further into the cold and darkness below me. But I remained fully conscious of everything: the slow pull towards the bottom, the muffled sound of a boat overhead, the underwater echo of my bubbles trailing away, the taste of dirty water in my mouth. I couldn't help noticing my own sense of calm as I stared at the rippling surface above me. It was blue, so incredibly blue. Time had stopped. There seemed to be no separation between river and sky, no boundary between me (and all the other fish) and that big world out there, that world filled with all my oxygen. Both water and sky, each brilliantly blue, were captured under what appeared to be a big blue bowl overturned on New York City. Way above me, at the highest point of the bowl, two suns shimmered like a pair of fiery eyes.

The next thing I became aware of was my wallet floating in the water directly in front of my face. It had blown out the bottom of my back pocket, squirted right through the seams by the force of my fall. Again, with a detached calm that I could have never summoned with my conscious mind, I reached out and snatched it in my fingers. There was $250 in there, and it suddenly occurred to me that people who survived jumping off the Brooklyn Bridge probably had to pay a fine. I would need that money and most likely some form of identification. It seemed that the proper thing to do was to get to the surface, talk to the authorities, calm everyone down, and straighten out the matter in such a way that we'd all be home for dinner. What money I had left could go towards cab fare.

I waited patiently to see how much further I would sink. When I stopped sinking, stopped "not" breathing, stopped waiting for death or something else to "happen," it was then that the thought of using my willpower came back to me, striking me absurdly (as one who has been banging on a door might suddenly realize that he holds the key).

Renewed with this option, I scissor kicked and shot upwards, breaking the surface of the water and waving my wallet triumphantly in my hand. Immediately I was seized with pain, my body beginning to register the trauma from the fall. It was as though I were in the grip of a crab's claw. My lungs felt vacuumed clean, nearly collapsed and pinching for air. They hurt so badly I couldn't draw breath. My heart throbbed in my throat and the blood pumped with roaring pressure against my ears.

It felt like being born. The East River had acted as my doctor's slap and I, the infant, tried frantically to call forth some kind of give-and-take between oxygen and lungs. I thrashed the water and tried to bite the air. But my lungs seemed frozen in the closed position. Finally, as though they had been squeezed down as far as they could go, burning, aching from emptiness, I sensed that I could do nothing by trying, and that they had to wake up on their own and grab the substance that fuels the machinery of life.

I relaxed. The gagging subsided, and after a moment, in rushed the wind. Pain, pain, unbearable pain. It felt like all my ribs had been cracked and my heart beaten to a pulp. But I took air, great gulps of air, the oxygen coursing through my veins, infusing vitality and restoring my sensations. I tingled with electricity.

For a long time I bobbed in the middle of the river, treading water while I steadied my breath. My focus was blurred, and all I could do was watch the two bright suns pulsing in rhythm to my throbbing heart. A half minute passed and I calmed down, noticing that as I did so, the two suns slowly merged and became a singular ball.

***

"How would it make you feel," I said, "if I unplugged the phone before we made love tonight."

Susan rolled on her back and spread her arms out, crucifix style. It was a warm night in early May 1983. She exhaled slowly and rolled her eyes to the ceiling. "But we just made love fifteen minutes ago," she sighed. "You either have a bad memory or you're taking Superman pills. Or," she said, furrowing her brow and pursing her lips thoughtfully, "I'm not doing a very good job."

I sat at the foot of the bed (actually, a giant futon on the floor of my loft) and drank in the sight of Susan's body, paying particular attention to the fresh perspiration on her neck and belly and the wedge of black, curly pie still gleaming from semen and saliva.

"Susan, what I meant was, how would it make you feel if part of my behavior was to unplug the phone every time before we made love?"

"I'd probably be alarmed," she said, stroking her palm

against her moist belly. "After all, you're not the most popular man in New York City—no offense—but your phone isn't exactly ringing off the hook every time I'm here. I guess I'd think you were trying to hide something from me. Like maybe someone you were afraid might call."

Susan reached far the damp washcloth she always brought to bed with her. "I take it there's a lesson in this?" she said, dabbing the cloth between her legs, lifting her rump and wiping the sheets beneath her. Finished, she tossed the rag at me. "A boy scout is always clean," she said, smiling.

I applied the cold cloth to my crotch. "I'm having trouble with a character in my play," I said.

Susan sighed, rising on one elbow and taking a sip of bottled water. "That again," she said.

"Yes."

She held out her hand for the washcloth but I tossed it over the railing. I took a sip of Evian, which was tepid and devoid of fizz.

"So what's your point about the phone?" she said. "What's that got to do with your play?"

"I'm stuck again," I said. "I want the actions of my characters to speak for them. Right now, as it is, it feels like they're just standing on stage, making speeches."

I looked out the window at the condo across the way. A tall blond woman was lighting candles at a table and two men appeared to be examining a bottle of wine.

"You see, if I did something like unplug the phone or . . . or dash to the bathroom . . . and come out with white powder in my nose—"

Susan laughed.

"—that would speak volumes about my character, right?" I motioned for Susan to slide over and stretched out on my stomach beside her. The damp spot from our lovemaking felt cool like a military medal pressing against my chest. Through the open window a tomato/basil smell drifted up from the Italian-Argentinian restaurant on Columbus Avenue, plus the ambience of horns and traffic, and the fanciful work of the retired concert pianist on the sixth floor, whose strains of Chopin and Brahms rebounded off the other side of the alley.

"I need to create more action, Susan. Something like Willy Loman. You could just tell where he was headed, that he was going to kill himself. His actions were making it clear."

***

Like most people, my eyes are located about five inches above my chin. As I bobbed in the East River my chin rose perhaps eight inches above the water's surface, making my point of view—at wave crest—approximately fourteen inches high. That's considerably less than the proverbial bird's eye view, as I had enjoyed, however fleetingly, from the bridge. It was also a great deal less than the relatively lofty perch my eyes were normally accustomed to when I stood on my feet. What I had now was the vision of a beagle, the viewpoint of a log, making the Manhattan and Brooklyn shorelines seem impossibly far away. The only things I could see well were the objects above me: the tops of the World Trade Center and the towering span of the Brooklyn Bridge. I gaped at hundreds of people on the walkway, waving at me.

Maybe it was my imagination but could I be hearing laughter? Cheers? Shouts of encouragement? My God, I thought, I had done the impossible. I had leaped to my death and survived without a scratch. I held proof of the miracle— my wallet in my hand. Its presence in my grip, complete with its $250 and condom "O" crease on its side, was proof I had snatched victory from the dark waters of defeat. With joy and abandonment I shouted, "Who needs this!?!" and threw my wallet high in the air. It hit the water and sank out of sight. With it went the money plus my driver's license, automatic teller card, and employee I.D.

The party over, I became aware of the swift current carrying me out to sea. It dragged me along and the bridge seemed to be pulling back in the other direction, getting smaller and smaller. What an absurdity, I thought, that after trying to snuff my own life, I was now faced with having to swim hard in order to save it. Even more absurd was when I asked myself which way to go. I heard a voice—a voice more like someone else's than my own—that said, "I'll take Manhattan," and with a few bars of music, other voices chorused that that was the direction to go.

At first I liked it, this feeling of self-recognition, this rare and unusual role as a doer of a spectacular feat. In a matter of seconds I had gone from unknown playwright to Guinness World Record material. It was like being a star in a movie of my own making. But it wasn't long before a slow surge of panic began to grow inside me. Swimming took forever. My pants and baggy shirt fought against me, dragging on every stroke. My shoes made kicking nearly impossible; it was as if I had rocks tied to my ankles. My throat burned as I gulped mouthfuls of water. No matter how hard I swam, the Manhattan side seemed the same distance away. It looked like I'd wash out to Staten Island before I ever swam to shore. The panic worked itself into a frenzy, a nervy series of mental explosions every time I had a negative thought. My movements became jerky and several times I went under, the panic overcoming me like a school of piranha.

Ten minutes passed and I still paddled against the current. Near exhaustion, I cursed the absurd treadmill I seemed to be on. Why couldn't I just *die*? I pleaded—and a sinister thought occurred to me. Maybe I had died, I reasoned. After all, it had been deathly quiet under the surface. Perhaps I had passed out of my body. Perhaps its dead flesh was at this moment tumbling on the river bottom, bouncing around the garbage and abandoned cars, getting hooked on an open door or radio antenna, or maybe just sinking stone-cold into the muck.

I couldn't swim much further and Manhattan still looked to be over a mile away. Was it my imagination or was the shoreline pulling back from me with every stroke?

"Welcome to hell, buddy," said the voice in my head. "First a little diving lesson. Now we're going to swim. For eternity. Getting tired? Too bad! We've just started. Maybe you'd feel better without those aching limbs. Think about it. Think what could take off your limbs."

A shark, I thought.

"Shark?" said the voice. "A shark you say? You want a few sharks? Glad you thought of it, buddy. Of course we can have sharks. We can have all the sharks you want! This is hell. We can do it all. Anything's possible when you put your mind to it, friend."

The dialogue ran back and forth, with the old, familiar voice of "me" getting seduced and badgered by the second, malevolent "me."

"How would you like to swim in hot lava, friend?"

"Leave me alone!"

"Aren't you tired of choking on all that water? Wouldn't you rather choke on—"

"Hot coals? I mean lava. No, I mean—"

"Excellent! A hot lava mouthwash. We'll have to try that for the *next* thousand years!"

I pushed on, swimming and crying, asking God for a second chance. It seemed hopeless. I was doomed to paddle against the river forever.

I finally reached shore at the point of exhaustion. The police waited for me. Behind them was an ambulance, a crowd, and Susan, waving, her red shoes still in her hands. Two cops in rubber hip boots waded in the water and hoisted me up on wobbly legs.

I stood still to catch my breath. My eyes traveled from the crowd, to Susan, then over to a giant baby doll crumpled on the rocks by the water's edge. It was an actual-size doll, propped in a sitting position, looking hideous, like some evil artifact guarding the mouth of a cave. Its tattered, yellowed dress and mud stains on its face suggested it, too, might have been tossed from the bridge. Glass eyes stared back at me.

Of course, I thought. I *have* died and gone to hell. It happened during the calm as I floated to the bottom. My spirit separated and must have slipped into a subterranean world, I thought, a double world completely separate from Susan and the others. It was like a snow shaker upside down. Back on earth, I reasoned, Susan was watching them haul my body from the river. The doll was a symbol to remind me. A little joke of the Devil's. Meanwhile, my spirit was in this other place, cut off from help. These weren't real cops, real EMTs, real bystanders. They were demons. The Susan I stared at was also a demon. As strong arms steadied me and pulled me from the river, the voice grew louder in my head. Swimming the river was your first test, it said. There's plenty more where that came from.

CHAPTER 6

Paul Gorman, M.D., looked up at the ceiling, sighed, and stopped writing. He placed his gold Cross pen in the binding of his patient's chart and shut the chart, pulling on the tip of the pen so it stuck out like a bookmark.

He chuckled sadly. "This guy is happy to be here," he said, shaking his head as he ran his fingers over his thinning black hair. "He's delighted, completely overjoyed. He knows the routine, he says he likes the food, and he can't wait until morning when he gets to meet the rest of the staff. What do you do with someone like that? Can anyone tell me how I'm supposed to go in there and convince him he's got a disease?"

"Give him time," I said. I looked at the clock in the nurses' station. Five minutes to one in the morning. On the desk beside Gorman I could see his hastily written medication orders. Haldol now and Lithium for later, after his bloodwork. "Yep, give him time," I said. I grabbed the flashlight and clipboard in preparation for hourly rounds. On the clipboard I penciled the name of our new patient, Terry Donofrio, for room 713.

"Is he on any special precautions?" I asked Gorman.

"Yeah, happy precautions. Don't let him have too much fun."

Susan bustled up the hall as I made my way to check on our patients. She held Terry's clothing—folded jeans, sweatshirt, shoes, and socks—in a wire basket.

"Terry's asking about you," she said, winking. "He seems to think you have a pretty good handle on his problem." She laughed. "See you in a little bit," she said.

We passed each other, lightly brushing hands. I clicked on my flashlight and looked in room 701.

It was May 23, 1983. My twenty-seventh birthday. (Also the one hundredth birthday of the Brooklyn Bridge.) In six and a half hours Susan and I would dash out of the Mitchell-Walker Psychiatric Clinic on Manhattan's Upper East Side, deposit our paychecks, then catch a train at Penn Station, heading for the white sand and sea breeze of Long Island's Jones Beach.

I had been working full-time nights since November as a psychiatric nurse aide. That's where I had first met Susan; we started work on the same day together. But while she worked all three shifts and had some semblance of a normal life, I left work at dawn five days a week and caught a subway to Greenwich Village where I continued as a full-time student in NYU's Dramatic Writing Program. I had a play ready for production and scrambled around the clock trying to find actors, technicians, a director, anyone interested in helping me. Most days I got home around four or five, growing very edgy on the A Train and feeling the elasticity in my knee joints as I walked the last two blocks to my apartment on West 74th. I lived on the third floor but usually took the elevator, resting my back against the handrail as it chugged up slowly. Once in my apartment I pulled my books out and tried to look at homework while I wolfed down a plate of Kraft macaroni and cheese. My body starved for sleep but by some cruel formula the need for it made it impossible to acquire. I lived numb. My mind was restless, nagging me in what little sleep I got, my dreams those of scaffoldings and stairways, of hallways and too many doors, of chasing manuscripts blown by the wind. I learned to sleep between classes and even on the subway between the Village and home. But every time I started to slip into unconsciousness, my mind tried to yank me back, recalling one more item I had overlooked—a piece of dialogue, classroom notes, something from the store—my whole lifestyle a battle with the dread of falling behind. I made things worse by drinking too much coffee; I was a slave to the rhythms it created.

But school had been out since May 17. I was beginning to gain some weight back and was sleeping enough to erase the shakes and the shadows under my eyes. In the early morning of my birthday I looked forward to falling asleep on the sand.

I worked my way to the end of the hall. Everyone was sleeping except Beverly, the fifty-five-year-old redhead who was masturbating, as usual. The sight of her knees up under the covers and the sound of her moisture no longer bothered me. I marked an "M" next to her name.

The light went on in 713. I walked to the doorway and peered inside.

"Pssst. Hey, buddy. Take a look at this." Terry, naked except for a pair of baggy white undershorts with a coffee stain on the front, sat with his legs crossed on the foot of his bed. He motioned for me to come in his room. He was a young man of twenty-five with short, brown hair, dark eyes, and an athlete's knotty shoulders tensing and relaxing like rubber bands. He had an appreciable V of dark hair on his chest, topped off by a gold cross dangling from a chain.

He held up a short, sharp object. "They didn't take my pen," he said, grinning. "I suppose that means I'm not on suicide precautions." He chuckled, pretending to stick the pen in his eye.

"That's good," I said flatly.

"You bet that's good, but the nurse didn't give me anything to write on, so I'm taking notes on my flesh."

Terry pointed to his left leg. Blue writing decorated his thigh. "Listen to this," he said, looking down. " 'There once was a patient named Stan/Who lived in an old coffee can/When he wanted some speed/He found that his need/Was supplied by the beans in his hand.' Pretty good, eh?"

I focused on the pen. "Are you going to keep writing on yourself?" I said.

"Sure am. Unless I run out of ink. Or space. In that case I'll go next door. I saw a real fatty sleeping by the window. I could probably do 'The Waste Land' on her and still have room for more poems of my own."

"Please," I said, "don't try anything like that."

Terry's eyes twinkled with mischievous fire. "How come so glum, chum?" he said. "Have a seat by me." He patted the bed. "Plenty of room for the wanderer. You know, it's great to see you, Mike."

"It's Mark," I said.

"Oh. Sure it is. How could I be so rude. Wasn't more than a month ago, was it?"

"About that. Maybe six weeks."

"Well, it's great to be back," he said. He held out his hand.

"Welcome," I said, matter-of-factly. I stayed where I was.

Terry slapped his hands together. "C'mon, it's past midnight. Let's have a little fun. At least a smile. Jeez, what you need is therapy, pal," he said. "Let's start with word association. I'll name the parts of a woman's body and you name your favorite fruits, okay? Let's start with nipples."

I replied with silence. Privately I thought, "Grapes."

"C'mon, lighten up," he said. "What's it take to getcha feelin' good about yourself?"

"Sorry, I got rounds," I said. I waved my flashlight.

He laughed. "Don't we all," he said. "Don't we all."

Terry Donofrio was a manic depressive. This was his third time on the unit since I had been working there. He always came in on an "up," usually after sabotaging his medication. On his previous admission he came to us strapped on a stretcher with four security guards in escort at each wheel. "Hey, Mike, look at this," he had said. "I'm the lead float in the St. Patrick's Day Parade!"

I remembered thinking then how manic depressives were so lively that they should be on television game shows where their talents could be put to use. They had a way of infecting you with silliness, and nurses and aides on the unit admitted to each other that a manic patient was good to have around when all the others were depressed. But as Sir Isaac Newton was fond of saying, what goes up is pretty messy coming down. Manics crashed once the drugs caught up with them. That, and lack of stimulation. Then Terry and all those like him would sit and stare for hours, the older ones falling asleep in their chairs, their heads on their chests, sometimes a line of drool trickling down. They lost concern for their appearance, sometimes needing to be fed and bathed, and it wasn't totally unusual for a suicide attempt now and then—rebellion against being normal. You could always spot a manic on the day he came down—he wore that vacant look, that hopeless, burned-out stare, the look of someone who's lost his best friend or has been booted out of heaven.

Terry had talked to me on the down side the last time he had been at Mitchell-Walker. He was lethargic, completely overcome by a sullen mood, spending a second day in bed with a washcloth on his brow. I was in and out of his room all night long, checking his blood pressure because I feared we might have overmedicated him.

"Do you have any idea what being manic is like?" he had asked, surrendering a limp arm to the blood pressure cuff.

"No," I said, lying. He peeled back his washcloth and opened one eye.

"It's like having all the money in the world," he said, "but nowhere to spend it."

***

That afternoon Susan and I nestled in the sand together. We scraped out a shallow pit beneath one of the many dunes topped with sharp grasses, digging in behind a driftwood log that gave us additional shelter from the wind. It was a lackluster day, the sun pale behind thin, high clouds, the breeze cool and at times peppering my arms and legs with grains of sand—and with goosebumps like little sand dunes themselves, each topped with a blond blade of grass. We were alone except for a father and son running by the water's edge, the boy flying a red, diamond-shaped kite. The man carried a radio and Latino music rose and fell with the wind—as did his son's laughter, the cries of gulls, and the churning of the waves, all of it blending into a soft, sleepy texture, soothing and distant. Susan and I snuggled low, hugging each other between two cotton towels. Susan wore a black, two-piece bathing suit with stiff, pointy breast cups that reminded me of speaker cones.

"What did you think of Act II?" I asked, placing one of my tennis shoes on top the pile of papers that was my play.

"It made me laugh," Susan said. She placed her arms around my neck and drew me to her, engaging my lips in a long, moist, reptilian kiss, sans lipstick.

"Did you feel anything?" I asked.

"Feel what? You mean like emotion? I can't say I was deeply moved, Mark. Why, was that your intention?"

"Come on. What do you mean, was it your intention? Of course it was my intention! I wanted you to feel something."

"It's pretty hard to feel something about a bunch of school kids playing hooky from a nun." Susan strummed her fingernails across my back, stirring up a fresh patch of gooseflesh.

"It's more than that," I said, grabbing her hand.

"Yes, but I'm talking about general impressions. Overall impression. Look, you told me to be frank. You said you wanted to be compared to the best there was—"

"I remember what I told you, Susan. That's great. Now, what about subtext?" I said.

"Oh, you've got some character development going on," Susan said, "but it's too preliminary to make me feel anything significant. All I can really comment on is the plot."

"And you don't like the plot."

"It can be more original, Mark."

"But there's a lot of subtext," I said. "All kinds of things are going on." I took Susan's hand and removed it off my body.

"Let's forget it," she said. "I can see this isn't going the way either of us wants it to. I'm sorry, I have to be honest. We talked about this before. It's already been done, Mark."

"But it's me," I said. "I've spent almost a year on this."

"Sure. And it's good for that reason. But you've got to think of an audience too. And I don't think there's much of an audience for a play about kids. Especially after you told me that you're going to cast adults for the parts. I think that's dangerous to begin with. This isn't Charley Brown."

"Damn right it isn't Charley Brown."

"And that's good too. But it's your first play, Mark. It's an exercise. Why don't you think of it as a good first step and move on to the next? Try something else now. A year is hardly a long time for a really great play to be written. Many take a lot longer than that."

"But I can produce this now," I said. "I talked to Steve and Barry and they told me how much their play cost at that Presbyterian Church."

"You mean that one we saw back in March? That was terrible. *Piano Player on the Titanic.* Yuk! They didn't get a single review." The wind kicked up and Susan tucked her legs into her chest, her whole body rippling with shivers under her towel. "How many people were there on opening night?" she said. "Maybe fifty? Did they tell you how much money they *made* on it?"

"They lost a few hundred, I'm sure. But that's not the point. I'm ready to lose money, too, if it means putting something up on stage."

"Why don't you save your money for another play?" she said. "Or use it for a trip somewhere?"

I slipped out between the towels and sat on the driftwood log. We'd been through the "nurturing girlfriend" scene several times before, enough to make our conversations seem like play rehearsals themselves. Susan did the "I love you/I support you" role well, but at the same time, being a native New Yorker, she felt she had a lot more on the ball when it came to Broadway and knowing what the public was willing to pay for. It hurt to agree with her, but she was usually right. What she didn't know, however, was that I had already taken her advice on how to spend my money. I had just bought tickets for a vacation in July. Susan wasn't invited.

"I got a letter from Kelly," I said, looking on the other side of the log for a blade of grass, a straw, a gull feather, anything to pick my teeth.

"I think I saw that on your table the other day," Susan said. "I forget—is that a male or female friend of yours?"

"Male. My best friend from high school."

"How come he calls you the fifth Beatle?"

I laughed, remembering the address on the envelope. Good old Kelly Scott. The skinny kid with the Elvis Presley crop of hair. Winner of the Most Changed Personality Award. As far back as first grade he and I were the darlings of the out crowd, instigators of rebellion, captains of calamity, always on the ropes against the nuns. Together we fought them for eight years (my play was an attempt to show Catholicism as being diametrically opposed to puberty) and then in public high school, getting suspended together for pranks or things we had published in the school paper. When we emptied the biology lab of two hundred crayfish and dumped them into the back of the driver's ed car, we made an everlasting name for ourselves.

Ha was with me on my first LSD trip. And my last.

Then out of the blue, Kelly changed. College turned him into Achievement Man. He quickly became the most unavailable best friend I ever had. While I was still bumping around between the local colleges, searching out West for "where it's at," and sidelining myself for two years in Alaska, he went on to nail down an MBA, feeding me one terse letter for every two or three novellas I mailed to him. But I never let it put me off, believing instead that his higher calling justified my relegation to second place. I was willing to wait. Good times would roll in again, as soon as Kelly came out of his "serious" phase. For as long as we had known each other we had shared a maniacal, stoned humor that I believed was my core connection to everything I valued. It was laughter without reason. When we got together everything took on a perverted twist, and we were forever explaining our viewpoints to others or, just as well, turning away to laugh at something else. We often read each other's minds. It seemed I'd never find a friend who knew me like Kelly.

Just when this connection had seemed irreparably cut, a new set of circumstances brought us back together. In 1980 I got a job as a house orderly at Ronson Lodger Medical Center, a 380-bed institution built on old swampland a few miles south of Erie, Pennsylvania. Kelly had just landed a personnel manager's position with a large paper and pulp firm in Meadville, only a few miles away. On one of my many visits to his rented house (which were received with less and less warmth) I mentioned a position was being vacated in the administration department of Ronson Lodger. Kelly's attitude toward me changed dramatically. Did I know any of the other administrators personally? Could I find out about the guy leaving, what kind of things he was responsible for? Sure, I said, I can help you out. I floated through Ronson Lodger pretty easily and had a good rapport with just about everyone: doctors, nurses, heads of the departments.

I greased the door very well for Kelly and he stepped right in, taking over a post with public relations. I made sure he was well spoken for and to the best of my knowledge, none of the other applicants had a representative already there at the hospital, beating the drum for them. He was almost a "known" before his first interview, and there's not a soul at the hospital who'd deny I paved the way for him. He thanked me profusely —then once again, went cold. It was like he never knew me. A few months later I spotted him in the cafeteria with a couple urologists and a reporter from the local paper. I joined them at the table and got this terrible feeling like he threw up an invisible wall. After that, if I passed him in the hall, he'd smile at me weakly, always patting his suit coat pocket to let me know there was something he forgot and needed to be on his way. Not even the highest-paid surgeons treated me like that.

I will say one thing in Kelly's defense. He was trying to get on with the rest of his life. I reminded him of the old days, the party daze he'd just as soon forget. While I still hurt from his rebuffs, I wasn't too thick-headed to realize that Kelly's career was on a different track than mine, and that his desire for intoxication had probably changed as well.

A year later, Kelly was changing again. Just before NYU got out I received a letter of his inviting me to his cottage on Lake Erie. The tone was warm and full of nostalgia—lots of references to things from our junior high days, a few private drug culture phrases, sprinklings of rock-n-roll lyrics that still held their power. The letter tapped into that part of me I once shared with him, setting off a chain of memories, flooding me with the essence of bygone times—sights, sounds, smells—as though it were a music box that had played beside my bed as a child.

***

Kelly was baiting me.

"I'm going back to Erie in July," I said to Susan. "Kelly bought this cottage he rented last year and he's invited me to his housewarming party."

Susan rolled on her back and lifted a leg under the towel, the wind catching a corner of the cloth and lifting it to expose her thigh, and above that, where he legs joined, the black triangle of her bathing suit. She said nothing, only put an arm behind her head and sighed, looking up at the hazy sky. With her other hand she felt for the towel and tucked it around her waist.

"I take it you're going alone?" she said.

"Yes."

The rest of the afternoon our conversation rose and died

like a candle struggling in the wind, like flower buds trying to rebound against a succession of frosts. Returning later on the train, Susan tried to bridge the silence one more time by asking me again about the fifth Beatle.

"It's Beetle," I said, "B-e-e-t-l-e. But that's just the name of the club. So we don't get sued. When I was up in Alaska we had this joke going that the first person to get to New York City was to open up a nightclub called the Fifth Beetle. We wrote really long letters. At least I did. Anyway, I drew a logo for it, a bug with a body shaped like Paul McCartney's guitar. He was their bass player, you know. Played left handed."

"I know." Susan smiled cruelly.

"The gimmick was that we'd have one of those number counters like you see at a deli—you know, the kind that tell you which customer is next—and every so often the number would turn over and we'd buy drinks on the house."

"I don't get it," Susan said.

"The number is for the amount of fifth Beatles in the world. Every time there's a new fifth Beatle, the number changes."

"Like fifty billion served?"

"Yeah, you got it."

"No," Susan said, scratching her head. "I *don't* get it. What's a fifth Beatle?"

I looked at Susan and smiled, thinking, Damn if I ever tell you. I recalled the line Kelly came up with years before (which, incidentally, he had used to close his letter):

"Love means never having to say, 'I guess you had to be there, man.'"

CHAPTER 7

Photos of another woman:
- Catherine Hayes in bare feet and faded jeans, sitting on the trunk of my car. Her jeans have a hole in the right knee and her skin pokes through.
- Catherine in the morning at one of our camping trips, stooping over a smoky fire while cleaning out an iron skillet, beside her a tin dish with soapy water balanced on the rocks that ringed the fire.
- Catherine with two girlfriends in front of a red wooden covered bridge.
- Catherine at sunset, face in shadow, underexposed.
- Smiling Catherine, lobster dinner, upstairs at my place, Erie, Pennsylvania
- Catherine with author
- Author and Catherine
- Close-up Catherine, golden-haired Catherine, Catherine of the bobbed nose, the freckled shoulder, the red lines on her ass from the seat of her resilient 10-speed, the brass Buddha incense burner, the ear-splitting whistle when she called Duke, her black Lab.

If Kelly had been baiting a mouse trap, then his mentioning of Catherine had been the big cheese. Catherine had been a fellow student at C. Emily Barrett College, a branch campus of Penn State University, where I went out with her for a year and a half. She had left Erie last January for New Mexico, to live with friends and start her life all over. (That's how she put it, "Starting all over." Catherine was twenty-three.)

But now she was coming back, at least according to Kelly. Her mother, a widow, was getting remarried. The wedding was the same week as Kelly's housewarming party, and his letter implied that I already knew.

I didn't know a thing about it and the whole affair troubled me. Catherine was never far from my thoughts—sometimes right smack in the middle of them when Susan and I made love. Susan didn't know about Catherine, of course, except when I mentioned her briefly on one of Susan's and my early dates, playing down the importance of the old relationship because I was coming on to Susan as a fully equipped, compassionate male, heart still pink and fleshy and ready to bleed in the name of love. It was pure bullshit. It was also habit. I had used the "tormented, intellectual, alienated" writer ploy so often that it was second nature to me. When I really refined my act, adding a touch of shyness and sincerity, I found I attracted very nurturing, attentive females, the kind of women who save themselves by finding someone to save. I loved being saved.

My little game also kept anyone—myself included—from asking why I was twenty-seven and never married yet. It also helped me minimize my feelings for Catherine, whom I had really loved, because I was too scared to let go of her completely. I believed that I'd always be in love and that I'd always be single. It was just a matter of orbiting around and around; in time Catherine and I would cross paths again.

The day I got Kelly's letter I called Catherine in New Mexico. No answer. The next day no answer. I started thinking about her during school. I tried again; no answer. I called her mother. Congratulations, I said. I heard you're getting married. Yes, the wedding was on, she said, and Catherine would be there. And where was she now, I asked. This week she thought her daughter might be skiing. Keep trying, she said. I thanked her. The next day I bought my ticket.

But it didn't occur to me until the train ride back from the beach that Catherine knew very well that today was my birthday. Yet I hadn't received a card. Perhaps tonight she would call. I was dying to hear her voice again.

Photos of me after diving off the Brooklyn Bridge (page four of the *Post*):

• Wading out the last few feet from the East River, my breathlessness evident from the hollow cheeks and pain on my face. I looked like someone had punched me in the stomach.

• Cops in black wader boots, yanking me up by my arms after I had fallen ashore.

• A group of EMTs escorting me to the ambulance.

• By far the most dramatic photo, the front pager featuring your author being held under his shoulders by two police officers, the three of us knee-deep in the swirling water with me staring directly at the camera. My shirt, proclaiming "Kent State" in huge white letters, blazed like a billboard across my chest.

As I stumbled dazed and dripping to the first of many ambulances, every thought, every perception, every chemical or electrical occurrence in my brain was operating on the belief that demons were going to kill me. I felt for certain that I was in hell. No person, no evidence was going to change that.

Two EMTs sat me on the back of the ambulance and a woman snipped off my shirt with scissors. I expected her to slash the blades across my throat. Or jam the point into my ear. Instead, she had me bow my head, placing a white towel over it. I thought, Aha! So this is how they behead you in hell. Cover the head and off it comes. But she went on to dry my hair, humming some silly song, checking my head for injuries in the same way the old school nurse used to check us for lice. She looked into my eyes with a flashlight and asked me if I knew my name and what day it was.

The two men came back over and helped her lay me down and strap me to a stretcher. So they aren't going to kill me here, I thought. They'll take me somewhere else where they can torture me for days. They'll kick me and cut me into little pieces. They'll hack off my penis and stuff it in my throat. They'll smash my balls with a rusty hammer. They'll make me drink Drano. They'll jam a blowtorch up my nose. Burn out my eyes in their sockets, then turn the flame on my balls.

The list went on and on. My mind refused to stop naming tortures. It painted scenes from medieval castles, dank torture cellars, from the dreaded experimental labs of the Nazi death camps, from Africa with its anthills and poisonous snakes, to North Vietnam's POW camps. All this pain was destined for me, filling up my future like a dance card in hell. Demons would soon be swimming in my blood.

But not here, I thought as they shoved me in the ambulance. Not with all these spectators. What they were doing was taking me where they could work undisturbed.

Where they took me was Bellevue.

***

September 6, 1983
(Afternoon session)

Yesterday Doctor Bowman and I agreed we can work together. She promised to meet with me at least three times a week. I've got new slippers on my feet, and the ward clerk informed me that sometime today I'd get my clothes back, after they finish sewing name tags into them.

It's almost one o'clock, time for our meeting, and I go up the hall towards the little office, looking down at the forest-green carpet blackened from burning cigarettes, hundreds of long, dark scars that look like divots on a golf course.

I open the door and Bowman's waiting inside. My chart is

open on the desk and she glances up, nodding and motioning for me to take a seat, then she returns to the chart, jotting notes.

On one of the chairs is a folded blanket. I sit on top of it and wait for her to finish writing.

"Okay," she says, setting her pen down in the chart and closing it on top. "Yesterday we didn't talk about why you were here. I believe you wanted to know what's expected of you. Why don't we get that out in the open, before we go into anything else?"

"That's fine," I say. "I guess it goes without saying that I'm on a locked unit." I stretch my hands out in front of me, palms together, then pull them apart as though stretching taffy.

"Very true. You were delusional your first forty-eight hours here, Mark, so I don't know how your memory is of the past week or so. Are you up to hearing all of this?"

Bowman leans forward and locks her fingers, resting her hands on her desk. She's wearing a dark blue blazer and I notice an expensive gold watch glinting from the cave of her sleeve.

"Go ahead," I say. "I want to know what I'm up against."

"Basically, you're a ward of the state. You're to remain here up to a period of one year, at which time your treatment may be extended indefinitely—"

"Indefinitely!?!" I gasp.

"—or you may be released on probation. Depending on your evaluation—*my* evaluation—you might also be released back to the court, where you would stand trial."

"Trial? Trial for what?"

"Do you recall stealing anything recently?" Bowman asks. "About two weeks ago?"

"Oh. That," I say, hanging my head. "But I didn't mean it."

My mind is swamped by memories of pain: running, fighting, handcuffs, steel bars in a jail.

"Somehow I expected you to say that, Mark. That's what a lot of other people believe, too. That you didn't mean it. Which is why you're here. The judge has asked us to try to determine the state of your thinking at the time. Based on what we come up with, that'll indicate what form of long-term rehabilitation you'll need."

"I have to stay here a year, doctor?"

"Up to a year, if necessary. Do you also recall jumping off the Brooklyn Bridge?"

"Doctor, that's not exactly the kind of thing one easily forgets."

Bowman weaves her fingers together and stretches her arms out like a piano player loosening up. Two knuckles crack, delicately. "The judge holds the opinion that your state of mind when you went off the bridge was the same state of mind when you committed your recent felony. He sent you here to find out if that's true. If it is, you won't be charged."

"Charged? You mean I can go to prison?"

Bowman opens my chart and runs her finger down a page. "The issue is insanity, Mark. You've worked in this system. I'm sure I don't have to tell you what's at stake. In a month or two I've got to call a preliminary staffing for you. That's when you go before the other doctors and anyone else who's worked on your case. At that time we'll review our options. The entire team—not just I—will make an initial recommendation back to the judge."

"Jesus," I sighed, sinking low in my chair. "How can I get out of this?"

"Get out? What do you mean?"

"I mean how can I help. I don't have a year to lose. I want this matter settled quickly and I'll do anything to help it along."

"It's good to see you motivated," Bowman says, smiling. "You want to help? You can start by being honest, Mark. I've got the reports from the other hospitals here," she says, tapping my chart, "and quite frankly, you looked to be playing with about half a deck. Am I making myself clear?"

I nod, looking down.

"You've been anything but honest. Even to your own

family members. That's got to stop. You see, to help you I need information. Very important information. And most of that I've got to get from you. It's vital for both of us that you let me know what's been going on inside of you."

CHAPTER 8

"If you don't talk about your problems they have a way of building up inside of you."

Susan said those words on the highly refrigerated, dark-windowed bus as it dieseled down to Asbury Park on the Fourth of July, 1983. Once again the subject was my play, *Can of Worms*, which was now moving into the preproduction phase, due mainly to the fact I had offered Barry Gordon, fellow playwright, the director's chair at $350 a week. I did this, of course, without consulting Susan. She knew nothing until she walked in on the end of my phone conversation with him that morning. It was she who brought the subject up on the bus.

"It's no big deal," I said. "The only reason why it's such a big secret is because you're trying to make me feel guilty for not telling you."

"I'm not trying to make you feel guilty," Susan said. "It was plain to see you felt guilty all along. It was on your face."

"It was not."

"When you hung up you knew I had caught you."

"Caught me nothing," I said. "You don't know what you're talking about."

"Look," she said, sitting forward and slapping her hands together as though for prayer, "the issue isn't whether you hired Barry to be your director. I don't care if you hired Sam Peckinpaw and plan on using real blood. The issue is that you feel you have to keep secrets from me. Isn't that true?"

I looked out the window at the New Jersey scenery

blurring by. "There are secrets," I said, "and that's what they are, secrets. Everybody has them. Even you, Susan. But there are also parts of my life that I just live and make decisions about, and I don't stop every five minutes and wonder if it's something I should be getting your opinion on. I didn't realize we were becoming Siamese twins."

It was to have been a holiday, a great day at the beach. Susan was dressed for fun in a floppy yellow sun hat, a maroon tube top, and a soft cotton black pleated skirt. Her shoulders glistened with cocoa oil, leaving a stain on the seat. We had the seat with the emergency exit, and before Susan had started the little firestorm over Barry, she had been lying back against the door with her legs stretched over mine. I had been rubbing oil onto her calves and knees, happy as a drug addict in a hypochondriac's bathroom, except whenever Susan winced because I had been pressing too hard. Even though the bus driver had made a public announcement forbidding us to do so, I had opened the window a crack and was working contentedly on those magnificent legs while she had struggled to read the *New York Times Magazine* with the wind flapping her paper. She ended up folding it commuter style, just wide enough to read by the column.

I can't remember how the conversation started, exactly. We had been talking about my moodiness and my inability to express my feelings. At one point she had said something about my need to protect my ideas. "You think you have a lot to hide," she had said. "You think whatever's in your head is so unusual that no one out there will understand you. You've got to watch that. A bad case of it is called paranoia."

I considered her remark, considered it for what seemed like an eternity of silence. However, a very stalwart and soldierly voice, a voice like Errol Flynn's or, more precisely, Winston Churchill's, commanded from some inner island that we should, to the last dying man, defend our beaches, our streets, our towns and villages. We should, with no exception, ever lay down our arms before the foreign invaders. Encroachment. Relationships were filled with wars of encroachment. And spying and surprise attacks. I thought of a two-line lyric from Steely Dan, which was at that very moment prominently scratched on one of the men's room stalls in the film school at New York University:

Low black cards can make you money
So you hide them when you're able

I was *always* hiding things. Always. What made this woman think I was going to change a lifetime habit just to be on the sunny side with her?

Then she made the remark about Barry. Got me to admit I didn't want her to know. She told me I was nuts to offer him $350. She said I was nuts to offer anybody anything at all.

"This town has names for people like you," she said.

"Chump?"

"No. Victim. Barry's going to appreciate your little gravy train, I'm sure. But if he ever had any talent—and God knows that play last March didn't exactly reveal an ocean of talent—well, let's just say that whatever talent he has, has just been undermined by your offer to pay him."

"But he really wants to do it. Besides, three-fifty is hardly anything to a guy like Barry."

Susan reached behind her and pushed the window shut. "Don't believe what you see, Mark. I met him at that party of your sister's, remember? He dressed the part but believe me, he's like everyone else in this town, living hand to mouth. How old is he? Forty-five, fifty maybe? And he's still trying to get his first review in the *Voice*?"

"So? What's wrong with that?" I said.

"Nothing," Susan said. "I just bet he's got a lot of the same foods you do in his refrigerator. He's not what you think he is, that's for sure."

"I'm glad you're so certain about these things," I said, my eyes traveling down and away from her. "Sometimes I think you know too much, Susan. You always suspect the worst in people and you're so sophisticated that you don't believe in dreaming anymore."

That one got heard by several people in front of us. Unknowingly, our voices had been rising steadily and heads were now leaning toward the aisle, ears thrown back to catch the argument.

Susan stared at me in silence. When she finally spoke her voice was low, cool, and deliberately even. "Be careful when you use the word 'always' with me. I'm not 'always' anything. And if it seems I don't trust dreaming, it's only because I've got more experience than you and have been there to see what happens sometimes to dreamers. I only want to protect you, Mark. I care about you and only wish you'd take more time with things. You can get what you want but you have to understand timing. I think you're pushing this play. It's not ready yet. That's why I don't trust Barry. He mentioned he had read it at the party."

"He said he liked it."

"Yes, Mark, he said that. But in a certain way that I guess you didn't pick up on. Oh, God, this is hard." Susan folded her hands in her lap and looked down for a minute. "Look," she said, "if I had been working on it as hard as you, and going to school and working full-time nights, I would be real eager for positive feedback. And when you're that set on something, you don't always hear—"

"Okay," I said. "I get what you're saying."

"He was just being kind. That's why you need to be sure of things before you start spending your money."

I was sure. Until now, I thought. We rode some distance with neither of us speaking. Then out of the blue (and with no trace of malice whatsoever) Susan asked me matter-of-factly what weekend it was that I'd be flying to Pennsylvania.

The bus drew closer to Asbury Park. I stared out at the New Jersey beach communities rolling by. A fine, sunny day with people on bikes, people in convertibles, people going in and out of houses. The bus rolled through alternating patches of sun and shade with big, broadleaf trees winking by, and in between them, glimpses of the yards surrounding the giant Victorian houses, many of them rented out by the week. My eyes took snapshots of tanned, healthy, prosperous-looking men in white tennis shorts standing around smokey barbecues, backslapping each other and blowing the foam off their beers. And women grooming picnic tables with white paper tablecloths, holding down the flapping corners with masking tape, bowls of fruit salad, or ketchup bottles. I saw surfboards on cars. A trunk lid open, a red cooler on the curb. A pile of ice melting on the street. Pairs of tall teenage girls walking down the sidewalks with bright bikini tops and towels around their waists, their legs like tan scissors flashing through their towels.

I thought about how casual everyone seemed to be. People flowed in and out of those big houses, in and out of badminton games, Frisbee, volleyball, food lines at the picnic tables—and most certainly conversations—much more easily than I. They never seemed to be bothered by the same issues I always wrestled with, never talked about the craziness of love or what is real or not real, what is worth living or dying for. They appeared so light-footed, yet so sure, so unencumbered. They lived joke-to-joke, never getting heavy, never getting down. All my sister's friends were that way. So was she. And Susan. And probably every friend of Susan's as well.

"The glib shall inherit the earth," I muttered.

Susan's eyes were closed and her breathing slow and steady. I sighed. I wanted desperately to know what her intentions were—and how she'd react if she knew the real me. I wondered if she was aware that my allowing her to get close to me was threatening all my secrets.

She was getting closer all the time. She was picking up on my inconsistencies. She challenged my thinking by asking me how I'd feel if someone did to me what I proposed doing. The problem was that I didn't think of others as being anything like myself. They were too rich, too glib, too superficial. At work they were crazy. At school they were sharks. No matter what category I lumped them in, they were all inhabitants of another world. It was me against them.

It occurred to me then and there on the bus that Susan's proximity, no matter how threatening, was the only real thing going on in my life. If it wasn't for her challenging me, drawing me out, I'd have disengaged from her long ago. Somehow she was massaging my loneliness, working on my bruised defenses, healing me, a bit too rough at times, by allowing me to see my self.

Susan opened one eye, the big brown button looking me up and down. "What's wrong?" she asked, both eyes opening wide as she stretched and looked out the window. "What are you thinking about now?" she asked.

"Oh, just this thing I saw this morning. When we pulled out of the Port Authority."

"What thing?" she said. "What did you see?"

"A bag lady leaning against a jewelry store."

"Yeah? And?"

"Oh, nothing," I said. "Forget it."

***

September 7, 1983
(Mental meanderings)

Doctor Bowman is the living example of economy in motion. This morning she breezes through the nurses' station, holding her arms out in what is obviously a well-rehearsed drill. One by one the nurses get up from their chairs and pile their charts on her upturned palms like sticks being collected for a fire. Important items are pointed out by Patricia Seifert, the head nurse, as she slaps Post-its on the growing stack, or flagged by Carla, the ward clerk, who, if she's anything like the ones I've worked with, gets paid the least but probably knows more than anyone else how things really run around here. Bowman's like the queen bee collecting her royal jelly.

I want to call Bowman's face striking, exotic, though there's nothing particular that makes it so. I suppose it is a combination of features: her narrow, Arabian nose with its large, pear-shaped nostrils; her upper lip with the gull wing nick in the center; her bottom lip full and rounded like a wave at its crest; firm but slightly hollow cheeks that give her a glamorous yet predatory appeal, like a friendly barracuda.

I got my clothes back last night, including the laces in my tennis shoes. That's a good sign when you've been on suicide precautions. Today I've picked out my favorite chair on the unit, a cushy vinyl thing the color of a clay pot. I pulled it over near the window where I can watch the tennis courts through the thick, mesh screen. The courts are faded now, having been painted a rich, rusty red, only now they're closer to the color of my chair, or more precisely, the color of a pencil eraser. The net sags in the middle of the court, and today, as a harbinger of autumn, I watched a lone brown maple leaf crawl across the court, pulled by the wind like a lobster on a string, its pointed tips scraping quite audibly as it inched forward, finally impaling itself in the net.

I am meeting a lot of new patients. Some come up and introduce themselves, some are brought over and introduced by the staff, but most of them I'm getting to know by sitting in my chair, watching them closely while pretending to read a magazine. I am like the new animal in the zoo, checking out what's going on in the other cages.

Today marks the second day that two girls from the recreational therapy department have come over. They can't be twenty years old yet. They arrive at noon, cheerful as get-well cards. They wear bright, plaid tops over white or yellow pants, and like hummingbirds or characters from *Mary Poppins*, they zip through the unit with bright, singsong voices, clapping, coaxing, inspiring patients to rise and join them for a brisk, happy walk. "Everybody up!" they say. "This is fun, fun, fun." They look at me and the one girl runs her finger down a list."Nope," she says, shaking her head.

"Maybe next time," I say. "Maybe I can make a wallet."

They go next to Stanley, the scar-faced wino who's always pulling cigarette butts out of the can. He's slumped on the couch and they start tugging his arms. "C'mon," they say, "this'll be fun." Stanley mumbles and fends them off. They do not give up. Together they stand him, and his baggy pants slide off his hips. His underwear hangs below his shirttail, white with holes below the elastic band, sand-colored stains, sagging as though he might be hiding a grapefruit there.

Recoiling from the sight, one girl looks away, her eyes unintentionally catching mine, locking up with them as we both share a common revulsion, a sudden bond with all that is sad and hopeless about hospitals. There are no words for what we feel. We each have our face pressed to the glass. In between us, though transparent, is the difference between two separate worlds, two different histories, two different reasons for being in this space.

I smile weakly and the moment passes by.

I worry because sooner or later my discussions with Bowman will have to turn to the subject of dreams. I dread this because she is a student of medicine and science, a rational thinker. She may feel that dreams have nothing to do with why I am here.

I am not sure to what degree, but I believe that dreams have a *lot* to do with why I am here. I am not talking about daydreaming, flights of fancy, or the typical dreams of the sleeping mind. I am talking about dreams that come true. I am talking about trance states, scenes I had witnessed as a child and then, many years later, walked into in the present tense. I am talking about things that can't be explained, an unwanted gift of precognition that has made me distrust the "normal" flow of daily life.

This is exactly why I didn't want to come here in the first place. Even with my suicide attempt out in the open, I still fear talking about these dreams. They're much worse than my leap off the bridge. It sounds crazy. Even in a place like this.

CHAPTER 9

At Bellevue they placed me in a glaring white holding room that smelled of rubbing alcohol. On the counter behind me stainless steel instruments lay soaking in glass jars of tea-colored liquid. Silver bedpans and gourd-shaped urinals lay stacked on shelves behind a pair of glass sliding doors. By the sink, re-sterilized suture kits sat wrapped like packages in heavy white cloth.

Several people lifted me from one stretcher to another. The rails came up and my wrists were secured in leather collars. Everyone left except one short, dark-haired nurse who pulled off my wet pants, leaving my underwear on.

I heard Susan's voice outside in the hall, followed by Richard's Irish-Brooklyn brogue. Another man was talking to them, and I heard Richard say, "Don't worry, we're taking care of it." Then, a moment after that, "I don't care who started it, we'll finish this, all right?"

Damn, I thought. Was Richard one of them, too? He had been married to my sister for over three years, had adopted her girls, bought them a house, and had made a real family for them. He did a great job raising them, loved them immensely and treated my sister like she'd been sent to him by God. He had lent me money, helped me get my first job in a Brooklyn deli, and was instrumental in seeing me get started in Manhattan. There was nothing I couldn't ask him for, nothing he wouldn't try to give me.

How could he be one of the Devil's legion? I thought. No, it must be a trick. Someone was imitating his voice.

"Wanna see your family?" the nurse said, rolling my jeans into a soggy ball. She scuttled over to the counter, rearranging jars packed with cotton balls and washing her hands under the tall gooseneck faucet. I heard the clank of metal instruments being dumped in the sink. I pictured sharp, curved blades with long, flat handles. Blades with human tissue still dangling from them, exacto knives like we used to fillet frogs with in biology class. I imagined one of them in the hand of my brother-in-law, his other hand pressing tight against my throat, keeping me from jerking my head up. With his fingers he'd travel to my lowermost rib and just below it he'd draw the razor's edge against my skin, carving a thin fissure that would bloom open, red juice bubbling up as lightning rods of pain jabbed behind my eyes. With my side opened like a speared Christ, Richard—not the real Richard, but this double Richard —would grin like a jack-o'-lantern and hiss in my face. "I'm gonna carve you like a Christmas ham," he'd say. Then he'd cut again, spreading my wound, working his fingers into it as though prying open a clam.

The nurse dried her hands on a paper towel. "I'll get your family," she said. She looked around the room, grunting her satisfaction, and went out the door.

A moment later Richard and Susan came in, Richard remaining at my feet with his head bowed and his hands folded in front of him. Susan, however, came up to my face, bending down and kissing my forehead while stroking my hair. She put her lips to my ear and whispered.

"We're going to get you out of here," she said. "Be patient."

The nurse returned, shaking down a thermometer. She opened her mouth and I did the same, receiving the cool, glassy stick.

What if there's poison on the end of it, I thought. God, what I'd do for a little poison; that would be an easy way out. Most likely it was a drug to make me hypersensitive so that each little stab would seem fifty times worse. Soon hundreds of demons would be showing up, dressed in Nazi uniforms, and they'd start passing out knives like cigars in the delivery room.

A kinky-haired man came in wearing a long white lab coat. His hip pockets bulged with pens, a stethoscope, calculator, test tubes, tan-colored surgical tubing, and thin rubber straps. In a Spanish accent he introduced himself as Dr. Martinez, asking Susan and Richard to leave, closing the door behind them. Martinez withdrew my thermometer, turning it as he held it to the light. "Hmmm," he said, shaking it and dropping it in a glass jar of amber liquid where a dozen others fanned out like pencils in an office cup. Martinez proceeded to look in my ears, nose, and eyes with a tubular light. Next, he placed his cold stethoscope to my chest and asked me to breathe deeply, then tapped his fingertips against the back of his other hand, moving them downward across my chest and stomach.

"Do you know where you are?" he asked, jotting notes on a clipboard.

I locked my jaws together. I looked at the ceiling.

"Did you hear me?" he said. "I asked if you knew where you were."

I stared in silence.

"Hmmm," he said. "Do you recognize those people out in the hall?"

Again I said nothing.

"Very well," he said, leaning toward my face and pulling down on my lower eyelids. "Say 'Ah,' " he commanded. He flashed a tongue depressor from one of his pockets.

I opened my mouth and extended my tongue. But I did not make the "Ah" sound. Martinez waited.

"Very well," he said. He stepped back, made some notes, and stepped out the door. I heard the tongue depressor snap and saw him jam it in his lab coat pocket.

I grew cool under the single sheet. I listened to the air conditioning whir, imagining it growing louder like an airplane motor. Then another man came in and wrapped a cervical collar around my throat. He immobilized my head between a pair of triangular, gray foam pads. He left and an orderly in surgical scrubs came in and pushed me out into the hall. He picked up speed and my eyes hurt from watching the ceiling spin by as the road had done earlier when I had hung out the door of Richard's car.

Ahead of me I heard my sister calling.

"Mark! Thank God, it's so good to see you!" Joni came to my side and kissed my forehead. Her eyes were moist and mascara streaked the sides of her face. The orderly kept pushing the cart, and she walked backwards as we continued down the hall.

Wiping her eyes and smiling, Joni placed her warm hand over mine. "You took a detour, little brother, but we'll get you back on track," she said. "What we've got is a slight delay. But we're working on it. We're working on it right now."

Joni winked at me and gave my hand a squeeze. She seemed genuine to me, not one of the damned. I looked for some other indication, a light in the eyes, a hesitation or fear on her face, to be sure she was on my side.

We went through a crowded waiting area filled with crying babies and old people coughing. Joni was told to wait. The orderly pushed me through swinging doors and into another hallway where he parked me against a wall, leaving me alone. The light was dimmer here and I grew anxious being separated from Joni, whom I believed was the only person who could possibly save me.

I began hearing voices mixed with the messages coming over the intercom. When they paged Dr. Herman it became Dr. German. The thought crossed my mind that in hell you died a million deaths, each one more horrible than the one before. Richard's carving me up would only be the tip of the iceberg. I saw myself getting buried up to my neck in sand, thirsting for a thousand years. I'd be so crazy, so fry-brained that I'd beg for a hatchet, a chain saw, anything to come slice my head off. But after a brief blackout I'd only reassemble somewhere else, like in a shark tank or on a pile of burning wood.

Beyond the swinging doors I overheard Richard's voice. He was shouting. He was angry about something. I thought I heard him say, "Cut the boy twice," or, "cut him with ice."

(It wasn't until a full year later that I learned what his angry disposition had been about. According to my sister, a few weeks before I went off the bridge, Richard had found out a new union steward had been elected at his shipyard, a man supposedly on a mission for the mob. Richard had dreaded such situations, and often told stories about how the Mafia ruled the Teamsters and the concrete trade. He always said how lucky he was, that they had never offered him protection. But apparently they were knocking on his door now and someone—a mob "spokesman," a union rep, maybe just a worried employee—had recognized Richard in the waiting room and had engaged him in an argument. Unknown to me, Richard had been shouldering an awful lot of strain, though he was the type to never show it. The weekend after the Fourth of July I had stopped over his place and found him with a locksmith, getting an estimate on a home alarm. He was real nonchalant about it, but from what Joni told me a year later, there had been threats on her life and they had started sleeping with a gun in an open nightstand drawer.)

Meanwhile, someone wheeled me into a darkened room. Several people untied me and placed me on a cold, hard slab. Hideous machinery loomed overhead, arms and cones and wires and things that hung down like miniature satellite dishes. Here it comes, I thought, the buzz saw ripping up my crotch. I prepared myself for the Super Bowl of pain, the spinning blade cutting me up like kindling for a fire. I got ready to drown in my own screaming, drown as my blood sprayed the walls, the hot wheel biting through flesh, bone, and muscle, grinding nerves, chewing up my spine.

"We're going to do an X-ray," said a female technician.

I was rolled to my side and had more foam pillows tucked around me. Another woman in a lead apron asked me to hold still while they changed plates and aligned the crosshairs on the X-ray machine. "Hold still," she said, now behind a wall. There followed an electrical surge and a snapping sound as particles shot through me and peppered the film plate. They did this several times, my bladder signaling how full it was every time they turned me. The thought of requesting a urinal was out of the question; it would give them ideas on how to abuse me.

It was hard to tell where minutes stopped and hours took over. I went from hall to hall, room to room, undergoing all kinds of examinations. I was rolled, pinched, jabbed, and probed. Someone went up my ass with a flashlight and a grapefruit spoon. I was repeatedly asked if such-and-such hurt, what day it was, or if I knew why I had jumped off the bridge. I never answered. Finally I was parked next to the information booth in the emergency room.

Susan's upper body cruised into view. Tired, she smiled and covered me with a thin flannel blanket. "I've got to go home and get some sleep," she said. She stroked her hands against my cheek. To my left I could see darkness staining through a high, narrow window.

"What time is it?" I asked.

"Almost midnight."

Joni came up beside her. "How are we doing?" she asked.

I nodded against the collar under my chin.

"The X-rays are fine," Joni said. "Everyone's amazed. Do you realize what you've done?" She smiled at Susan.

Susan kissed my cheek. "You're indestructible," she said.

Joni turned her head and covered her mouth, fighting back a yawn. "Okay now, here's the game plan," she said, bending to speak in a lowered voice. I noticed her hair hung limp and her hazel eyes looked puffy underneath.

"We've stopped them from admitting you," Joni said. "The reason we gave them was because we think you did some drugs on that trip you took to Pennsylvania last week. Do you want to talk about that? You haven't said anything, Mark, but I know you. I remember from before. I know when my little brother is messing with things that get him in trouble."

"Is my neck broken?" I asked.

"No," Joni said. She and Susan looked at each other.

"Then take this collar off," I said. "I can't stand looking at the ceiling anymore."

Susan reached forward, pulling the Velcro tabs and sliding the giant Kotex out from under my chin. I sighed with relief.

"How 'bout these foam things?" I said, referring to my bookends.

"No," Susan said, "I think we should leave them there."

"Mark, I know this isn't the time," Joni said, "but you've got to help us. We're trying to get you admitted to that hospital in Kingston. It's the one Richard was taking you to when you jumped out of his car. It specializes in drug detoxification. Do you understand?"

I nodded again, this time feeling pain at the top of my neck.

"It would help us to know what you took back there in Pennsylvania. They could start treatment on you right away."

I closed my eyes.

"Was it pot? LSD?"

I had heard about witches, black masses, and human sacrifices. Members of covens came from all over the world. I figured they hadn't tortured me yet because everyone hadn't arrived. Devil worshippers were still flying in from Europe and Korea, getting put up in hotels like delegates at a torture convention.

"Look," Joni said. "We'll talk about this later. Unfortunately we have to leave now. The ambulance can't take you until tomorrow. You understand me? Open your eyes. I can't talk with your eyes closed. Do you think you can stick it out till then?"

I nodded.

"It's very important, brother. You can't do anything funny here. You understand?"

To answer, I shook my wrists, which were strapped tight to the sides of the stretcher.

"Is there anything you need before we go?" Susan asked. She tucked my blanket along both sides.

I shook my head. I heard bones grating in my neck. It felt like a fingernail file scraping out the inside of my skull.

Richard came up and gave my foot a squeeze. "Nice earmuffs," he said, cupping his hands beside his ears. He stuck his thumb up and winked. "You'll be in the right place before you know it," he said, "just you wait and see."

You devil, I thought. That smile doesn't fool me.

CHAPTER 10

In 1973 I was a member of a gang. Only we didn't think of ourselves as a gang, but more like a bunch of young guys you might find sitting on a couch in your basement, wearing odd little grins and joking about something you wouldn't understand. We loved loud music and were never home, except at meal times. What seemed like long ago we had once been paperboys, Boy Scouts, the sunburnt boys who, at their worst, shook up their soda cans, held spitting contests, broke the occasional window, but were always gracious when we mowed your lawn. We were neighborhood fixtures and—*always*—somebody's kids. You knew us by who our parents were. You said, "There goes David's boy. He's getting as tall as his father."

Only now we were older. And bigger. The size no one trusts anymore. Our hair was long. We seemed to come from another neighborhood. You could no longer pin it down who our parents were; it was as if we didn't *have* parents. It was in our voices. They were deeper and resonated with dishonest intentions. They betrayed our impatience, our agitation. There was also something in the way we walked, an arrogance that proclaimed we were on our own and that if you wanted to punish us or bring us to justice, you had better be faster and stronger and plan on doing it directly—not through trying to humiliate our parents. We were beyond them now.

These were the restless, awkward years when we had outgrown our bicycles but couldn't yet drive a car. On foot we came and went at strange hours, slinking through the streets and backyards of Youngstown's West Side. Those were our voices at midnight. That was me breaking glass. We arranged rendezvous, crawled out of open windows, bent back fences, moved between shadows, learning how to walk softly and how to dodge the cops.

Once, on a typical summer night, we were walking near the intersection between the old Sinclair refinery (where our arms used to get sore from throwing rocks all day at the big, silver storage tanks) and the firehouse bordering Mill Creek Park. We approached a car idling at the traffic light. I saw a lone woman at the wheel. She turned her head to observe us. Next, I heard the sound of her electric doors locking. Then she took off, even though the light was still red. I remember thinking, we were a gang all right. We were the people other people were afraid of.

There were four of us in our gang—Kelly, Danny, Reese, and me. Our chief aim was getting high. This consisted of chasing down any activity or substance that promised to fill the empty holes in our lives. None of us were geniuses. We didn't play team sports or belong to the Spanish or Drama clubs, or subscribe to Junior Achievers. Puberty itself had let us down, providing a brief flicker of paradise during those first ejaculations, but even that had become routine. Once the urge had subsided—or been satiated, as was usually the case—life became unbearably dull again, the horizon of the future about as flat and unappealing as the Ohio landscape itself. We needed kicks, excitement, adventure; something that challenged us, involved all our senses. The *Mad* magazines with the back covers accordion folded weren't going to do it anymore. Even *Playboy* couldn't do it anymore. Or fireworks or cigarettes. We wanted desperately to jump start the adulthood process.

At age thirteen, we found the first spark. It was Christmas time. Celebrating our last year of Catholic grade school together, Kelly, who was an altar boy, pilfered two bottles of wine from the church sacristy. He dropped the unopened bottles from a back window into the snow-crusted bushes below. I retrieved them after school; by that time they had tiny ice crystals forming in the necks; flat, shiny cells that swirled about as I shook up the bottles. Danny and Reese joined us as we drank them in the confessionals after school, hearing mock confessions, playing with the dimmer switches that worked the red lights. We finished both bottles and Danny and Reese missed their bus. They were clearly drunk as they walked off towards home, the sun going down already, their intoxication evidenced by the uneven zig-zag trails they made in the snow. The next day they told us of getting chased out of somebody's garage when they snuck in to get warm. I had a pretty decent buzz as well, and by the time I got home the only activity I was fit for was horsing around with my little brother, piling pillows at the bottom of the steps and daring him to jump onto them.

In ninth grade we graduated to beer and soda wines, getting drunk in the woods on green bottles of Ripple back when Ripple bottles still had the wavy lines in the glass. (This was 1970, and I remember being ecstatic over the advent of bell-bottom jeans. They were much more convenient to drink in because, once drunk, you could get them off easier. Prior to bell-bottoms, there had been a few episodes where I had vomited Boone's Farm strawberry wine on my pants and ended up sleeping with them on. One time I went to bed with them around my ankles and later tripped myself going to the bathroom.)

In those early days the most common way of getting alcohol was to steal it. An empty peanut butter jar allowed me to siphon off a shot or two from everything in my parents' liquor cabinet, which wasn't much. (I swear the cheap Seagrams they served at their fiftieth wedding anniversary was the same stuff we gave them at their twenty-fifth.) To get really good and drunk we only had to wait for the winter. People in Ohio are known for keeping their beer and wine cool in their garages, especially between Thanksgiving and the New Year's holiday, when we often hosted a series of "garage sales" once the sun had gone down. I had a couple of other tricks for getting what I wanted: one was my Government of Guam I.D. that I had altered in typing class to say I was twenty-three. The other was a sock. To steal single bottles of beer from convenience stores, I cut the toe off a black stretch sock, then sewed it within my bulky winter jacket, stitching it on three sides like an inside coat pocket. Imitating a detective, I practiced the quick unzip and the fast hand going inside my jacket, only instead of reaching for a gun, I was tucking away a can or bottle of beer.

In the summer after I turned sixteen I got a job at nearby Idyll Park, a tacky amusement park that drew a wild, riffraff crowd every night after sundown. The employees were a sorry lot, too. It was there I met Ron Conklin, a fellow about twenty-four whom I asked to go to the liquor store for me. I gave him thirty dollars back when cheap stuff ran five bucks a bottle. He came back with fifths of bourbon, scotch, gin, rum, and vodka, which I carried home from the park and hid above the acoustical tile ceiling over my father's workbench in the basement. It was a dark, difficult hiding place and a problem quickly developed: how to tell one bottle from the other by feeling with my hand. I ended up tying a different colored string around the neck of each bottle so I could tell what I was reaching for.

I have one memory in particular relating to that liquor stash. It involved the bourbon, a brand name like Colonel Lee, I believe. Kelly, I, and Barry Something—don't remember his last name—got hammered god-awful, adding the Colonel to blueberry snow cones during the last hour before we closed up at Idyll Park. (At Idyll, being drunk on, before, or after the job was as common as pukers on the Tilt-A-Whirl.) We sat at a picnic table on the hill, in the dark shadows of a pavilion, drinking until the neon signs on the midway got smeary and stretched out, as though they were reflections in one of the fun house mirrors. We locked up our booths while being quite drunk, and by the time we loped out to Barry's car, what liquor we had left we were drinking straight from the bottle. It wasn't until we got in the car and sat down and collectively felt the vehicle moving—though Barry hadn't started it up yet—that we realized none of us could show their faces at home for a few hours, and we were completely terrorized at the thought of any of us driving. Attempting to regroup, we decided to spend a few minutes listening to music in Barry's car. But no sooner had I leaned my seat back than Barry began throwing up in gut-wrenching salvos. Leaning out the driver's door with his arm on the armrest, he hurled mouthfuls of sour-smelling amusement park food onto the parking lot, forming a stream that meandered beneath the front wheels and downhill past my side of the car.

Lightweight Barry then passed out. Neither Kelly nor I had a driver's license. All the lights went out in the park and we were the only car left in the parking lot, and it was smelling too foul to just sit there and listen to Black Sabbath for the tenth time. The night was young and we were still charged up.

"You know what I've always wanted to do?" Kelly said, digging through the shoebox that held Barry's 8-track tapes.

"No, what?" I asked.

"I've always wanted to see somebody wake up underneath the big wooly elephant on the Lost River ride."

The Lost River was a tunnel-of-love ride featuring oarless rowboats that coasted in and out of darkness through an African jungle theme, finishing with a screaming plunge down a waterslide. At the entrance to the ride was a plot of fake jungle foliage, a fake thatched roof beneath where ticket holders got seated in their boats, plus a big plastic elephant with seaweed-like fake wool draped over it. The elephant had only one working part, its head, which raised and lowered all day long while jungle drums pounded never-endingly from a pair of speakers hidden in the bushes beside it.

"How much do you figure Barry weighs?" I said.

"Can't be more than one hundred thirty pounds," Kelly said. "They didn't even let him fill out an application at the

Army."

"We can park the car at the service gate," I said. "It's only fifty yards from there."

To make a long story short, we drove up to the service gate, where we hauled Barry out of his car and dragged him hammock-style by his arms and ankles, his purple T-shirt rolling up and exposing his belly.

Moving only alerted me as to how drunk we were. Every time we dropped Barry, scraping his poor, exposed flesh, I howled insanely. Kelly and I tipped, tottered, and tumbled like a pair of shoes in a dryer. We stopped to pee and crossed urine streams like two little boys having a sword fight, splashing each others 'shoes. Eventually we made it to the metal-plated canal where the boats passed through, a four-foot-deep trough lying between us and the elephant. Barry hadn't woke once, only mumbled an occasional word or let out a raspy, snoring sound, as if he were gagging and trying to catch his breath. Mostly his head rolled from side to side, practically lifeless.

We decided the only way to get Barry across to the elephant was to haul him over where the boats were docked, using the lead boat as a safety net in case we dropped him. I would go first, scramble across the boat to the other side, then take up Barry's wrists after Kelly lowered him in.

What ended up happening was that Kelly and Barry both fell in the boat, Kelly twisting his ankle pretty bad. Barry didn't wake up, but he uttered such a sound when he hit that we got scared he might have broken something. So, instead of trying to haul him to the other side, we released the boat and watched it go into the tunnel, Barry, slouched over the middle seat, looking like unclaimed baggage going back inside the carousel. We felt pretty certain that the gate would be up on the other side, otherwise Barry would go up the hill and come down the waterslide, the entire ride, including its seventy-foot, whooshing climax, taking place while Barry slept, oblivious. We did not stay to see if he came down.

By the time I was a sophomore in high school, illegally buying my booze became the most common way to get it. In the tough neighborhoods of Youngstown's lower South Side we hit places like Trixie's Deli, Ishmael's, and Mandy's Market, which were small, family-owned convenience stores that carried an unusually large proportion of beer and wine on their shelves. We had a special arrangement at Trixie's where the owner asked us to please buy our beer on any night but the weekend because the police were trying to catch him selling to minors. I dug a large pit in the woods near my home and dragged an old steamer trunk down, making an underground ice chest, camouflaging it with dirt and leaves so that we could buy on a Thursday and still keep it cold until Friday or Saturday.

Then the police switched off and started raiding on weekdays. Kelly got busted once and so did Danny. Danny had to testify against Ishmael's, which meant relations with that store ceased immediately. And that was probably for the best because the store was in the middle of an urban war zone and simply waiting in the getaway car nearly drove me nuts. That was the one store I was too chicken to buy at. It had no windows, not even on the door. I thought that if I went in there something would go wrong, I'd look at someone funny or fumble with the cash, and I'd get my brains blown out. Reese was usually the money man. He'd go in, pull what we needed out of the coolers, get it on the counter, and then stick his head out the door, signaling us to pull up to the curb. I'd jump out the passenger door, pop the trunk, while Reese paid up and jumped in the back. The owner, a skinny black guy who smelled like boot polish, bagged the beer and came out himself, clearing me aside while his big, bloodshot eyes looked both ways. Satisfied it was safe, the owner tossed the beer in the trunk, rapping on the roof as I slammed it down and hopped in, the car already starting to speed away, which made the whole affair feel like a bank robbery.

I was sixteen when I had a minor panic attack while buying two cases of Colt 45 at Mandy's on Indianola Avenue. It was a cold, snowy weeknight in January, and word was out that another eight inches were expected to fall and that schools were as good as closed. A perfect night for drinking, our tank full and the heater blasting, some Christmas lights still on the houses, and the roads pretty empty—whatever cars were out were mostly stuck, spinning their tires, or sliding sideways at the traffic lights. Danny dropped me off a block away, which was my request because I needed a little time to work on my act. I hitched up my collar as I walked in Mandy's, feeling pretty confident things would go as smoothly as they had maybe a dozen times before.

I recognized the thin man who always wore the dirty white shirts with the pearl buttons at the register. I thought he would recognize me, but when I dropped the Colt 45 on the counter he surprised me instead.

"Can I see some I.D.?" he asked. He looked past me to another man who had suddenly come up behind me in line.

I had never been asked before, but without a flinch, gave the thin man my Guam I.D. He looked at it closely, then glanced at the man behind me. Thin man seemed nervous. Instead of giving me back my I.D., he set it below the keys on the register, taking my money to ring up the sale.

An alarm went off in my head. It said, "Vice squad! Get out of there fast!" Room temperature climbed to a thousand degrees. Not waiting for my I.D. or my change, I grabbed the malt liquor and dashed out the door. I nearly creamed myself on the sidewalk ice but managed to stay up while I turned the corner and ran through the alley beside Mandy's, dumping the Colt 45 behind a pile of dead batteries and old oil drums. I thought I heard footsteps following but I never looked back. I ran through yards and jumped fences, outpacing barking dogs. I crossed more streets and ducked between cars that swerved in the snow, their rear tires kicking up white powder that arched like the stream of a drinking fountain. I took to the backstreets, giving up my chance to flag down Danny and the others, and ended up walking two miles home in the freezing cold.

***

September 8, 1983
(In the day room)

Someday I will be asked to speak at a junior high school in middle America. The principal will ask me to pass on a few words about teenage drinking.

Here they are:

(1) Smashed (2) Wasted (3) Plastered (4) Hammered (5) Totaled—as in "totaled the car" (6) Zonked (7) Snookered (8) Shitfaced (9) Fucked Up (10) Pukin' (11) Power Pukin' (12) Inebriated and/or Intoxicated (13) Drunk (14) Destroyed (15) Gone—as in "completely gone" (16) Zombied (17) Gorked (18) Stoned (19) Wiped (20) Maxxed, or To the Max—as in "fucked up to the max".

The list complete, I will implore the students to ask themselves this one simple question: Has there been any time when, after consuming alcoholic beverages, you found yourself referring to your condition by any of the above twenty (20) terms?

"If you answer, 'Yes,' " I will say, "then there are those who'd tell you that your answer indicates that you have a drinking problem. There are probably an equal number," I would also say, "who believe those others are full of poppycock."

***

Back in my high school sophomore year you couldn't have kept alcohol away from me if you had put toxic waste in every alcohol container. In fact there were many mornings when a cigarette butt floating at the top of a warm glass of beer was not so much a deterrent as a minor inconvenience, like eating olives with pits.

It was the Ride I was after. The out-of-control Ride. The feeling that we were bowling pins and alcohol was the ball. Up. Down. Roller coaster of semi-consciousness. Entire scenes snipped from the movie of life, rerun backwards or jammed into fast forward. The first-beer buzz. Then the second beer, like an earth tremor, like a change in wind before the storm. Then the third and fourth cans, when the sliding board gets extra slippery or the legs on the swing set start pumping out of the ground. The fifth, and the sliding board starts stretching like taffy. The sixth. Everything breaks up like an avalanche of pillows, like wild pheasants scattering, like straw men tossed in a wave. It's as though the evening consisted of Polaroid snapshots mixed out of order, or—if you're drunk on both wine and beer or wine and whiskey—fragmented in such a violent rush that you feel your entire being rolling with the cosmic punches, your existence scattered like 52-pickup or a clay pigeon hit by a 12-gauge round.

My first real drunk I crashed through the woods, kicking things, knocking fenceposts and small trees over. On the way home I pushed over a stop sign and trashed my neighbor's mail box. I loved it. I loved the anger and energy it released. Alcohol made me UN-responsible for whatever happened next, even if I did it. It was like hanging on to the tail of the dragon.

There was no better night than one that involved a lot of scene changes, a blurry series of encounters and getaways, a constant stream of strangers. Drunkenness restored mystery to my life. It gave to alcohol the power of a god, the power to move, destroy, or save me. Everything tilted and all the hard edges went mushy—like falling down the stairs. It seemed I never got hurt, and the next day they'd drag me back to where I had almost killed myself and no one could believe a person could fall like that and keep on moving. I earned medals for nothing. I loved falling and getting picked up in a heap, Kelly or Reese holding me up, steadying my feet.

I loved crashing through the woods in the dark. I loved crazy car rides, especially when we got lost. I didn't mind vomiting, either. Early on, there was a certain status to it. In ninth grade if you didn't have a good puke story for the lunchroom on Monday it was obvious you didn't have a very productive weekend. I was lucky. I threw up everywhere. One time I threw up in a dressing room of a department store. Another time I threw up in a school bus, on my way to a speech tournament where I took fourth place. I threw up out of a tree fort, then later fell off the platform and onto my vomit. Another time I threw up spaghetti out the rear window of Kelly's mother's car, a streak of white specks that resembled a painted decal like you might see on the side of a racing car. Hers was a green Dodge Dart. There were six of us in that car and it was cold out and we rode all the way to Pittsburgh and back for no reason other than to get lost because we had nothing else to do. When we pulled into a 7-Eleven for cigarettes, Kelly saw the dragon-flame of vomit stretching all the way to his mother's tail lights. He blasted me with verbal abuse while we cruised around until we found an all-night automatic car wash. Just when the soapy brushes were making the front windshield look like shaving cream, I had to let go of another gallon of bad beer in my belly. I was sitting in the middle and had to lean over to grab the window roller, which provoked a few slaps from Danny until he saw my cheeks puffing out and realized I wasn't kidding.

"You fuckin 'nuts?" Kelly yelled. "Don't open no window."

Too late. I cranked it down and leaned right into the brushes, my face peppered with bristles as I puked pasta pellets back at the beast. It was like vomiting into a hurricane. Hot, soapy water shot into the car. Jets of air, water, and brushes attacked my face. Someone pushed against my ass and tried to shove me out the window. I heaved through the entire car wash, my long hair turning into a stiff bed of kelp from the hot wax spray.

That night Kelly didn't even pull in my drive. They left me off in the street, and all I can remember is stumbling my way to the mountain ash tree that used to grow on the side of our house, hanging onto the trunk while I sang to myself and gathered my wits about me before I started looking for the back door key.

CHAPTER 11

In high school we often joked how marijuana had saved us from becoming alcoholics. (Needless to say, that joke was only safe in certain company. You never said it in front of straight people, of course, but you also didn't want to bring up the subject in front of guys who had "drawn a line in the sand" against marijuana and other drugs, yet remained content with their militant-style drinking. These were the jocks and greasers, the boys with the muscle cars and their girlfriends who chewed gum. They needed kicks, too. However, their principal problem with marijuana was its being illegal.)

Unfortunately, becoming a criminal was part of the dues the neophyte pot smoker had to pay. You had to be willing to go against the grain. Besides, you probably had been drinking for awhile already and were sick of alcohol and the whole loss-of-motor-control/falling-down/puking-on-yourself scene. If an altered state was what you were after, eventually you asked yourself if alcohol was the best—or only—road to take.

Aside from the lone puff on Guam—in which nothing happened—it took me over a dozen attempts to get my first high, living as we did off the table scraps from Reese's older brother, Carl, who was apparently buying a lot of parsley at that time. He gave us the shit he got burned on; dry, leafy concoctions that filled the torn corners of Glad sandwich bags. Like condoms in a lovers' lane, these littered the ground beneath the pine trees where we huddled and smoked in the dark beside a sleepy cul-de-sac, unconcerned with the occasional car rolling by or light that went on in somebody's kitchen. It was winter and we smoked during the six o'clock news. Often I could see the gray TV light flickering through Mr. Mateo's curtains.

We gagged on those early pipefuls and rolled clumsily joints full of bumps and stem holes. We performed an ironic ritual, which was to light cigarettes after we had finished smoking pot so that our parents wouldn't smell anything funny. It took about two months (and marijuana from another source) but eventually I got stoned, heartily accepting this new drug as my own personal savior.

Being stoned was different than getting sauced (21) on booze. Instead of the crashing, tumbling, punch-drunk heaviness I usually acquired, I now experienced a timeless hush, a dewdrop-in-the-spiderweb sort of feeling that descended unexpectedly on this angry and defiant sixteen-year-old boy. The change was radical. New words moved to the forefront of my vocabulary: High; floating; buzzed; Zen. Out with wasted. In with mellow. That first stoning I remember looking at the joint, watching it, observing it, observing me watching it, watching me watching me observing it, then nearly merging with it, fascinated the whole time as it slowly burned a hole in my father's vinyl-covered card table.

"Wow," was what I said.

"Wow," Danny echoed. Wow, wow, wow.

We put the fire out—observing ourselves putting the fire out—which made for a kind of laughter I had never before heard coming out of my own mouth. For the first time in my life I didn't take myself seriously. Prior to that, there had been a character living in my head whose only concern had been worrying about the future. Is the homework done? Are the parents pleased? Will Vietnam still be going on when I graduate?

Suddenly that character's voice got pushed to the background. All that ambient pain, low-grade anxiety, got stuffed back in the aspirin bottle, all that worrying hushed behind a soft wad of cotton.

Marijuana alters perception. It also transforms time. With marijuana, the mundane becomes significant. It's like your life is on film and there you are, standing, talking, taking a walk, taking a shit, brushing your teeth. But every so often the film stops and backs up briefly, and you do a double-take on your own behavior. At that moment you get this feeling that you stepped out of the movie for a split second, rising to the ceiling, perhaps, or stepping to the side for a different camera angle. For the first time in your life you ask yourself questions like, "Why do I brush my teeth that way?" or, "Look at the way my face feels when I smile like that in the mirror." Suddenly your eyes look in. When you do this a lot—or smoke dope a lot—that brief moment of being an observer gets longer and longer until whole situations, perhaps even days, occur under the scrutiny of this double observation. On one hand it's significant, profound even, because for the first time in your life you've adopted the view of the Other. Ego is no longer your soul reference point. You're no longer on automatic pilot. Suddenly you see those shoelaces you've been tying, that hair you've been combing, those lies you've been telling.

On the other hand, though, it's sort of like being a monkey grooming himself, only the monkey has a super intelligent brain. So every time you pull a tick out of your fur, you think it has fantastic implications, philosophical reverberations, and you're forced to consider revolutionary systems of thought. But all the while you're still a monkey, and the only thing certain is that you've got a bug in your hand.

No sooner had Danny and I put the fire out, cleaned up the mess, and gone outside than the next strange thing happened. We walked down Dogwood, barely ten minutes stoned, when a car pulled up beside us and the driver seemed to beckon for us to climb inside. "Seemed to" is the operative phrase. He also seemed to be someone who knew us, but we couldn't tell for sure. Was he looking at us or what? Danny and I shrugged.

"Why not?" I said, and we both grabbed a door and hopped inside the car. It took ten, maybe twenty seconds to realize that we didn't know this man at all and that, whoever he was, he hadn't motioned for us to get inside his car. The only reason he had stopped beside us was because traffic had backed up.

We laughed. It was absurdly funny. Here we were. In a stranger's car. Curious and a little nervously, I flicked open the armrest ash tray.

"WHAT THE FUCK ARE YOU DOING!?!?!?!"

There was no doubt where *that* voice came from. Danny and I bolted from the car and ran to the woods bordering Mill Creek Park. What sweet mystery! Now there was a new dimension to everything. Information—experience itself—came in through new channels, mingled with our senses in such novel fashion that a handshake was no longer necessarily a handshake; an arrow pointing in one direction did not mean a damn thing. All rules were broken; all bets were off. With marijuana, the boring became tolerable. And the tolerable became interesting. For the first time in my life school looked like it might be fun. I fell so completely in love with marijuana that I quickly progressed from buying $15 and $20 ounces to buying a $300 kilo for my own personal use. I stayed stoned almost every day of my junior year.

I handled marijuana like a coin collector might fondle his coins. Late at night the table in my basement became a workbench where I weighed ounces in plastic bags, removed stems one at a time, and separated the potent flower tops to mix with different strains of marijuana I would buy in smaller quantities as they arrived from Columbia, Panama, Thailand, or Vietnam. I searched unceasingly for the perfect House Blend. I was a hungry buyer and desired connections with anyone, anyone who could score me some pot. I walked into strange houses or met with strange people in the back of scummy bars. I made quick deals in parked cars. People came to our house and my mother thought they had car trouble or wanted directions. She'd say, *those* are friends of yours? You gotta be kidding!

When I wasn't smoking dope I groomed it like horses in a stable. I could stay up all night cleaning a quarter pound for seeds, watching them roll down the center of a Chicago double album, dropping like BBs into a 35 millimeter film container.

Having spent $300 on a kilo, I proceeded to bury several ounces in various spots throughout the city. Double wrapping each bag inside a one-pound coffee can, then sealing the can with masking tape, I'd march off with my shovel, pen, and paper, in case I needed to draw a map.

Marijuana was portable. With long hair you could walk the halls in high school with a joint behind each ear. Four joints fit nicely in a Tic Tac container. And it was totally illegal so you didn't have to worry about a fake I.D. You never had a pile of bottles or cans left over, and you didn't have to sweat about keeping it cold in the summer. You didn't have to force it down like Boone's Farm wine. Marijuana didn't make you throw up or piss a lot, and it didn't screw you up so bad you'd fall asleep in the snow or, like I did once on cherry vodka and slo gin, on a stack of wooden pallets behind the IGA.

***

In the fall of our senior year it was LSD's turn to infiltrate our ranks. Acid, as it was known, was hardly news. Ever since "Lucy in the Skies with Diamonds" and the color photos of hippies in *Life* and *Look* magazines, my friends and I had viewed LSD as a further frontier, an elite experience we'd approach once we had found the courage. Many friends outside our circle had tried the drug already. The news was intriguing. Supposedly you could taste sound, hear color, and sex became like an ocean of Vaseline stuffed into a fur-lined glove.

Danny was first to go. I remember the day after when he came over my house to tell me about it. We sat in the kitchen with the door closed and the television loud to drown out our voices. I was jealous and perturbed. Danny's stories were incredible. He said he saw music crawl down the wall, solid sheets of it, a different color for every instrument, rolling down like wallpaper unfolding. He told me how he watched a willow tree dripping fountains of color.

"Where were you when you first got off?" I asked, wanting to recreate the experience vicariously.

"Leigh Marie's," he said, naming a tiny restaurant that was basically a finger-warming joint for drunks in the cold and kids out of gas.

"Leigh Marie's? How sad," I said. "That must have been horrible."

"No, you should have seen it. It was wonderful."

"What was your first sign you were getting off?" I asked.

"The place got real warm and light, a strawberry light, and it seemed like there were prisms hanging everywhere, I mean up above and off the cream pitchers and napkin dispensers, everywhere. Everywhere you'd look there'd be lights blinkin'. There'd be this sort of a breeze thing, I guess, some kind of a wind, and the light would get brighter and all the prisms would go spinning and there'd be rainbows on all the walls."

"Where did the wind come from?" I asked.

"Fuck if I know."

Danny went on and on. Light hummed and sound bent backwards. Food became symbolic, he said; it was like eating pictures out of a *Good Housekeeping* magazine. Bread tasted like it had been baked in a computer. The best part, he said, was while driving around they had to stop the car several times because they were laughing at nothing. Eyes clogged with tears. Laughing at nothing.

"Things don't have to make sense," he said. "They just happen. They happen and they're really weird."

When I took LSD with Danny, Reese, and Kelly on the night of May 3, 1974, I experienced a most profound sense of weirdness. Everything around me—houses, trees, cars— seemed to be props on a stage. At twilight, when we walked through the ballfields behind the 7-Eleven, both Kelly and I felt an overpowering sense that we were miniature figures on a giant toy railroad set, the kind in department store windows. I kept looking to the sky for the giant hand that might pull up some trees, move some houses, or perhaps pluck me from the planet altogether.

At other times we shrank beyond small to microscopic. Walking through the park at night the leaves of trees became waving hands above us. When I stopped to observe them, they transformed into amoebas and paramecia, undulating and darting about as though we were below them on a microscope slide, the four of us in a drop of pond water, little creatures walking through a one-celled world.

Several times I had difficulty telling where I stopped and the outside world took over. An oil stain in the parking lot spun like a record and hissed at me, calling me by name. It changed color from blue to red and at the same time I felt a hot, red pain on my forehead, a laser light aimed between my eyes. As the oil stain hissed and pulsed color, my brow flamed hotter and hotter. The only way to deal with the phenomenon was to walk away from it. Later, from a hill above that same parking lot, I watched my own Blessed Family Church go up in flames. The school followed. It was like a photograph burning from the edges and by squinting my eyes I could make the flames jump higher. I became terrified that it was really happening and only by closing my eyes and praying hard could I make the flames go away.

This was my third LSD trip and by far the most dramatic. Flowers talked to me. Streetlights hummed. In fact, I noticed Danny was right, all light hummed, different colors at different frequencies. Approaching headlights sounded like leaves rustling or an ocean wave crawling up the beach. Neons crackled and the florescent tubes inside office buildings and stores at the mall gave off a numbing drone, a headache-producing vibration that made us a bit testy whenever we had to go to the store for any reason.

On May 3 it grew foggy late that night. Around four in the morning we hiked to the man-made spillway known as Newport Falls. It was a set of quarried rock steps where Lake Newport tumbled over, whispering loudly and fanning a mist. We stood on a rock ledge above the falls, feeling the spray, watching the fog creep across the lake, wisps of it dancing like ghosts or clinging from the trees like kites.

Suddenly, in a few short moments, the overcast cleared. The fog banks separated, and up above, the clouds slid by like a domed stadium opening. Everywhere you looked the fog swirled upward, wispy tails of it evaporating, drawn up like the resurrected dead. A full moon burst out, shimmering across the lake. The tips of pine and spruce began glowing milky white and everything pulsed with a silvery edge. The lake shimmered mercury. Above us the sky polished her jewels and opened her deep black jewel box, a million stars winking from the darkness, and between them, the vast, yawning space ready to swallow us all. The moon seemed twice its normal size and shone with a brilliance that lit our faces. I held out my arm and looked at my jacket sleeve. The moon had kissed my arm, and everything else, with a sprinkling of white dust, with talc.

Kelly jumped in front of me. He grabbed me by my jacket collar and looked me in the eyes. "Did you ever have a dream where you're looking at a giant sun?" he said.

I recalled the dream. Instantly. Instantly as he spoke.

"Yes!" I said. "When I was small. There's a car on a hill. I'm in the back seat. My parents are in front and Joni and my two older brothers are sitting next to me. A giant sun is coming toward us but everyone is pretending it's not there."

I looked at Kelly. He nodded, his face flushed with excitement. "Exactly," he said.

"I'm real excited because I've never seen anything like it," I continued, recalling the image that had come back and haunted me every few years. "It's huge! But no one's paying attention. And then I turn around and notice Joni has a worried look on her face. I can tell she knows something about it but she won't tell me. And I can't figure out why everyone's so scared."

It was my turn to grab Kelly. I shook him by the shoulders. "You mean you had that dream too?"

"Exactly," he said. I let go and all four of us stared at the moon. It was a white hole ripped in the sky.

Kelly lit a cigarette. "In my dream," he said, "everyone is scared but me."

"Yes," I said. "It's huge. A giant star. Or a sun. And no one knows what to make of it and you can tell they're all scared. But I'm not. But I think that maybe I should be."

Kelly and I looked at each other. "Reese, you ever dream anything like that?"

"No," he said. Neither did Danny. But Kelly and I had had the exact same dream. The dream was old; we must have been three or four when we had it.

"Look at the edge of that storm front sneaking away," Reese said, pointing.

Like a blanket's edge, the last of the clouds passed over our heads, receding toward the horizon.

"They just rolled right outta here," Kelly said. "Right over our heads. Christ, it's unreal. Here we are, right where they point on those weather maps, the very point where the clouds slip away. We're right at the front. The whole goddamned front."

He flicked his cigarette over the falls, the orange light arcing high then traveling down, winking out in the white ribbon of water.

CHAPTER 12

I left Bellevue on the morning of Friday, July 29, 1983, getting lifted off one stretcher and strapped down to another, this time with nylon belts across my legs and chest. They slid me in the back of another ambulance with two paramedics, male and female, who rode with me, sitting on a bench by my side. The ambulance swayed as the driver banked left and right. IV bottles swung from hooks like hanging porch plants on a breezy day.

My cervical collar was reinstalled. They also tucked a rolled-up hand towel behind my neck. The female paramedic, a heavyset woman with hooker-red lipstick and two diamonds in each ear, fed me ice chips with a plastic spoon. In a New York accent stronger than black *caaaaw*-fee, she asked me what I did before my accident.

I told her I jumped out of a car.

"I mean what you do for a living," she said. "You have a very interesting face."

"I'm a writer."

"Oh, so you're a writer?" Her face lit up. "I was a writer once, too. My name's Gretchen. Pleased to meet you."

She held out her hand, and her face flushed with embarrassment; my hands were strapped tight and there was nothing to shake. I thought that was very funny. She did too, and ended up digging an old tissue out of her pocket so she could wipe the tears from her eyes. It was a good start. The other paramedic—whose name I never got—relaxed a little and stopped looking at me like I was about to explode. Gretchen didn't take long to launch in about David Mamet, Eugene O'Neill, and all the plays she had seen on Broadway.

I told her theatre was dead.

"It's not dead," she said, "but the cost of parking doesn't make it any easier." She laughed and patted my face with her ice-cooled hand. Gretchen was a joker and I welcomed that. She also acted like she had known me for years. "So when is your next play coming out?" she asked. "I'm looking forward to reading it, maybe even seeing it if you can get it up there under the big lights."

"We'll just have to see," I said.

"Aw, that's nothing for a man of your talent," she said. "Just a matter of time for someone like you. I can tell, you know. I can tell just by lookin' at you. You've got what it takes. Ol' Gretchen knows about these kinds of things."

It's a funny thing about psychosis, how the paranoid record has its B side: delusions of grandeur. Only a few hours before I had been terrified that demons were going to hack me limb from limb. But as Gretchen continued talking, saying things like, "I can't see how you can fail . . . why, with all that talent . . . only a matter of time . . ." I became filled with a light, pleasant gas. Her words and manner soothed me and it seemed as if only good things were possible. Several times I thought I heard a marching band. I could see them in my mind's eye, hoisting up the trumpets, all that glittering brass. I imagined Gretchen could hear them, too. At any moment she'd have them stop the ambulance, swing open the doors, and reintroduce me to my adoring public. Yes, the doors would open wide upon a bucolic, New England town: Main Street swept clean as a Shaker museum. Its two-story brick and white-frame buildings; the hardware store with rakes and red wheelbarrows in the window; the barber shop with its spinning, patriotic pole; the hotel with its wide plank porchway. The town square would be a shady piece of Eden with its modest, columned courthouse perched behind a Civil War cannon, its muzzle erect as a Boy Scout thumbing through *Hustler* magazine. In the center of the square, a white gazebo. A crisscrossed trellis laced with ivy. "Welcome Back, Mark!" would be stretched across banners roped between the streetlights. Crowds would cheer and throw confetti, a paper snowstorm engulfing the band. White straw hats. All the old men lining the sidewalks would wear white straw hats. Film crews would be scrambling for footage. Like a thicket of cattails, hundreds of microphones would strain at my moist, smiling face.

That's psychosis for you. One minute, Nazis. The next, screaming fans.

When the ambulance doors finally did open, the only crowd to greet me consisted of two orderlies and a security guard who helped hoist me from one stretcher to the next under the covered entrance to Huntington Community Hospital, south of Kingston, New York. Joni and Richard were already there, Joni wearing her game face and Richard looking quite amused, though there was a certain tension in the crisp way he brushed off the sleeves of his powder-blue sport coat.

I was whisked up an elevator and wheeled onto a sunny wing that had classical music floating through the halls. They pushed me into a large white room with a single bed. Once more a small crowd gathered to cradle me by my sheets and lift me into bed. I came down a little hard. My head hit the pillow and there was no mistaking where I was—the industrial pillow, the vinyl pillow, the blood-resistant, mucus-resistant, all-manner-of-bodily-fluids-resistant pillow, crackled like a stuffed reptile, collapsing slowly like a leaking tire.

Just like that, everyone left. "The doctor will be with you in a moment," said the last nurse, a heavyset woman whose large, white butt waddled behind the others like a momma duck out the door. In the hall I could see an aluminum cart with its doors open, food trays with yellow plastic domes keeping the food hot on the plates. I smelled French toast and syrup.

Joni and Richard waltzed in my room. Richard sniffed about, ran his fingers across the surface of my nightstand. "Nice wickiup," he said. "I think you're in the right place, pal."

Joni handed me a vase with yellow flowers. "Saw it downstairs," she said. "Yellow means strength to face our hardships."

"That's very nice," I said.

"It was on the card," Richard said. Joni scowled as she removed a green wrapper.

"Can you put them by the window?" I said.

She put them on the ledge above the radiator, giving Richard's hand a squeeze as she went by. "See how special my little brother is?" she said. "*He* gets a private room."

"Hopefully *he* has insurance to cover it."

A tall man in a brown suit filled up the doorway. "So we're finally here," his voice boomed. "A day late but not a day too soon." The man came in and stood over me.

"Hello, Mark. I'm Doctor D'Aoust. We're going to be working together for the next few days." His hand swallowed mine in a firm, warm shake.

"Help me pronounce your name," he said.

We went over it several times, until I said, "Close enough."

"But don't you want people to pronounce it right?" he said. "This name is rich in history. Russian, isn't it?"

"Actually, Ukranian."

"Ukranian? Why, that's marvelous. Let's say it again. Wool-ish-en, right?"

"You got it," I said, looking at my sister.

"Wolyczin. Hmmm. I like it. You know, a person's name carries a history," D'Aoust said. "It's up to us to keep that history alive. And pronouncing it in the Old World manner is the first step you can take. It's a beautiful name, really." The doctor looked at Joni and Richard. "And now is a beautiful time for you two to excuse yourselves," he said. "You may wait downstairs, but I must advise you that this will take some time. What's more, there may be nothing conclusive, certainly no accurate prognosis this early on."

"But doctor," Joni said, "I've been talking to him in Bellevue and I believe—"

"If you wish to speak to me, you may wait downstairs. I'd like to be alone with Mark now."

Joni started to say something but Richard tapped her arm, then tugged it gently until she followed him out the door. As Richard went out he darted his eyes towards D'Aoust, then looked at me, rolling his eyes towards the ceiling. He whistled a low note as he disappeared into the hall.

Dr. Frederick D'Aoust was a sight to behold. His eyes bulged like ping pong balls behind his thick, horn-rimmed glasses. He had Howdy Doody ears—big, flappy skins of putty that stood out like handles on tea cups. Surrounding these cranial wings (and, thankfully, helping to camouflage them), a savage head of slept-on hair spiked upwards in all directions, the left side particularly snarled and rising up like tufts of pampas grass. He was obviously eccentric, a cartoon of a man —but just as obvious I sensed a smoldering passion that could be easily converted to anger. Beneath a narrow, beakish nose he twitched a thick, wiry, caramel-colored mustache, yet his eyebrows were so small in comparison and so tarry black that they seemed not to be his, but rather stolen from someone else. That was the thing about him—he seemed built from used parts, even his brown slacks appeared a shade lighter than his sport coat. To me at least, his haphazard appearance advertised quite loudly that he was a man who spent his hours gazing on the inside. I imagined he spent many nights alone, slipping out of bed after the wife had nodded off, easing into a favorite chair in the dark and theorizing this and that, getting high off thoughts, the way they collided in discovery. His eyes (did I say ping pong balls? Excuse me. Golf balls. No, eggs.) those giant peepers of his seemed to capture everything about him, seemed to scrutinize every object in the room as though frisking reality for concealed weapons. And when he spoke his voice seemed unnaturally loud, as though he relished the very act of speaking and believed that those within hearing distance would do well to listen to the sound of his words. He was most theatrical.

"Can you roll on your stomach?" he said. As if on cue, a dark-haired nurse entered the room and strolled to the other side of my bed, helping to guide me over. With a quick rip of velcro, D'Aoust removed my cervical collar. He pulled my pillow from beneath my head, and the next thing I knew he was leaning over me, pressing down on my spine with his wrists locked in CPR fashion. Moving up from my tailbone he delivered several sharp thrusts.

"An osteopath," I muttered, my breath squeezing out.

"Absolutely," he said. "Do you have a problem with that?"

"Absolutely not. Some of my best friends are osteopaths." I thought of Bobby and Carol from Erie, neither of whom could get in regular medical school.

D'Aoust concentrated on a point between my shoulder blades.

"Ouch," I said, "that's painful."

"Relax," he said. "And don't talk while I'm working on you."

He lined up the target with his fingertips, then pressed down. I heard a crack that coincided with a popping in my ears. A strange and refreshing feeling radiated from the center of my chest. I felt a tightness leaving me, as though a window in my heart had been thrown open and a fresh breeze allowed to blow through.

"Ah, that's great," I said.

"Okay, you can turn over now."

I obliged. The nurse lifted the head of my bed by remote control. She was a white woman about forty years old with thick, dark hair sparsely populated with silver strands, plus a face that reminded me of a child's red crayon scribbling with her uneven lipstick and overly rouged cheeks. Stout and muscular, she also sported two fistfuls of mammary gland pressed tight against her uniform top. She was called Joanna

DeLeon, according to a blue name tag perched on her right mammary, which, like a sinking ship, angled at thirty to thirty-five degrees.

D'Aoust produced a tongue depressor. "Say 'Ah,' " he said.

I opened my mouth and uttered the sound. D'Aoust pressed close enough for me to smell his aftershave. I caught a glimpse of his perfect fingernails; cuticle crescents followed by a band of pink, then topped again by white, square-clipped edges. His hands smelled like aspirin.

He withdrew the stick, wrinkled his nose, and made a clucking sound. "You're going to need antibiotics," he said, tossing the stick in a waste basket that opened like a clam. "You have a throat infection from swallowing dirty water. We'll start you on those today." He spoke the last words extra loud, looking over at Joanna. He named a drug that ended in "-xillin" and she jotted it down. "I'm also going to give you a shot of B-12," he said, "plus put you on large doses of vitamin C. That seems to lessen withdrawal symptoms, if there should be any.

"Get him changed and you can go now," he said to Joanna. She pulled the top sheet over me and asked me to slip out of my river-stained shorts. "I can't believe they let you lie in these," she said, handling them like a dead animal. "Where were you?"

"Bellevue," I said, receiving a pair of karate-style white pajama bottoms, pulling them on and tying them at the waist. Joanna took my shorts and left.

D'Aoust flipped open a brown plastic chart. My name covered a white label on the spine. "Your sister tells me things have changed quite a bit since you came back from a trip to . . . let's see, where was that?"

"Pennsylvania."

"Yes. Let's start by talking about your trip to Pennsylvania," he said, scanning my chart with his enormous eyes. "When exactly did you go?"

"I guess last weekend," I said.

"Do you remember the dates?" He looked at me over the top of the chart.

"Twenty-first, twenty-second, something like that," I said.

"What did you go for?" He tugged at the knot of his blue-and-brown-striped tie.

"S'cuse me?"

"Why did you go?" he said.

"To see some old friends." I cleared my throat.

"Did you see them?"

"Yeah."

"Did you have a good time?"

I felt moisture on my palms. I slid them under the sheet and wiped them against my pajama legs. "A good time?" I said. "That depends."

D'Aoust pushed his glasses back on the bridge of his nose. His eyes enlarged as though behind magnifying lenses. "Depends on what?" he said. "What did you do?"

"Oh, swam, mostly. Swam and ran around."

He sighed. "Ran around," he said, looking out the window. He shook his head. "Did you do any drinking while you ran around?"

"Oh, some. You know," I said.

"No, I don't know," he said. "What did you drink, pray tell?"

"A few beers."

"How many, exactly?"

"Just a few. You know, the usual. I always have a few."

"A few," he repeated. He tapped his pen against the inside of the chart. "Always has a few. And did you do anything else?"

"Oh, yeah," I said, perking up. "I went white water rafting. Quite unexpectedly."

"I meant other than alcohol," D'Aoust said. "Did you do anything besides drinking? Did you take any drugs?"

I looked up and noticed the ceiling tile was peppered with tiny black dots. Amazing, I thought. A veritable constellation of dots. All those square tiles, all those little dots. And in the middle of the ceiling, two light bays with the glare of their florescent tubes softened behind the ribbed texture of the plastic refracting screens. A texture, I thought, comprised of millions of tiny pyramids, rough as a cat's tongue.

"Mark?"

"Yes?"

"Did you take any drugs?"

"Drugs?"

"Drugs. Did you take any drugs when you visited your friends?"

"Sort of." My voice squeezed out my throat, sliding up the scale as well.

"Sort of what?" Again D'Aoust struck my chart with his pen.

"I smoked a joint."

"Ho, ho! A joint of marijuana!"

"Do you have to say it so loudly?" I looked out the door. A dietary worker shut the doors on the cart. He had long hair and a suspicious manner.

"A joint?!?" D'Aoust boomed. "Just one little joint? One teeny joint? One itsy, bitsy, teeny joint?" He threw his head back in laughter.

"Okay already. A few joints," I said. "Maybe two or three. Or three or four. But no more than four."

"No . . . more . . . than . . . four," he said, jotting mechanically in my chart with heavy, rough strokes, once for each word.

He's putting me on, I thought.

"Anything else?" he said. "Any pills or cocaine?"

"No. Marijuana was all."

"Marijuana and alcohol, you mean."

"Right. I forgot. Hey, do we have to talk so loud?"

"No one's talking loud."

"It seems like you want someone to hear you," I said.

"Maybe I want *you* to hear me. Now let me ask you again, were there any other drugs?"

"No, sir."

"You're absolutely sure about this? It's very important."

"Honest. No other drugs."

"That you know about," he said.

D'Aoust undid the top button of his collar. He set the chart on my mobile table. He leaned back against the wall near the door, looking into the hall, then out the window, then down at his feet, sighing.

"Tell me," he said, "are you hearing any voices?"

"Sure," I said. "Yours, mine. The intercom."

"Don't be smart. I mean *voices*, Mark. In your head. Telling you what to think. Or telling you to do things. Are you hearing anything like that?"

"Not now."

"Were you hearing them before?"

"Kinda. I kinda heard some stuff when they were doing my X-rays."

D'Aoust lifted his right foot and placed his brown wingtip shoe against the wall.

"Where was that?" he asked, rubbing his hands together.

"Bellevue."

"I see. And what were these voices saying?"

"Oh, the usual. Kill myself and stuff like that." I waited for him to shout it down the hall.

"Did voices tell you to jump off the bridge?"

"Not exactly," I said. "That was mostly my decision."

"Did you hear voices in between the time you smoked marijuana at this party and when they were taking you across the bridge?"

"God, yes. All kinds of things were going on."

"Hmmm, I see. I also understand you work at the Mitchell-Walker Institute." D'Aoust brushed the knees of his pants and moved away from the wall. "How do you think they're taking this back there?"

"I don't know. I suppose they're wondering something."

"Do you enjoy working there?"

"Sure do," I said, sitting up. "I love people. I love helping people. That's what hospital work is all about. Service. I love being of service. You know, I never burn out like other health care workers. Don't know why. But everybody tells me that. Even my patients notice."

D'Aoust rolled his eyes skyward, the dark irises disappearing like fruit on the wheels of a slot machine when the handle gets pulled.

"Well, we want to be of service here, too," he said. "We want to help you, Mark. And the best way to do that is by being honest. We have to both be honest with each other, right?"

"Right."

"Good. Now part of that means you need to tell us whenever you start hearing voices. That's very important if you want to get well. We have to know how you're feeling, okay?"

"Sure."

"I'm not kidding. Total honesty, Mark. You understand?"

"Cross my heart," I said, X-ing my chest.

"It's very important."

"Of course it is. I'll do everything I can, doctor."

D'Aoust picked up my chart, flipping pages. "Now I want you to stay in bed for a few days. But soon you'll be up and moving around. We've got plenty of activities on the unit. You'll like the people and there's lots to do. You're in the right place, Mark."

"That's what Richard said."

D'Aoust stared at me, his brows arching dramatically. "Who's this Richard?" he asked.

"My sister's husband. You know, that guy she was with."

"Oh, of course," he said, nodding and stroking his chin. "Anyway, don't forget what I told you about voices."

CHAPTER 13

A short time after D'Aoust left Joni and Richard reentered my room.

"How does your neck feel?" Joni said, bending over to brush my hair back and kissing me on the forehead.

"Good as ever," I announced.

"Whew, your hair stinks, though," she said. "Once you get a few privileges, don't be shy about asking for a shower."

"Forget that for now," Richard said. "What really counts is that you're safe. And that's great. What do you think of your doctor?"

"He's an osteopath," I said.

"Don't you have a friend who's an osteopath?" Joni said, brushing the sheets at my feet, clearing a spot for her rear.

Busying himself as hospital visitors often do, Richard lifted up my toiletries—"admission kit"—to examine it further. Inside a clear plastic bag was a tiny box of tissues, toothbrush, a sampler-sized tube of Pepsodent, two matchbook-sized bars of Dial soap, a blue plastic cup, a black plastic comb, a pink plastic spittoon, and a cable TV channel guide from HBO featuring color photos of coming attractions on the cover, the photos having rounded corners to simulate a TV screen.

"Oh," Joni said, putting a hand to her temple, "Mom called."

What was left of the East River rose in my stomach. "Did you tell her about *this*?" I said, gesturing to the room.

"We didn't talk. I called home a few minutes ago and picked up a message on our machine. Mark, I don't know how but somehow she found out about the Brooklyn Bridge."

"That doesn't make any sense," Richard said. "How can she know that?"

"She said the whole town knows."

"What town?" I said. "What are you talking about?"

"Damn," she said, crossing her legs and dangling her foot from the bed, flopping her shoe heel up and down. She sighed and slapped her thigh. "We're both in it now, kiddo. I hope I can handle this."

"You mean you weren't going to tell her?" I said.

"Would you? Listen, we're not out of the woods yet. We're still trying to find out what happened back at that party of yours. There's so much we don't know yet that I wasn't going to tell her anything—not until you and this whole situation got stable."

"Is this thing in the papers?" I said.

Joni and Richard looked at each other like two actors who both lost their cues. Richard sat on the bed, turning his back to me and flashing Joni the "quit" sign, scissoring his hands apart like an umpire signaling "Safe!" at home.

"I saw that," I said. "Somebody's not being honest with me."

***

No one here gets out alive.

That line describes very well what it meant to grow up in my family. Why else would two adults, Joni and I, involved in a life-and-death drama, care one way or another how their mother feels about the thing?

Part of the answer rests with Dad. Since his first child was born in 1944, my father, Raymond Wolyczin, ruled his household by means of two paramount laws:

1. When you leave a room, turn out the lights
2. When you're eighteen, you're outta here

All his six children learned the value of electricity. They learned about watts and volts and how the electric bill is paid. It's paid with your father's sweat and labor, that's how it's paid. And since you don't pay it, kid, you better go along with the program, that is, do what I tell you or you can go get your own place to live and run all the lights, see if I care, and leave the music up loud and have all your friends over and don't give a shit if you wake up in a dirty house with no clean sheets, but until then you respect your mother and your father because I get up every day and go to a stinkin' job so my ungrateful kids can go to school and eat and wear all them fancy clothes. I didn't get none of that when I was your age.

(I was wrong. I guess part of the answer rests with my dad's parents, for making him scared that the universe would shortchange you, if it could.)

Poor Dad. He never learned the art of giving spontaneously. Because of how *he* was raised, he thought that you gave because you *had* to. Johnny be good—or else. So ol' Johnny becomes a daddy and ends up giving to his kids in a forced and painful manner—all that pain coming from the memories of his parents' coercion. Dad, never receiving appreciation as a child, couldn't conceive that *we* were appreciative of what he did for us. He didn't trust. Sure, we tried to help him, appreciating harder and harder, until appreciating became damn hard work.

Which is why Rule number two was so important. It established the limits of the father-and-child contract. When you're eighteen, Joni, you're outta here. I don't have to worry about you not appreciating things anymore. You think you can do better? Then go ahead. No one's stoppin' you now.

All six children can give their father credit for his honesty.

He lived through the Great Depression. His view was that it's a tough world; you either sink or swim on your own. Better find out sooner than later.

However, rather than admiration for his honesty, Rule 2 created an opposite effect. We were terror stricken. High school graduation meant the end of the world. We had to leap without looking, and incredible pressure made us grab, one at a time, for the first thing floating by. Dale became a teacher without giving it a second thought. Scott went in the Navy because his grades weren't very good. (Dad said it was the Navy or nothing.) When my sister's number came up, she found her career already selected for her: nursing. That's it. Dad would help with some tuition, but of course it meant moving out. Any other career choice and she'd get no help at all.

But Joni had a plan of her own. It was called Prince Valiant in a sports car. The end result was a hasty marriage, but nevertheless her prince provided the necessary exit visa and, at least in the beginning, offered her some hope of a better life to come.

The rest, they say, is *his*tory. Joni and he were not a good pair. She finished nursing school with a real show-and-tell project in human fertilization. She heard the words "I told you so" so many times from her own parents that she probably should have embroidered the phrase on a sweatshirt and worn it every time she came back home.

Clearly she hadn't measured up. She was divorced and living alone shortly after her second daughter was born. Her husband, bless him, had found somebody less challenging, somebody more inclined to defer to his vision of the world.

This "measuring up" business screwed over our whole family. Totally screwed us. Fucked us up. Made us neurotic, guilt-ridden—Mom, Dad, the whole fucking family.

I think it started with Sunday mornings when our whole family scrambled like RAF fighter pilots to make it to Catholic church on time. The TV was blasting. I was fighting with my little sister, Mary. Joni was trying to wrestle the bathroom away from the older brothers while Dad searched the house, complaining about not being able to find the Sunday sports page or his church contribution envelopes that he filled with money and sealed the night before. Mom, the ever plump, slightly jowly woman with red dyed hair turning naturally to silver, ran about, throwing a roast or a chicken in the oven, scrounged for her makeup that Mary had misplaced, monitored our dressing routines, telling us what we could and couldn't wear. She was vicious pulling those white T-shirts over my head, that tiny hole would lock around the bridge of my nose and practically rip my ears off. At one time Mom carried a lot of fat on the backs of her arms; I remember the skin hanging down from her triceps like ear lobes, remember those arms flailing about as she directed traffic on Sunday mornings, stopping me like a top in motion, planting her hands on my head and tilting my face back for inspection, wiping the dirt smudges off by licking her white handkerchief and rubbing until my skin burned.

The ride to church was an exercise in letting our parents know how much we hated it. "The Pope makes mistakes," Scott would say. "He's only human, you know." We had other things to grumble about: our stiff, scratchy clothes, Sunday chores, Sunday dinner that promised peas and carrots or some other punishing vegetable. Often we'd be embroiled in an all-out argument just as we pulled into Blessed Family and approached the church doors. Then the Miracle of Serenity would occur: all fights would suddenly cease as we entered the hushed congregation, our heels echoing off the marble floor, strangers looking our way, the sanctimonious organ music, the candles and stained glass lighting alerting us to His Holy Presence, like a face slap, and most importantly, alerting us to the Right Way to Behave. Bow that head! Fold those hands! Look up, look down, look pious. (Perhaps there was one last chance to kick my little sister as we filed in the pew.)

Mom loved it when we sang those hymns. Why, not singing or saying the Apostle's Creed was a guaranteed way to earn her wrath. Quite often she reached over at the beginning of mass and shoved a prayer book in my hands. If I did nothing, she'd take the book and open it to the page we were on.

"Mom! Okay, already. I'll pray, all right?"

My favorite church story concerns the time I was under the influence of mortal sin due to the fact I had been trying to instigate my own wet dreams—a very serious offense according to the church pamphlet "God, You . . . and Masturbation" that I stole, with considerable nervousness, after eyeing it for weeks in the fifty-cent rack at the back of the church vestibule. I was several years short of puberty yet, but being the precocious lad I was, I had certainly *heard* about wet dreams, and orgasms, but of course, having no actual experience only made me more susceptible to believing that perhaps I *had* had one and not known it yet. The pamphlet could clarify it. I was in love with Diana Rigg, the secret agent in *The Avengers*. Ever since I could remember, bedtime had offered me the chance to snuggle up to a cool, fresh pillow and practice my kissing and make-out lines. I was all over Diana. Even when I was a lad of barely seven, I would slip under the covers, taking my surrogate girlfriend with me, and act out all sorts of fantasies involving submarines, caves, army tanks— any small enclosure that my undercover world could be. These were simple, puppy-love feelings, and it seemed only natural to fall asleep with visions of Diana Rigg dancing in my head. And then, in later years, on occasion I would wake from a particularly vivid dream. Perhaps it was of ponytailed Rebecca, who sat in front of me in fourth grade geography class. Or Carol, who rode the bus. They were wonderful dreams, full of kissing and touching. Touching my little hard-on became a morning ritual for me, no more unusual than the clock radio coming on or the smell of oatmeal from the kitchen downstairs.

Then I had my brainstorm. I wondered if perhaps there was a way to create the dreams I wanted, to sow a romantic seed or two before I fell asleep. I took to vivid fantasies, praying that in sleep, they'd come true.

But according to the pamphlet, this was very bad. Any conscious volition on my part, any attempt to will sex into my dreams was a sin, clear and simple. Perhaps a *mortal* sin, if I were to believe what the nuns had taught me. Back in first grade Sister Cecilia had diagrammed the soul. I still remember the good Sister—a jouncy, heavyset woman with catfish whiskers curling from her chin—as she drew a giant circle with chalk on the board.

"This is your soul," she had said.

She then proceeded to pepper the circle with tiny dots. "Those are sins," she said. "Venial sins. They're very small, but as you can see, class, they add up like dirt."

"Now here's a mortal sin," she said, taking the side of the chalk and brushing over the circle in long, broad strokes. Great streaks of white filled the soul in until it was completely dirty. The thing about mortal sin, she went on to explain, was how it blocked off the "grace of God." With a mortal sin on your soul you were completely disenfranchised, and no amount of praying or good deeds or going to church would make it go away. Only confession would clean it up. Confession was the only cure. In fact, if you knowingly went to communion in a state of mortal sin (that is, took the host on your tongue which represented the body of our Lord, Jesus Christ), then you were guilty of a double offense, heaping one mortal mess upon the other. And another thing, she said, was that if you kept making the same venial sins over and over—even though they were only microscopic dots—they sort of coagulated and eventually formed a mortal sin. It was spiritual cholesterol.

Everyone knows it's not as literal as that, but I'll be darned if ol' Sister Cecilia hadn't made a lasting impression. And there I was a few years later, manufacturing venial sins every night like a squirrel in his den, gnawing on the Devil's acorns. By now I was aware of the grievous state I was in; a soul so bespeckled with sex and sin that only a lengthy, choke-voice confession could erase them, otherwise not a single beam of light would ever penetrate the gloomy cavern—formerly my soul—where my spirit now hovered in sickness and shame.

But getting to confession wasn't exactly a high priority with most schoolboys my age. You didn't go unless someone made you.

So there I am, at church with Mom and Dad when the big moment comes. Communion time. Music up. The priest gives the cue. Everybody is rising and going to the communion rail. Mom looks at me, and I have to make a dreadful decision. Do I take communion, knowing full well that I'm doubly damned for inviting Christ into an unclean soul? Or do I stay in the pew and prepare myself for the first question she's sure to ask the minute mass is over: Why didn't you go to communion?

No way was I going to open *that* can of worms. I'd rather deal with God in the afterlife than have to deal with my mom yelling, "What do you mean, mortal sin? How could a boy your age be guilty of mortal sin?"

CHAPTER 14

I'm sorry. We were talking about measuring up.

So let's pick it up where we left off, exiting church on Sunday mornings. As I mentioned, Mom usually had a roast in the oven and there was always an hour or so before dinner would be ready, so part of our Sunday ritual included stopping over the grandparents before we went back home to eat. My mom's parents were fat, happy Slovaks. Dad's were thin, stern Ukrainians, beady-eyed and worrisome as the day they fled the Ukraine during the Russian Revolution. Over Mom's folks we could usually count on getting some ice cream, Popsicles, or soda. Over my Dad's folks, zilch. They didn't have toys. They didn't have games or coloring books. We had to sit there in our stiff Sunday clothes and count the time going by. (Actually, that was one of our games: "Guess how many minutes have passed?") We weren't allowed to watch TV. And we had to ask Grandma to use the bathroom, which was such a traumatic experience that my brothers and I chose to hold it instead. Whenever we found out we were going to visit the Ukrainian grandparents, Scott would say, "Oh oh, Church, Part II."

Inevitably, on the way home we kids would try to get Mom and Dad to promise that we'd never go back again. It was here we learned that our own parents weren't exactly dancing with joy over the idea, either. It had to be done, though. It was expected of us. That measuring up shit. It was only one hour a week, dammit, and besides, as soon as we got home we could go back to being ourselves again.

I can't speak for my sister but I would guess she absorbed some conditional loving patterns much as I had. Everything was predicated on behavior. If you acted good, you were good. As Bradshaw puts it, we were human *doings*. Bring home an "A" and you got a pat on the head; bring home the birds and bees, and you got hit with a bucket of cold water. Growing up was largely spent wondering how you were doing so far.

As a consequence Joni became the ultimate fixer. She loved to fix people's behavior—especially if it reminded her of the old family patterns. She was the peacemaker, the mediator. One time Dad and I were to the point of blows over my refusal to get a haircut. He threatened to cut it himself if I didn't go to a barber. Joni stepped in and got us both to agree to letting her cut it, though she ended up taking off more of my hair than any barber would have done.

Joni was bright and usually gave herself the time to think things through. One day I guess she caught on to how backwards our childhoods had been and then set out to eradicate the problem by doing the very opposite—loving unconditionally—whether the one she loved wanted it or not.

Enter me. The teenager whose hair she used to cut is now twenty-one and the failing child, the experiment gone bad, the black sheep grown to the size of an enormous black hole. I couldn't drive a car or keep a job. Everyone else had given up on me. The doctor in charge of my second institutionalization had told my mother flatly, "Your son's a schizophrenic. Be prepared to live with the fact he'll be in and out of hospitals for the rest of his life."

Nevertheless Joni took me in to live with her and her two little girls. I was two notches above a cauliflower, a Thorazine zombie not even fit to be her babysitter. I was on such a high dose of the drug that often I couldn't hold objects like spoons in my hand. I walked like a robot and fell asleep several times a day. I woke up every morning with a puddle of drool on my pillow. It took a major effort just to tie my shoes. But Joni wouldn't give up. She nurtured and fed me health food, weaning me off the Thorazine, until eventually I got back on my feet again. To me it seemed she was the only person who cared if I lived or not.

Those were strange times in Erie, Pennsylvania. Nurse Joni was young, divorced, and beautiful, and drew male doctors to her like cobwebs down the throat of a vacuum cleaner. It was dirty for dirty, with Joni going out on weekends partly because there was nothing else better to do, and at least on the outside, the men who asked her appeared successful and stable. Often it took no longer than the first or second date for her to realize how misleading appearances could be.

An image I recall very clearly is the one where she came over my apartment at one in the morning, unannounced, and told me she had gotten out of this guy's car at a nearby traffic light because he thought they were going back to his place. My apartment had a raunchy loveseat sagging in the corner by the radiator, and I can still see her yanking off her boots and jumping up and down on it, protecting her head from the ceiling, the dust puffing out the cushions, her brown corduroy skirt ballooning, her voice cursing men, men, and men in its loudest, angriest tones. I think it was the only time she was ever happy to see beer in my refrigerator.

I mention these things because most of her life, Joni was compromised. She knew people had trouble dealing with a strong woman, but her survival depended on her being strong. She needed a good man in her life but the reality for Erie was that you got whatever was available. She was a good nurse but the reality was that only kiss-asses and old crusty butts got the supervisory positions. She did great things as an intake nurse for Ronson Lodger's psych unit (where I was later to work), but whenever she proposed a new pilot program the doctors scuttled it because they couldn't control it or hadn't thought of it themselves. And she was a great mother but couldn't help feeling the burden that single parenting placed on her.

Her moving to New York was the ultimate risk. Not only was she just another new face in town, but she vowed to never take up nursing again, even if it meant starving to death. Needless to say, her meeting Richard was God's grace, indeed.

***

So there we were six years later, together again, only this time I'm in a hospital once more and though I'm financially solvent, living among Manhattan's upper crust, pulling down good grades in a demanding art school program, working full time nights, dating a beautiful woman, and on the verge of launching my first stage play . . . I'm in trouble with Mom again.

Actually, *we're* in trouble with Mom again. Joni had some explaining to do. What went wrong, my mother would want to know. I thought you were handling him, she'd say. I thought you said he was doing better.

***

September 11, 1983
(Morning interlude)

My prize vinyl chair—the chair with the view—turns out to be a sweat-producing contraption. I throw a blanket over it before I sit down. A pleasant breeze wafts through the open window, tickling the hairs on my arms. Summer is holding its breath as it crosses the finish line. On the other side of the tennis courts the oaks and maples are squeezing out their last ounce of green. Nature is drawn tight as a bow. That certain back-to-school smell is in the air, the smell of a season ending. The cicadas scream only at high noon now, getting in their last licks before the cold kisses them goodbye.

I can't conceive of staying in this hospital for another year. To sit here and watch four more seasons change behind a wire mesh screen—that thought sickens me.

I meet with Bowman later today. She says she has something important to discuss with me. That has got me thinking about my dreams again.

I always thought it was a movie on TV, because there were definitely times—like when my cousin pushed me out of a tree onto the driveway—when illness or some other reason prompted my parents to let me stay up with them at night, watching something on the television that would have normally been denied to me because of lateness or perhaps the program's content. So for many years I thought the image of the three giants was some clip from a science fiction film, some image I had stored from when I was barely able to sort fact from fiction in my brain. The scene went like this: There were these mammoth concrete creatures, giants of white stone that marched all over the earth. Everyone was afraid of them because they sucked the energy from the planet, drawing it up through their feet as their feet struck the ground. They'd march for a while, all the humans fleeing in front of them, then they'd stop. When they rested they looked like giant hourglasses, pale concrete towers tapered at the waist.

As years went by this dream image resurfaced every now and then. It would superimpose itself on whatever I was doing, like a music box tune or the smell of candied apples, then evaporate and leave me with a hollow, mysterious feeling. I never knew for sure if I had dreamed it or seen it on someone's TV. Even more puzzling was its nagging reoccurrence, the way it haunted me like the big sun dream. Why should it be that important to revisit me again and again?

I was about twenty-five when I went to a party off-campus at Penn State. Catherine Hayes was with me; I remember she left me for a moment to chat with some friends. I didn't know many people there so I started browsing through some magazines scattered on a coffee table. I picked up a recent copy of *Time*. On the cover was the famous photograph of the Three Mile Island nuclear power plant, the ominous reactor towers captured in twilight. With a cold chill crawling on my flesh, I recognized the towers as the ones in my dream.

I can't remember if I told Catherine about the incident or not. I was quite shaken and couldn't sleep that night, and I also lost my appetite the following day.

Not long after that incident I had another dream. It took place in New York or another big city, where I was in company with one of my sister's closest friends, Patricia, an actress. I was beside the woman at a swimming pool, and the pool was on the top floor of a very high building. All around I could see the tops of other skyscrapers. But what I was really taken with was the water. The pool was so clean and blue. I turned to Patricia to remark how pure the water was, and I became aware of her figure in her two-piece bathing suit. It was nothing more than a typical impure thought, but I knew I shouldn't feel that way, being an acquaintance of her husband as well.

I began fighting the impulse to look her over. As I did, she turned to me and said, "Yes, the water is very clean here. However, you must go to where the water is dirty."

Suddenly the scene changed and I was overlooking a broad, muddy river. The scene altered again and I was beside the riverbank, pushing people in wheelchairs up and down the tangled, muddy slopes.

I awoke from the dream sensing that this one, too, was like Three Mile Island. It was going to come true. I've had thousands of other dreams before and since, but there was something about this one—and don't ask me what—that told me I couldn't escape its happening later.

At that time I was having trouble at Penn State, and since both my sister and her friend lived next door to each other in Brooklyn Heights, I reasoned that this time I should try to help the dream come true. I took it as a sign. A few weeks later I had applied to New York University. I called my sister and gave her the news. If accepted, my sister promised she'd help me get started with a new life in New York.

(Later that day)

Bowman is dressed in black. On the desk in her office, where my chart usually sits, it is bare. She sits next to me in the other wooden chair, facing me, her legs crossed and her hands on her knee. She turns her palms up, examining them before speaking.

Mark, this is difficult so I want you to bear with me. The staff has been observing you for a few days now, and it is our recommendation that you begin treatment with antipsychotic medicine."

Bowman's hand makes a tiny fist. "I'm aware that part of your problem is chemical dependency. I don't want you to see this as a setback in that regard."

"But I'm doing better, doctor. I'm doing better every day."

"This drug will help you stay focused, Mark. I think it will help your recovery."

"What drug are you talking about?"

"Thorazine."

CHAPTER 15

On May 4, 1974, the morning after the full moon and my third and final LSD adventure, I drove Kelly, Danny, and Reese to Kent State University. It was Saturday, sunny, and the drive had started with no particular destination until a radio disc jockey mentioned the traffic congestion around the university in commemoration of the fourth anniversary of the National Guard shootings. As soon as we heard that we all looked at each other and knew where we wanted to go. I gunned the motor and turned the wheel of my first car, a white 1967 Pontiac Bonneville convertible with a four-barrel 454 "rocket" V-8 engine, an automobile that drank gas so fast the fuel gauge bounced from F to E like a parkinsonian teeter-totter. The car's charm, however, rested entirely in its open-air capabilities; it was a riot to take the top down, roast ourselves on the black vinyl seats, and cruise seventy miles an hour on old state routes that passed through sleepy towns like Niles, Girard, and Newton Falls. The car's old shocks gave it a boat-like ride, a spongy, delayed response to dips and curves.

"God damn, Kelly," I yelled above the wind, watching yet another cigarette ash hover above the ashtray before rising, swirling, and blowing over our shoulders. "God damn, I can't believe we had the same dream. Doesn't that freak you out?"

"Not after talking about it for five hours straight," Kelly said, glancing back at Danny and Reese.

"Didn't you sleep at all this morning?" Danny shouted from the back.

"Nope," I said. "No need to. If you really think about it, sleep's a waste of time. I can't believe I've wasted so much of my life sleeping." I laughed. "But that was then, fellas."

I turned up the volume on the cassette player. Yes's latest album, *Tales From Topographic Oceans*, blared over my inadequate speakers.

"What happened to this song we once knew so well?" said the lyrics. "We must have waited all our lives for this moment, moment, moment."

"I feel like we made a special connection, Kelly. It's like we were destined to remember that dream, and to remember it exactly at the same moment."

"Right," he said, holding down his long, dark hair. "How much further to Kent State?"

"You know, I feel really good about myself. I've never felt like this before," I said. "It's like the time we both saw that giant ring around the moon. Remember that? That circle filled up half the sky. And just the two of us seeing it, standing on that hill. What'dya think, Kelly? Are the two of us destined for something?"

"I think there's four of us in this car," he said, turning down the volume.

Two, four, six, eight—drugs'll make you radiate. The third trip's the charm, ol' Mark-y boy, said a voice in my head. You always wanted something to give you a purpose, to set your ambition on fire.

It was true. I felt like I was jumping from ride to ride in my own little Disneyland, everything full of mystery and meanings, the whole world lit up from behind—and a whole new person inside of me emerging like some pivotal character who arrives late in a play. Iceman cometh. Iceman born again.

"Wasn't that weird last night when I said I saw that cigarette going out the window of that car, only it hadn't happened yet?" I looked in the mirror at Reese, his face shadowed by two days' worth of whiskers.

"Guess you saw it before it happened," he said.

"It was great. It was like being a split second ahead of reality. The whole night went like that, don't you think?"

"Hey, Mark, you wanna stop at a 7-Eleven somewhere so I can get some cigarettes?"

"Sure. And how 'bout when Danny lost his contact lens in the woods and I just reached in there, right into the darkness, and pulled it out of the dirt?" I said. "God, what were the odds of that?"

(What were the odds that my ego would piss on my parade?)

If I had been teetering on the brink while driving to Kent State, what I saw when we arrived completely pushed me over the edge. A giant crowd milled about the grass, clusters of people sat on blankets, watching from the knoll. Down below, on stage, Daniel Ellsberg read from the Pentagon Papers. Posters featured caricatures of Richard Nixon with one word, "Dick," below a nose drawn to resemble something out of *A Clockwork Orange*. Jane Fonda was rumored to be arriving. Grateful Dead music trailed from speakers high in the dorms. LSD seemed to have opened a door for me, a door to a new kind of energy. I could feel raw emotion running through the crowd. As though I were X-raying personalities with my eyes, I sensed that I could read peoples' intentions, that I had developed some type of radar that detected the subtext beneath peoples' actions. At last I was connected. Even my own behavior became transparent to me, all the kowtowing I had been doing for my parents, all the pretense and manipulative games. The old me peeled off like excess skin and I felt free, open, unashamed of who I was. I had cut the strings from the puppet.

The Answer was everywhere about me: It was on the face of the hippie mother breastfeeding her child. It was a dog leaping for a Frisbee. It was a baby girl in a stroller, gumming a pretzel. It was a bearded young man asking for a light. I was on the cusp of something magnanimous. An entirely new voice thundered in my head. I felt "chosen" to explain this vast mystery, this pure and joyful Life denuded of all wars and games and fear. The Answer was obvious.

I grabbed Kelly by the shoulders. "*This* is what needs explaining!" I yelled. "This! This! This world without fear!"

Kelly smiled but didn't say anything. I let go and felt myself tingling in the balls of my feet. Slowly the feeling rose until an electric current leaped wildly up my spine, rushing soft fire and blood to my brain, raising the very hairs on my head.

Overload.

I collapsed on the grass and curled into a fetal position, letting out a storm of tears like I had never known before. My friends stood by me, then slowly backed away. Quite a crowd passed by, some stopping to stare, others nodding and continuing their way. I cried until I was weak and light as a feather. I didn't care who watched or who thought what. At last I knew that I knew that I KNEW. The one hand clapping had slapped me in the face.

***

Somewhere among all of this was a dream, a shared dream, of a giant sun. No one could tell me that great forces weren't taking shape. I was so drained from crying that I gave the keys to Reese and rode home in the back with Danny. "Where to?" someone asked and we all started laughing. The V-8 fired up and the Ohio countryside rolled by, blond and green, the fields arranged like patchwork between oak and maple woods. We crossed creeks that glistened from sunlight, riding over old iron bridges that wobbled from the weight of our car.

We parted, and when I got home I paused at the back door, overlooking the yard where I had played as a child. It had been a perfect day. The late afternoon sun was soft now and thick like honey and a large ray slanted against the trunk of the big oak in the center of the yard. The tattered remnants of my tree fort still clung to the lower branches. My eyes could pick out the donkey-tail end of the rope swing, which had frayed long ago. I could see the rusty nail heads in the wooden steps climbing the trunk, the first step skewing to the left, the next one to the right, and on and on up the tree like poorly spaced railroad ties.

Of course, I thought. That's where I need to go. I crossed the yard and climbed up to the old rotted platform. I grabbed the rope and gave it a tug, then let it swing like a graduate's tassel. It seemed like only yesterday when the rope had held the big tire we used to spin on, leaning over to scoop up pennies, marbles, or toy soldiers in the grass.

Everything is perfect, I thought. It's all perfect right now.

Gary Sabo, a neighbor ten years older than me, gravitated to the backyard fence in order to talk. We hardly ever spoke to each other, mostly on account of the years back when my mother didn't like the gangs of older boys who spent time in their backyard, foul-mouthing, drinking beer, and tuning up their cars while playing Rolling Stones music from the black, naked speaker cones planted like ears on the automobile roofs.

Interestingly, on this particular occasion Gary and I talked like long-lost brothers. The Isaly Dairy had just shut down. Yep, Gary said, Youngstown's economy was in for hard times. "You just wait," he said. "The steel mills will be shutting down next." We talked about space exploration and how NASA's technology was useful for American businesses, too. Gary was smart. He was a middle school teacher. Next we talked about tennis and Japanese beetles. He told me why Japanese beetles loved roses so much.

We finished talking and I went in the house, amazed that after so many years of silence, Gary and I could pick up a free-flowing conversation just like that. As I entered the kitchen I encountered my parents and became sensitive to their inquisitive glances.

"Where were you all day?" my mother asked. Her arms, flabby and dotted with liver spots she had inherited from her mother, busied themselves about the kitchen, cleaning up after a meal.

I told her we went to Nelson Ledges, a state park north of Newton Falls.

"You know your father and I didn't know you were home until he looked out the window. Considering that we didn't know where you were all day, you could have come inside and let us know you were back—"

"Sorry, Mom."

"—instead of climbing like an idiot up in that tree. I'm sure it's not safe anymore."

"And dead, too," my father said, "ever since you drove fifty dollars' worth of nails in the thing."

My father rose from the table. "What did you and Gary have to talk about?"

"Nothing," I said. My instinct told me to avoid him. I went to the basement to be alone. He followed me, puttering around his workbench in the adjoining room as I put on Pink Floyd's *Dark Side of the Moon*.

"Keep that music down," he grumbled.

I began undressing to take a shower. My hallucinations had stopped but I was continually struck by hues of light that seemed more brilliant than they normally were. The reds pulsed in the gingham curtains and the stack of different-colored bath towels struck me as a cross between a rainbow and a stack of Chiclets. Actually, *everything* seemed brighter, or as Kelly had put it on the drive home, "Everything looks wiped squeegee-clean." I became entranced by details: the condensation glinting in the far corner on the basement wall, lint balls clinging to the heels of my socks, two tiny holes under the left arm of my father's white T-shirt.

My father was a big man. Tall, not barrel chested, but with long, powerful arms from years of working with his hands. He had a grip that wouldn't quit. That afternoon he watched me as I seemed to take forever to get undressed. I folded each item of clothing, receiving subtle information about the fabric, the color dyes, the types of stitch. I stopped to admire the grooved design on the bottom of my tennis shoes.

"I wonder who came up with this," I said to my father, holding up the pair.

"Came up with what?" he said.

"The tread design," I said. "Do you think they tested it?"

"Tested *what*?" He seemed perturbed.

"These grooves here. See? They're different in front, by the toe. Do you think that's because they know something, or they just do that to make fun designs when you walk in the mud?"

"Stop being ridiculous," he said.

I had just removed my underwear when a large spider dashed across the basement floor. Reacting quickly, I grabbed a small cardboard shoebox and dropped it on top of him.

"There," I said, "now there's no escape."

"What'd you catch?" my father said, coming toward me.

"A spider," I said.

"Kill it."

I grabbed my Pink Floyd album and slipped it under the box. I wrapped a towel around my waist and retrieved the box, holding it on top the album jacket as I carried them both outside where I tossed the spider into the grass. When I returned downstairs my father grabbed me by the shoulders and pushed me against the wall. He locked his rough, beefy hands under my jaw, lifting up so hard that I had to stretch on my toes to keep from choking. My towel dropped to the floor.

"Dad! What's wrong?" I said through painful, clenched teeth.

"What's wrong!" he screamed. "You're what's wrong! Why didn't you kill that thing?"

I reached up and pulled his fingers from my throat. "'Cause I didn't . . . want . . . to kill it," I said. He released my neck but still held me, his hands pressed against my chest.

"It ain't normal," he said, his dinner breath buffeting my face.

"Dad, it's killing that isn't normal. I didn't kill it because there's no reason for it."

"You never needed a reason before," he said. "That's why it ain't normal. What's gotten into you?" He released his hands but didn't step away. The concrete wall cut into my back. "You didn't eat dinner," he said. "You didn't even look to see what we had. In all my life I've never known you to walk past a plate of hot food. You can't tell me something hasn't gotten into you."

"Nothing's gotten into me except—" I didn't finish.

"I've been watching you," he said. "You're acting goofy. Something isn't right."

"Something *is* right, Dad. Something's right for the first time in my life." I backed along the wall until the other room opened up behind me.

"Something's wrong when my son stops to pick up a goddam spider."

"Something's right," I said. "*I* am right. I'm right because I'm changing my life."

"Oh, bullshit." He looked away while he shook his head. "What's so right about climbing trees and talking to Gary Sabo?" he said. "What's so right about walking around here with a shit-eating grin on your face? Staring at your clothes like they're talking to you or something. Huh? You tell me!"

I backpedaled toward the shower. "It's . . . it's love, Dad. I care about Gary."

"Jesus Christ," he moaned, smacking his forehead with his palm. "What brought this on all of a sudden? Since when did you care about Gary Sabo? Or anyone else for that matter?"

"Since today. Since I found out what love is."

"Oh, my God," I heard my mother from upstairs.

"Saul, why are you persecuting Me?"

I'm not sure Who said that. Did it come out of my mouth, or my mother's, or did it just go off in my head?

I said something else and my father talked back but I wasn't listening anymore. Words flew around like a bunch of moths butting into a street lamp. Pretty soon words weren't even there anymore, just mouths flapping, my mother coming downstairs and joining the fray, her mouth a big black oval like one of those singing angels on a Christmas card. I grew distant from the whole scene, felt myself shrinking smaller and smaller like the dot in the center of an old-fashioned black-and-white television set, turned off but lingering there in the middle of that blackness, hanging like a lost star until I finally winked out. Only hours from heaven, I was getting my first taste of hell.

For the next two weeks I lived under house arrest. My parents, especially my mother, suddenly developed a keen interest in whatever I was doing. Who did I ride to school with in the mornings? What was that smell? When exactly did school get out? Where was I going after dinner, and could they have a phone number to call? For the first time she questioned the five-leafed plant in the center of a patch I had sewn on my jeans.

Odd things started happening. My family doctor, an ex-neighbor of ours, made a surprise visit one day. I hadn't seen him since I got vaccinated for my trip to Guam. He had stopped making house calls ten years before. Yet there he was, stopping by for a friendly visit. He asked me how I was doing, if my grades were good, if I had lost my balance in the last few months. We all sat in the living room, making painful conversation and enduring the strange, in-between silences while he seemed to study me like a test tube turning color.

A week later, my mother took me to a psychiatrist. He gave me Valium. I thought that was funny. Very ironic in a way. I had just sworn off Valium. So I gave it to my friends. Mr. Lowry, the health counselor at school, caught me dispensing the drug, and he took me to his empty classroom during lunchtime where we had a conversation I couldn't make heads or tails of. Soon after that an ugly rumor started and there was talk I wouldn't deliver the class address at commencement that year. I was the class speaker, having awarded myself the title after losing the election for class president by three votes. Before

May 3 I had been working on a speech that promised to be the best ever delivered by a student at Major Thomas Bewlay Memorial High.

The last days of school rushed by in a disjointed frenzy, time expanding and contracting in a way that little insignificant moments, like talking to some little kids who were throwing rocks in the creek, seemed charged with special meaning. Yet other things—homework, chores—seemed like activities more appropriate for a different planet. I messed up commencement practice by not getting in line with everyone else. It seemed like they were playing a game, all my classmates making fun of me with some silly version of Simon Says. "Who needs this phony May parade?" I said, my voice snatching everyone's attention in the auditorium, ringing back in an awful silence. The girl next to me stood up and abandoned her seat. There was a low whisper and everyone slowly filed out, leaving me, the only person in a five-hundred-seat hall. My head was swimming with anger and fear, with a sense that everyone was betraying me. You fucking sheep, I thought. Blah, blah, blah. After what seemed to be an eternity Mr. Lowry tapped me on the shoulder and said if I wanted to, he would take me home.

But it didn't end quite yet, even though my classmates and favorite teachers began treating me differently. No more jokes about gurus and Tibet with supercool Mr. McCallister. No more hall passes from the yearbook advisor. Someone rifled through my locker. My padlock was stolen. Other students became afraid of me, pulling away in secretive groups as they watched me come down the hall. Kelly and Reese no longer got high with me at lunch. I couldn't get a ride home from school. I'd walk home and end up in a different neighborhood, sometimes miles from my house. Bits of litter on the street fascinated me; I began picking them up and reading them, certain that messages were being planted around the city like a breadcrumb trail that was supposed to lead me to . . . what? Glory? Safety? I think I was supposed to end up at a big surprise party of some kind. Not only would all my friends be there, but rock-'n'-roll celebrities and movie stars as well.

For five days after my Kent State visit I experienced the weirdest thing; I couldn't eat or sleep, couldn't sleep no matter what. There was all this music in my head. Angelic symphonies seemed to spring from nowhere, animating me, distinct as any sound coming from the outside world. I heard them as clearly as one hears birds in the woods or waves at the beach. There was a soundtrack to everything I did; music for walking, for eating, for sitting in the dark, asking myself questions and answering them immediately. I stayed up night after night, writing poems that only certain people could understand, and for only a short period of time.

Finally, a few days before graduation and my eighteenth birthday, my dad shoved me in the car and dragged me to the local institution. (That was after they were supposed to pick me up from school but I burst free from the principal's office and ran out the door.) Once I was safely locked away, my mother went on an emotional bender of her own, parading down the street, stopping at all my friends' houses. She demanded that whoever was responsible for me—the drug pusher and his parents—should come forward and accept their blame.

1974 turned out to be a long, hot summer. I received my high school diploma during visiting hours, having it slid to me under a chicken wire glass window. The place was called Woodside Receiving Hospital, and they counted the silverware plus you only saw women at meals or during outdoor activities. Outdoor activities were brief because most people, me especially, were given Thorazine, a drug which makes the skin burn from sun exposure.

Woodside was only four miles from where I lived. As little kids we knew what it was, and what kind of people were there. We called it the Funny Farm. Whenever my father drove by, we used to play a game, ducking down in the back seat and holding our breath. The game was that, if you weren't careful, you could get mental illness by inhaling it from someone else.

CHAPTER 16

"Now get this. It's a regular night in the loony bin, right? We got this movie going, an old-time flick like *State Fair* or something like that—you people know about *State Fair*? I hear some laughing. Good, glad you're enjoying the show—but anyway, the movie's got three reels, right? So I'm in charge of the movie and we're already through half of the second reel when I get paged to go to the front desk. I find out we got an admission. No, not your brother, Sarah. Finish your drink and shut up. So like I'm saying for anyone who's still interested, I got this new patient coming in so I tell someone else to run the movie for me. Well this other nurse doesn't know much about movies and when the second reel is over she puts on the first reel again. But no one knows the difference, see? They watch the first reel all over again. That's what's so cool about being a mental patient. You just sit there with your popcorn and watch the show. God, you've been a great audience. It's been a pleasure. See you next Thursday night!"

King's Rook Club, Erie, Pennsylvania. Sometime in the winter of 1980. For a short time I was a regular feature on amateur night, a stand-up comedian whose act featured stories about Ronson Lodger Medical Center, where I worked as a psychiatric nurse aide.

If you can't beat 'em . . .

***

In.
Out.
In and out.
In. Out. In and out.

Dr. D'Aoust looking dapper, a twinkle in his eye. The blood reports are most interesting, he says.
(In.)

Spiderwebs hold me in bed. They fasten to my lips and when I speak, my words get caught in the filaments, fluttering before my eyes like helpless flies.
Someone whimpers in the next room.
In the lavatory I urinate a split stream, a "Y" of yellow liquid, and I am frightened the nurses will find me and start reading my mind again.
(Out.)

"Here's a get well card from your brother in Alaska." (In.)

"How was your baked chicken, Mark?" (In.)

My eyes can't focus. I look at something and it rolls up, dragging my eyesight with it.
My head aches so bad I think someone has been pummeling me in my sleep. (Out.)

D'Aoust again. Throat infection cleared up. Increasing vitamin C.
(In.)
We need to talk some more about Pennsylvania, he says.

Who's taken over my sleeping, I want to know. Something comes through my wall every night and dives into my dreams, a machine shaped like a coil and dripping blood.

It waves a pointer at me and talks like a teacher. An angry teacher. It forces me to look at lessons, at endless replays of the same old crime.

(Out.)

I stole it, I say, I stole it when you weren't looking.

(Out.)

(Out.)

Who's that in the hall? What are they feeding me? Don't they know I can see through these mirrors?

(Out.)

(Out.)

(Out.)

Some nights a policeman comes into my dreams. We wrestle among the stars, we wrestle through eternity because we both represent opposite points of view.

Did I really get out of bed last night? Who brought me back? Where was all that yelling?

I have to wear a restraining jacket. I've got floor burns on my knees and elbows.

No way will I touch that food. Not now. (Out. Out. Out.)

"Mark," the nurse says, "I'm going to give you this little sedative." In, out, in, out. "Mark," D'Aoust says, "you've got to tell me what you took in Pennsylvania."

"Geese were flying south in V formation. The thermometer grew red and hot in my hand. A rattlesnake was warning me but I couldn't see him. I got left there by my friends, dumped out of the car in front of a mobile home park in the country. Hot, flat country. I was naked. Dirty from road dust. I remember the postman and his car with the steering wheel on the other side. He was standing beside the car, wiping his brow with a white kerchief, and opening a long row of maybe fifty mailboxes, all nailed to a kind of hitching post that sagged in the middle. They were different colors and sizes, and with their jaws hanging down their open holes resembled a pan flute, a giant pan flute, and then the postman turned and saw me standing there, naked. That's when the arms came out of the mailboxes."

"We're losing him, doctor!"
Scorpions on the ceiling.
"Let's try a pulse."
"Get the cart in here!'"
A big opening, a windy place. Lightning on the horizon.
Heat lightning. Soft action. Something way off over the plains and a prickly feeling rolling up the hairs on my back; a storm is coming. And just when the shutters start trembling, the awnings flapping like a wounded bird—just when I should be in my mother's lap, her warmth pressing me tight—a big opening swallows everything beneath me.
I fall through. I claw at nothing. I keep on falling through a dark and windy place.

"Get Doctor Maholtz, stat!"
"C'mon, get that IV going!"

"Mark, for God's sake, tell us what you did in Pennsylvania!"

***

My good doctor, if you insist on knowing the details of my recent trip, I can tell you one thing for sure. I had my misgivings.
On the flight to Buffalo I remember liquoring up quite substantially. I'm sure you can understand this, doctor. I had gotten ahold of Catherine—at last!—in New Mexico and she had sounded pleased to hear my voice. She was even more surprised when I announced that I would be seeing her in Erie in just a few weeks. It never occurred to me that I was inviting myself to her mother's wedding, barging right into a family

affair.

But doctor, if you're to truly understand the odd combination of things that made me jump off the Brooklyn Bridge, you must try to imagine what my life was like all those years in Pennsylvania. However, I'll spare you the slosh and drivel of everything that happened to me between the years 1974 and 1980. Slosh, drivel, and droll. The best way to imagine it would be to picture a rocky, lifeless island somewhere off the coast of Antarctica. Now imagine a fog rolling in and sealing off the island for a period of six years. That's pretty much the story.

Let's concentrate on the victories instead. Back in '74, I guess I had beaten my father's system, staying home past the age of eighteen, mostly due to the fact that when I finally got discharged from Woodside, I was on eight hundred milligrams of Thorazine a day, which left me incapable of anything except short walks and television viewing. At its worst the drug made me feel as though I were walking through knee-deep water. Only it affected my arms and head, too, making it seem as if rubber bands were attached to my body and constantly pulling me backwards. Without my parents knowing it, I weaned myself off the drug throughout that winter and by March of 1975, I was ready to leave home.

A friend and I packed up all our belongings and drove across country to Juneau, Alaska. That was during the great Alaskan Pipeline boom and I entertained somewhat murky visions of getting rich welding things on the tundra, completely unaware that I had no union card, no trade skills, and no Alaskan resident status. It wasn't long before I settled in as a bank teller, cashing all those big paychecks that never became mine.

Victory number two: I learned how to feed myself. And my rent was always paid. But, dammit, my wandering mind wasn't satisfied with the vast reaches of Alaskan wilderness. Prompted by a little bit of marijuana, I began going "indoors" again, wanting another ride on the Kent State Express. All aboard! Train now leaving Track Number Nine for Vision Valley, Misty Mountain, Paranoid Junction, with final destination, Straight Jacket City and Alaska Psychiatric Institute (good ol 'A.P.I.).

To put it simply, eighteen months after my first hospitalization, I repeated the scenario, going to jail this time, then to a hospital, then to the state correction center, then back to the hospital, then finally to the state psychiatric hospital in Anchorage during the depths of winter.

Victory number three: While undergoing treatment in Anchorage, I figured out what that crazy dream meant, the one about the giant sun. It was a dream about the future. The big ball of fire was Halley's Comet and it was going to destroy planet Earth. I figured that out in 1976, a decade before the scheduled disaster, and I believed myself to be one of very few people to realize it. What a lonely place to be. I watched friends get married, buy houses, have children. I watched them invest in their futures. I watched little boys and girls run out the door to play. All along I was sickened by knowing the end was near, and that the end would be horrible. I saw this knowledge as a curse; there was no way I could ever share it with anyone, unless, of course, I wanted to be committed again. By the time I joined my sister in Pennsylvania a serious death wish had taken hold of me, infecting my attitude towards everything long-term. I didn't care; I couldn't make myself care. I verged on heroin addiction and tried seriously to kill myself at least a half dozen times. Eventually I destroyed my sister's car trying to roll myself off a logging road in the mountains.

Victory number four: In Pennsylvania I bought a 35-millimeter camera. I mastered it well enough to produce an impressive portfolio, full of dramatic, colorful landscapes, and also stark, emotion-filled black-and-whites. However, going back through the vast majority of color slides I took, one notices that most of them were of cemeteries. I used to camp out alone near them and shoot the sun coming up over the tombstones.

Victory number five: About the same time Joni moved to New York, I enrolled at the Barrett College of Penn State University. Barrett was a branch campus of the great Penn State machine, a beautiful, sprawling, busy place with lots of students and lots of energy. Energy radiated from the workouts on the soccer fields, from the acclaimed stage productions of the Barrett Players, from the superb minds in the English Lit Department.

That's where I first met Catherine Hayes, in the office of the *Collegian*, the campus paper, where I resided as editor-in-chief. Catherine walked in one day, dressed in a baggy T-shirt and paint-stained blue jeans, looking about as though she might be lost. She said she had some poems that might be right for our publication. I wanted to tell her that we didn't publish poetry, that I hated poetry, but I rarely spoke my mind on such matters, especially to attractive women. Not particularly tall or ample busted, Catherine had an interesting face nonetheless: very open, very oval. Blue eyes. Perfect, piano key teeth. Beneath her tangle of natural blond hair she beamed a nonstop smile, a glowing advertisement for optimism. It was the same smile I would encounter often throughout the dark, cold nights of the winter of '79, when drugs and insomnia would sabotage my sleep. I smoked dope by myself a lot and sometimes those sessions grew horrific and boundless, as though I had cast myself into a bottomless swamp of negative thinking. I'd grow terrified and lonely in my apartment and dress hastily, jumping in the car my sister left me, driving through the snow at two in the morning to arrive at Catherine's apartment door. This happened once or twice a week, my ears cued to her feet padding across the kitchen floor, the door opening a crack, and her face, blank and sleepy, looking me up and down to assess my condition. More often than not, after some coaxing, that famous smile would emerge, blossoming slowly until it curved like the safety chain that dangled between us.

"Come on in," she'd say, sliding back the chain.

She always let me in. She shouldn't have, though. I was prone to mistreating her.

CHAPTER 17

Catherine lived on the top floor of an old, Victorian house, complete with a six-sided, pointy-roofed tower where she hung her potted plants and kept a writing desk that boasted of neatness. Her living room had thick, red carpeting, and that's where I often crashed on my drugged and demonic nights, allowing her to take my coat and boots off, then to hold me while she softly hummed some unrecognizable song. After she warmed up my hands she'd usually make peppermint tea, and I can still see her in the kitchen wearing her father's flannel robe, all the lights out and a strip of moonlight angling through the kitchen window, flashing ivory on her leg whenever it poked through the slit in the robe.

Catherine's job was to listen. In the two years we were in school together she must have heard enough paranoid delusions to last a lifetime. She spent the better part of these nights trying to reassure me that I wasn't crazy, holding me, rubbing my shoulders, trying to get me to laugh.

She meditated and burned incense all the time; her bookshelves were filled with volumes on yoga and astral travel. I swear there was a calmness to that apartment, especially at night, when the shadows seemed to whisper and shift around, grow softer as though invisible medicine was being released in the room. After a while I'd calm down. I'd finally be aware of the clock in the bedroom ticking like a faucet dripping, while outside, the night was massaged by the bark of a dog, the peal of a distant train, or maybe two cars racing between some faraway traffic lights.

In the person of Catherine I discovered a soft, pliant, spiritual force. Initially, however, our relationship was founded on pure physical attraction. Suffering as I did from SOB Syndrome (Sex On Brain Syndrome), my first interest was in Catherine's behind, which, though not nearly as large as one, was nevertheless shaped like a Weber grill. Each cheek was a perfect half-pear, each a lobe of a perfectly drawn Valentine's heart. Undeniably, the earliest aim of mine was the manipulation of reality until a situation should arise whereby we both might find her lying naked on her belly, her rump arched skyward, and I would dive face-first between those curvy mounds, my tongue seeking their valley, my nose their warm springs, my hands gripping her cheeks like binoculars.

Alas, Doctor, such sweet union was not in the cards for Catherine and me. At least not very often. There were several attempts at such joining, but most were so bizarre by nature —one was in an abandoned railroad switching hut—that we ended up talking about them before we had even finished, critiquing ourselves as if we had been in the audience of our very own play. We were, after all, writers. We kept journals and swapped them every few weeks. It was fun making guest star appearances in each others' lives, but also with that came my mention of other women, sometimes lengthy, detailed passages, and it didn't take long for Catherine to realize I was not the "settling down" type. (More like the "tying down" type.) I would never censor my writing because I believed in honesty at any price—even if the honesty warned others to stay away.

What I needed was a girl to talk to who didn't mind me talking about girls.

And of those times when we did sleep together, you might say we made love by accident because we never knew from one moment to the next if we were going to become intimate. We were always intimate of mind, but only occasionally intimate of body. I was never sure if I wanted to be responsible for it.

"You need healing," Catherine had said, and yes, it was a

lot like waking up with a full bladder and someone pressing on it—you bet I was sensitive. The whole issue of intimacy was distorted in my mind; I viewed intimacy as a surrender of control, a giving up of freedom and autonomy. But just about *everything* in my mind was black-and-white back then. I was never sure if the thoughts I was having were "good" thoughts or "bad" thoughts; I didn't trust myself as my mind's own guardian. After two full-blown psychotic episodes, I was uncertain over what kind of thinking would get me in trouble again. One general rule, however, did seem to apply: the more simple, safe, reality-based thinking I did, in other words, the more conservative and unimaginative I was, the more those thoughts seemed to be accepted by others, and along with it, so was I. However, should a daring idea enter my mind, it was usually accompanied by a voice who cautioned, "The others won't like that, you know. Don't risk it."

At this point in my life I would have accepted a phrase like "Ideas are dangerous" as being true. I could not step back or find the confidence to distinguish between genius and insanity. It had been three years since last blinded by Thorazine, and by now my writing talent and some of my thinking skills had reemerged. In fact, my intellect was rolling high numbers. I had created a special parody section in the campus paper and in the fall of my second year had written a piece on the local volunteer fire department called "Firemen in Pantyhose," in which I claimed the town's firefighters drank beer, drove recklessly, and removed the personal possessions from people they allowed to perish in the flames. I claimed they wore pantyhose as part of a firefighting ritual inspired by the fire chief. I also used the actual name of the fire department, a big mistake, because on the night before we went to press, a dorm fire broke out at Barrett and they came and extinguished the blaze. The firemen thought my article was a strange way to thank them and, with the aid of an attorney, pressed their point with the college dean.

The time was Christmas, 1980. My Penn State days were

numbered. So were my days at Ronson Lodger, and my days as a comedy king. I had scored several ounces of Turkish hashish and was keeping all of it for myself, smoking it nightly, except on special occasions like the time I joined Catherine for Christmas dinner at her mother's.

It had been a long time between periods of sobriety. We arrived at her mother's house, which looked like a frosted sheet cake with the green Christmas lights looped across the front porch hedges and the whole lawn a flawless plain of fresh, white snow except for a single stitching where the paperboy had trudged across the center. The green lights reflected moodily off the snow. It was so beautiful I didn't want to go in. But I dared not mention that to Catherine and, gathering a deep breath, followed her through the front door, which was like stepping into a scene from a TV Christmas special: toys, red ribbons, and wrappings on the floor; a little boy crawling in front of the couch, dressed in green shorts and red suspenders over a white shirt; mulled cider steaming on the stove; overly dressed strangers in little cliques, looking self-conscious and awkward and talking partly into their highball glasses, as though everyone had a microphone in their hand.

Altogether there were twelve of us at the table. I had to eat with my elbows tight at my sides. But I was grateful for such a fine meal and I piled my plate high, mixing all my foods together. Tiny Christmas tree lights winked from the next room, a soothing ambience that made me feel sleepy. Pine smell filled the house, and the stereo played lots of songs with Christmas bells.

But an hour after the meal I became weary of Catherine's relatives, who were, after all, total strangers. I grew tired of discussing only "safe" topics, doubly on edge because of keeping my promise not to drink that night. I thought if I had to explain the ethnic origin of my last name once more I would scream. When Catherine's cousin, Ron, an electronics salesman, heard I had lived in Youngstown, Ohio, he asked me if I knew Robert Cruikshank, an IBM dealer who operated out of Akron, some forty miles away.

"Bobby Cruikshank?" I said. "You bet. Best damn dealer in the territory."

Then I said I knew his wife, who was thinking about volunteering at the public library.

"Incredible!" he said.

"The Midwest is like that," I said. "It's one big family."

Later. Downstairs. With the basement door shut. Just Catherine and I. Everyone else is a muffled laugh or floorboards groaning.

"I get nervous around new people," I said. "It's like there are two of me battling over which one comes out. I don't know if it's better to be phony or maybe stand up and say, 'Kick me. Kick the *real* me.'"

"When was the last time you got high?" she asked.

"Dunno. Few days ago, I guess."

Catherine's mother used to be a basement beautician. The cement walls were marred by four unpainted rectangles where mirrors used to be.

"Still hide your dope in the bathroom?"

"Why? You think I should move it?"

"No, it's just that anybody who goes through all that to hide something, you know, wrapping it in cellophane and whatever else you do—"

"Sticking it behind the tub."

"—yeah, whatever, well, I was just thinking."

"Thinking what?" I asked.

"Well, anything you have to hide like that, I mean, when you really think about it, maybe it's not good for you."

If advice could be a hockey puck, this one struck the net. However, I would not pursue that subject.

"People have a way of pressuring you to conform," I said. "It's very subtle. Subtle as a handshake. Do you know what happens when you refuse a handshake?"

"What are we talking about, Mark?"

"Some of those games, especially your cousin Ron's."

Catherine sighed and looked away.

"What's wrong?" I said. "Did I say something wrong?"

"No, not really."

"But I can tell. You're mad at me. It's on account of what I said about Ron, right? Okay, then, blame me if you have to. I'll take the blame. Sorry."

Catherine sat up. For an instant her eyes grew wide. "Tell you what, Mark. Why don't we blame it—I mean blame it all—on the mosquito man."

"The what?"

"The mosquito man. Mom always teased me that I was a little strange because when I was a young girl I liked to inhale the insecticide when the mosquito man came by. We used to ride our bikes behind him whenever he sprayed the neighborhood. I loved the smell."

***

A long time had passed between that Christmas dinner and my arrival in Buffalo just before I jumped off the bridge. Not only was it just occurring to me that I had never been invited to her mother's wedding, but I was totally uncertain as to what kind of Catherine would be meeting me at the airport.

"What if she's met somebody else and he's attending the wedding with her?" I asked myself. But she wouldn't have agreed to pick me up at the airport if she was in company with another. At least it's not the kind of thing I would do. But maybe this was different. After all, we had hardly been lovers in the traditional sense when we dated back in our *Collegian* days. Who knows how she felt now? The possibilities nagged me. "You shouldn't butt into people's lives," I told myself, "or go butting into the past." If you did you could never be sure you were truly welcome or just being tolerated for the sake of good manners.

"To hell with it," I told myself. "Halley's Comet is going to torch our asses anyway, so who cares?"

Another set of possibilities haunted me. What was I going to tell Catherine about my life? How long could I play up the NYU scholarships, my coming theatrical debut, the apartment on West Seventy-Fourth Street? In reality I was fucking tired. There was so much I didn't like about Manhattan, about the crowds, the conflicts, the senseless pace of things. When I really thought about it (*dared* to think about it) I reduced my existence to simplest terms: I didn't care for my lifestyle. Or my life. In a little more than a year I had sunk into self-hatred, depression, despair. Final result: after all my moving and Catherine's moving and my striving and Catherine's striving, after all the shuffling and reshuffling and time apart—all I had to show for it was being unhappier than ever.

Damn, if only I believed in my play. But I didn't. It was clever words and nothing more. It had no taste of blood, no passion, no feeling of completion or triumph. I was getting opinions from too many sources, and even though I was the only one banging out the words, their influence made it seem as though it were being written by committee.

One other item bothered me—what to tell Catherine of Susan.

I loaded up too fast on my drinks, earning a scowl from the flight attendant, who made herself scarce. I picked the smoking section, a major mistake, because that put me in the very last row, privy to the sound of flushing toilets and the fresh blasts of odor each time someone came out of the restroom. On top of that was the nonstop roar of the tail engines and the wobbling and bucking that's much more pronounced in the back—all for the love of a cigarette. I rotated three cough drops in my mouth as I stepped off the plane.

Catherine greeted me warmly in the airport terminal. She was alone. She wore a very sheer blouse tucked into a pair of white shorts. The blouse had Hopi Indian designs, thunderbirds, serpents, animal tracks, etc., scattered over a white field of cloth that hardly obscured a lacy trimmed bra underneath.

"Quite a top you've got there," I said, breaking our embrace.

"I made it myself," she said. "It's cotton. We import the fabric from India."

" 'We?' Who's 'we?' "

"Corinne Topper. She's a fashion designer. Remember? I mentioned her on the phone. I'm helping her with her new line of summer clothing."

That struck me as odd, Catherine becoming a fashion designer. So suddenly, too. On the way to pick up my luggage I found myself looking at my own clothes, comparing them to whatever flashed by on other people in the terminal. When my suitcase slid out onto the baggage carousel, I was struck by the shabby quality of my imitation leather bag and was embarrassed to claim it.

It took ninety minutes to drive from Buffalo to Erie. It was only in the last few minutes, after we had gotten off the interstate, that anything significant was being said.

"You miss this old town?" I asked.

"Nope." Catherine pumped the brake as we approached a light.

"You sound pretty unqualified there," I said. "I thought you always liked it here."

"I did. But that doesn't mean I miss it. The West has a lot to offer, you know."

"So I take it you're happy out there."

"Very." The light went green and we shot ahead.

"Would you like to explain?" I said.

"Explain what? Happiness? It's just that the world's a lot bigger once you're out of college. If I regret anything, it's that I put in four years of school and ended up with the wrong degree."

"What's wrong with an English degree?"

"If you have to ask that question, Mark, then you'll never understand what I'm talking about. Look, any degree is fine for you because no matter what you do with your life, you'll just go down the road, writing about it. Good for you, you're a writer. But I'm not. Not like you, anyway. I've got to do something that's going to produce things in my life. Like an income. That's why I'm excited about New Mexico. It's very creative out there. I like making things and Corrine is already established. She says I have a lot of talent, and I've been thinking myself that maybe I'd like to make jewelry for a living."

"Jewelry?"

"Yes, jewelry. I like working with my hands." Catherine turned off Parade and onto the street where her mother lived.

"But you don't know anything about jewelry," I said.

Catherine hit the brakes. "Stop right there," she said, turning to face me. "I've got a whole house full of people right now who are talking just like you. 'Why this?' 'Why that?' They're all testing me, trying to get me to explain myself. I've got brothers and sisters and cousins who've never done a single thing with their lives, yet they feel real good sitting there, telling me what I ought to do with mine. Most of them have never left Erie, never taken a chance on anything. Please don't become one of them, okay? I don't know if I could take it from you."

We pulled into the drive and Catherine cut the engine. The house was all lit up.

"Listen," she said, "it's real awkward in there. Too many people. Let's go in for a while and you can meet some strangers, which I know you love, but I have to tell you something, Mark, ah, we can't sleep together."

"Can't . . . sleep . . ."

"I've got my sister in my room with me so I think it's best if you take the little camper parked out back. I've made the bed and I can help you with your things, but I'll have to get back when the lights start going out, okay? Sorry, I don't know how to better explain it."

"You've explained it enough," I said. If there was one

consolation—a consolation I repeated again and again like a mantra as I fell asleep that night—it was that our conversation hadn't touched on my bad feelings about New York. I reminded myself that if I kept playing my cards right the following day, perhaps my unhappiness would pass unnoticed. I'd be able to get out of town with my secret intact.

CHAPTER 18

The next day Catherine explained to me that we'd have to part company later that afternoon; there was a family dinner, afterwards, the wedding rehearsal. She said it was no trouble to drop me off at Kelly's, where the party would be later that night. Sunday I'd be on my own to get to the wedding. She gave me the church address and told me it was at one o'clock. Good, I thought, I'll have time to buy some clothes. And of course, "unless you get a better offer," she promised to drive me back to Buffalo for my red-eye flight. In the meantime, though it was cool and overcast that morning, we decided to go for a drive in the country.

We motored down Highway 97, passing over low hills and through tiny towns, eventually stopping at a place called Seagull Lake, a shallow, brown patch of water not too far from a pheasant farm.

"You know, Mark, every now and then a person has to butt right in and let their feelings be known." Catherine shut off the engine and rested her chin on the steering wheel, turning her blue eyes to me.

"I'm really sorry about this whole thing," I said. "I guess it was really rude to invite myself to your mother's wedding."

"I was speaking for myself," Catherine said. "It was about being honest—and about what I've been meaning to tell you."

"What's that?" I leaned back and tried to rest my arm on the door but found it rather painful because the window didn't roll down all the way. It was like resting it on a razor blade.

"Mark, I don't know if it's school, or work, or the city, but you're looking thin and kinda nervous-like. Do you know what I mean? I don't know how to tell you this but you . . . you just don't look too good." Catherine bit down on her knuckle and looked the other way.

"That's great," I said. "Normally I'd jump right in and say that makes two of us. But I won't. In the first place it would be a lie. And in the second, you're right. Thank God school's out. At least now I can keep food in my stomach. I swear to you I don't know how I'm going to pull it off when things start up again in the fall."

We got out and walked the broad, flat trail which followed the water's edge. Little by little I opened up about the problems I was having with my play. I told her there was no one I could trust at NYU. That was ironic because as I told her, I was already thinking that I couldn't trust Catherine anymore, couldn't trust her to understand me and my problems. It was funny because on the flight over, my fantasy was that Catherine could understand everything. Certainly she could understand me much better than Susan ever could—at least that was my thinking then.

We slowly circled the lake. Tiny diamonds winked on the water as a breeze kicked up and the sun came out from behind the clouds.

Just as Susan had done, Catherine cautioned me about going too fast, about trying to prove myself instead of enjoying what I was doing. Even though it turned out to be her standard pep talk, I hadn't had one from Catherine in a while, and it worked. I got light enough to momentarily care about another human being.

"I can see you're happy about your move to New Mexico," I said. "It shows."

"Thank you."

"I just wish it could have worked out between us two."

"C'mon, you don't really mean that, Mark."

"But I do." (Well, maybe I didn't—at least not when I

thought of Halley's Comet.)

"What about 'Freedom for All/Marriage for Morons' and all that stuff, Mr. Writer? What about your license to steal and all the good things that go with camping alone?"

"Maybe I'm getting soft," I said.

"No, I just think you're hoping *I'm* getting soft—in the head, that is."

"Oh, come on, remember the switching station?"

"I can't believe all those places you used to take me to," she said, laughing. As we neared the car she took my hand. Her fingers were soft and cool.

"Those places were pretty scary," I said.

"They were condemned, my friend."

"You still have your journals?"

"Of course," she said, smiling. "I plan on keeping them forever." She gave my hand a squeeze as we stopped in front of her car.

"Remember the time we climbed out onto your roof and sat naked, listening to that other couple fighting all night?"

"Oh, God, that was horrible! What did she do? I forget now."

"Left Chinese food sitting in the back of the car," I said.

"Oh, my," Catherine cooed, releasing my hand to fish her keys out of her pocket, "you know what's going to happen if we keep talking like this."

"We're either going to get horny or throw up," I said.

We stood at the doors and Catherine opened hers a crack, placing her foot on the running board and resting her chin on the roof, grinning at me with her blue eyes flashing.

"Well, which would you prefer?"

"Do you really need an answer to that?" I said. "It's been a long, long time."

"You mean it's been a long time with me," she said, smiling.

It was a small car—a Plymouth Valiant, I believe—but we managed to pull off something that any department store

Santa would have given a hearty Ho-Ho-Ho for, provided his laptop girls had been a little older. She moved in such a way, darting left and right, that my brain lit up on one side then the other, eventually every little nerve coming alive as though the tissue mass had been an airport blackened out during a bombing raid and her lovemaking had been the All Clear signal, throwing the switch that activated the tiny blue landing lights once again. Afterwards a delightful state of mind ensued, a giddiness that enveloped us both as we lay there, speechless, then gathered ourselves like confetti after a New Year's party, leaving the lake and heading home.

Somewhere near the town of Wattsburg we crested a hill and passed a house on our right, an unremarkable ranch-style dwelling with a big garden and doghouse, the dog's black head and paws protruding out the door. Near the doghouse several clotheslines sagged between two T-shaped poles. Beside them, as a centerpiece to a little circular rock garden, stood a Virgin Mary on the half-tub, the bathtub buried halfway in the ground, the inside surface painted blue and forming a Hollywood Bowl type of enclosure over the holy woman standing with her hands outstretched.

I was working up a wry comment on the thing when the road curved and we approached another house, on the left, that had a giant flat rock standing in the front yard. Painted on the rock—which was bigger than a king-size mattress—was a silly old cow with a bell around her neck.

"A giant cow!" I said.

"You've never seen this before?" Catherine said. "We call it the big blue cow. It's been here for years."

It was blue alright. The sky behind it was painted rich China blue—the same color as the bathtub down the road.

I heard a gong in my head—a great big Oriental gong.

"Oh my God," I said. "Don't you get it? It's a sacred cow. They're making fun of the Virgin."

"What virgin?"

"The thing we just passed at that other house. Didn't

you see it? It's a parody. A visual parody. Wow, that's really something. They must be Hindus."

It didn't matter whether she had seen it or not. Catherine didn't make the connection, didn't see any significance at all. It was just a big blue cow, some silly thing she'd been driving by ever since she had been a little girl.

But for me, however, that painted rock was about to enter my world, and once entering it, to help throw me upon a new and dangerous course, a course I could have little foreseen.

CHAPTER 19

Catherine dropped me off at Kelly's, a quaint, white frame cottage with red trim around the windows located on the Pennsylvania border just west of the summer resort town of Dunkirk, New York. The cottage perched above the cliffs overlooking Lake Erie. Beside it a tiny creek trickled by, the opposite bank rising to an overgrown vineyard consisting of unruly, twisted vines, the rows barely recognizable because of the weeds between them. On the other side of his property an apple orchard languished in equal decay. I could see—and smell—apples rotting on the ground.

Catherine spoke briefly with Kelly and Pete Sheridan, a mutual friend of ours, and some other woman whom she apparently met before. But no sooner had we dropped my bags in a musty back room than she was saying goodbye, reminding me about the time and place of the wedding.

"Don't worry about me," I said. "I wouldn't miss it for the world."

Catherine reached up and hugged me, allowing my kiss to linger on her lips just long enough to rekindle my loneliness. She broke the embrace and I walked her to the car.

"Amazing how time marches on," Kelly said, slapping my back as we watched Catherine's Valiant trailing dust back to the highway. "I'd have to say in her case that time has been especially good. She looks great, doesn't she? Must be that Arizona sun."

"New Mexico," I said. "New Mexico sun."

"Well, unfortunately some get away," he said. "Come on, there's a lot of other people who are dying to meet you."

"Isn't that what we used to say on the hospital floor?" Mandy, one of the nurses from Med-Surge, came up from behind and hugged me. "Good to see you back again," she said.

"Hello," I said. "It's been awhile."

I was what you might call "missing in action" as I chatted with Mandy, who, fortunately, did most of the talking. I listened distractedly, using the moment to size up the appearance and manner of my oldest friend. Kelly, who at that moment picked up a stray volleyball and tossed it to a waiting player, radiated confidence and success. His chief feature remained his Berlin Wall of a brow, a prominent forehead sheltered somewhat by his thick, black hair, now businesslike and short with a few rolling curls that I supposed were due to a body wave. He was tall but no longer thin; in fact, he carried the physique and strut of a professional baseball player. He struck me as being cool and detached, as though by some attitude or force of will he could regulate everything in his presence, taking care of each person or matter in his own good time.

Kelly motioned for me to follow him back to the volleyball game. "Beer's over there," he said, pointing. "And food will be out in an hour or so. Hope you're hungry."

I greeted some of the old gang but declined to join the game, fearing that if I coughed I would be exposed as a smoking fool. I grabbed a beer instead, content for the moment to watch my old friend, Kelly, move about and orchestrate the party. He was doing very well monetarily, that much was obvious. A nice place in the city and now this spot out here. He looked and acted nothing like the guy who had helped drag Barry to the rowboat on the Lost River.

People waved and I exchanged a few greetings; I knew just about everyone there. While that should have given me some security, a feeling of homecoming, perhaps, little signs of change seemed to prick me with sudden disturbance. Rick

Jeffries, the X-ray technician who always had teeth the color of a soft-boiled egg yolk, now sported a smile that was oyster white. Todd Barringer, who had for years lugged around an old Rambler that begged for a mercy killing with every last turn of the ignition key, arrived at the party behind the wheel of a brand-new Ford Thunderbird. His girlfriend, Rita, someone informed me, was now his wife. I walked toward the car, and when she swung open her door and got to her feet, I saw that both of them had been very busy in the family way—she wore a tent-sized blouse and looked like she was trying to shoplift a lampshade. I remembered when she had turned me down for a date. Other things had changed, too. I heard Ronson Lodger was building a new sports medicine complex. A competing hospital had added another CAT scanner and had bought Ivar's Bar and torn it down to make way for a new emergency heliport. And Carolyn Dobbs, an ancient flame of mine, was now married and appeared happily so, sporting a diamond the size of a mothball on her finger. I watched her at the volleyball net, shaking her red hair after coming down from blocking a shot. Her rump looked tight inside her tan shorts and her legs looked lean and taut with muscles as she jumped up and down.

Out of nowhere I experienced a grieving pain, a stab of remorse accompanied by an image in my mind of Catherine driving back to Erie, herself upset over something involving me. I tried to imagine what it was. Instantly I regretted making love to her in the fashion that I did, taking pleasure from her as though she were a postcard I bought to remind me of my trip.

"So how's the playwriting business, my old companion in crime?" Kelly approached my side, his arm around Deborah Colfax, the gorgeous RN who had joined the Ronson Lodger hemodialysis unit shortly before I left.

"Mark, you know Debbie, don't you?"

"Yes, I believe we've met," I said, recalling my initial reaction to the attractive new face in the hospital cafeteria. There hadn't been a male staff member—married or not—who hadn't been drawn to her like defense contractors to a

Pentagon budget spokesman.

"Kelly says you're working on a play," Debbie said. "It wouldn't happen to be about the hospital business?"

I took a long gulp, finishing my beer. "Afraid not," I said. "You've got nothing to fear."

Debbie looked askance at Kelly, who shrugged his shoulders. "I shouldn't think so," she said.

"Can you tell us what your play *is* about?" Kelly asked, motioning for me to follow them back to the cottage. "Food's ready."

"Let me get out of these long pants first," I said. "I think I might want to join that volleyball game." I dashed ahead of them and ducked into the cottage. In the back room I encountered a tall fellow slipping out of a wet bathing suit.

"Oh, sorry," I said.

"No problem. Hey, you're the playwright, aren't you? Remember me? I was your replacement."

I looked at the man's face: lean, dark eyes and hair, a stubble of whiskers on the chin, and below, a red shaving rash around his Adam's apple.

"Tony Sinfield," he said, extending a cool, wet hand. He nearly lost his balance as he kicked off his bathing suit.

"Mark Wolyczin," I said, shaking his hand. "So you came on before I left."

"The very last day you were there. I don't expect you remembered me with all the partying going on. Man, you were popular on that unit. They're still telling stories about you, you know."

"Thanks. I'm flattered. Did you see an old suitcase around here?"

"I saw a vinyl one earlier. Why don't you check under that pile of towels."

"Here it is," I said.

"So you've been in New York this past year?" he asked, slipping on a pair of denim cutoffs.

"Yep."

"Guess you missed Edward Albee then. He was here to direct *Who's Afraid of Virginia Woolf?*"

"Really?"

"The talk of the town. Barret College did a great job, as usual. Too bad you missed it. Albee did a little seminar on creative writing. I fancy myself to be a little bit of a writer, too, and I went along, you know, just to see how I measured up to someone like that."

Tony toweled his hair.

"So how'd you do?" I asked, forgetting my suitcase.

"Amazing," he said, raising his chin, his face seeming to leap out from beneath the cavern created by the towel over his head. "When you meet that man there's only one thought that goes through your head—you know he knows. Get what I mean?"

Tony slipped the towel to his shoulders and tapped the side of his head. "He Knows, my friend. He really Knows."

With that, Tony slipped out of the room. I remained there, trying to remember why I had come into there in the first place. Vaguely I recalled being on the run from something, and that thought triggered another image of Catherine in her car, cursing me all the way home.

I rejoined the crowd, most of whom were attacking the food table and loading up plates with pork steaks, burgers on buns, mounds of potato salad, and red, smiling watermelon slices. There must have been forty people, the majority gathering to eat in a sunken, shady knoll around a wisp of a fire that would, in a couple of hours, be transformed into a cheery blaze and a centerpiece for the late stayers—usually the more serious drinkers of the group.

What a waste, I thought. If I were in New York now, I'd be involved with high-level meetings, organizing the play production, doling out responsibilities, and shaping the architecture of my future career. Instead, I was in company with male nurses, orderlies, and other types who celebrated life by wolfing down hot dogs and belching out loud.

I grabbed some food, another beer, and settled in with the others. Still feeling like an alien, I reminded myself that most people didn't give a good shit if I fell off the end of the earth, so that when they asked me how I was doing, I only needed to say, "Fine," or something equally superficial and that would probably be as far as anyone would want to go. Besides, I was obviously an alien for a very good reason: I lived in New York, which meant I operated on a frequency vastly superior to these people. In fact, the only way to stay connected with them was to drink a lot of beers—catch up, so to speak—and then perhaps at a point of common denomination I might be drunk enough to appreciate the kinds of things they were saying.

Tony Sinfield, however, seemed to be an exception to this rule. I couldn't keep my eyes off him. Several times I caught him looking up from another conversation, nodding in my direction, seeming to include me in what he was doing, or at least an acknowledgment of my presence. He was intriguing. I had never met anybody who had interested me so much in such a short amount of time.

Shadows lengthened as the sun dropped low and pink over Lake Erie, accompanied by a rowdy countdown from some respiratory technicians who had already exceeded the safe drinking limit. Kelly rebuilt the fire, asking a few guys to roll down one of the kegs from the cottage so that people wouldn't have to go far for a refill. The few doctors and executive-type friends of Kelly's had long since left. Moon madness was fast approaching. An evening breeze wafted off the beach as Kelly covered the embers with kindling, then half-cut logs. Dry branches of pine crackled and caught fire, the flames leaping up and making faces glow orange.

I took a seat around the fire between Pete Sheridan and the keg, hoping that the ensuing darkness would envelop me in a safe, "wallflower" state. I fantasized about Catherine and the wedding.

"Hey, Mark," Kelly called from the other end, "are you

ready to talk about this play of yours?"

"Well," I said, feeling the eyes upon me, "what do you want me to say?"

"Why don't you start with the title?"

I looked down in my cup, swishing the foam of my beer. "*Can of Worms*," I said.

"What's that?" Pete asked.

"*Can of Worms.*"

There followed an awkward silence.

"Look, folks," Tony interrupted as he strolled to my side, "you have put this poor man on the spot. Obviously you have missed the point by asking the wrong question in the first place. What you want to know is what the play is *about*. It's foolish to expect to learn that from the title. That's like asking Mozart to hum a few bars, isn't it?" Tony clapped me on the shoulder.

"You bet," I said.

"What we should do, people, is to ask the author what the play *isn't* about," Tony said, refilling his cup. "For instance, would you say your play is anything like Pinter?"

"Not in a Pinter sense," I said. "Too existential."

"So then it's un-Pinteresque," Tony said, waving his cup to the circle, now hushed in a different manner. Then, directing his words at me, Tony said, laughing, "Don't you just hate people who use suffixes like '-esque 'at the end of an author's name?"

"Like Kafka-esque," I said. "Woody Allen covered that in *Annie Hall*."

"It was *Manhattan*, I believe," Tony said.

"I'm pretty sure it was *Annie Hall*, Tony."

"Could've sworn it was *Manhattan*."

We both shared the spotlight. Sensing some fidgeting in the crowd, I tried to think of something that would steer the conversation onto everyone else's level. "Actually, what I hate the most," I said, "is people who stick the word 'fuck' into the middle of an adjective, like 'fan-fucking-tastic.' "

Apparently I had underestimated my audience. No one laughed, except Kelly, and I had a definite impression it was not *with* me.

"Well, I'll have you all know," Tony said, quick to patch the damage, "that I'm from Rochester, New York, where the term 'can of worms' has a clear and colorful meaning. It's even on the city maps. Can of worms, you see, describes a certain spot on the beltway where about a dozen interchanges take place and more accidents occur than at a demolition derby. From the air the whole thing looks like a plate of spaghetti that's been knocked on the floor. It's sheer misery during rush hour traffic."

"Amazing," someone said.

"Yep," Tony said, slapping my back again as he returned to his seat, "can o' worms, the old c.o.w."

CHAPTER 20

Imagine, if you will, that there existed a cosmic link between Tony's remark about the "c.o.w." and the impression made earlier by the big blue bovine painted on the Hindu's rock. (Please remember that at the time my mind was not well. In fact, it was so busy recoiling from the Kelly's and Catherine's and Deborah Cofax's out there, that it was, in essence, yearning for some metaphysical occurrence to come my way, some miracle, some redemption machine, some astral ace in the hole, a pair of magical wings to soar over my head, grab me, and haul me away from my earthly dangers. I wanted imagination to replace reality.)

Try thinking of lightning going off in your brain. Or reaching in your pocket and pulling out a humpback whale. Or a thousand crows flying into your face, each of them covered with confectionery sugar. That was the impact of Tony's mentioning "COW" to me.

It became the answer to all of my problems. Tony had just given me the key in the form of a new title for my upcoming play. Out with *Can of Worms*. In with *Sacred C.O.W.S*, to be subtitled, *Cans of Worms*. I cannot stress enough what a bolt of insight this turned out to be. There and then I decided to rewrite my play, shift the focus off a bunch of grimy, dirty-mouthed boys, and instead, attack the very foundation of the Mother Church. I would lay waste to all that was wrong with Catholicism. This would be a philosophical triumph, a challenge to the pillars of reason. It would be *Death of a*

Salesman, Hamlet, The Tempest, The Crucible, all rolled into one. For a brief second I considered writing a companion book, a novel entitled *A Treatise on Truth,* but that idea faded before the million bulbs lighting up the marquee for my play, now a hundred feet tall on the Broadway in my brain, employing the world's largest bathtub and sheltering the world's most mammoth Mary, an exact duplicate of the one looking down from the mountain on Buenos Aires. I would be rich, rich, rich.

Instant zeal. Kent State all over again. I had had enough of the unpleasant facts of life. Ever since birth my brain had been filled with millions of interesting connections, dreams about to come true, insights and ideas just waiting to rub sparks together. Thanks to Tony I had been given a free ride. I felt like Einstein the moment after E equalled MC squared.

I sat beside the fire, assessing Kelly and his intentions toward me. He was hostile, no doubt about it. Everything he said seemed barbed with some effort to upset me. I watched the way he shmoozed up to Debbie. Well, at least I had the last laugh there. Unknown to anyone but Debbie and me, I once had the great fortune of seeing her at her very worst. It was in the hospital cafeteria one morning a few weeks after she had started her job. I was in early, grabbing a quick breakfast before going up to the unit. As I paid at the register, I noticed Debbie sitting alone by one of the windows. The cafeteria was deserted. Wanting to finally speak to the slender Cleopatra who had so lately raised the common blood pressure around Ronson Lodger, I grabbed my tray and made a beeline to her table. After all, even if she rebuffed me, I'd at least gain an independent impression of the woman and be able to file her on my emotional Rolodex, so to speak.

As I walked toward her, she looked up and her eyes grew wide with terror. In reflex I looked behind me, wondering if there were hit men or gorillas following. Just as I approached the table and was ready to set my tray beside hers, I suddenly realized the cause of her alarm. She had farted, and quite recently. A rank, pungent odor—like rotten eggs, like a cattle truck in a traffic jam, like when you take the Tupperware lid off boiled, refrigerated broccoli—hovered in the air, causing my nostrils to flare and my mind to reassess the situation. So moved with compassion was I that I completely forgot my entrance line. I thought of bad timing and the other injustices of the world. And I pondered the sorry, undeniable fact that Debbie had no one else to blame it on.

I set down my tray and mirrored her worried expression. The only thought that could come to mind was this little tidbit I had overheard on the radio that morning. According to an AM talk show, Pennsylvania's trout season had kicked off with a bang.

"Do you like to fish?" I asked.

Basically, that had been the extent of my relations with Deborah Colfax. Now, by the flickering fire, it was easy to see that she avoided eye contact with me. Tony Sinfield, on the other hand, kept making overtures that I found quite welcome. Several times he motioned for me to join his little group and often he asked my advice on this and that. At one point we joined each other for a little male bonding while urinating over the edge of the cliff.

"They could probably arrest us for industrial pollution," he said, laughing. "I never did like keg beer."

"Thanks a lot for what you said about the c.o.w.," I said. I squeezed hard, trying to force some urine out.

"Cow? Hell, you oughta drive it sometime. There's nothing to thank me for."

"Well, it's just that you put things into perspective for this guy."

Tony zipped up. "Christ, are you here to enjoy the view or are you gonna take a piss someday?"

"I got bladder problems. You go on ahead."

"No problem. Hey, so that Kelly guy is an old friend of yours, I take it."

"Yeah, we go way back." I shook my dick. No results.

"Hmmm. Seems like you got some friction there. Wanna

talk about it?"

"Friction with what?" I eyed him suspiciously.

"Between you and your friend. Is there something eating you up?"

Finally, my stream spurted lakeward. A little choppy and thin, as though pinched from bladder spasms, I had to inch up closer to the edge of the cliff in order to deliver it safely to the water below. Such a weakling, I thought, worried that a sudden breeze, even a slight one, would be enough to deflect it back against my trouser legs.

"Things haven't always been kosher," I said, "but it's not really worth talking about. If Kelly's happy, I'm happy." I added an appropriate "Ahhhh!" to mark the release of pressure.

"Well, rumor has it those two are getting engaged."

Oops! End of stream. "Damn," I said.

"Yep," Tony said, "they'll be good for each other. He's Mister Cocksure, and Lady Deborah strikes me as the kind of girl whose shit don't stink."

"Au contraire, my friend, au contraire." I zipped up, my fingertips wet with dribbles.

"Hey, what's this over here?" Tony said, bending down to pick up something that was already in his hand. "My, where did this come from?"

He held up a marijuana cigarette.

"Mmmm," I said. "Great timing. But maybe we ought to go somewhere where no one will disturb us."

"My thoughts exactly," Tony said, heading toward the creek. "You know, people like yourself are decidedly different. You shouldn't feel bad because you don't fit in."

I followed in the darkness. "I guess it's easy to notice," I said.

"Yep, like a square peg in a small-town hole. But you've got nothing to worry about, my friend. Your day is going to come."

We each picked a rock at the edge of the creek. In the distance behind us flames licked up and danced along the tree trunks. On the overhanging branches, heat stirred the leaves.

I could hear laughing. Human shadows stretched across the ground, long, rubbery arms melting into the darkness outside the circle of light. The fire popped and crackled distantly, contrasting the cold, hard rock I sat on and the hush of the creek rippling by. Tony's face glowed as he struck a match.

"This is muy bonita marijuana," he said, inhaling.

We come once again to another difficult spot. How does one describe a world beyond meaning?

I lost my mind that night, lost it more fully than the time at Kent State or my incident in Alaska. Somehow I believe Tony orchestrated the whole thing by playing little games with me until I could no longer distinguish between fact and fantasy. One thing he did was to deliberately stop his phrases. In that way I would finish his sentences for him, allowing him to gauge my predispositions, in other words, "where I was coming from." Like a dog getting his biscuit, he'd say, "Yeah, that's right, that's exactly what I was thinking of." This gave me the impression that we were reading each other's minds. Pretty soon he'd just nod in a certain way, and I'd take that to mean the endorsement of everything I was thinking. I don't know if there was something else in the marijuana, but after two joints we rejoined the party and I felt everyone else was functioning on a knee-jerk level, doing some kind of compulsive dance in response to what I was thinking and feeling. At first they were like puppets, moving to or away from me, depending on what I was thinking. This was terrifying because I didn't believe I could control the nature of my thoughts. The only way to deal with it was to leave the firelight circle and pull myself together in the shadows by the creek. I stumbled off through the dark and soon my friends and their laughter became like ghosts, phantoms, some distant reality growing pale against the hallucinations rising inside of me.

Tony and another fella joined me and we smoked more marijuana. Pretty soon after the last joint I had the distinct impression that both of them had disappeared. It was like they had been sitting beside me one moment, and in the next, had been erased completely.

Not long after they faded away, I too began to dissolve. I roamed the woods by the creek bed and felt myself to be walking among and through the trees, oblivious to solid obstacles. I floated and felt like vapor. I came to a spot on the cliffs where there was nothing but lake and sky. The stars seemed to be three-dimensional boxes connected by thin dotted lines. I lost all sense of my body, coming to believe that there was nothing in the universe but voices, voices traveling through space. My legs went away; I watched them dissolve from the ankles up, as though someone were blotting them out with black paint, leaving a hole in their place, a hole as dark and deep as the lake, as empty as the sky. Next, my arms melted away and then the rest of my body. I became a clear glass jar with nothing inside.

"Here I am," I said. "But where is that?"

Then the most amazing thing occurred. My inner voice—that fearful, excited, lusty navigator—dropped off too, and for the first time in my life I was conscious without any thinking going on, aware but without ego. It dawned on me that this is what "nothing" is—the experience of timelessness in a deep, dark void. I was breathing. I was breath. Then I was the space between breaths, an opening so wide that a million lifetimes could fit inside. I was eternal now. Dead but not forgotten. How could "I" forget? "I" watched with complete compassion. My body was there but invisible, a black silhouette cut from night's darkest cloth. I was not flesh but essence. Void looked back at void. Then even void was gone. Essence was gone. Finally, "I" was gone. Every star, every thought, every light out—every shred of my identity completely gone, gone, gone.

***

I awoke under a tree, my head on my suitcase. My first awareness was that of bird sounds, and a weak light growing from across the highway. I lifted my head and saw that I was in the apple orchard, about a quarter mile from the party. The growing light was dawn. Mist hung in the branches above me, and through the dull, grayish haze I could make out tiny black things darting limb to limb. Something landed on the ground. Then something struck my leg. "Caw! Caw!" screamed a crow above me. "Get up! Get up!" The crow knocked down another apple.

I got to my feet and picked up my suitcase. My neck was stiff and out-of-joint to one side. I staggered back to Kelly's, examining the dirt and scratches on my body like someone might sift through their house's belongings in the ashes of a fire.

A tiny whiff of smoke still spiraled from the gray mound where the party had been. Cups littered the lawn; most of the benches and lawn chairs were knocked over. The volleyball net sagged and there were two paper cups hanging in the netting. On the ground next to the keg a few paper plates were wrapped like cabbage leaves around half-eaten ears of corn, margarine stains soaking through. A few human bodies lay prone on the ground, reminding me of a Civil War photograph of corpses on the fields of Antietam. One couple lay covered with blankets. Another snuggled close to the fire. As I stood there, surveying the damage, Kelly banged open the cottage screen door and marched out on the back porch, stretching.

"All those going rafting," he called out, "it's time to rise and shine!"

"Time to wake up and smell the coffin," said a voice behind me. I turned. It was Tony.

"Ready to take on a brand-new day?" he said.

Panic gripped my gut; I had forgotten about him until that very moment. Pieces of the previous night flashed before my eyes.

"What happened?" I said. "How did we disappear?"

Tony cocked his head with a look like, "You mean you don't know?" but didn't say anything, only smiled and seemed to want to change the subject. He waved at Kelly. "Got a volunteer here," he called.

Though I didn't show it on the surface, down inside I grew terribly alone, terribly afraid. I didn't want to have to sort out the pieces from the night before. I remembered Catherine and her dropping me off—and the wedding—but it seemed irrelevant now. I needed someone to explain what had happened, how I had come to disappear then reappear again. Everything was tilted, a little off color. I wasn't sure if I was back in the right world or not.

Kelly strode toward me, nudging a few sleeping bodies. "Hey," he said, looking at my suitcase, "So glad you're not a man of your word. Do you know last night you accused me of trying to poison you?"

"I what?"

"Yep. You said I was going to murder you in your sleep. Then you grabbed your bag and left. The last thing you said was that you never wanted to see me again."

"I'm sorry, Kelly."

"Aw, you probably don't remember it at all, do you?"

"I'm not sure what I remember."

"Well," said Tony, approaching us, sipping a glass of tomato juice. "You didn't throw up on yourself or make love to any ugly women. My friend, there are many who would consider that kind of night an unqualified success."

I looked around. I was in no shape to go to a wedding. And after hearing about my paranoid accusations, I was too embarrassed to ask for a ride to the airport. It was too early anyway.

***

So it was that I rode over two hundred miles in four hours, my world inside my suitcase that was now inside the trunk, joining two carloads of people for an afternoon down the Youghiogheny River, south of Pittsburgh, spilling over the rapids known as Ohiopile. I talked to rocks. I talked to trees. I saw ancient Indian encampments and established rapport with various fossils. I had mental contact with the force of the river. I incurred the quizzical glances of Kelly and the others, and at some point near the end of the adventure Pete Sheridan's wife got the information from me that I had to be on a flight in Buffalo only a few hours later.

A conference gathered, everyone standing around me like a team of physicians. At the car they went through my suitcase, finding my ticket, discussing the chances of their patient making his flight. My drama was a group thing now, and as a consequence I felt more and more helpless. People were taking turns watching me, showing me where to sit. This went on for quite a while until Kelly had an idea and went inside the raft expedition company, returning in a few moments and announcing he had called Pittsburgh International. If we rushed, he said, my airline could transfer me to their last flight leaving from Pittsburgh. In the meantime, how was I feeling, old pal?

More blackouts. A scene of total confusion, me and the others running for the airline gate. I'm on board—no—wait —there's some trouble with my ticket. God. Thump, thump, thump, the beat in my heart, the clock in my foot, pounding the floor. My suitcase. There's no time to check my baggage. Forget it. No, wait, you can carry it on. Goodbye! It's been real. Who painted that cow on the rock? Push—shove—and I'm through the metal detector. Is that me they're calling over the terminal PA?

I climbed on board and felt the stuffy, airtight seal of the tubular enclosure. The jet took off, the ground pulling away as if against gravity's will. An hour later and I was staring at the lights of Manhattan. More confusion at Newark International. I missed the shuttle. Later, after I got home and dropped off my suitcase, I grabbed a cab to Mitchell-Walker. At this point I wasn't sure if I worked that night or not. It seemed I wouldn't have let myself cut it that close, and with the Pittsburgh flight and the other delays, I was now over three hours late. My watch said 2:15 a.m. and the streets were deserted.

I came up on the floor, trying not to jingle my keys as I let myself on the unit. It was deathly quiet, the main hallway slipping in and out of shadow between the low-watt security lights. Before I reached the nurses' station I passed the day room and noticed two patients sitting in pajamas on the couch. A young man and a woman. They stared at me and my eyes locked up with theirs. I got the look. It's the look of someone who knows who you are, who knows you're one of them. My worst fear came true: I was in the wrong world after all.

"So good to see you're back home," said the man. The woman laughed like a demon.

"I guess you'll be staying here for a long time," she said, cackling. "And to think, this one's getting paid."

I dropped my sweater and ran. Down seven flights of stairs. Out the door. Across East Manhattan. Scurrying for cover in the shadows of Central Park. That's where I stayed, near the band shell, huddled in the brush until dawn.

Throughout the next four days my world increased its tempo. I became convinced that it was not safe to sleep at night. I built a small signal fire on my floor, burning the first fifty pages of *Can of Worms* in a leftover Jiffy Pop tin. I played music to hide my thoughts, to keep the evil ones from stealing my soul during my brief afternoon naps. My neighbors banged from all sides, held conferences at my door. There were threats to my life, real threats. The phone rang and was full of bogus voices on the other end. Someone was imitating Susan. If they had gotten to her there was no telling how far the conspiracy had spread. I couldn't trust anyone. I hammered a box of nails into the fat end of a baseball bat. I was out of food. I was prepared to die.

PART TWO

THE LONG WAY BACK

Last night I invented a new pleasure, and as I was giving it the first trial an angel and a devil came rushing toward my house. They met at my door and fought with each other over my newly created pleasure; the one crying, "It is a sin!"—the other, "It is a virtue!"

KAHLIL GIBRAN, THE MADMAN

For some, sex leads to sainthood; for others it is the road to hell. In this respect it is like everything else in life—

HENRY MILLER, THE WORLD OF SEX

The crystal ship is being filled, A thousand girls, a thousand thrills

THE DOORS

CHAPTER 21

"Doctor D'Aoust, is that what I think it is?"

The doctor's eyes followed mine to the cart parked at the foot of my bed. It was a crash cart, a portable device carrying medicine, an EKG monitor, equipment for installing an artificial airway, and on top, the ominous pair of defibrillation pads, which, when applied to a dying patient's chest, shot volts of electricity intended to kick-start their heart.

"It's been here for three days, Mark."

I didn't remember seeing it before, didn't recall much of the past seventy-two hours. I could tell by the pink, raw skin, though, that I had been tied up with washcloths and tape around my wrists.

D'Aoust crossed his arms, his one hand still clutching my chart, and looked out the window. "To me it resembled a good old-fashioned case of delirium tremens, although classic alcohol withdrawal should have started way before that. After you ran away from Mitchell-Walker, did you do any drinking while you were in your apartment?"

D'Aoust set my chart on my meal table and hitched up his trousers to sit on the end of my bed. He wore another brown suit, this time with a yellow shirt underneath sporting a crop of tiny fuzz balls where his neck joined the collar.

"I drank some," I said. "I was having a hard time sleeping."

"According to your sister, your neighbors were, too."

I laughed. My ribs and stomach ached. When I crossed my arms in reflex, I noticed bruises from IVs on the insides of my arms. My left forearm was spotted like an overripe banana.

"I went through hell, didn't I?"

"Let's put it this way. You've got half the nursing staff calling you Linda Blair. I wouldn't have believed some of it if I didn't see it myself. It was like an electrical storm. You're lucky to be alive. You had a heart rate over one-eighty there for a while."

D'Aoust paced back and forth from the window as he spoke, flipping open my chart and tracking something with a downward sweep of his index finger. When he found what he was looking for he grunted and closed my chart. "The real irony," he said, "was that in order to get you through this, we had to give you the same stuff that we're weaning everyone else off of. I've never seen anything like it. What makes it worse is that we don't have anything conclusive, either. It was too late for anything to show up in your blood, but if you're telling the truth about that party of yours, then my best guess is that there was PCP in that marijuana you smoked."

"Angel dust," I muttered.

D'Aoust tipped his glasses down and his eyes, much smaller above the thick lenses, stared at me imploringly.

"So what's the next step?" I said.

"There's not a whole lot we're going to do right here," he said, picking up my chart again. "We'll get you stabilized, get that shit out of your system, but after that you're going to need to spend some time in a treatment center."

"How long will that be?" I asked.

"When did you start drinking?"

"When I was twelve. But what does drinking have to do with PCP?"

"Everything, my friend. As a general rule, I allow one month for every year of substance abuse. That's fifteen months in your case, in which I'd recommend a year's minimum in some sort of halfway house or extended treatment facility."

"A year? You're nuts!"

D'Aoust leveled a glance in my direction, his brow knitting together for a moment, then relaxing as a faint smile crossed his lips. "You should hear yourself when you say that," he said.

I looked down and sighed. "I'm sorry, I didn't mean it that way. It's just that I've got this play put together and I know the director is worried. He needs to hear from me. I've got school this fall and an apartment that needs me as its renter. I'm sure you understand. You know how hard it is to find a place in Manhattan to begin with. Just think if I end up homeless with a lot of—"

D'Aoust chuckled sadly, waving a hand for me to stop. "Save your speech," he said. "I'm not interested in what you destroyed on your way here. All I can do is try to save what's left. Believe me, *every*body's got a story like yours."

I looked up at the ceiling, the florescent lights and acoustical tiles all bleached white. I felt a headache coming on.

"I'm giving a lecture tomorrow night," D'Aoust said. "If you continue to improve, I'll expect you there. Meanwhile, I want you to think about something." He took off his glasses, which caused his face, now somewhat stripped of its Mr. Potato Head quality, to assume a worn and lean affect, as though it were the face of a field surgeon in World War I, the face of one who had seen too many battles, too many deaths and sufferings.

"Have you ever heard the expression," he said, " 'In the land of the blind, the one-eyed man is king?' "

"I don't think so," I said.

D'Aoust put a hand over his eye. "See you tomorrow," he said.

Later that day I went for my first walk on the unit. I was overcome by the amount of pain in my body, not just the muscular trauma in my neck and back from the fall, but stiffness in every joint and deep, throbbing pains in all of my organs. It was hard to piss. So hard, in fact, that all I could do was hold on to the towel dispenser above the toilet and pray over my limp dick, all the while feeling that if I pressed any harder, the piss would burst out a hole in my side. It felt like someone had shoved toothpicks or wooden matches up my penis. My kidneys felt tender, my pancreas sore, my bladder stretched tighter than hide on a snare drum. My lungs were shot, too. The slightest laugh would make me cough— any sudden breath and they'd react with spasms, leaving me a choking, salivating idiot, doubled up in a chair or on the floor.

Fortunately, I was not alone in my pain. The unit, which held thirty or so sufferers, was filled to capacity with heroin addicts. I was in one of three private rooms. Everyone else shared four-bed rooms, spacious cubes with divider curtains and huge contraptions in the center, a television receiver with four separate screens reaching out on long, metallic arms, an octopus that reminded me of a dentist's X-ray machine in the way each little box floated down from the ceiling and hovered in front of your face.

Feeling bored, I eased into one of these rooms and introduced myself to the four guys lying in bed. Enthusiasm was in short supply. I got a cursory nod from one guy and ignored by the rest. I remained standing by the door, looking for a chair.

Finally, the guy in the nearest bed, the one who had nodded, mumbled something like, "I'm John," or, "Hi, I'm John."

John was not a bad-looking guy, medium height but well built with dark, defined Italian features, a great lock of shiny black hair curling into his eyes. He tossed off the covers and took several minutes to lower himself into a sheet-draped chair beside his bed. He moved as though recovering from recent back surgery, with short, strained breaths, his face tightened from pain, little pearls of sweat popping out across his brow. I moved to help him but he held up his hand. I saw the number next to his name on his I.D. wrist band: John was twenty-six. I couldn't help noticing the marks on his arms, marks that made my arms seem pale by comparison.

"The fuckin' shit really does a number on your joints," he said, landing with a sigh. He noticed my stare.

"Fine, go ahead, look at this," he said, holding his arms out. "Do you think Cinderella wants this for a prince?"

"Sorry," I said. "I didn't mean to look at you that way."

John's arms were tracked with countless light and dark ovals, some with skin freshly wrinkled as though he had left a cigarette burning there or had poured lines of Elmer's glue on his skin and had forgotten to peel them off. The old scars were darker and looked hard as bark.

"Shit, when was the last time you even used your arm, John?" said the guy near the window.

"Go fuck yourself, pardner," John said.

"He wouldn't know how to begin," chorused a third voice.

"Get the nurse in here," said the guy by the window.

"Why's that? You gotta look at her to get a rise?"

"Here? You mean the nurses here? You'se gotta be kiddin'."

"Go on, get outta here," John said to me. "The only thing worse than a bitch is a bitchin' dope fiend. Christ almighty. I don't know how these nurses do it. If it was me I'da taken a gun and wasted every cocksucker in this joint. Blown their brains out. Told 'em they was gettin' what they deserved. Who wants to hear a bunch of dope fiends whinin' all the time?"

The fella across from John—the only one who hadn't spoken—moaned and tossed beneath his sheets.

"Why'dncha go get me a Coke?" John said.

"I don't know where they are," I said.

"They're in the fridge. We got twenty-four-hour kitchen privileges, man. Christ, we never had that at home, right, fellas?"

"What kind of home you talkin' about?" said the man near the window.

"Go fuck yourself," John said. And then to me, "Go get me a Coke."

***

For whatever reasons (the obvious being that I was not from New York nor addicted to heroin) I was not destined to gain friendship among the junkies on the unit. The best I ever did was that first night, when they asked me to join them in a game of poker, using cigarettes for betting chips. There was something downcast about them, some damp spark that seemed to remove them from any hope, excitement, or sense of possibility. They lacked a future. It was as though, via the golden tunnel of the heroin rush, they had gotten a glimpse of the afterlife—and found it wanting. Their humor was morbid and defeatist; there was something sick in the way they bonded to each other over their scars, injuries, inabilities to achieve an erection. It was the status of pain. They kept to themselves, mumbled monosyllabic stories, and gave me the feeling that they viewed me as an oddity, a "druggie celebrity."

I had little time to consider relations between me and my fellow addicts for I soon developed my own set of problems. The demons who had taunted me in the East River and had promised me executions au jour—they were coming back now, slipping through the cracks and floorboards, dropping down like tiny spiders on invisible threads. The day room looked out on a clover field and a distant hillside terraced by a four-lane highway. In the tree line above the road I imagined devils waiting, a small army of twisted souls camping by night, sharpening their weapons over campfire flames. Every serial killer in the country had one target: me. They were stalking me, waiting to pounce, waiting to drag me away to some rock pile, some makeshift altar, where they'd pelt me with stones then tie me down, slice me up slowly, and make me drink my own blood and urine. They'd tear off my legs and make me eat them after beating me with them to get the names of my family. I'd cough up any name, any government secret, give them ways to torture everyone I knew. I'd give them addresses and phone numbers. The pain would be too great. They'd get cousins, old friends, my entire high school yearbook. I'd be like a worm under a magnifying glass, twisting, confessing to anything.

Though I did not mistake Dr. D'Aoust, his staff, or the other patients for demons, I imagined that they knew what a horrible creature I was, what a fake, a weakling, a groveling Judas, ready to turn over his friends. I imagined they had a list of my sins and held little sympathy for me. In my mind they all wanted me to leave the unit, get out there and get it over with as soon as possible. No pleading, no cowardice. Just get tortured. I believed that John and the others were barely putting up with me and would have killed me themselves if it wasn't for the Devil demanding to do the job personally.

The Devil was getting closer all the time, wiggling through the air ducts, disguising his voice behind a rattle in the wall or the hum of machinery. He searched for me room by room, peering through the television sets. The hospital received cable and HBO's two featured films that month were *Arthur* and *Foxfire*, both of which held a secret message for me. While *Arthur* poked fun at my addiction, it was *Foxfire*, with Clint Eastwood, that festered my paranoia. I couldn't get away from it; it came over every set on the unit, reappearing at odd hours as HBO played it again and again. In the film Clint Eastwood steals a top-secret Soviet fighter plane. The plane's controls, it turns out, can only be operated in Russian, and there were several scenes where the plane is flying low over the ice fields and Clint Eastwood says, "Think in Russian." That line drove me nuts. I'd be getting medicine from a nurse and she'd ask me if I heard any voices and at that moment I'd hear Clint on someone's television warning me to think in Russian, which was my cue that my thoughts were being read somewhere and I had to "not-think" whatever I was thinking. I was like the little boy who plugs his ears, counting to a thousand to drown out the taunts of his playmates.

I thought about Halley's Comet. I saw it squatting in the sky, about to hatch us. I saw myself staked to a mountaintop, nearest to the flames, with all the world mourning the day I had been born.

CHAPTER 22

September 16, 1983
(Morning session)

"Does the television talk to you, Mark?"

Bowman's face is bright and cheerful. Is it me, the sunshine, or is she just in a super mood? For the first time I notice a wedding ring on her finger.

"The television? Sometimes it has," I say.

"I mean right now. Do you hear voices?"

"No."

"I see here in your notes," she says, flipping open my chart, "that some of the staff feels you get distracted by the TV. You rarely go to bed until ten p.m., after the television's turned off. And sometimes during the day you run into the lounge for no apparent reason, other than to stare at the TV."

"An old habit, I suppose."

Bowman wears a purple blouse with a string of white pearls dangling beneath her collar. She runs her finger along them, spreading out the loop so that it's curved like one of those velvety ropes that keeps you in line at the bank.

"Why didn't you get along with the patients on Doctor D'Aoust's unit? Were you afraid they were trying to hurt you?"

"Sort of," I say. "They didn't want anything to do with me because I would have ratted on them. They called me a Judas."

Bowman's eyes narrow. "Are you sure that's what you

heard, Mark? Did someone actually say that? They called you a Judas?"

"I just knew it, doctor. Some things you know."

Bowman releases her pearls. She picks up my chart and changes her mind again, mumbling "Hummph" as she lays it aside, picking up her pen. She twirls her pen in her fingers, looking at it for a long time without saying anything. Then she looks up, her face displaying the by-now-familiar, knowing smile. "Did you ever experiment with heroin?" she asks.

"No," I say. "Absolutely not."

***

The winter of '77 battered the Great Lakes with a series of deadly storms. Parts of the Lake Erie shore recorded snowfalls of over a hundred inches. For weeks on end the temperature never reached above 15 degrees. Dozens died, getting buried in their cars or freezing to death in unheated homes, the bodies of the elderly often found in pairs, huddled and stiff in their beds.

During that winter I worked for Cee/Kay (as in "If You See Kay") Construction Company, a ragtag outfit that hustled along the shores of Lake Erie from Cleveland to Buffalo, specializing in poured concrete foundations for homes and small buildings. The term "laborer" described it well; there wasn't a moment on the job not filled with some grunting, thankless task. I hauled eight-foot metal forms on my shoulders, yanked thousands of them off the fake brick walls we made, pulled them out of giant mud holes, slipping on the banks, sloshing through knee-deep water—which turned to slush, then ice, as the winter beat down.

We were a sorry lot, a collection of losers, the gravel-throated foreman and his scar-faced brother both alcoholics, the rest of us drinkers, potheads, and, in growing numbers, heroin addicts straight out of prison because one of the crew, an ex-convict, was using Cee/Kay as a back-to-society pipeline for his inmate friends.

Every job took about three days to complete. After the footer was in we'd set up the walls on the first day, pour and let dry the second, then strip it the third day and hustle to the next site. No matter where we went someone always knew of a tavern nearby. I didn't have a car so I became a prisoner of the after-work quaffing sessions, usually three-hour binges that ended in a drunken ride home with just enough time to pull off my stinking work clothes and collapse into bed. This scenario repeated itself four or five times a week.

Late in December we found ourselves outside of Cleveland, working like dogs to pour a series of foundations before Christmas arrived. On the day before Christmas Eve a bitter storm rolled in, a blizzard out of Canada that dropped power lines, cracked water pipes and engine blocks, and froze to death a pair of sparrows sheltering in the straw we had packed on top the freshly poured walls the night before. I was the first guy on top the walls that morning and already my nose and fingertips had been stinging by the time my hoe had struck the birds. They were light and hard, like the straw itself.

The foreman's brother, an ex-Marine maniac who often bragged how he had tossed Vietcong from helicopters, developed frostbite and we quit early that day. Word went out from the main office that we'd hold up until the day after Christmas, then strip the job and try to pour another. We were already bunking at the Six Gun Lodge, a flimsy motel with a sputtering neon and one crippled ice maker in the manager's office, a big aluminum box that coughed and rumbled while we were checking in, upchucking fresh ice cubes onto a pile in its belly. The best Cee/Kay could do for us was to place four guys to a room and promise us meal reimbursements totaling fifteen dollars a day.

All night the storm blasted Cleveland. Wind buffeted the windows and the little air-conditioner-turned-electric heater hardly neutralized the cold draft blowing beneath the door. Bill Blakeman, who was one of those guys who thought he didn't need to shower because he splashed Brut under his arms in the morning, thought it was real cute to take my sweat socks and stuff them into the cracks around the door. I didn't give a damn; I considered Blakeman homicidal, and if that was the extent of his abuse, I was content and even found it mildly entertaining. I was not exactly Mr. Congeniality either. I paced the room, complaining about the weather, the work, my leaky boots, the paltry meal reimbursements. Eventually I upset even the most negative of the other guys. I also bummed cigarettes, scrounged for old donuts, and ate the cheese off the top of the previous night's pizza box.

Boze, the ex-con I was telling you about, a steely-eyed, rat-faced creature who used to live near Cleveland, had managed to persuade one of his old girlfriends to brave the storm and drive over to join us. He called during the six o'clock news and it took her about an hour and a half to get there. Then it took us about ten minutes to realize it was her and not the wind knocking at the door. When Blakeman finally opened it, Grace, a fairly pretty thing with bangs and straight brown hair, pushed through the door and started things off by accusing Boze of "making her" drive all that way. She tossed her coat over the dresser and proceeded to make herself at home on top the bed that should have been mine. She propped a pillow behind her back, kicked off her shoes, and stuck her feet under the covers. She had a cold, she said.

Ted, who had been asleep in the other bed, rolled over and looked at our newest companion. "Well, what do you think of our pad?" he said dreamily.

"This fuckin' room's freezing," she said.

When Boze didn't remind me of a rat or a weasel, he reminded me of a lean, hungry hawk. He got out his wallet and removed a piece of paper. "With a little luck," he said to Blakeman, "I can find an old connection who used to deal at the Flats."

Pot-bellied, ponytailed Ted, who often drank himself into a permanent grin and whose only redeemable quality was his ability to make chili on a hot plate, sat up in bed and told

Boze that scoring some heroin would be a pretty good idea considering he had brought his syringe along in his shaving kit.

Christ, I thought. I had figured Ted for an alcoholic.

"Might have to drive a ways to meet this dude," Boze said.

"You can't go out there," Grace said. "You'll get yourself killed."

"Only someone like *you* would get herself killed," Boze said, fingering the paper as he dialed the phone. "Believe me, I'm not crazy enough to let you do any driving."

"Who says you're going to do any driving at all?" Grace hissed, holding up her keys. "It's my car, little boy."

"Watch your mouth," Boze said, cupping the phone.

"You're not going to get killed and destroy my car."

"Kiss my ass," Boze said.

"I thought you called me over here because you wanted to see me, not make some—"

"Shut up!"

Someone answered the phone on the other end.

"Jerry," Boze said, smiling and flashing Ted the thumbs up, "Jerry, my man with the steady hand." Boze cradled the phone and turned away from us. "How ya doin', Jerry?" he said in a lowered voice. "It's me, Boston . . . Boston. That's right, your old buddy from Boston, Mass."

There's a certain decorum when you're around somebody making a drug deal—especially somebody who's not using their real name—and it involves minding your own business. In deference to my friend's privacy, I turned my attention to his girlfriend, overcoming my initial prejudice and abhorrence of her personality by glancing at her slender neck, her Bambi eyes, the two conical lumps under her red wool sweater which I judged to be the size of the frozen birds I had found that morning. I wondered how warm her body was and how warm and cozy the sheets must be with her lying on top of them. I thought there was a chance—granted, a slim chance—that I could reclaim my half of the bed since I had slept there two nights already, and in so doing, earn the right to sleep with this woman since she had freely chosen that spot as well. Realizing that this particular fantasy couldn't hold water, not even in *my* head, I pretended that Grace would announce a contest that night whereby each of us men would try to show her the most concern, compassion, and attention, with her keeping score and then sleeping with the winner.

Grace yawned and checked her watch. "You guys got cable?" she asked.

By the tone of his voice I knew Boze had found what he wanted. I heard him close with a line like, "This better be good," and after hanging up, he renewed his fight with Grace over using her car. Meanwhile, Blakeman, who had excused himself and was now hatching a thunderous bowel movement in the bathroom, yelled out that Boze should look on the dresser for a set of keys, and for Boze to take the company pickup. "Don't let it get too low on gas," he yelled, and we laughed at that. "No one's gonna come out and get you," he said.

Boze grabbed the keys. He took a collection. He wished himself luck. He zipped up his coat and opened the door. Wind roared like a jet engine, and invisible hands yanked the door from his grip, slamming it against the wall. Snow whirled in the room. Outside, just beyond the door, flakes zig-zagged like tiny white billiard balls after the break. Beyond that roared a streaking blur. Cursing, Boze grabbed the door with both hands and pulled it closed behind him.

Two hours later Boze came back. He squeezed through the door, the cold rushing in and big flakes swirling behind him. I looked out across the parking lot where the slanted fury of the storm had piled snowdrifts against a pair of parked cars, rounding their shapes. The wind howled, blurring the landscape beyond the lone mercury light at the edge of the lot.

Boze carried a brown paper grocery bag filled with Doritos, Slim Jims, and two six packs of beer. He set the bag on the bed, stripped off his coat, and after blowing on his reddened hands, pulled from his pants pocket a cigarette-sized tube of tin foil crimped at the ends.

"This is good shit," he said, opening the foil. Blakeman, Ted, and Grace flocked close, Blakeman checking the adjoining door to the foreman's room and pushing in the lock.

I, too, moved closer for a better look. Boze peeled open the foil, exposing a trough of white powder, a dingy white line with tiny bits of what looked to be burnt wood. It resembled what you might get if you spilled a box of baking soda on a busy restaurant floor and swept it all back up again.

"Looking at it won't get us high, boys," Ted said, rolling up his shirtsleeve. "Let's get this show on the road."

"I'm first," Boze said.

"Since when?" Ted said, going to the dresser and unzipping his shaving kit.

"Since I went out there and got the shit," Boze said, rolling up his own sleeve. "Nearly got killed about a dozen times."

"Poor baby," Blakeman said, grabbing a beer and sitting on the bed.

"Don't give me 'poor baby' shit," Boze said. "If it wasn't for me you wouldn't be looking at a fix right now. I'm the man with the connection."

"And I'm the man with the works," Ted said, displaying a dirty, battered syringe and burnt-bottom spoon.

"I had to put a half tank in that truck just to get back here," Boze said. "Almost froze my hands off at the pump."

"Who cares?" Blakeman said. "Deal goes first," Boze said.

"Works first," Ted said.

"Bullshit!"

"I believe half the money was mine going into this thing," Blakeman said, leaning to the side and lifting his rump off the bed. He released a stream of flatulence that sounded like the side of a rubber shoe being dragged across a wooden floor. Everyone looked at Grace for a moment then went back to what they were doing.

"I paid for more than your ride, Boze," Blakeman said, "so

if you wanna be needle-shy, just hand over our share and we'll start the party without you. Can't get more fair than that."

Blakeman barked another fart. Grace, with a look, moved away from him and sauntered over to the far bed, turning up the volume of *The Rifleman* on TV.

Angry, Boze folded up the tin foil, clutching the tube in his hand.

"C'mon, man, it ain't like you're not gettin' your share," Ted said. "Tell you what, I'll cut the lines and you can pick which one is yours, okay?"

"I get choice, right?" Boze said, relaxing his fist.

"Right."

"And second on the needle, okay?"

Ted looked at Blakeman. "Fine with me," Blakeman said.

"No problem," Boze said, handing the foil to Ted. "Start cutting."

"Fair is fair," Grace said over her shoulder.

"You shut the fuck up," Boze said.

Ted poured the powder on the dresser top, breaking it into four little piles with the edge of a pack of matches.

"I'll take that one there," Boze said.

Ted nodded, grabbed the spoon and syringe, and went to the bathroom. He filled up the sink and drew fresh water through the syringe, squirting it back into the sink several times, then drawing up a small amount and leaving it in the tube. Next, he took the spoon and went back to the dresser, carefully scooping his pile onto the inside of the match cover, then pouring that into the center of the spoon. He pulled a cigarette out of Blakeman's Marlboro pack and peeled the paper off around the filter. Peeling it like a banana, he took a strip off the filter and rolled it into a tiny ball.

Ted went back to the sink, taking the spoon and my Cricket lighter with him. Rolling up his sleeve some more, he clamped the syringe between his teeth like a pirate's knife, looking around and finally deciding to tie off, tourniquet-style, above his left elbow with the cord from the venetian blinds.

To do so he had to set the syringe beside the spoon below the bathroom mirror and pull the cord tight with his teeth. I watched it pinch his skin and turn it blue at the circle. Next, Ted thumped the inside of his forearm with the backs of his fingers, whipping them against his skin to make his veins rise. He pulled the cord tighter, thumping harder and turning his arm as though inspecting for mosquito bites. Finally a vein surfaced, a little roll in his skin, standing out like the only wrinkle in a well-made bed.

"Mmmm," he said.

"Mmmm," we echoed.

With his right hand Ted took the syringe and squirted a thimbleful of water into the spoon, making a little puddle surrounding the island of white powder. "Here goes," he said, taking the spoon in his left hand and clicking on my lighter, running the flame underneath. The spoon bottom torched black and the heroin bubbled up, turning brown with a black-brown rim around the puddle. Pieces of dirt floated to the surface, turning over like vegetables in a boiling stew. I caught the smell of burning hair.

Ted set the spoon down and checked his arm one last time, pumping his fist. He tossed the filter ball in the spoon and stuck the needle in the center of it, dragging the tip over the spoon's surface until he sucked up all the liquid, the larger chunks of dirt caught by the filter. The needle bent and made a fingernail-on-blackboard type, metallic scraping sound. Finished, Ted held up the syringe as he squeezed out the excess air, thumping it with his middle finger until the needle's eye shed a single brown tear. I could see specks of dirt floating inside the syringe.

Locating the barely visible vein in the middle of his forearm, Ted pressed the needle at an angle, expertly sliding the point into his skin. I winced. He squeezed the plunger slowly and every drop went up his arm. Blood flushed back into the syringe as he withdrew the needle. He squirted that into the sink, a thick, red ribbon like a jet trail sinking to the bottom, eventually breaking up into a pale, sickly pink.

Without even a grunt of satisfaction, Ted untied his arm, bent it forward, and went out into the room. "This better be good," he said, passing Boze near the dresser. Ted lay down on the bed, lighting up a cigarette and parking an ashtray in his lap.

With minor variations on arm tying and vein thumping technique, Boze and Blakeman repeated the act, each of them sucking burnt tar from a spoon, sticking it boiling-hot into their arms, then clouding the sink with fresh spurts of blood.

When Blakeman finished he handed me the needle. "You gonna be next?" he said.

CHAPTER 23

September 16, 1983
(Morning session, continued)

"Back in high school," Bowman says, "when you were running around with your friends, what role do you think you played in your group?"

"Role?" I ask.

"Were you the general, a captain, a private?"

"I was probably a captain," I say, "but I always felt like a general."

"Did you see yourself as a leader?"

"I always thought so."

"But not the general?"

"Maybe at times. But it always seemed like people who were generals got overthrown after a while," I say.

"Do you think you would have made a good general if you would have been given that position?"

"No one *gives* you that position," I say, rubbing my chin. "Besides, it wouldn't have made any difference how I got the job—they would have overthrown me."

Bowman smiles. "Why do you say that?" she asks.

"It happened every few years. I got iced by the 'in' crowd, if you know what I mean. I guess it came with the territory."

"Why's that?" Bowman asks.

"I always thought I was smarter than everyone else."

***

Until the night he gave his lecture I was quite content with thinking Dr. D'Aoust to be rather comical, nothing more than a caricature of a man, full of idiosyncrasies—the kind of person who ritualizes his bathroom functions, who parks his shoes in the same place every night, the sort of genius who either never knows when the garbage goes out or knows it so well that he's got the entire process diagrammed on the wall.

But at the lectern that night he became a beast of a different order. There must have been a motivational speaker hiding inside him, a latent showman, a dormant preacher, a visionary driven to impart his knowledge. He stood taller. His voice boomed more than usual. He made wild, sweeping gestures that seemed to charge the air.

"No matter how bad you think you've got it," he began, pushing back his glasses. "No matter how close to death you came, or how close you think you are, you people in this room are the luckiest people alive. You want to know why? Because you're about to be handed the sacred tablets."

The guy next to me raised his eyebrows.

"That's right," D'Aoust continued, "the sacred tablets. These tablets come in the form of the only working cure for an addicted world."

There were about fourteen patients in the classroom, along with another dozen or so family or friends of patients. Susan was there, looking like a relic from my greatest hits catalogue, my ambassador from the past, a sharp, stunning reminder of how things had been before my big splash in Manhattan. Susan was in her butterfly dress, a tight, white taffeta cocoon that displayed her curves like a mummy's wrapping, then blossomed into a multi-layered collar with lapels of red, yellow, blue, green, staggered like pages of an open book, each ready to flutter like a rainbow with wings.

I was surprised to see her; I didn't know she was coming.

She arrived after I had been seated. D'Aoust kept the room divided anyway, with two empty rows separating us addicts from Susan and the others, and beyond a knowing smile and purse of her lips as she airlifted a kiss in my direction, I knew for certain that the good doctor would not tolerate ongoing distractions.

An overhead projector whirred and bleached a movie screen with harsh, white light. D'Aoust paced back and forth in the light, handwriting from the first transparency crawling over his gray silk suit. He made a few more grandiose remarks by way of introduction, thanking everyone for being there, then wrote the word "Responsibility" on the overhead.

"Why are you here?" he asked a patient in the front seat, a tall, thin, young man with straight blond hair.

"Think about it," he said. "Take as long as you need. I want you to think hard. Why are you here?" D'Aoust placed his palms on the young man's desk and leaned into his face, repeating the question again, his eyes boring deep, the silence unnerving, embarrassing everyone. I felt the atmosphere thicken in an already tense room.

"Well, have you figured it out yet? Do you know why you're here?"

"The judge sent me," the young man muttered.

"The judge sent you! The judge?!?" D'Aoust smacked his own forehead with the palm of his hand. "Look at that word up there, fellow," he said. "Look real hard." D'Aoust stood up and pointed to the screen. "Slaves!" he bellowed, his eyes scanning the room. "You're nothing but slaves!"

Quickly he drew a diagram of something that reminded me of a pair of railroad tracks.

"Listen up, people. Take a good look here. This is the pathway of normal experience," he said, tapping his black marker against the transparency. With the marker tip he followed the parallel rails. "This is the direction of a normal, healthy life." He drew more railroad ties. "These are events that add stress to your life," he said, pointing to the ties. "They're typical, they're universal, they're the little piss-offs that make up an average day."

D'Aoust came down the aisle and leaned into John, who sat two chairs in front of me. "Can you name a few things that piss you off?" he said. A few people started to laugh but they quickly stifled themselves. D'Aoust stared at John.

John looked down. "You want me to be honest?" he mumbled, talking to the floor.

"No!" D'Aoust bellowed. "I want you to lie! I want you to think real hard of something that never pisses you off but I want you to tell it to me anyway to throw me off the track."

D'Aoust shook his fists and looked up at the ceiling. "Slave!" he yelled. "You don't know when someone's being serious with you, do you? You don't know what matters anymore. Tell you what, John, I'll make it easy on you. Does someone sticking his face in your face ever piss you off?"

D'Aoust crammed his mug right into John's, his eyes round and white as 100-watt bulbs behind his glasses.

"Yeah, I guess so," John said.

"Good. Now let's suppose my getting into your face is the first rung on this ladder," D'Aoust said, standing up and moving to the projector. He pointed to the bottom tie on the railroad tracks. "Imagine this spot represents nine a.m. on Monday morning. This is your first fight with your boss. Some of you still remember what a boss is, don't you?"

A few junkies laughed. D'Aoust pointed to the ladder.

"Now, every one of these lines represents more stress. This is a fight with a customer," he said, pointing to the next tie. "Here's a bill you haven't paid yet, and here's the sonofabitch bill collector who's harassing your wife."

D'Aoust's marker moved up the tracks. Then he stood up and pushed his glasses back on his nose. He came down the aisle, pausing with every patient. Slowly, inexorably, he moved closer until he leaned on my desk.

"Mark, you know what regular people do when they encounter stress?"

Everyone watched me. I wasn't afraid to look D'Aoust in the eye, but at the same time I felt my feet grow weak and noticed a tugging sensation at my tailbone, so that little by little, I started sliding down in my seat.

"Well? Do you ever wonder how other people handle stress?"

"No I don't," I said.

"SLAVE! Knowledge is power!" he yelled, pounding my desk. "We are all carriers of information and don't you forget it. Carriers of information. To not know something limits you. Limitation is slavery. With limitation you will always be the last to know, the last to get, the last to arrive at anything. And in this world, the last shall be last, amen! They will do the bidding of others. They will be no more than slaves. You hear me? Slaves!"

D'Aoust looked across the room. "Someone from that side be so kind as to inform this man what the simple folk do when it comes to handling stress." D'Aoust moved back up the aisle and crossed in front of the screen, the light glinting off his glasses.

Susan raised her hand. "Some people work out," she said. "You know, jogging. Aerobics. Some people get counseling or just go for a walk."

"In other words, they handle it," D'Aoust said. "Rule number one: life is a series of stressful events. There's no getting around it. I don't care if you live in India, Indiana, or with the Barnum and Bailey Circus. I don't care if you're a woman, a man, or still undecided. I don't care if you're stoned, sober, or so whacked out on needles that you think some sidewalks feel better than others. Stress is a reality of life. It's one of the *main* realities. And because of that there's a lot of shit out there, a lot of advertisers that want you to believe that their little pill or bottle of beer is going to take all that stress away. Make you feel better.

"Slaves! Believe that and you're doomed. You can't change anything on the outside, you understand? Nothing you swallow can change a thing. It only covers up the feelings. The pain. That's the game you dope fiends have been playing since you took your very first drink or your very first drug. Here's what you've been doing. Now watch."

D'Aoust drew another set of railroad tracks. They started at the same place as the first but veered off to the right. "Same day, Monday morning," he said, pointing to where the tracks overlapped. "Boss sticks his face in yours. But instead of handling it, running, jogging, fighting, discussing, whatever, here you go now, your first high for the day. You see, you didn't get through the situation—you went around it. And at eleven o'clock, when more bad news comes, you turn on again, and this time you're further removed from the actual stress of life. What happens is you create a whole new pattern, a whole new set of steps that become reality for you. Whenever you hit stress, you've trained your body to go this other direction. Not through life, but around it.

"But there's one important factor to consider. You got on this other path by means of a chemical substance. It's the drug that gets you in this little groove where you don't have to deal with stress. And guess what, boys and girls?"

D'Aoust stood up from the overhead, perspiration shining on his forehead as he stepped from the light.

"Here's the killer," he said. "Here's why you're here. You see, we've gone and taken your little chemical away. Or like this fellow over here thinks, the judge took it away. Doesn't matter. What you've got is no more medication. No more holidays. And guess what? Here comes that ol' stress again. And no way to jump over here to the other track, to the drug path. So now you've got to go back through every level of stress, relearning every situation, re-experiencing all the pain. Ain't that great? What fun! While the rest of the world gets stronger and stronger, gets better and better at dealing with stress, you lucky dogs get to go back to first grade. You poor bastards. You have to start all over again. You slaves! Do you have any idea what you've done?"

That's pretty much the gist of a Dr. D'Aoust lecture. High drama, and a moral in the story, too. Everyone had to attend the show at least once before discharge. Then you got his blessing and an escort out the door. As a rule he didn't keep you long, just until the poison got out of your bloodstream, about five to ten days. I was lucky. I stayed long enough for two of his lectures. Still, when it was time for me to go he told me he didn't have much faith in my future. "There's something we're missing with you," he said. "I got all your charts and history here in these pages. I have X-rays, blood reports, your entire chemical profile. And I still don't know if we're even scratching the surface. There's something inside you, some kind of secret, and I don't know what it is."

We were all going to be killed, *that* was the secret. Toasted like a marshmallow in the center of the flames. Except that's not the kind of news you pass on to your doctor—not if you ever want to be out on the streets again. The goddam comet was supposed to take us all by surprise, but I had gone and opened up Pandora's box, or, to use a more appropriate tale, I had strapped on my Chicken Little outfit and had run around, screaming, "The sky is falling, the sky is falling," only I was sorry for it now but it was obviously too late. There'd be hell to pay. And I was the one stuck with the bill. I was going to be cream of demon soup as soon as they got their hands on me.

Susan visited with me after the lecture. I was feeling somewhat overwhelmed by it, and more than a little downcast at the thought that I was a slave and a social and emotional retard when it came to handling stress. D'Aoust's remarks about needing a year in a halfway house reverberated through me as well.

"So how's my white knight?" I said to Susan, admiring her dress with the broad lapels. I sat up in my bed, my feet under the covers.

Susan came to my side and placed her rump on the bed.

"White knight is fine," she said, "and it looks like prince charming is doing a little better, too."

"I oughta be," I said. "I passed the lecture. I heard that after that, they don't keep you much longer in this place."

"That's if all goes well," she said. "Don't forget, three days ago they were scraping you off the ceiling."

"You heard?"

"I tried to come up but they wouldn't let me see you."

"I probably wouldn't have recognized you anyway, Susan."

Susan covered my hand with hers. I tried to focus on the beautiful woman who was trying to help me. It was difficult to feel good about her, about our relationship, in light of my adventures in Pennsylvania and the fiery catastrophe of the world ending soon.

"Think in Russian," I heard from the other room.

"Can you shut the door?" I said.

Susan got up, closed the door, and returned to my side, unfastening the two clasps behind her lapels and placing my hand against her breast. Susan's touch acted as a tonic. She stroked my face, my hair, drew me to her and let me smell the warmth from her cleavage.

"I guess I'm just getting to know you now," she said, cradling my head against her bosom. My fingers found her nipple, worked it hard as a kernel of Indian corn.

"This is the stuff I didn't want you to know," I said.

"Yeah, well, you're a pretty good actor. But you know, I thought something was in there. All that secrecy. Can you understand now that I would have never judged you?"

"How do I know that?" I asked.

"I'm still here, Mark. Doesn't that prove anything? You've got to believe that I'm not going to leave you."

CHAPTER 24

There is a story about a drunk who stumbles out of a tavern during a winter snowstorm and freezes to death. He becomes a snowman. The next morning the children find him. They put a carrot in his nose, buttons down his belly. They give him sticks for arms and they give him a name. For the first time in his life, he's happy. He's dead. But he's happy. He doesn't have pain anymore.

Mr. and Mrs. Richard Kerrigan picked me up at Huntington and drove me to my next destination. "It's called New Beginnings," Richard said. "It's a rehabilitation center."

"It's called the New Beginning Center, dear," Joni said, "and they like to be referred to as a recovery center."

"Yeah? Well, whatever," Richard said. "I just know the program is called New Beginnings. Pretty nice name, eh?"

"You talking to me?" I said.

Joni flashed me a smile. She had been doting on me for the last couple of hours, insisting that I wear the new pants she bought me, standing over me while I cleaned out my belongings from the hospital room, talking to the floor nurses in a high-strung, superficial manner. It was like she was Mrs. Normal and we were the healthy, Normal Family, like we were going to the beach instead of a recovery center.

"Do I have to stay at New Beginnings for an entire year?" I asked in the car. I sat between the two of them, with Joni keeping her right arm over the door lock.

"An entire year? Heavens no. I think what we're looking at is a matter of weeks, don't you think so, Richard?"

Richard shrugged. It was a stupid question anyway. I was sure my gang of serial killers were breaking camp by now, dowsing their fires, packing their weapons. Their point man was probably on our tail. I would have turned around to check for myself, only I didn't want to make Richard paranoid again. Still, I could see them in my mind's eye: mean-faced, muscular men in combat fatigues, men with scars and Castro beards, men strapping knives to their calves, pinning grenades on their chests, throwing .50-caliber bullet belts over their shoulders. No doubt the bones of small forest creatures lay charred in the ashes of their fires. Nothing could stop them; these savages would follow our car to New Beginnings or wherever else they were taking me. It really didn't matter.

"Look at this," Joni said, handing me a stack of Get Well cards.

What a joke, I thought.

"So how's Jennifer and Courtney?" I asked, enjoying the irony. How old would they be when the world blew apart? When the hot, molten fastball punched a hole through one side and out the other, knocking us off our orbit and sending us into the dark, frozen tracts of space?

"They're fine," Joni said. "They'll be up to see you next time we visit. And by the way, I hope you don't mind that I gave your apartment key to Susan. She said she'd pick up the rest of your mail and get more clothes for you. I can't believe the stuff you packed in that suitcase."

"Joni," Richard said.

"That's true, sorry," she said. "You didn't know why you were packing."

The New Beginning Center, formerly a Catskill ski resort located outside of Kerhonkson, New York, looked impressive as we approached it from the highway. The main lodge was characterized by big, oval oak doors with iron latches and trimming—the kind often kissed by battering rams in English castles. The doors greeted us at the top of a long, white limestone driveway. Joni rolled her window down as we approached, and white dust floated in the car and I could hear the tires churning up the stones. Richard parked the Lincoln in the turnaround in front of the doors, and I got out and took my suitcase from the trunk, looking up at Old Glory atop a sixty-foot flagpole rising from a grassy mound in the center of the drive. Wind luffed the flag and the rope clanged against the pole.

We went inside where it was, ironically, as dark as a tavern. As my eyes adjusted I beheld a roomy lobby with large wooden beams running up to a high, pointed ceiling. A stone fireplace sat dormant in the center, a pair of grinning moose heads flanking either side. It was library quiet. An old, thin man in a white T-shirt with a poorly cropped beard sat on a couch near a stack of firewood. In the far right corner two women stood reading a pamphlet together. To our left was the office and receiving area, marked by bright florescent lights behind Dutch doors where Richard went over and asked to fill out some papers. Behind the doors a big man got up from an old leather office chair and greeted him. He opened the door and walked toward me, extending a giant, rough-looking paw.

"Hi, I'm Mike," he said. "Welcome."

I dropped my suitcase and we shook hands. "I'm Mark," I said. "Glad to meet you."

Mike released my hand and turned to embrace Richard. Their hands slapped each others' backs. The top of Richard's head barely reached Mike's chin, and Mike seemed capable of hanging him from the wagon wheel chandelier that dangled from chains in the middle of the lobby.

"So you're the new kid on the block," Mike said to me, breaking their embrace. "You think he's a candidate for the club, Rich?"

"He'll make a good one if we can get the bugs out of him," Richard said.

Mike laughed, the buttons on his short sleeve shirt pulling

against the muscles on his chest. He was a bulldog of a man in his late forties with a graying, ultra-short crewcut, a long, thin scar like a white crease visible through the stubble above his left ear. He had a round, ruddy face with a bottom lip so full it looked to be puffy from a fistfight. He had a tree trunk for a neck. It pressed against his shirt collar even though the top button was open. That voice of his! It seemed to rumble from the bottom of a cave, bounce off the insides of an oil drum, groan like a diesel truck winding out first gear. It sounded like the public address system for hell.

Joni and Mike exchanged pleasantries, Mike receiving her brief kiss on the lips, the proper New York thing to do. Everyone told everyone else how fine they were looking.

"You folks wait here while I show Mark to his room," Mike said, leading me through the back of the lobby down a long, sloping hallway. "I hope you're not accustomed to luxury," he said when we reached my room. It looked like a cheap motel room with two twin beds, a pair of mismatched old dressers, and thin, paneled walls with a framed copy of the Lord's Prayer, complete with praying hands, at the foot of the nearest bed.

"I just got out of Huntington," I said, glad to see there weren't any TVs.

"You're rooming with Danny," Mike said, pointing to the ruffled bed nearest the bathroom. "Put your things on the bed for now and wash up, if you like. In thirty minutes you can attend a meeting. After that it's free time till five, then dinner. You can talk to some of the guys. But after dinner I'd like to see you alone."

"Where at?" I said.

"Don't worry. I'll find you. By the way, I take it you understand why you're here."

Mike placed his hands on his hips. He took up half the room.

I shook my head. "They brought me here."

"New Beginnings is a treatment center," he said, "for

drug and alcohol abuse. You're here on Doctor D'Aoust's recommendation. Do you have any idea why he'd send you here?"

"He thinks I'm a drug addict, I guess."

"What do you think?"

I set my suitcase on my bed and sat down next to it. "I'm not sure," I said. "All I know is that I didn't ever want to go to another hospital again. But here I am. I've probably lost my job and won't make it back to school this fall. I don't know where else I can go."

"Do you think you can stop worrying about your job for a while?" Mike asked. "Just while you're here. I want you to think instead of all the drugs and drinking you've done over the years. That's what we're going to focus on."

"Okay," I said, "then what?"

"Then you might realize you're probably in the right place, Mark. Why don't you listen to the other guys at the meeting and tell me what you think."

"Sure," I said. "I'll try."

"By the way," he said, holding out his hand again for another shake, "I'm a recovering alcoholic myself. Just about everyone you'll meet here is a recovering addict of some type. You don't have to feel you're alone, you understand?"

"Yeah, sure," I said, letting him smother my hand.

"See you after the meeting," he said, and left.

I was on my own for the first time in over a week. I quickly encountered my first problem: my dresser drawers were stuck. After some effort I freed the top one and threw my clothes in, noticing the drawer was lined with old, yellowed newspaper, a page from a grocery store ad with drawings of apples and peaches and big, bold numbers stating the price per pound. Curious, I looked for the date or the name of the newspaper at the top of the page but couldn't find either. Not knowing what to do next, I examined the bathroom for a few minutes, looking at the shower and toilet as if perhaps they might function differently from any other shower and toilet in the world. I heard some laughter outside and then a crow cawing in the distance. Something about the crow frightened me. Serial killers, I thought. They were taking up new positions.

I walked back to the lobby. Joni was busy with someone at the reception desk and Richard was in front of the fireplace, joking with someone who looked like he might be the cook. The man wore a white, blood-stained apron around his waist. He *could* be the cook, but then again . . . As I approached them I heard the man say that the food was as bad as ever; in fact, he said, it had to be bad in order to teach everyone humility. That got a big laugh from Richard.

I stopped in my tracks. How could I have been so blind, I thought. Of course Richard knew that this would be the place for me. He had been here before. As a patient.

CHAPTER 25

Even though I had attended a Twelve-Step meeting at Huntington, I had been too paranoid to realize what was going on. But at my first meeting at New Beginnings I was a bit more clear—clear enough to realize I'd have trouble with their philosophy.

It was the afternoon of my first day, not too long after Joni and Richard had left. At that first gathering I learned why the lobby had been hushed like a church. All activities were segregated, said a man in an opening statement. The man, a staff counselor named Paul, said sex was a big problem for addictive personalities. "It's a distraction," he said. "It'll keep you from facing your other problems." He informed us that the punishment for talking to women was immediate expulsion from the recovery center.

He informed us that later in the week there would be a special meeting on the subject of impotency. Apparently this was another big—perhaps I should use the word "major" in this context—problem facing male substance abusers once they cleaned up their acts. Someone called it the "softer way" meeting and there was a good-hearted laugh at that, something which I interpreted as an "in" joke. A few jokes were made on top of this one, several about Mike, he being the counselor they regarded most qualified to chair the meeting.

Announcements over, the meeting officially began with some guy introducing himself by first name—Jerry—and saying, "I'm an alcoholic." "Hi, Jerry," everyone chorused. Holy shit, I thought, it's one of *those* groups. It reminded me of a bunch of kids saying, "Good morning, Teacher."

Jerry, an average-looking fellow in his middle fifties, proceeded to recite this long speech called "How It Works." He read it off both sides of a laminated sheet. This took about seven minutes and contained a list of twelve suggestions—"Commandments," I remember thinking—that were coincidentally on a giant poster taped to the wall. They were called the Twelve Steps. I knew this because the guy next to me nudged me and pointed solemnly to the poster. I obliged my friend by displaying a hefty dose of false interest, which, throughout my career at these meetings, was to become a common mannerism for me.

As if by silent cue, people began lighting cigarettes. There were about forty guys in the room and before Jerry had finished reading, I was one of only three guys who weren't smoking. (I was proud of my accomplishment of not smoking since I had jumped off the Brooklyn Bridge.) Within five minutes I couldn't see the other side of the room.

The meeting groaned on and seemed somewhat less structured, except that every person who talked introduced himself as an alcoholic, which was followed by the sing-song chorus. Hi, Bobby! Hi, Bill! One fellow said he was a "grateful, recovering alcoholic," and I took special notice because it indicated, at least to me, that the guy had enough gumption to innovate.

However, I couldn't for the life of me see what the hell he had to be grateful about. He was the skinny guy I had seen by the fireplace logs when I had first come in. His hands were shaking and I figured he had been the one to trim his own beard. Either that or someone had played a joke on him while he was sleeping. His pale skin seemed stretched tight over his bones—little sticks for bones—and his too-large T-shirt draped over his chest like a drop cloth on a small statue. But damn if he didn't chirp, chirp, chirp about how good it was to be alive. "Today I'm clean and sober," he said, "and, God willing, this evening will make another twenty-four hours that I haven't had a drink. That's a victory for me."

Some fuckin' victory, I thought. Try saying that with a tavern next door.

When he finished about three guys clapped. I squirmed in my chair. The next one to speak was this short, Italian-looking guy who could've been tossing pizzas any night in an Eighth Avenue pizza palace. He, too, had been spared by the bottle for this day at least. But it wasn't more than a month ago that he had been stealing car stereos to pay for his habit. Then another fella spoke, this one confessing he had been drinking Gumout barely a week before.

I sunk lower into my chair. After hearing story after story I formed the impression that alcohol was the vampire and your daily "Twelve Step" meeting was the cross you wore to protect you. Nobody gave himself credit for anything—especially for getting better. It seemed taboo to blow your own horn, unless you were sounding off about what a miserable life you had. In fact, the whole program seemed to be just that: You told everyone what a fuckup you were and then you waited to see if the next guy could top you. I figured we'd end the meeting with a vote and maybe prizes for the best hard-luck tale. I felt I had an inside shot with the Brooklyn Bridge.

The meeting couldn't have ended too soon for me. The ashtrays were full and my eyes burned. I walked out of there feeling that a huge mistake had been made. These people weren't my type. It was going to hurt Mike when I told him, but I needed to spare him, myself, and my family all this time and money. I walked down the hall, putting some bounce in my step. Who knows? Maybe this was what I needed to cure me. One good meeting was all it took. Yessiree! No way would I do drugs again. Not if it meant hanging out with these people.

I met Danny back at our room. He was lying on his bed, reading a little red book. He had a slight build, thin, blond hair John Denver length, dressed in blue jeans, a New York Mets T-shirt, and leather sandals on his feet. He was about my age, maybe a year or two younger.

"Hi, I'm Danny," he said, rising up.

"And don't tell me," I said, "I bet you're an alcoholic."

"That and then some," he said, laughing. "You must be new to the program."

"That's right. I'm not programmed."

"Doesn't matter," he said, standing and extending his hand. "The only requirement for membership is a desire to stop drinking." He tapped the book. "It's right in here," he said.

We shook hands. Something about Danny alarmed me. He was overly friendly. He seemed eager to please, eager to have me speak. Just too damn eager, I thought.

" 'A desire to stop drinking,' " I said. "Where have I heard that before?"

"It's in the preamble. We say it at every meeting."

"That explains a lot," I said, looking around the room, looking for a way out. "Do you guys always talk like that?"

Danny laughed. "You mean the cliches? Oh, a lot of us do, I suppose. I keep forgetting what a turnoff that must be. But you'll understand once you get into the program."

"I have no intention of getting into your little program," I said. "I don't beg for biscuits, I don't do tricks." With that I turned away from him and checked my clothes drawer to be sure my clothes were still there.

What's it like to be brainwashed, I wondered. Is it like running around in an ant hive? Carrying a Bible and reciting verses? I looked at Danny. How long had it taken for him? Was it like the body snatchers? Did he wake up one morning and find a pod next to his bed?

Does a program take away your urges, your feelings, I wondered. What would it be like to never have another thought I could call my own?

Then I remembered the Nazi serial killers still hot on my trail. I looked out the window, shivering at my recollection of laughter the last time I had been in the room. Strange laughter.

There had been a crow, too, just like in Pennsylvania. Danny might be one of them, I thought, an agent planted to soften me up, to lower my guard until the others were ready to jump me. That explained his friendliness.

"What's wrong?" Danny said, leaning over the bed and watching my face. I turned away from the window.

"Nothing," I said. "What's there to do around this place? Play cards and look at last year's *Readers Digest*?"

"You want a tour of the grounds? This place is great," he said, rising slowly and checking himself in the mirror. "C'mon, I'll show you. We got a lake, a pool, two tennis courts. All kinds of stuff."

The New Beginning Center was great, all right. Well-terraced lawns spread out between little patches of woods, the woods thinned like the breaks between golf course fairways, knolls of clustered shade trees with the underbrush cleared away. We stopped at the swimming pool and I could hear cicadas humming in the hot August air. Danny, limping slightly, led the way down a winding path by the tennis courts. Large oaks and maples stretched their branches over us and the sun speckled behind them. Their leaves moved slightly, like the hands of beauty queens passing in a long parade. My legs felt good as they limbered up, renewing themselves as we stepped over roots, rocks, and furrows.

We passed several women coming the other way. I made a point of bowing my head and averting my eyes. But after passing one particularly attractive blond, I surrendered to the urge and turned my head. I caught her looking back at me, too.

"Uh-uh," Danny said. "It ain't worth it."

The lake turned out to be nothing more than a large, brackish pond. Deadwood littered the edge. Large, fallen branches stuck out from the brambles propping them up. At the far shore a thin film of yellow algae spread like cream of wheat between tall reeds and a cluster of cattails, their fuzzy brown tops reminding me of corndogs at the amusement park.

A man jogged past us, a peninsula of sweat penetrating the front of his tattered gray T-shirt. "Keep an eye out for that snake," he yelled.

"Snake? What snake?" I said.

"Aw, some of the old timers say there's a copperhead roaming around," Danny said, holding his side. "Personally, I think they just want the lake off limits."

"Off limits? Why?" I asked.

"Jealous. They're too old to handle a walk so they don't want anyone else enjoying themselves, either."

"By the way," I said, "I noticed you're limping. Are you all right?"

"As right as I'll ever be."

"Oh yeah? Can I ask what's wrong? Or is it personal?"

"No," he said, resting against a tree. "Nothing's personal anymore. It's my liver. But I won't bore you with the details. You'll probably hear about it at the meetings. It's the kind of story you're probably sick of already."

CHAPTER 26

Ol' Mike was one hell of an audience. He sat back and let me tell him all about the Brooklyn Bridge, about the cops and paramedics and ambulance rides. How thrilling and dangerous I was to myself. By now the bridge was a 175 feet tall. The swim to Manhattan took an hour and a half. I told him all about the party in Pennsylvania, how I tripped my brains out on PCP until I thought I was walking on Lake Erie itself. I admitted that I drank a lot in New York City. I drank like a fish, I said. I held nothing back from good ol' Mike, my brother alcoholic. Based on how those other guys talked in that first meeting, I figured that's how you got your points, got popular.

"Well, that's some story," Mike said, crumbling up an empty pack of Lucky Strikes. "You think you can write that down?"

"I definitely plan to," I said. "I'm a writer, you know. Someday it's going to be a whopper of a tale."

"No," Mike said, "I mean write it down now. Tonight. I want you to write your whole personal history, only I want you to start with your first drink. Better yet, I want you to start with your childhood. Write down everything that ever happened to you. Good or bad. I don't care. Write it all. Don't tell me your intentions or what you were thinking at the time. Just your behavior. What you did. I only want to know what you did."

He opened a black leather appointment book and took up his pen. "You think you can make enough of a start so that we can look at some of it tomorrow?"

"Tomorrow?" I said.

"Yeah. As in the day after today." Mike opened and closed his jaw a few times, exercising it. His neck muscles fanned out as though stretched over harp strings.

"You mean share it with you?" I said.

"Why not? You're going to publish it anyway, right?"

"Yeah, but my childhood? That's not very exciting compared to the bridge and all."

"That's okay. I'm not your publisher."

"But it won't even be exciting for me," I said.

"Sure it will," Mike said. "For instance, what's your very first memory?"

"First memory?"

"Yeah. How far back can you remember?"

I sat there in silence, looking at the floor. I crossed and uncrossed my legs. "Hmmm," I said. I looked up at the ceiling and closed my eyes.

"Time," Mike said. "All we got is time."

"Ah, I got it. I was young, real young. Maybe two or three. I had the croup. You know, where you can't breathe and you cough up blood—"

"I know the croup," he said.

"Anyway, I had the croup and I coughed up blood all night. But the next day was a school day and my older brothers and sister got up and got ready. So I had to sit there in my crib and watch them. None of them came in to see me. I remember showing the blood on my pillowcase but they kept on going past my door. No one came in."

"You mean no one paid any attention to you," Mike said.

I left Mike's office feeling depressed. His final question was if I could recall any childhood dreams. I told him no. No dreams.

I didn't sleep that first night. I lay awake and imagined I heard killers shuffling through the woods. Had they drawn straws for who was going to kill me? Maybe they had picked a specialist, a knife man, who could stalk silent as the wind, his eight-inch blade sharp enough to split whiskers on a kitten. He's slip in my room and with one hand he'd cover my mouth, pushing my head deep into the mattress. I'd get a moment's look into his eyes, a brief communion of terror, then the other hand would whistle as the blade curved across my neck, a deep flap opening and a river running red along the gash. The pain would flash and roll over me, my eyes frozen on this man's leering face. As I sank towards darkness, death pulling me down, he would lean forward and whisper a final curse into my ear.

I sat up in bed. I didn't like the curse part. It was like getting bad directions in the afterlife. I wanted to go out with more pleasant thoughts than that. No, I thought, more likely they would probably use a jellyfish; they'd drop the jellyfish on my face, which wouldn't kill me, only stun me and muffle my cries. Then they'd carry me away and at least serve me breakfast before the real carnage began. They needed names and I could buy some time with that. In fact, when I really thought about it, it was even more likely that they'd take me out with a crossbow; cool, silent, deadly quick. One minute I'd be standing around, talking to friends, and the next, dropped over with a shaft through my heart.

"That's not so bad," I said to myself, but then I remembered I was scheduled for several days' torture. It would never be a one-shot deal.

Thoughts like these kept me up all night. Toward morning I imagined my heart had stopped beating. I lay there, sweating, trying to find my own pulse. I couldn't wait for the sun to come up. As bad as the company was at New Beginnings, I was anxious to be around other people—if only to get away from my murderous thoughts.

In the morning I followed Danny to the dining room for breakfast. It was a large but cozy hall with an elevated stage on the right, flanked on both sides by large windows. At the back of the hall the chow line ran cafeteria-style. The clank of silverware and dishes plus eighty or so voices filled the hall with an ambient din. I joined Danny at a table with four other guys. One fella, Steve, I recognized from Huntington. He was dark haired, heavyset, with thick eyebrows and a big, black caterpillar of a mustache. He had worked at a pharmacy and gotten himself addicted to morphine and Dilaudid.

The table next to ours was filled with women. I noticed the blond who had passed me on the path. I could watch her without being seen, her mouth moving as she talked. She'd smile and bring her water glass to her lips or tilt her head back in laughter. She had a long ponytail segmented with rubber bands. It hung to the center of her back like a wind sock waiting for a breeze.

Danny nudged me with his elbow, pulling me into the conversation at our table. Going with the only thing I knew, I asked Steve if any of the other "D'Aoust Boys" were due to show up at New Beginnings. As I looked about the cafeteria I was surprised not to recognize anyone else from the detox unit.

He laughed. "I don't believe you asked me that, man."

"Why? What's the matter?" I said.

"Christ, you're such an uptown idiot," he said, dabbing some biscuit gravy off his mustache with a white paper napkin.

I stared. I didn't understand his attitude.

"Mark, those guys are junkies," Steve said. "I mean street gypsies. The only reason they made it to Huntington was 'cause some social worker or parole officer had the strings or the bucks to get them fixed. Most are on and off methadone for the rest of their lives. Dope or methadone, that's the choice. When they get out of D'Aoust's they got nowhere to go. 'Cept back to the streets."

"Or jail," Danny said.

"Or someplace cold with a tag on their toe," said the guy next to Danny.

Steve looked around the table. Two guys nodded. "You

know what a place like New Beginnings costs?" Steve said. "Those guys like John, they ain't got a chance in hell. They knew that but you didn't. That's why you couldn't get in their clique. You go chummin' 'round the unit like everyone's gonna be pals when they get outta there. Meet at Lincoln Center for coffee or something. Christ, the day you meet those guys on the street is the day you're in the wrong fuckin' neighborhood."

Late that afternoon I went out and sat by the swimming pool. The sun slanted long shadows off the wooden deck chairs arranged in little circles on the lawn. The chairs were painted bright red or blue or orange and had ribbed wood backs and ribbed seats with a large right arm designed—ironically—for holding drinks, like the school desks of long ago.

Steve and a few other guys were in the pool. They threw a soccer ball back and forth, ducking under as they aimed at each others' heads. I got up and kicked off my shoes, then went to the pool's edge and put a foot in the water.

"The pool's off limits, Mark."

It was Mike. He had come up beside me, both of us watching the guys horsing around. "I don't understand," I said.

"It's off limits for you. On account of your special circumstances." Mike looked out towards the sun, shielding his eyes, then worked a finger around the inside of his collar. "Hot, ain't it?" he said. He tugged on my arm so that we both backed up from the pool.

"Mike, if anyone can swim, you know it's me."

"That ain't the point," he said. "I saw that cervical pad in the box with your stuff. I have a good mind to see that Doc Bailey looks you over before you take part in *any* activities here, you understand?"

"But it doesn't hurt. Even D'Aoust took it off."

"This isn't D'Aoust's territory. We have our own rules here." Mike moved to the edge of the pool. His lips moved and he nodded as his eyes traveled from one swimmer to the next. "Seven," he counted.

"I take it you play lifeguard, too," I said.

Mike stepped in front of me, blocking the sun, his body imposing on me like a refrigerator tipping over. Our eyes locked only a few inches apart.

"Call it a hunch," he said. "No more than a feeling. But I don't want you going in that pool, you understand?"

"Yes sir."

Mike moved away. He jerked his thumb up and shouted at the swimmers. "Okay," he said, "swim's over. We got a meeting, then dinner, then another meeting at eight."

The guys moaned like kids being called by their mother. Someone threw the ball and it whistled past us, nearly hitting Mike's legs and trailing a line of water as it zipped through the grass.

"Barrister," Mike yelled, "you got fifty push-ups for that one!"

"How about fifty chapters in the Big Book?"

"That's more like it," Mike said. He turned back to me. "By the way," he said, nudging me towards my chair and my shoes, "you got a call from your girlfriend. I think you should call her back."

CHAPTER 27

The lobby contained a pair of pay phones in a converted coat check room near the front door. A cardboard sign tacked above the phones said, "Don't Slam the Phone Because You Can't Handle AT&T (Alcoholic Temper Tantrums)."

Something was wrong with Susan. She seemed different, removed, emotionally flat. I tried to get her to talk about it but she wouldn't. I kept saying, "It's me, isn't it?" but she wouldn't tell me, instead promising to see me tomorrow, which was a Saturday.

As I hung up I felt something go loose inside, something slipping like the earth's crust just before a major quake.

The pre-dinner meeting topic was "helplessness." There was no shortage of material in that regard.

Dinner was loathsome as well, consisting of canned, overcooked peas, instant potatoes, and salisbury steaks swamped in gravy. Detesting it entirely, I surprised myself by loading up my plate nevertheless, telling myself that a full belly would help me sleep that night.

After the meal I found a pad of paper, a pen, and a cubbyhole where I could write. "Just tell me what you did," Mike's voice echoed inside me. "Especially with drinking."

***

The first memory that came forward was one concerning

my older brother, Scott, who, when I was ten years old, had come home from boot camp in the Navy. He had spent a weekend in New York City. He brought back souvenirs from Greenwich Village: incense, cloth patches with peace signs, and several protest buttons attacking Viet Nam and LBJ. One button offered particularly strange advice: "Smoke a Banana." I showed it to Kelly and he said a song by Donovan, called "Mellow Yellow," was all about getting high on banana skins.

Even at ten years old the idea of getting high was not foreign to me. I knew that inside myself was a labyrinth of feelings, of different states of mind. In fact, my memory now sharpened by the need to write things down, I was able to recall that at two years of age I had already developed an instinct for bliss. Around the back of our house we had a laundry exhaust for my mother's dryer, a hole with a tin rain guard that channeled the exhaust downwards, along with the lint fuzz that gathered in the tall grass beside the house where the lawn mower couldn't reach. When I was just able to walk, guiding myself with a hand against the house as I clumped along in those painful, foreign things called shoes, I rounded the corner one spring day and encountered the exhaust. It was a mystifying experience. I could smell fresh clothes, the same smell that always accompanied afternoons in front of the television set when my mother would bring up a hamper of warm sheets and towels and dump them on the floor, letting me play in the hamper while she did her folding, watching "Guiding Light." I was boggled. Here was that same smell and warmth, but somehow on the outside. Blowing like steam from a box. It was the essence of prior experience, like being in two places at the same time.

According to Kelly, smoking a banana could do the same thing.

Thursday was grocery day and—because I had requested them for my school lunches—Mom came home with a fresh bunch of Chiquitas. I broke one off and scraped the strings from the insides of the peels, baking them on a small square of tin foil in the oven. Mom was there when I did it. I told her it was a science project. The strings never dried, turning instead to a black, tarry paste. Later that day Kelly and I took off for the woods, full of wild ideas as to what the drug would do to us. But the paste would not ignite, not even when we rolled it up in notebook paper. Finally we smeared the concoction on a pair of cigarettes, choking violently while trying to hold the smoke in our lungs. Even though we didn't know what "high" was, we pretended to be it. Nothing happened, of course. But the experience awakened my desire for far-off places.

***

I didn't write anything down beyond that. I sat in my cubbyhole, pen in hand, overcome by the assault of memory. Had I written at all, there would have been fifty pages before I got to the part where I took my first drink.

One memory stayed with me longer than the others. As I folded up the blank sheets and headed for my session with Mike, I was consumed by this picture of myself at the age of seventeen, a passenger in Kelly's car as we rode along the country backroads on a wet, wintry night. It was before Kent State. I had a six-pack of beer in my lap. We had just stubbed out our second joint. The ashtray was full of cigarettes, overflowing like a bag of McDonald's french fries. I had a buzz in my brain, a feeling of being empty, like a television with the sound turned down. I stared out through the rain-streaked window at the dark shapes blurring by. Everything was flat, one dimensional. Barns and silos were cardboard props. Bare trees scraped the sky with fishbone branches. Low clouds choked off the stars and clamped down on everything, seemed to hold us under a darkened barrel.

We were lost and I didn't care. I was numb in the comfort of the heater on my feet, nodding to the whir of the wheels. We were too high to talk. There was nothing to talk about anyway. The only thing I cared about was the ride. I wanted to keep riding. The longer it lasted, the better. I looked over at the fuel needle. Half tank. I raised my beer.

"You know what scares me more than anything, Kelly?"

"Wha's that?"

"Arriving."

Kelly's eyes looked right. He nodded and grinned. "I s'pose when you got nowhere to go, ya sorta get used to it."

"I know," I said. "The thought of actually getting somewhere scares the shit outta me. Don't tell anybody I said this, okay? It's just that I don't know what's going to become of me. I mean, what if I wake up someday and I'm in the wrong job, or house, or doing something that I don't want to be doing?"

***

"I want outta here, Mike. I want outta here now."

"Don't say I didn't warn you about the food."

We were in Mike's office. He kicked his feet up on the desk.

"I'm not joking about this, man. This place isn't the right program for me."

Mike pointed to a chair. I hadn't sat down yet.

"Do you have any idea, Mark, how many other guys say the exact same thing?"

"I don't care about them. I'm—"

"I know. You're different, right? Well, let's see just how different you are. What are those papers in your back pocket? Is that the stuff I wanted you to write?"

"Not exactly," I said, reaching behind me with a hand on the scrolled papers. I pulled them out and sat down.

"What do you mean? Where are they?" Mike dropped his feet and sat up in his chair.

"I couldn't do it," I said.

"Did you try?"

"Yeah, you bet. But there's too much stuff. I get confused thinking about it all."

Mike got up and went to a file cabinet. He opened the top drawer and pulled out a manilla folder. "You ever steal liquor?" he asked.

"Yeah," I said. "A few times."

"You ever steal money to pay for liquor or drugs?" He opened the folder, looking down at me.

"Probably," I said.

"Probably. Good answer. Tell me, what do you think of the meetings so far?"

"I hate 'em," I said.

"Is that why you want to get out of here?"

"Yep," I said, sitting up in my seat.

"Let me guess," he said, laying the folder on the desk and turning it around so I could read it. "You don't like the meetings because of all the bleeding hearts. Because those stories make you sick, don't they?"

I nodded. I looked down at my file.

"See that? Not a thing in there about what you've done to get here. Nothing about you drinking liquor or stealing to drink liquor. Nothing about drugs or jail or anything illegal that you might have done. Nothing about the goddam bridge. You know, Mark, every single file in there is exactly the same. We got their names, addresses, and vital statistics. That's it. Look there," he said, pointing. "You're a pulse, a blood pressure, a list of allergies. It's the same for everyone. Everyone's equal. Now the problem with you, as I see it, is that you think, when it comes to the meetings, that you're somehow different. It's on your face. You can't stand to hear what goes on around the tables."

"I can take it," I said.

"Oh? I wonder. I wonder if you're one of those guys who changes his tune all the time. Are you? If you are, believe me, you won't be ready to hear the truth—not yours or anybody else's."

"I'm ready," I said.

"Oh yeah? Then why didn't you do any writing?"

***

"I bought them for you a couple of days ago," Susan said. "Richard told me they had a pool up here."

I held up the dark blue Speedo bathing suit. It looked very small.

"They have a pool," I said, "but I'm not allowed to use it." I sighed. Susan and I sat alone in the dining hall. We had a table near the window which overlooked the back lawn and a utility shed. Hoes, shovels, and rakes leaned against the shed, half-empty bags of fertilizer lay stacked beside an incline walkway marred with dirty tracks from a wheelbarrow going up and down. The bags moved in the breeze, their slit tops raising and lowering like old people trying to touch their toes. A storm was coming. The clouds were bunching up and turning the color of slate.

Susan was not herself. She sighed repeatedly and drew a lazy circle on the table with her long, red fingernail. With eyes so large, it was easy to see them looking down or away at those moments they would normally be looking into mine. A smile would begin at the corners of her mouth but before it could stretch and round out her cheeks, it sagged into one of those expressions you see on people at the airport when they hear that their flight's been delayed.

"It's really good to see you," I said. She had brought two Bloomingdale shopping bags filled with clothes. A rubber-banded stack of mail jutted from the top of one bag.

Usually when Susan was angry she'd drum her nails. Or deliver her most potent weapon, the Pout. But neither was in operation; I couldn't read her. She seemed scared, withdrawn, waiting for the right time to say something important.

Finally our eyes made contact. "We need to talk," she said.

I inched back in my chair, appreciating the table between us. "Okay," I said. "What'll we talk about?"

"About that blond woman you've been seeing."

Wind sock, I thought. But I barely spoke to her. How could I be in so much trouble?

Susan folded her hands and looked to the side. "Mark," she said, her voice breaking with emotion, "when I went to your apartment I saw some things. Shocking things. Do you know what I'm talking about?"

My mind traveled to West 74th Street and hovered from my ceiling. I scanned the sleeping loft, the bathroom, the main room with its tiny braided carpet on the bare wooden floor.

"I'm not sure," I said. "What did you see?"

"Photographs. Your mirror was on the floor and you had photographs taped to it. Photos all over the place."

Susan brought her hand to her face but not in time to catch the icemelt rolling down her cheeks. Two beads landed and winked up from the table.

"Oh, God," I said, "I'm sorry."

When I had gotten back from Pennsylvania, hallucinating up a firestorm, I created this fantasy that I could summon Catherine from New Mexico by beaming her through my full-length mirror. I pulled it off the wall and set it on the floor, making a landing pad which also doubled as an altar. I taped old photos of Catherine to the mirror frame and, filling that up, made little tents with the remaining ones, like you do when building a house of cards. I chanted, burned incense, and scattered her letters and some dried flowers she had sent me, all in an effort to better visualize my target. I was going to bring her through, just like the transporter in *Star Trek*. In one fevered session I filled up a notepad with our most private sayings, the little pet names we had used for our genitalia, our code names for heaven. I had taped those to the wall, surrounding the "do-not-remove-by-punishment-of-law" tag I had ripped off the couch from her mother's house where we had first made love. Lastly—and I prayed they were no longer there—Catherine's blue silk panties I had stolen from the last time we went camping. I had draped them over the top of the mirror and looped a St. Christopher medal through the crotch.

Patron saint of astral travelers.

"Susan, I was sick."

"You were sick when you did that, Mark. But were you sick the whole time you were seeing her while you were sleeping with me?" Susan fished a Kleenex out of her purse. "Is she the one you saw in Pennsylvania?"

"No," I said. Technically, she had met me in Buffalo, New York.

"How can I believe you?" she said. "What's her name?"

I bit my lip. "C-Catherine," I said.

"Oh, yes. Catherine. The Catherine who didn't mean anything anymore. The Catherine who never came through when you needed her the most. The same Catherine, I suppose, who broke your heart. The girl you said left you long before you came to New York."

Susan wiped her eyes. "You lied to me, Mark. You lied."

"I didn't lie. I led you on."

Susan pushed her purse and it fell off the table. She buried her face in her hands. When I bent down to pick up her bag my eyes traveled to the shadow beneath her white skirt. Suddenly her hand chopped down the center of the skirt and she squeezed her knees tight.

I raised my head like a fox caught with a mouthful of feathers. I held out the bag.

"You lie, you lie, you lie!" Susan tore her purse from my fingers.

"I'm sick," I said. I looked down at the table.

"That's why you were going away all the time," she said, "isn't it? To see someone else. How could I have been so stupid?"

"Don't blame yourself," I said.

"Oh, don't worry," Susan said, pulling out a mirror then tossing it back in her bag. "I know better than to blame myself. I just wonder what was going on in my mind that made me believe you. I don't know why I'm surprised to find out you've been cheating on me."

"But it wasn't cheating, really. I mean, what did we have?"

"Exactly," she said. "What did we have?"

Susan got up and went to the window, raising a leg to sit on the ledge sideways. She looked outside, upset with the mascara on her fingertips after wiping her face. She was quite a picture; a beautiful, brokenhearted thing. A woman at a window looking out on a storm. For all practical purposes, she could have been a woman at the railing of a cruise ship, a cruise ship pulling out from port. And I was stuck on shore, watching her sail away.

Ten minutes later Susan was gone.

CHAPTER 28

September 18, 1983
(Afternoon session)

"I'm a user of women—what more can I say?"

"You've said a lot already. But I want you to remember that it's you who are making that claim," Bowman says. "Only you can judge yourself."

"But the evidence is there," I say. "I'm guilty."

"According to whom? Why don't you try telling me why you sought so many relationships? What were you looking for, Mark?"

***

Before I worked in the mental health unit at Ronson Lodger, I worked the floors as a house orderly. My duty list included everything from restraining confused or dangerous patients, to saving lives with CRP, and then to the more menial chores of giving middle-aged men their pre-prostate surgery enemas or helping an elderly woman raise herself off the toilet.

My real reason for going from floor to floor, however, was to hunt young, available women. If, for instance, the eighth floor employed a nurse who had caught my eye in the cafeteria, you can be sure I found some work to do on that floor. I would come up, ostensibly to check up on a patient who had fallen out of bed the night before, but really I was there to brush uniforms with my current love interest. So many times I helped Mr. Jones or Mrs. Smith wiggle themselves onto the cart for surgery, when all along I was panting for a flash of cleavage as my target nurse bent forward, her stethoscope dangling, her face upturned and smiling as I made one of my many corny jokes.

Student nurses were my favorite. They would arrive in groups of ten or twenty and populate the halls like shy, pretty flowers. They were so young, so innocent. And also gullible enough to take orders from someone like me. Their faces beamed, pink with blush. Often they wore strong, fruity perfume, the kind of stuff that hugs the floor the day after a teenage slumber party. So young were they that sometimes I noticed a bit of baby fat as my eyes appraised their necks, bare arms, calves, and ankles beneath their bright little uniforms. I loved it when they wore bobby socks. Bobby socks were like invitations, love letters, little white flags flashing by. I remember many times walking to work, whistling "Good Ship Lollipop," as I planned my patrols for that day. I had a sweetheart on every floor. If not, I didn't visit that floor very often.

Sex entangled my brain like an overloaded switchboard. One night I had the dreaded enema shift, a routine of going from room to room with a plastic bag and tube in my hand, explaining in a user-friendly voice how so-and-so's doctor had ordered a pre-surgery enema for him and how easy and painless it would be. "Standard procedure," I'd say, "I do these all the time." I would fill the bag with a thousand cc's of soapy water—twice the size of an average water balloon—and in my kindest voice suggest that my patient roll onto his left side so I could fill up his tank.

Getting patients to cooperate gave me a strange sense of power. Smiling as I had them unhitch their pajama bottoms, I realized I was on equal terms with any physician who had ever told a patient, "This won't hurt at all."

There was nothing pleasant about the experience—

something I knew but they didn't. In fact, I made a point of clearing the way to the bathroom, removing any suitcases, visitor's chairs, et cetera, to provide them with a clear runway to the toilet seat. I even put their slippers on in bed because I knew that once I was through, time itself would compress as they bolted like horses from a burning barn.

But as for my obsession with women and how it affected me, there was one incident which involved a routine enema on an otherwise routine night. I had been making rounds, acquiring the names of my victims from lists at the nurses' stations. As I went from room to room, each time I entered one, an insulting show was being broadcast on the television. It was called *Battle of the College Cheerleaders*, or something like that, a thinly disguised excuse for panty shots and heaving bosoms. It was a big hit. All the men's rooms had it cranked up loud.

Personally, I found it disgusting. Couldn't they package all those tight butts and gleaming thighs into something more acceptable, like a beauty contest? How could anyone let themselves be used? As I entered a patient's room on the fifth floor and filled his enema bag in the bathroom, I could hear the canned cheers and pseudo-expert commentary by the lucky guys hosting the show. I smirked. The damn show would probably win an award. There'd be sequels and probably a high school version, too.

I came out of the bathroom and approached the foot of my patient's bed. I held the bag high like a hooked fish in one of those sportsman's postcards you get in Minnesota.

"What's this?" the man said, his eyes growing large. He seemed to look behind me. I followed his glance. I assumed he wanted my comment on the television show. On the screen above me, seven nymphs in micro skirts climbed on top each other's backs, forming the beaver-enriched "pyramid," a real show stopper at football games.

I sighed. "It's cheap sex," I said. "How anyone can stoop so low beats me."

The man's eyes grew wider. He clutched the covers and pulled them to his chin. It was then I realized he had been asking about the bag in my hand.

***

September 18, 1983
(Afternoon session, continued)

"Okay then, I'm a sex addict. There. I said it."

"Doesn't prove anything. Doesn't change anything."

"What can I say then, doctor? How can I change it?" I look through the beveled glass in the office door. Weird shapes go bending by.

"Maybe changing it isn't what we're after," Bowman says, stretching then checking her watch. "Have you ever thought about acceptance?"

I sigh. "How can I do that?" I say. "That stuff was horrible."

"You know, it's funny, but I must admit I detect a hint of bragging about all this sex stuff. It's as if part of you, your superego for instance, wants to punish you for being a bad boy. And yet, there's this whole other side of you that's pretty smug, kind of happy you got away with it all. That's what I hear in your voice, Mark."

"No way," I say.

"I also suspect you're having a hard time reconciling the two because a part of you isn't so sure you might not do it again. You don't know if you really want to give it up. And because of that, you don't trust yourself, do you?"

Bowman stretches as she stands up, then pushes her chair under her desk. "Look," she says, "we covered a lot today. Most of this is stuff you're going to have to deal with long after you get out of here. But that's all right, you've got the rest of your life. However, I want to tell you one little story before we break off, okay?"

"Sure," I say. "Fire away."

Bowman closes my chart and tosses her pen in her white, beaded purse. "I used to live in Colorado," she says. "When we got married, my father gave my husband, David, a brand-new pickup for the backroads. It was one of those real nice ones, shiny red with a camper on top. Only it drove me nuts because David wouldn't take it anywhere. His excuse was that we hadn't broken it in yet. I couldn't believe it. He would not take it on the backroads. We fought over it every weekend. Anyway, we took it into town one night and parked it on the street while we went to a movie. When we came out, we saw that someone had hit the side, leaving a pretty major dent. David went nuts, as you might expect. But you know, that dent was the best thing to happen to that truck. You know why?"

"Yeah," I say, "I bet he started using it after that."

"That's right. It wasn't perfect anymore. He could treat it like a regular old truck."

***

New Beginnings (once again):

Susan was gone, demons were back, and Mike was on my shit for missing a meeting. Another counselor was upset because I hadn't made my bed, either. We had a big, three-way fight in the lobby. Mike said he'd talk to me some more after lunch.

"Fuck it," I said, "I ain't going to lunch!"

I stomped down the hall and Danny, coming the other way, caught my arm and tried to stop me. "Leave me alone!" I yelled, windmilling my arm and running into our room. I slammed the door and jumped on the bed, curling up into a ball.

A few minutes later the sky poured down. Wind rushed through the window and rain drove against the screen, pelting my face and bare arms with a fine, cool mist. A thunderclap exploded and rumbled down the valley. The rain swelled, pounding hard and steady, rattling on the roof like dice in a cup.

I slept through lunch. I slept through dinner and the evening meeting. I slept through the entire storm. I woke up around two a.m., fragments of a dream dissolving as my eyes scanned the unfamiliar dark of my room. I had dreamed I was in a row boat, paddling with a stop sign.

Danny snored lightly in the other bed. I could hear water dripping from the spouting, hitting something metallic like a trash can lid. I got up, my shoes and pants still on, and pulled a sweatshirt over my head. I tiptoed past Danny's bed and peeked out into the hall. Seeing nothing but little half-circles from the night lights on the floor, I ducked into the hallway and walked quickly to the nearest door. I slipped outside, holding the door so it closed silently behind me.

I stood in the courtyard that opened out to the swimming pool. With feet sloshing on the wet grass, I hurried through the darkness towards the pool, hearing night crawlers suck back into the soil, alarmed by my approach. I took off my shoes. The cool, wet grass felt spongy beneath my feet.

There were no lights around the long, rectangular pool. From a shed nearby I could hear the hum of the circulator pump, but other than that, the pool was a dark, silent, inky mass, a giant door opening to a silent world below. I stood at the edge and shivered, looking around, wondering where to go. A white towel lay curled at the base of the diving board. I walked over and touched it, determining that it was soaked. I picked it up, gathered it into a ball, and tossed it in the water. A circle of ripples spread out as the towel disappeared. I took off my clothes and stepped up on the diving board. Thinking that I would only get in one good dive—and not caring what kind of sound I made—I bounced high off the end and pointed myself headfirst through the water.

The impact snatched my breath away. I was jarred as if

landing from a much greater height, and something seemed to snap in my neck. There was a sudden flash and I thought for a moment that I had reinjured myself, broken my neck perhaps, and that I would lose consciousness and sink to the bottom. The feeling of being submerged horrified me. I feared that the pool was indeed a doorway and that through this passage the demons I had escaped could now lay hold of me. A terrible death waited down there.

I kicked and clawed my way up. Breaking the surface, I gasped for air, reliving the trauma of the Brooklyn Bridge. I paddled to the edge of the pool and held on to the side, my heart revving with pain, my mind wild, battling the panic. I pressed my face to the cool, wet cement.

It was several minutes before I could stand on my feet. I expected all the lights to go on and the staff to come down and haul me away. But nothing happened. Still shaking from the experience, I stepped into my clothes and snuck back to my room. Danny's snoring was a welcome sound.

CHAPTER 29

Sunday breakfast. Pancakes stiff and dry. Eggs that weren't soft boiled, yet weren't completely hard boiled, either, with firm whites on the outside and orange yolks that barely retained a drop or two of thick, gooey moisture.

We were the same fellas at the same table and I wondered that morning—as I fielded questions from Danny about Off-Broadway plays—if it wasn't too late to change, that is, to select another table for the next meal and perhaps meet some fresh, interesting people.

"That's incredible," Danny said, "a New York playwright. It amazes me that there are human beings out there who can put thoughts and feeling into words. It simply amazes me."

"Personally, I don't think it's so great," I said. "I'm more impressed with anyone who builds with their hands. Someone who builds their own house, now there's an artist for you."

Mike came up to our table and bent down low by my side. "Are you going to church this morning?" he asked.

"I wasn't planning on it," I said.

"Well, if you're not, then I'd like to see you in my office. How about in fifteen minutes or so, right after you finish breakfast?"

"Sure," I said.

Mike left. My eyes searched the faces around our table. "I wonder what that's about," I said.

***

I looked at the bottom of Mike's shoes as they lay crossed on his desk. The soles were like irons, with stitches coming down from the toes like little holes for steam. Mike lay back in his chair with his hands folded behind his head, his elbows sticking out like wings.

"Has Doc Bailey seen you since you've been here?" he asked.

"Just that one time when I first came in," I said, recalling the old man taking my pulse and blood pressure.

"How's that neck of yours?"

"Fine."

"Any problems?"

"Nope."

It had been throbbing all morning.

"Mark, let me get to the point here," Mike said, taking his feet off the desk and lighting up a cigarette. "We don't have an official rule for it but we do put a lot of emphasis on the daily meetings. We figure without meetings you don't have much of a program. Without a program, you don't have recovery. Now that makes sense, doesn't it?"

"Yes."

"We figure there has to be something really important going on for a client of ours to miss a meeting. Now maybe you weren't aware of that. So I'm spelling it out for you—don't miss another meeting, you hear?"

"I'll do my best," I said, sitting up and eyeing Mike's ashtray, which was a clear, round piece of glass inside the center of a miniature rubber tire. "Can I borrow a cigarette?"

"What? You gonna return it or something? Here, take a smoke," he said, chuckling as he tossed me a Lucky.

"By the way," he said, "they told me at the front desk that your girlfriend was by yesterday. Would she have anything to do with missing those meetings?"

I lit up my cigarette, propping my feet on his desk, too. "As of yesterday morning," I said, exhaling a gray, thick cloud, "my girlfriend and I passed through a vital crossroads, Mike. At which point I believe each one of us has selected a different route."

I smiled. Mike merely arched his eyebrows, looking thoughtfully at the back of his hand. On the next puff a wave of nausea swept over me. I felt dizzy, little pockets of the room growing dark brown and fuzzy like little brown polka dots blotting out the light. I heard a roar in my ears and felt my head grow heavy. The feeling and the darkness grew until it seemed I was sliding headfirst into a double-thick grocery bag.

"What's wrong?" Mike said. "You sick?" He leaned forward and steadied my shoulders. He took the cigarette out of my hand.

I stopped short of passing out. After putting my feet up and taking my vital signs, Mike and I agreed I was well enough to attend that morning's meeting. On the way to it he asked me about my autobiography. I had to disappoint him once again.

The meeting turned out to be the one on impotence. It was a packed house, guys sucking cigarettes like they were nicotine nipples. I purposely sat next to a guy who smoked Vantage, probably the most impotent cigarette in the world. I bummed one as the meeting began, mentally crossing my fingers as I lit up with the rest of my brothers.

Aaron, one of the counselors and a former New York City cop who got knocked off the force after getting a DWI while on patrol in the Bronx, opened the meeting by saying, "Everyone knows booze'll give ya the limp dick, but what they don't realize is that booze for us is courage. Booze is how we got the guts to go get laid. Unfortunately, for some of us that meant leaving the old lady behind."

He got a few laughs and I realized his opening line wasn't a spontaneous remark, but more of an ice breaker like you might hear at a Rotary function. Then he went on to talk about feelings—probably the most-used word in a Twelve-Step meeting. Some of it was getting old already; a lot of it I had heard from D'Aoust and his staff. The idea was that liquor and drugs blocked off your feelings. And that once the blockage was removed, negative feelings resurfaced and made healthy relationships impossible.

"With all these new feelings pouring on," Aaron said, "it's normal to start questioning yourself. That might keep your dick gravity-bound for a while. You might find out you don't know love from liverwurst. Or you might find out what a shitty lover you really are. It can get very tense and you might have to separate for a while to see where your loyalties lie."

"Loyalties lie," I thought. Interesting phrase.

***

Poolside on Sunday afternoon. The sun was hot but the air was not as humid as the day before. Everything smelled clean from the previous night's rain and a gentle breeze rose and fell, caressing the hairs on my legs. My chair was the furthest one from the water, angled away from the pool area, which was populated exclusively with women clients and their women friends, some of them standing in the shallow end, talking, the majority sunning themselves on towels in the grass, flopping about randomly like seals on the beach.

I had my mail with me, and a diet Coke. Out of the corner of my eye I could see Blondie, her hair long and loose as she strolled waist deep through the water, tipping her head back and splashing little droplets on her face and chest.

I imagined a Twelve-Step meeting for people who dreamed the future. As main speaker I'd announce: "Halley's Comet made me a slut. I used the end of the world to justify fucking everyone I could. I lived without hope of heaven, without fear of hell. No wonder I thought sex was such a big deal all the time."

I played out my imaginary speech as I glanced at my unopened mail, fanning the envelopes with the rubber band still in the middle, looking in vain for a letter from Catherine. She had no idea what had become of me.

"That's right, people, Halley's Comet took away my values. Made me an insensitive man."

A bee landed on my Coke and crawled in the hole. A voice spoke from behind me. "Did you know this is women's swim only?"

I turned around and my eyes traveled slowly, hungrily up a pair of long, bare legs topped with a "Hugs Not Drugs" T-shirt. Like a No Trespassing sign, the shirt draped a neon pink bikini bottom winking seductively from the shadow where the legs came together. My eyes continued upwards to a face I recognized as belonging to one of the female counselors.

"I didn't know the pool was segregated," I said.

"Well, it is, so you're not supposed to be in the area. Besides, you have someone over there calling you." She pointed behind me.

I turned around. Mike stood at the door, wagging his finger.

I sighed. "My mistake," I said. I grabbed my things and walked toward him.

"Let's go," he said, dropping a hand on my shoulder. "What did I tell you about that pool, eh?"

"You said not to go in it."

"Near it, friend. You got a phone call. The pay phone by the door."

I walked off ahead of him.

"Remember, my friend," he called after me, "no more pool."

I reached the phone, hoping for Susan. It was Joni. She said they weren't coming up to see me today. Something about Richard working yesterday and needing the day off. She asked me how I was.

"Fine," I said, smiling because at today's meeting Aaron had defined that word as meaning Fucked-up, Insecure, Neurotic, and Empty. Joni said she was glad I was feeling fine. Then she asked me if I had my checkbook with me. I looked down, fanning my mail.

"No, I don't see it here," I said.

"Susan said she found it and brought it out to you. You didn't find it with your things?"

"I didn't put them all away yet," I said. "Maybe it's in the bottom of the other bag. Why? What's the matter?"

"What do you think your bank balance is right now?" she asked.

"I don't know," I said, feeling guarded until I could find out what she was after.

"You don't know how much money is in your checking account?" she said incredulously.

"I'm not saying that," I said, "I just wanna know why it's so important all of a sudden."

I heard Richard in the background, saying, "Come on, you can talk about that later."

"We just got the bill yesterday for your ambulance ride."

"What ambulance ride?"

"You know, when we took you out of Bellevue. The five-hundred-dollar ambulance ride."

"Jesus!" I heard Richard exclaim.

"I get it now," I said.

"Well, the reason I'm calling is that Susan said you had a few bills in there and I figured you probably haven't paid your rent yet, either, right? Your rent for August, Mark. Now I'm not saying you don't pay your rent. But anyway I thought that maybe, since you had your checkbook there, you ought to go through your mail and look for your bank statement, you know, just to be sure you know where you stand. You don't want to let these things slip by. In fact, if you need stamps, I can get you some stamps and the next time we come up we can sit down and make sure your bills are all caught up and maybe plan out how we're going to manage those resources until you get some more paychecks coming in. By the way, Susan said last Friday was payday and that you probably worked some hours from before you went to Pennsylvania, don't you think?"

"Maybe." My head felt clogged and throbbing with pain.

"Well," Joni continued, "Susan said that they're holding your check and that you need to notify them in writing to send it on to your address. Do you have any deposit slips with you? We'll have to mail it in but that's no problem. Richard banks by mail all the time. By the way, Richard says hi. How was your visit with Susan yesterday?"

I disconnected. First in my mind . . . then by hanging the phone up, carefully, as prescribed by the sign above. Hanging up felt so good that I wanted to hang up again, maybe a little harder the second time.

CHAPTER 30

Later that day I went back to the room and found Danny with his wife, a pretty, dark-haired thing with a cute figure and a pair of flashy green eyes that matched her green skirt below her ivory blouse.

"Sophie, I want you to meet my roommate, Mark. Mark's a really great playwright who's got a show going off Broadway."

"Oh, it's not that close to production," I said, feeling that the whole writing scene was a world away right now. However, his remark reminded me to look for my checkbook. Meanwhile, Danny took off his shirt and went into the bathroom.

"Sophie's joining us for dinner tonight," he said, his voice echoing off the tiles.

She smiled at me demurely, turning down the volume on her body language now that she was the only one on the bed. "Danny says you're a fabulous writer."

I found my checkbook. My last two entries were to Barry Gordon, star director. Seven hundred dollars and we hadn't picked our first actor yet, hadn't even found a place for the play.

"Do you have any samples of your writing with you?" Sophie asked, folding her hands in her lap.

"I don't believe this," I mumbled under my breath, too low for Sophie to hear. Seven hundred dollars for nothing.

"Beg pardon?" she said.

I forced a smile and told her politely I was here to gain a broader perspective, to hold the reins on my prodigious writing talent, for the time being, at least, so that I could clear up some lingering "suicide stuff" and a recurring death wish for the entire planet.

I went out the door desiring one thing—to be left alone.

Dinner was lovely. Sophie was lovely. Another guy at our table had his wife with him, too. He told me there were several rooms above the main lobby saved especially for weekends, when partners could spend the nights together. I thought about Susan and felt the flavor go out of my meal.

Danny said there was going to be a big meeting that night, an open meeting with singing and a guest speaker. It was an alumni night. The speaker, he had heard, was supposed to be funny.

After dinner I had an hour to myself. I turned down a game of tennis, electing instead to stroll towards the pond, ruminating how everyone in my life had their teeth in me to some degree, had some expectations I was supposed to fulfill. Susan demanded my loyalty. Joni expected fiscal fitness; she required I balance my books and pay up on time. Mike wanted me to play the game, the repentant alcoholic, so he could write a progress note or two. Danny and his wife—why, to them I had to be nothing short of Eugene O'Neill, and a grateful, graceful one at that.

But nobody listened to me. Or so I thought. I reached the pond and deviated from the path, selecting a secluded spot with a patch of moss on the bank where I could rest my feet against some exposed roots, hooking my shoes into them like stirrups. The gathering twilight subdued the pond. The sun, slanting behind tall trees on my left, burned no brighter than a 40-watt bulb. The pond was diffused, softened as though viewed through a misty lens.

It was all absurd to my way of thinking. The last couple of days I hadn't heard any voices. Good. But I was paying for that with real-life conflicts in every direction. To continue on that road meant the promise of even more conflicts, with all my interactions graded by the wardens of my life: Joni, Susan,

Mike, and people like D'Aoust. If I continued down this road the end result, it seemed to me, was an anonymity of the truest sense. I was to be nothing more than a compulsive do-gooder, a people pleaser, an ex-boat rocker, another hand raised at a meeting, a polite, smiling head nodder, a yes man, one more grateful, recovering drunk blabbing his stream of cliches.

Something rippled the water a few feet from shore. I half smiled at the thought that any moment there was a poisonous snake ready to snatch my life. And if the snake didn't get me, who would believe me when I told them there was a gang of killers waiting to do the same? Yet here were people who were supposed to be my friends, people with the audacity to think that they knew what was best for me. Totally absurd. No one could stand in my shoes, no one could take away my pain by calling it (as someone had at the most recent meeting) "terminal uniqueness." They didn't know the *meaning* of terminal uniqueness.

***

I returned in time for the alumni get-together, though I arrived about ten minutes late. They had just finished "How It Works" and all the announcements, and I chose an appropriate pause to enter the dining hall and slip into an empty chair at a table near the back. Mike, standing like a sentry with his arms crossed on the other side of the room, saw me but didn't register any emotion. The speaker, a well-dressed black man, was joined by his wife and family on the stage. After he and his wife spoke, one of his daughters dusted off the old piano and they entertained us all with gospel music. A couple of aluminum coffee pots were filled with hot water; people helped themselves to packets of instant hot cider, Sanka, and herbal teas. An assortment of cookies were cradled in three wicker baskets with paper napkins stuffed in the bottoms.

After the meeting I joined everyone milling about the lobby, talking to a fellow named Paul, who had been admitted only yesterday. Someone tapped on my shoulder and I turned to face Doc Bailey, a bearded, bookish man in his early seventies, New Beginnings' resident physician who squinted a bit and ambled with a stooped posture.

"Can I see you for a moment over here?" he said, motioning that I should follow him towards the admission office. We walked together and he opened the Dutch doors, asking me to follow him into a tiny office in the back. "Please sit down," he said.

I pulled up a wooden chair and noticed my file lying open on his desk. "How are we doing tonight?" he asked. He grabbed a stethoscope and blood pressure cuff off the top of a metal file cabinet.

"Pretty good," I said. "That was a great meeting."

"I've seen better," he said, removing his glasses and rubbing one eye. "You mind if I take your vital signs?"

"Not at all," I said. "Is there some kind of a problem?"

"Apparently not," he said. "That's why I asked *you*." He popped a thermometer in my mouth.

After he finished the doctor asked me if I had been hearing any voices.

"No," I said.

"Have you ever been admitted to a hospital before?"

"For an injury?"

"For any reason." He stood back and looked at me, squinting.

"Yes," I said, "I've been in the hospital for mental illness."

"Once?"

"Twice. But that was a long time ago."

"I see," he said, jotting some notes and then stroking his chin. "And were you given any medication at those times?"

"Yeah, but the stuff was horrible," I said. "Thorazine. I had all kinds of side effects."

"And let's see," he said, "I have here you're not allergic to any medications."

"That's right," I said, "but that Thorazine is a killer. There's no way I could ever take that again. You aren't planning on giving me any, are you?"

Bailey closed my file. "No, I'm not planning on giving you anything. My job is basically to administer drugs that have already been prescribed by another physician. Some of the folks here are on antidepressants and blood pressure medication, things like that. But, considering you came here from Doctor D'Aoust's, I'm assuming you are on no medication at the present time."

"Correct," I said.

"That's all," he said.

That night I couldn't sleep again. After several hours of listening to Danny's clockwork breathing, I decided to dress and go for a walk. Once again I snuck into the back courtyard, this time slinking close to the shadows because the moon was out, three-quarters full. I crouched low among the hedges and skirted the pool, avoiding the area in front of the tennis courts because it was illuminated by a pair of walkway lamps mounted on wood posts. I snuck behind them and cut across the path, heading for a road I believed was on the other side because I had heard cars going by in the daytime. After traversing a short stretch of woods I came upon the road, a narrow, country lane, and followed it uphill and around a few bends until I was far from New Beginnings. There were few houses on the road, now and then a distant light shone behind the trees, and no cars passed either way. A half mile further I came to another bend where, on my right, a dirt lane cut into the hillside. I followed that route and came immediately upon a large excavation, an open pit, where some kind of mining had been taking place. A deep bowl had been carved from the hill, the sheer rock sides glowed skull-white from the moon. I could see my shadow as I walked to a bulldozer stranded in the middle of the pit. The dozer rested like a dinosaur, alone. I looked around but there was nothing to be afraid of. I grabbed hold and climbed over the treads, raising myself to stand beside the driver's seat.

"Where are you?" I asked, first in a low voice, then shouting aloud. "Where are you?!?"

I turned and faced the moon. I wanted my old friends; Kelly, Danny, Reese. I wanted them to see this, to talk to me and share my feelings. They'd like it here. They knew what it was to live on the edge of night. They'd understand this need to dip into the darkness, to trespass a little, to howl at the moon.

**

After breakfast the next morning Doc Bailey took my blood pressure again. He asked me if I felt dizzy or experienced anything else out of the ordinary. I told him I hadn't, and if I did, he'd be the first to know.

I attended the morning meeting and afterwards joined Mike for another session, this one in a small conference room downstairs from the lobby. I ended up smoking three of his cigarettes but didn't get dizzy at all.

"You know what I did on the morning after my very first drunk?" I said. "I went back to the woods where I had puked my guts out, just to see the mess I made. I did that quite a few times. I'd go back and check out the beer cans, the place where I had fallen down, the fire where I burned my jacket sleeve. It was like going to Gettysburg to relive the battle. I'd stay there for an hour, maybe, just seeing it in my mind again. Isn't that nuts?"

"Funny you should mention that," Mike said, opening up his big palms and looking into them. "I'm from Pittsburgh. I don't know if you know anything about Pittsburgh, but it's famous for its neighborhood taverns, these little places right on the corner. I went back about five years ago to visit my brother for the holidays and wouldn't you believe it, there in the Sunday paper was this photograph of a tavern they were going to tear down, you know, to make way for some condominiums. Anyway, I got real sad and all because that place had been a home to me. I had been a big customer and knew everyone who drank there. I kinda got choked up, you know? I never expected it to hit me that way."

***

September 19, 1983
(Overheard on FM radio)

> "And you may find yourself
> living in a shotgun shack
> And you may find yourself
> in another part of the world
> And you may find yourself
> behind the wheel of a large automobile
> And you may find yourself
> in a beautiful house, with a beautiful wife
> And you may ask yourself—Well . . .
> how did I get here?"

(Morning session)

"Whoa! Stop right there, Mark," Bowman says, sitting up and pushing her chair back. "You're going on with all this forgiveness stuff but I think you need to listen to yourself talking. You're acting like, 'If everyone would just forgive me, then I'd be okay.' "

"That's right," I say.

"Are you prepared to go meet all these people and ask their forgiveness?"

"Looks like I'll have to," I say.

"Personally, I believe you're already forgiven. Just suppose for a moment that everyone forgave you for everything you ever did. How does that make you feel? Do you feel forgiven?"

I sit there and say nothing.

"Can you possibly imagine that the only person who has to do any forgiving is you, Mark?"

I sigh and look at the floor. I think about the days remaining in the month of September.

"Tell me, when you were younger, Mark, where did you think you'd be when you were twenty-seven?"

"And you may ask yourself
How do I work this?
And you may ask yourself
Where is that large automobile?"
And you may tell yourself
This is not my beautiful house!
And you may tell yourself
This is not my beautiful wife!

***

At the end of our conference Mike asked me if I had gone anywhere during the night. I stared at him and told him no. There's a rumor you slipped out last night, he said. Someone told him they had seen me going out the door.

"Be careful," he said.

During lunch I caught Doc Bailey watching our table and I remarked to Paul how I disliked the man, how suspicious he seemed.

"Does anyone else bother you?" Paul asked.

I told him about Mike and a few of the other counselors, how they were big on rules but short on compassion. I made some pretty vicious statements and gained no sympathy from Danny and the others as I attacked New Beginnings and the program in general. I got fired up, and after the meal I took a table in the little elevated game room of the lobby and set out to write my autobiography, once and for all. I was determined to put it all down and be damned for it, too. When I caught Bailey watching me as he passed by the fireplace, I decided to have a little fun, figuring he was spying anyway so why not give him a little show for his money? As I formed my words and started writing, I decided to mouth them as well, knowing that, to an esteemed physician such as he, my moving lips would be construed as an indication of mental illness—the psychotic equivalent to the universal choking sign.

I wrote. Lips moved.

Sometime later—and God only knows how time passes in such states—I got approached by Paul, who asked how I was doing. A second later Mike was behind him, hulking over, and asking me to join them both on the couch by the fireplace. He scooped up my papers and took the pencil out of my hand, keeping a firm clasp on my shoulder as they led me away.

"You know there's a meeting going on," Mike said.

"Oops."

Doc Bailey was the next to approach me. And behind him, Aaron, the counselor, and Danny, with my suitcase in his hand.

"I just got off the phone with Doctor D'Aoust," Bailey said. "He's expecting you."

CHAPTER 31

"What went wrong at New Beginnings?"

Dr. D'Aoust's marshmallow eyeballs seemed to bulge out and press against the back of his lenses. He blinked a few times and fixed me in a cold, hard stare, his face holding an odd little half-smile as he waited for my answer.

"That's just it," I said. "Nothing went wrong, Doc. Nothing happened at all."

"Then why would they send you back?"

"Don't you have their notes or something? Why don't you read what the nurse took down from the guys who brought me here?"

I sat up in bed. I was not in my old private room, but in one of the rooms with the four TVs. D'Aoust had pulled the curtain for privacy but it was certain that the other guys were listening. You heard every burp, fart, and phlegm in a semi private room.

"I'm more interested in what *you* think happened," D'Aoust said, touching the knot of his tan wool tie. He was sans suit, just a long white lab coat over a blue shirt.

"They said I was spending too much time alone. That's a lie, of course. Everything was in groups. Swimming, meals, meetings. I don't know what they were talking about. If I had a little free time, sure, I might have kept to myself. I just didn't feel like asking permission each time I wanted to do something."

"Why couldn't you go with someone else?"

"I didn't like anyone else. They're all old farts and all they talk about is the goddam program. It makes me sick. They form a crowd and feel sorry for each other."

"You think so?" D'Aoust pulled over a metal stool, sat on it while flipping through the pages of my old chart.

"Look," I said, "I skipped a few meetings. That I admit. But most of the time I didn't even know they were having a meeting."

"Did you ever leave the grounds?"

"No, of course not."

"Not at night?"

"No."

"Not for any reason?"

"Nope."

"I notice your knee shaking under the covers. Is there a reason for that?"

I looked down at what appeared to be a puppy suffering from hypothermia. I said nothing.

"What did you think of the doctor there?" D'Aoust asked.

I laughed. "Bailey? That guy's a joke." I swallowed and controlled my voice, which was choked and unnaturally high.

"He says he saw you talking to yourself."

"Damn!" I pounded my fist on the bed and looked up at the ceiling. "Naturally you're going to take his side," I said. "Why would you ever believe me?"

D'Aoust cocked his head. His big eyes seemed to shrink a little, to pull back in their sockets, while at the same time his whole face seemed to grow more relaxed. He reached out and tugged at the curtain, closing up a small gap behind him and encircling us fully. He leaned over and placed his hands on top of mine. "Do you think someone is reading your mind?" he asked quietly.

I heard one of the TVs mumbling about it being unsafe to do something but I couldn't hear the message clearly.

"Everyone's reading my mind," I said. "I feel like I'm on trial or something."

"Is that why you're disappearing when you should be at the meetings?"

"I don't know," I said. "It's like I got this voice inside me that's always behind whatever I say or do. I could be talking to you and I hear this voice that says what a liar I am and how you better not find out what I really think of you. Even if I tell the truth—and know it's the truth—it goes on anyway, accusing me of being phony, of being falsely sincere. That's why I can't stand the meetings. I wanna stand up and say what's really bothering me but my mind tells me what an ego trip that is, what a crazy game I'd be playing to get everyone's attention and sympathy."

D'Aoust sighed and gave my hand a squeeze. "Believe it or not," he said, "I understand that much more than you'll ever know." He removed his glasses and rubbed his eyes. "Can I ask you if you hear it now?"

"All the time," I said, rolling away from him. "I don't get a break. Yeah, maybe a day or two goes by and I forget this stuff, but then something happens and it starts all over. I don't want to live like this, Doctor. If you guys want to kill me so bad, why don't you hurry up and get it over with? Just give me a shot or put poison in my food."

I heard a laugh from the other side of the curtain. "Tell fuckhead poison *is* in the food," someone said.

"Do you really think we want to kill you?" D'Aoust said, placing a hand on my shoulder and rolling me back.

"Maybe not you," I said, "but someone will."

After more questioning I admitted to Doctor D'Aoust that I was in fear for my life; I described as best I could the gang of killers who had pursued me since the Brooklyn Bridge and I further illuminated him on the nature of the bloodbath awaiting me. I told him I believed some of my fellow patients (as well as his staff) might be part of the conspiracy. When he asked me specifically about the television, I denied that I heard voices coming from it. Hell, *every* psychotic got his messages there; it was an unfortunate cliche. Of course I didn't mention

Halley's Comet either, as that would raise questions about the future for everyone. More rumors would only earn sanction for the crazed torturers eager to skin me alive, quite possibly swelling their ranks.

I promised to notify D'Aoust, his nurses, even the fucking dietary workers at the exact moment I began hearing voices or suspecting that someone was about to kill me. I promised to report all paranoid thoughts. I swore it and meant it.

He asked me if I would go to any length to get well. I said I would. He asked if I was willing to follow his instructions to the letter, even if he recommended taking a year off to regain my health. Again I said I would.

We shook hands on the deal, mine being taken in his firm, decisive grip.

There were some new junkies on the unit and some old faces as well. The staff treated me kindly, helping me refamiliarize myself with the routine. Needless to say, I began to miss the freedom of New Beginnings: the woods, trails, green lawns, the spacious dining hall, and the main lodge with its fireplace flickering peacefully at night. On Huntington's locked unit, I was limited to one tiny day room with its box of battered Zane Gray paperbacks plus its nightmare of board games, a closet stuffed with Clue, Monopoly, Life, Parcheesi, each box smashed flat at the corners. I dreaded lifting their tops off because I would no doubt witness their guts scattered in a manner that would only reinforce my depression—the missing battleship, the missing wheelbarrow, a homemade St. Charles Place deed drawn with a purple crayon—and make me loathe my childhood, my compulsive, orderly mother, and further mirror my pain-filled search for the missing pieces in my soul. Beyond that I could do nothing but lie in bed, stand before an open refrigerator, or walk round and round the same locked unit.

Nurse Carla was the first to remark that I was feeling low. "Just a little setback," she said, turning the valve on my blood pressure cuff and squeezing out the air.

Setback? True, I thought. Am I thinking of killing myself? Yes, I said, all the time. Especially during commercials.

The junkies teased me. Cream of tomato became "suicide" soup. I became Steve Brodie or "Brodie Man," my nickname given in honor of the nineteenth-century playwright who leapt his way to fame off the Brooklyn Bridge. In its most poignant usage, my new name became a verb, as in "Yeah, my roommate's the guy who Brodied off the bridge last month," which I overheard from someone at the pay phone in the hall.

Speaking of pay phones, Susan called. It was not good. It was not bad. She shared her condolences, telling me I'd be back on my feet in no time, and promising to see me whenever I truly recovered. The word "truly" stuck in my gut. I wasn't so stupid that I couldn't see the positive side of her phone call, but I was also depressed and the overall effect of hearing her voice, hearing her talk about work and the sights of Manhattan—the overall effect produced a bittersweet feeling, a sense that she might be forgiving me, but that it was all in vain. I was going to die and that was the end of it.

Clint Eastwood still fucked with my brain. Those goddam steely eyes above that pilot's oxygen mask. That set jaw. His cool, deliberate determination. He mocked everything I had allowed myself to become. So did the television announcers for a New York Giants pre-season football game, all of them studly and jocular and confidently male, wrapped in their all-male vocabulary. Deep pass. Tight end. Score. Appropriate baritone laughter. Manly as lug nuts in a hub cap, manly as greasy hands lathered with kerosene, manly as cleats, as a dirty towel rotting on a locker room floor, as an overturned hard hat with a stainless steel thermos sticking out, rivets on an I-beam, the cigar smell of the foreman's shack, the peg board hung with tools, bowling trophies on the shelf like the heads of wild game, a photo of the company-sponsored Little League team next to last year's Rigid calendar, the page corners smudged with fingerprints, fingerprints on the model's breasts.

I was a wimp and deserving to die. In the examining room I felt like a corpse standing on the scale. My pulse seemed weak. There was only one word to describe my condition: emaciated. I was dried and brittle as a milkweed pod. Beneath my hospital pajamas I was certain I was wasting away, no more muscular shoulders, no more definition of chest. I returned to smoking as to a favorite sport, fulfilling a death wish with every puff, imagining with morbid detail the little black pockets of tar, the nicotine collecting and filling up my lungs just like Sister Cecilia's chalk marks on my soul.

D'Aoust saw me every day. I had no trouble confessing my delusions. "They were in the parking lot last night," I'd say, "tossing stones at my window. I think they're going to use chopsticks. In my eardrums. Chopsticks dipped in cayenne or poison." I shared my paranoia with the nurses as well. I requested one of them to help me draft my will. They handled it with nonchalance. I don't know if they had been coached to downplay my anxieties, but by not arguing with me about the validity of my suspicions (other than a kindly pat on my hand and a murmuring of "We both know that can't be true,") the end result was that I believed they, too, saw and heard the same demons and voices and were watching the time tick down to my final day and execution. I gave up. The nursing staff—accustomed to the bizarre PCP abuser who last admission had performed *The Exorcist* live—were understandably relieved to be handling a much more sedated individual the second time around. Because I wasn't fighting it, my situation didn't appear to be dangerous. But deep inside I was all the more convinced there was nothing to be done for me. Nothing, that is, except to be allowed to stray into the forest, to fall before the wolves.

CHAPTER 32

Sometime around my third or fourth day back at Huntington I was awarded off-floor privileges, which amounted to nothing more than an escorted trip to the hospital gift shop. I went with four other guys, all of us in our pajamas, foam slippers, and robes. As I strolled aimlessly, pennilessly by the stuffed pink rabbits, the balloons, the get well cards, the chocolate-covered cherries, and the real and artificial flowers, the magazine racks and the Baby Ruth candy bars, I was seized by a feeling I couldn't comprehend.

(We had come down in the elevator, joking, slapping palms, punching arms, accompanied by Bernie, the male nurse who didn't discourage our hooting at the nurses. We had come down as a gang of friends and for a moment I forgot who I was and the evil waiting for me. I laughed and whistled with the rest of them, enjoying for the brief moment a sense of comradeship and effortless humor.)

Initially, the feeling was pleasant. It was déjà vu, a sense that I was young again, maybe ten or twelve, and that the patients I was with, the strangers, were my old friends who used to accompany me into stores—

—to shoplift. We'd come in and split up, going down the aisles, our deft little fingers working candy bars down our pants or up our sleeves.

The memory turned sour. Then it went from sour to worse, becoming a mild sensation that I was losing control. The memory of stealing bottles of beer, sticking them in my inside coat pocket, then stealing from neighbors, from friends' parents, flooded me to the point that I grew dizzy and hot. I had to hold on to the cashier counter, knowing full well that I was alarming Bernie—and everyone else, for that matter. It was as if I were reliving the incident, the guilt and fear like sweat, like emotional poison oozing out my pores.

I had to be taken back in a wheelchair. Later, I related the experience to Doctor D'Aoust, who was comforting, but in an obscure manner. "We're all in the same church," he said. "We just move from pew to pew."

D'Aoust had a special meeting with me the next afternoon. It was in the examining room, where he personally checked all my vitals.

"You know I really can't keep you much longer," he said. "And that scares me. But there's nothing more I can do for you here. You can attend my lecture again tomorrow. But that's it. It's all I can give you—except the strongest advice to take a year to recover. You have no idea the abuse your poor body's been through."

"I'll consider that," I said. "I really will."

"Can you indulge me for a moment?" D'Aoust said, hopping up on the exam table and setting my chart down at his side. "You know, I often say that we're carriers of information, but I get the feeling not too many people understand what I'm saying."

"I'm not sure about that one, either."

"Part of it is my own personal philosophy, Mark. It has a lot to do with being a doctor. I wasn't always in the detox business. I used to be in internal medicine. I had a practice in conjunction with a pair of surgeons—two of the best, let me assure you. However, it was my constant impression that people came to me to make them well. What I'm saying is that they came to me like you might go to an automobile mechanic. 'Fix me,' they'd say. 'Give me a pill and make the problem go away.' Nobody ever wanted to take responsibility for their own health."

D'Aoust crossed his legs and swung his feet gently, his hands on the padded edge of the table, his fingernails clean and uniformly clipped. "The information I try to carry is a message of individual power. I try to be the one doctor who takes the pills away, who tries to get my patients to see that they're the ones who got in the mess, and it's their responsibility to get out."

"I think I understand that," I said.

"No one is even close to fully understanding the link between experience and electrochemical changes in the brain," he said, rapping his knuckles on my chart. "However, you, my friend, are the direct product of how this theory functions. Repeated behavior ingrains certain chemical pathways in the brain. Your neurotransmitters run on these paths. Neurotransmitters are the guys who carry your messages. Every time you repeat an action or experience a strong emotion, you're creating a type of habit, wearing a path. That's why practice in sports produces great athletes. It's also why escape artists often end up drunks or dope fiends. To change behavior, especially addictive behavior, means creating new pathways and new chemical reactions."

I tried to follow him but my face showed the difficulty I was having. "Oh, forget it," he said. "That's enough for now. Tomorrow I sign release papers for six more people just like you. I'll tell them everything I just finished telling you. And you know what? I'll give them the same odds, too. Honestly, Mark, it's about one in a thousand. No matter how simple the solution seems to be."

He sighed and hopped off the table. "I suppose another way of looking at it is like being the bugle blower for the troops ready to charge into battle. I really want to see you get through this one."

Doctor D'Aoust, the oddball creature with the Einstein hair and the Mr. Potato Head features, the googly eyes, the slug for a mustache, good ol' Doctor D'Aoust removed his glasses, and looking at me—looking *through* me—reached out and hugged me, and I caught by electrochemical transmission some small amount of the love he had for me. He squeezed me like he might never see me again. For a moment I was lost in his warm embrace.

"If you're going to be a carrier of information," he said, his arms still around me, "then you're going to have to start with what little you know. Try to understand recovery, Mark. If you make it, you've got to pass that on. No matter how bad you think you've got it, there's always someone worse off than you. You may not know this now, but helping others is a very selfish thing."

***

Richard, Joni, and her two children drove me back to New Beginnings. Jennifer and Courtney wore white sundresses, both beaming with cherub complexions and golden hair looking as though they were making their first communions.

"How's work, Richard?" I asked. The Catskill scenery slipped by, sun and shade rolling over the windshield.

"Things could be a lot better," he said. "Right now we're long on orders, short on help."

"He's got union problems," Joni said. "Maybe you can get a job with him when you're done with the recovery center."

"And you can try the East River again," Richard said, "this time with concrete flippers."

"Richard, it's not that bad."

"Courtney has something to show you, Mark." Jennifer smiled, tugging at something in her sister's hand.

I turned around. "What do you have there?" I asked.

Courtney covered her blue eyes with her hand and held out a crayon drawing. "What's this?" I said, taking the paper and looking at a stick figure dropping upside down into a body of water.

"That's you going off the bridge," Jennifer said.

Richard smiled, shaking his head slowly. Embarrassed, Courtney buried her face in the car seat.

"Courtney has something to ask you," Joni said.

I looked up from the drawing.

"She wants to know if you're going to have an operation," Jennifer said, poking her sister. Courtney appeared to be on the verge of crying.

"I'm not going to have an operation," I said. "Do you believe that, Courtney? Come here. Do you want to sit in the front with me?"

She nodded, stretching out her arms for me to take hold.

After I was readmitted I rejoined my family in the lobby. Joni presented me with another stack of mail. "Maybe we should go back to your room," she said, "to be sure your checkbook's still there."

"The girl at the desk told me they put it in the safe," I said.

"Good. Well, open this one here," she said, pulling out a large gray envelope. "I think it's your grades from the university."

Richard waved to someone, excusing himself from our company. The girls began fidgeting. I opened the envelope. A computer form listed my courses for the past spring semester, and beside them was a letter grade.

"Not bad," Joni said, leaning over. "Three As and one B. And this envelope, I believe, is your scholarship for next year."

We opened that and both smiled, as I had been awarded an additional three hundred dollars.

"How'd you get my mail?" I asked.

"Susan dropped off the key," she said, restraining Courtney, who was tugging on her sleeve. "Okay, girls, you can go off and play. Outside somewhere is a swimming pool."

Two little white dresses dashed off down the hall.

"I heard about your fight, little brother."

"Susan told you?"

"No details, but the reason was pretty obvious when I went

inside your place. She's taking it pretty badly, you know."

I dropped the mail beside me and slid low on the couch. "It's a mess," I said.

"I'd sure like to know what happened back in Pennsylvania. I would think by now you'd have serious reservations about those friends of yours—and I use that term cautiously, believe me."

"I'm dealing with it," I said.

"You're just going to have to find better friends. I hope that Catherine wasn't part of it." Joni and her had met on one of Catherine's trips to New York.

"Leave her out of this," I said. "Please. In the first place, she wasn't there. In the second, it wasn't anyone else's fault, either. I did it. I did it to me."

"Mom called yesterday. Did I tell you?"

"I guess not. But go ahead, what's the verdict?" Doc Bailey and Mike walked by, absorbed in conversation. Mike looked up for a moment and nodded to me, then continued on his way.

"How's Mike?" Joni asked. "Richard just loves him."

"Mike's okay. So what's the latest on Mom?"

Joni leaned back and put her arm around the back of the couch. "Basically, she's calming down. I talked to Dad and he said she's stopped going to church all day. I imagine she's worn down a few sets of rosary beads, but she sounded fairly level, you know, ready to deal with the facts of the matter. Of course, like everyone else, she wants to know how this all came about, especially with you doing so well in school and on the verge of becoming a playwright."

"I take it you're handling my press releases," I said.

"Hopefully not much longer," she said, sitting forward and pulling some things out of her purse. "Here's some postcards," she said, "and stamps. They're small postcards so you don't have to say much, if you don't want to. It's just a way to let everyone know you're feeling better. And look, here's a Xerox of my address book. I copied the pages with your brothers' addresses, in case you forgot. I also found a canceled check of yours so I went to the bank and had them make up some deposit slips. Do you know what this is?" she said.

I took a white window envelope out of her hand. "It's my paycheck," I said. "Thanks."

Joni sat up and squeezed her knees together, placing a hand on top of mine. "Look," she said, "I understand your anger with all of this. I can even accept that you're angry with me. I'm not trying to run your life. I honestly don't mean to make things worse for you. But please let me help you, Mark. I don't want to see your world fall apart because of this one incident."

She squeezed my hand and I turned it over, clasping hers firmly in return. "I'm sorry for hanging up on you," I said.

"I deserved it," she said. "But can you see it from my point of view? You didn't die, Mark. It had to be for a very important reason. You don't talk to the doctors the way I do, little brother. This Bailey guy, Mike, Doctor D'Aoust—they're all totally amazed at what you've been through. You're blessed. You really are. And I love you. I'm not going to let a few bill collectors or your school or your boss back at Mitchell-Walker stop you from achieving your goals. You're meant for big things, Mark. You didn't come all the way to New York City to wind up a failure. It's important to remember that. You hit death head-on and came out without a scratch."

"Thanks," I said, giving my sister a hug. "I'll go through all my mail and see where I stand. I'll let you know if there's anything you can do for me."

Joni looked across the lobby. "You know Richard will loan you anything you need."

"Hey, did I pick up that he's having trouble with his workers, or was he just making a joke?"

"Unfortunately, he's got very serious trouble in some areas," Joni said. "But don't you worry. No one knows that business like Richard does. Look, here he comes now."

I followed my sister's gaze, catching sight of her husband coming toward us, Jennifer and Courtney each holding a hand.

Sunlight poured through a stained glass window, passing over his shoulder, making the three of them look like an Easter card. From nowhere, rising as an empty feeling in my stomach, came a shudder at the thought of the whole world ending. Courtney and Jennifer had only three more years to live.

CHAPTER 33

Soon after dinner Joni and the others departed. I collected my checkbook and clothes at the office and moved back into my former room. Danny had been discharged. He left a note on my bed. "Good luck and take it one day at a time," it said. Below that was his name and phone number.

Returning to the lobby, I passed Doc Bailey in the hall. He stopped me and advised me—very kindly, as a matter of fact—that he was obliged to take my vitals every morning. He also reminded me that I could go nowhere alone, and that attending meetings was compulsory. "Mike agrees with me," he said. "Miss one meeting and I'm afraid we'll have no choice but to view that as noncompliance. The result will be discharge on the following day."

"I'll do better this time," I said, entertaining a picture of me on the front steps, suitcase in hand, saying goodbye to New Beginnings. All in all, late August was not a bad time for travel. I could go by foot across New York to Erie. I could camp out at night and eat wild game and berries. I'd head for the bulldozer and get my bearings there.

I went to the evening meeting. I volunteered to read "How It Works," sucking up all the " 'Atta-boy" peer support and oh-my-what-a-good-servant-you-are feelings my ego could generate. I had a session with Mike afterwards, the big guy keenly interested in my somber mood, or, as I had often charted on my own patients at Ronson Lodger, my "flat affect."

"It's important to look beyond this depression," he said.

"Sometimes it's merely the beginning of acceptance." Once again he stressed the importance of writing my history down.

I went to my room that night and opened all my mail. The bills were small and manageable. I had a rent due notice. And a letter from a high school friend in California, someone who had no idea what I was going through.

I fell asleep listening to the breeze and crickets outside my window. The last thought on my mind (whispered, it seemed, from another source) was: "Make friends with the executioner. Now *that's* acceptance."

Waking the next morning, I recalled a dream about a bird in a tree. I was scared for the bird because my father—or maybe it was Mike—was chopping the tree down, trying to get at the bird.

***

Flunking out: that was the feeling. I felt I had let everyone down. Even the poor old winos, the wetbrains, the guys with no livers, they seemed to know something I didn't, seemed to be more ready to roll with the program.

All that next day my anxiety grew like a cancer. I missed Doctor D'Aoust. I wanted to go back to Huntington and hide beneath my sheets.

A subtle change was taking place around New Beginnings. Just about everyone I had known was getting discharged, going home. A new crop of fellows appeared: mean, crude, ugly. It was a massive changing of the guard and I became alarmed because the thought occurred to me that the hit squad, those demonic killers who had been stalking me at a distance, were now infiltrating the recovery center, disguised as patients, and preparing the area for a bloodbath feast. I finally figured out who my friends were; it was everyone who was leaving. I went so far as to imagine that Mike was involved with the demons, attributing to him the name Bludgeon because of his powerful arms and chest. He seemed like he'd prefer me to be standing, with my back against a concrete wall, perhaps, so he could whop me good with a two-by-four. Very blue collar. Doc Bailey, on the other hand, would want to spend the minimum of energy while keeping his fingernails clean. Obviously, the name for him was Injection. He'd shoot me full of drugs that exaggerated pain. Aaron, who wore a size 13 shoe, by my estimate, would assume the role of Ballkicker, or perhaps Shoe-in-Face. Paul, the little rat who had turned me in, got the name Icepick because I sensed he wanted to stand behind me, unseen, and ram a cold steel rod through the base of my brain.

Sitting there in the lobby, appearing calm by outside observation, my mind nevertheless entertained a fiendish version of the Miss America talent competition. As each new patient walked by, I assessed their apparent strengths and weaknesses in the area of physical torture. Skinny guys got the knives and branding irons. The more husky fellas were awarded clubs and brass knuckles. A large Native American checked in at the desk and I called him Arrow-up-the-Ass, releasing my most repressed vision of an unpleasant hereafter.

It was clear to me that time had run out. Whatever was going to happen was going to happen right here, right away, and right at the hands of those who stood around me.

As if on cue, the white tooth of a priest's collar caught my eye as a man in black entered the lobby.

"Father," I called, getting up to chase after him. "Father."

"Yes?" He turned and faced me. He was a man in his late forties with a round, unremarkable face and straight black hair that, though slicked down, revealed itself graying and receding at his forehead and temples.

"Father, I have a confession."

"Confession? You, ah, you are in need of a witness in Christ?" His voice—which I would have preferred to be strong, resonant, assuring—was rather unsteady, betraying an irritation of some kind. His eyes looked past me and I sensed he was preoccupied.

"I've got to talk to somebody right away," I said.

It wasn't until he grabbed my arm that I realized I had first taken hold of his sleeve, clutching it with unusual intensity. "I'm only here to drop these off," he said, holding up some stapled sheets of paper that appeared to be hymns. I looked at him imploringly, my eyes locked up with his, my body blocking his further progress. He cleared his throat, turning his wrist in the manner that businessmen consult their watches.

"I suppose we can sit somewhere for a few minutes," he said. "Wait here while I take care of these and I'll go find a room we can use."

"Thank you, Father. Thank you so very, very much."

I went back to my seat in the lobby, feeling the weight of everyone's eyes. They know now, I thought. They saw me take the bait. One of the new guys sat hunched over with his knees spread apart, rubbing the palms of his hands together as though warming them over a fire. The show was about to begin.

In a few moments the priest returned. He signaled with his hand, and I followed him up a winding staircase that led above the admissions office. He opened a door to a small, narrow room with one tiny window at the back. A bookcase brooded against the left wall, and beside it two wooden folding chairs sat facing each other. We each took a chair, the priest in front of me with the window light behind him.

"I'm Father Patrick," he said. "How can I help you?"

He was anything but my fantasy priest. He had an impatient, breathless quality. I thought for sure he was anxious to get out of there before the massacre started.

I folded my hands and hung my head over them. "Father," I said, "I'm in bad shape."

He placed a hand on my right shoulder. "All the more reason to talk to God, my son."

I looked up. "But will he forgive me?" I said. "I've got to know. I've got to be forgiven."

"God is all-forgiving. It's we who find it hard to forgive."

"But I'm scared, Father. How will I know I'm forgiven?"

Father Patrick leaned back and folded his hands in his lap. "That's the faith part, my son. But if you are truly sorry for your sins and vow never to repeat them again, it is our Father's will that you be forgiven. He loves his children, He really does."

"Not me," I said. "Not after what I've done."

"Perhaps telling me can help you ease your burden."

Tell him I did. I spoke of everything that had been held back from Mike, D'Aoust, and all the others. Stealing, adultery, lies, and blasphemy—I confessed to stealing drugs from a dead woman as I wheeled her body to the hospital morgue. I confessed to stealing my own father's pain medication that he needed after his kidney surgery. I had sniffed glue. I had boiled Paragoric. As far as sex was concerned, if women had been chickens, I would have been Colonel Sanders.

An hour later I was through. Father Patrick seemed somewhat transformed by the exchange. He was no longer edgy and impatient. When our eyes met at the finish, he seemed to look deeply into me, recognizing the bag of filth that had become my soul. He seemed to know, finally, that he was in attendance to the Anti-Christ, the most horrible human being to ever walk the earth.

Father Patrick clasped both hands around my head, pressing his palms against me tightly as he pronounced several prayers. He asked me to say my Act of Contrition, and I knew it was curtains because I couldn't remember one word of the all-important Catholic prayer. We said it together with me stumbling on every word.

Lastly, the good priest gave me some penance—ten Hail Marys and an Our Father—which was like dabbing your nose with sunblock to protect your face from a nuclear blast. Penance wasn't the word for what was going to happen to me.

I left the room and descended the stairs. I looked one last time over the lobby, imagining what it would be like, only minutes from now, stained with my blood: the moose heads, the Bill Wilson portrait, the wagon wheel chandelier.

Right in front of me on the black vinyl couch sat the big Native American, holding up a leather pouch from which he pulled—as though my fear had placed it there—a long, steel-shafted arrow. He smiled at a fellow sitting across from him as he lifted the arrow and eyeballed the shaft, turning it as though inspecting the rifling of a gun barrel. He ran his thumb along the four razors of the arrowhead.

My adrenal glands emptied. A voice of panic gave one clear command: Get out! NOW! I took one last look at the arrow and dashed out the front door. I raced down the steps and out across the drive, running past the flagpole, the big, silver chopstick with the rag tied on top.

CHAPTER 34

I picked a hot day to run away. Waves of heat radiated above the sticky tar road. I ran along the edge, feeling the heat through my tennis shoes; it was like running on a frying pan. I looked over my shoulder to see if I was being followed. I saw no one but I was scared anyway. I started looking for a side road or perhaps a path into the woods where I might hide. Unfortunately, both sides of the road were bracketed by barbed wire or clumps of jagged brush. Mailboxes, resembling silver loaves of bread, topped posts at the entrances to long, dirt driveways, which told me the land had owners and that I'd probably find trouble if I trespassed off the road.

About a mile from New Beginnings I heard the sound of an automobile coming up behind me. I turned and saw it was an old blue Ford Galaxy, the kind with the vinyl roof that looked like it had been through a razor blade car wash. It pulled alongside of me, matching my pace as I trotted slowly, growing more winded by the moment. Someone yelled something from inside the car. I bent down to see who it was. There was an old man behind the wheel, and beside him, an old woman, both characters in their late sixties whom I recognized from the treatment center. The man was an employee. I had seen him blowing leaves off the tennis courts with an air compressor. The old woman was either an employee or a patient; I remembered her face but, of course, had never spoken to her.

The car came to a stop and the man gestured for me to get inside. I grabbed the front door handle.

"Get in the back," he said.

I opened the front door. "*You* get in the back," I said, locking my fingers around the woman's wrist. I pulled her arm, attempting to slide her off the seat. I did not know she was the old man's wife.

"Bastard!" the old man shouted. He leaned over and caught his wife's leg. In doing so, his foot came off the brake and the car rolled forward. I yanked the woman halfway out the car and for a moment we tugged on his wife like two kids fighting over a piece of taffy. I pulled harder and she lurched forward, her left hand catching the window raiser. She had a red vinyl purse on her left shoulder and it slid down to her elbow. In desperation the old man caught hold of that. I pried her left hand loose and for one brief moment the only thing still attaching her to the car—holding her in the air, for that matter—was the purse strap caught at the bend of her elbow, the purse clutched in her husband's fingers.

The car rolled faster. "You're killing me!" she shouted.

"Fucking witch!" With a final tug the purse strap broke. I swung the woman free and dropped her on the road. She cleared the rear wheel, rolling off the berm and into a ditch.

Now it was the old man's turn. I caught the passenger door, reaching inside to lock claws with my adversary. His face twisted in terror. "Get out!" I yelled. But his other hand still gripped the wheel. Out of my periphery I could see we were rolling faster, the front wheels pulling us to the other side of the road. Cursing, scratching, slugging, I forced his other hand free and climbed over him to secure the wheel. We wrestled on the seat and I gained control, switching positions as I pushed him towards the door. With my legs I pushed him out, his fingers digging into the upholstery—in vain—as he slid off the seat. Head and chest disappeared first, then the legs with a flurry of frog kicks, his body hitting the road and sounding like a stack of apples spilling on a supermarket floor.

I got behind the wheel and gained control of the Galaxy.

The highway twisted before me. I hadn't driven in over a year. The slightest pressure on the gas delivered incredible power. It seemed like I could accelerate to the moon and back. I checked my speed: thirty-five miles an hour. But instead of racing away with complete abandon, I did just the opposite. I checked my side and rear view mirrors. I checked my fuel. I felt for a seat belt and made sure my hands were positioned correctly on the wheel.

"Let's not break any more laws," I warned myself, trying to engender a feeling of good citizenship as compensation for the deed I had done. For a long time I remained understandably nervous, but, crisis behind me and car in hand, I grew remorseful as I considered the consequences for stealing the car.

"Fuck," I said. "A felony." I had dumped the old couple out on the road. There'd be assault charges. And more hospital bills, this time for my victims.

"Better kill yourself," an old, familiar voice said. "Yep, you messed up so bad there's no fixin' it this time, pal.

"Better kill yourself. Better do it right this time."

I agreed. What I needed was a bridge abutment, one that was visible from far away. I was too scared to drive over the speed limit, so I wanted to be able to see my target ahead of time rather than go whipping around the curves and end up in a ditch and still be alive. It had to be a flat wall, plain as day, with a nice stretch of highway in front so I could accelerate, once I was sure I couldn't miss it.

I completely forgot I was escaping the demons. Ballkicker, Shoe-in-Face, Arrow-up-the-Ass—they meant nothing to me now. My new enemy was myself. Or, as the voice in my head had me believe, my new enemy was failure. I was terrified of trying to kill myself and not achieving some results.

But I still couldn't stop driving cautiously. Several times I passed beneath an underpass—one a very fine underpass, a black iron railroad bridge supported by big black stones. It was perfect. But I couldn't do it. Bad enough I had stolen the car, I thought, no need to wreck it.

"But you're going to kill yourself. It won't matter."

"Yes it will. I'll probably fail. I'll be in real trouble then."

My knuckles grew white from gripping the wheel. At the bottom of a winding valley I came to a town, a congested little burg tucked beside a river. At the first intersection I grew overwhelmed by all the highway signs. There were Routes 23, 10, and 17. I could go east, west, north, or south. I could head for Albany, Binghamton, or down to Poughkeepsie. I could turn right, left, or stay where I was. Should I put my blinker on? Do I ask for directions? Or do I cut the wheel and never turn back?

The light changed and the person behind me tooted their horn. Bearing right was the easiest thing to do, so I turned the wheel and headed past a series of gas stations, convenience stores, and small brick buildings. A gas station up ahead looked like a nice place to stop. I pulled in, put the car in park, and shut off the engine. Leaving the keys on the seat, I got out of the car and started walking up the road. (I was to learn later that the old couple had been making a bank deposit for New Beginnings; there was six thousand dollars in the glove compartment.)

The road wound uphill and I trudged on, totally lost, totally uncertain as to what might happen next. There was no sidewalk so I made my way along the shoulder, the traffic whizzing past me only a few feet away. A group of children appeared at the top of the hill, descending on the other side. They waved candy bars and soda cans. I swore they knew who I was, that they were talking about me. In fact, with each car that passed in the opposite direction, I imagined that the occupants knew damn well who I was and were glad I was finally getting around to killing myself. I was the mad dog who needed to be shot. Every driver who passed wished it would be his car I would choose for my sacrificial altar. All I had to do was pick one, close my eyes, and leap in front. Physics would do the rest.

I crested the hill and reached a clearing bordered by a tall chain-link fence on my right with some kind of light industry on the other side. A white car with lights slowed ahead of me, pulling to the side of the road. A blue-uniformed man hopped out of the driver's door, talking into something he held in his hand. He went for something at his side, yelling at me, "Hold it right there!"

I turned and ran the opposite way. I could hear his footsteps gaining on me, a sound like coins in his pocket and things jingling from his belt. The stampede sound gained behind me, and I felt a tremendous weight slam against my back. My legs buckled, and our momentum carried us both into the fence, my face and arms pressing into the silver squares. I felt like I had been made into a waffle. We bounced off and landed on the ground, the officer hauling me up and pushing me against the fence again, my face once more pressing into the metal grid.

"Spread 'em!" he yelled, kicking the insides of my shins apart while he muscled my arms behind my back. I felt cold steel bracelets lock on my wrists.

It was the best feeling in the world. I was no longer under my own power.

Hurray. The war was over.

CHAPTER 35

Ronson Lodger Medical Center, 1982:

"Doctors Bruenell, Horschak, Ms. Meyers—I want you to meet Mark Wolyczin, who'll be your personal guide through our security section."

Nurse Danetti smiled nervously. The two doctors and the woman with them nodded upon my introduction, but they held onto their clipboards, not offering up their hands to shake. Too much time. I found them hopelessly morose—just the kind of people who visit places and award certificates of approval. Later on at lunch, no doubt, they would make safe, bland comments about safe, bland food.

"We're pleased to show the members of the accreditation committee a whole new section since you've seen it last," Danetti said, fingering her lapel. "Go ahead, Mark, show them the bathroom first."

"First off," I said, leading them around the corner and into the heart of the security wing, "notice the rubber fixtures for the hot and cold water. They bend, never break. And thus, can never be used as a weapon." I bent down and turned the faucets on the tub.

Doctor Horschak laughed. "Where's the water?" he said. "Looks like you failed to put in the plumbing."

"Precisely," I said, walking back to the shatterproof window and rapping on the glass with my flashlight. Todd flashed me the okay sign and turned a valve below the desk.

Water gushed out of the faucet. "We control the plumbing at the nurses' station," I said, "simply with a flick of the wrist. This achieves two goals simultaneously, ladies and gentlemen." I raised a brow at the woman, holding it there for dramatic pause.

"Our first goal, we protect our patients from accidental hot scalding situations and, of course, the odd possibility of a suicidal drowning—or, for that matter, any flooding or other mischief. But at the same time, with unit policy specifying no running water unless manually controlled, well, it more or less guarantees that our security-risk patients can never bathe without proper supervision. And that, of course, eliminates the risks I previously mentioned."

I had never been pumped up so much in my life. I was running on four cups of coffee and a surplus of anger. The night before, Rhonda, pediatric nurse extraordinaire, had told me to take a hike.

I smiled at Head Nurse Danetti and she beamed her approval.

"I take it supervised bathing is not a policy for the rest of the unit," said Ms. Meyers, noting something on her clipboard.

"Heavens forbid," I said. "Of course not."

"Show them the towel rack," Danetti said.

"First, how about our implanted mirror?" I said, directing attention at a round metal disk. "It was built right into the wall. A further precaution against someone . . . what? . . . perhaps bludgeoning themselves against the side of the tub, I suppose. It won't stop them, of course, but we'll have a ringside view whenever they do it."

Ms. Meyers lowered her chin and peered over the top of her glasses. "But what if the patient's behaving?" she said. "Doesn't the mirror expose the patient unnecessarily before the entire staff?"

I laughed. "You know, I never thought of it that way. Mostly we get guys in here. You know the type."

Danetti laughed nervously, clearing her throat. "Anyway," she said, crossing in front of me, "as you can see we've taken out the metal bar that used to be our towel rack—"

"Just a rubber hook now," I said. "You couldn't hurt yourself if you cleaned your ears out with it."

"Mark, do you know who's relieving Shari in the game room?" Danetti said, holding out her hand for my security keys. "Why don't you do a bed check, then see how Shari's doing. I think she can use a break."

***

Erie, Pennsylvania, 1979:

I lived fourteen blocks from my sister's house and I didn't have a car. One way of keeping in touch with her was to haul my laundry over her place once a week, a necessary chore since my apartment was small and the air fouled up quickly with all my Cee/Kay construction work clothes stinking from concrete, oil, and diesel fuel. Often she'd have a dinner waiting and sometimes she'd let me spend the night. If it was convenient she drove down and picked me up, but more often than not I chose not to call her, electing instead to stuff a giant duffle bag, lay it atop my shoulder, and travel the distance on foot, traversing the network of alleyways and side streets that crossed the railroad tracks between her place and mine. Usually I traveled at night, slinking through the industrial corridor between West 12th and 16th Streets: tool and die, metal finishing, rubber stamping factories, junkyards, and the like.

I often rested near the tracks just down the street from her place. I'd drop my bag and sit on it, watching the trains go by. They came through quite frequently, the rail lines intersecting main thoroughfares, which made being late because of a train a common excuse for people in Erie.

For my own part, however, the trains were a tempting way to arrive on time. On time, that is, if the afterlife was your destination. I wanted out of Erie, PA, out of my dead-end, menial job, and out of life—and it seemed the steel wheels were the perfect way to do it. I had already made several half-hearted attempts, involving those last-moment dashes to the side as the conductor blew his horn. One time, however, I did make a serious attempt near the Cranberry Street crossing gate while several carloads of people looked on. It was raining that night. I strolled up beside the flashing red lights, ducked under the black-and-white striped arms of the gate, and knelt down beside the track of a slow-moving train. It was just pulling out after switching tracks. I decided to time the passing wheels, develop a beat, then on the fourth beat, stick my neck over the rail and have the next wheel remove my head. I set the laundry bag down and crawled close enough to kiss the boxcars passing. Wheels screeched and grinded. Grease and hydraulic fluids blew rancid in my face.

It was just a matter of leaning forward, I told myself. All I had to do was close my eyes and fall flat. One beat. Two beat. Three. I tightened up and started wavering. My body would not obey. Several drivers started honking their horns. "Are you crazy!?!" I heard someone yell. I imagined the mess and all the trouble I'd put the witnesses through. They'd be late, even later than usual. And if there were kids in those cars, it would be my fault if they needed therapy.

"Fuck it," I said, grabbing my laundry bag. I stood up. Raindrops pelted me, some trickling down beneath my collar. There seemed to be nothing to do but call it a day, to go home and go to bed, then get up and go to work the next morning.

How I hated that.

That same year I tied a rope in a tree not far from the Cee/Kay cement factory where every morning I had to show up for my five bucks an hour. I made a strong, tight noose out of a rope I had taken off the panel truck, the rope we used to secure our ladders. I climbed a large maple and anchored myself in a fork some twenty feet from the ground. I broke off a small, dead branch and tightened the loop around it, dropping the rope with the branch inside. It made a ping! sound and bounced back up, looking like it would snap my neck a good ten feet from the ground. But I never did it, never even put my neck in the noose. I sat there for maybe an hour, high in the branches, wishing I could get more days off—*this* was a day off—and also wishing I wasn't so depressed all the time.

***

"Let's go," the officer said, grabbing my sweatshirt behind my neck and pulling me off the fence. He hustled me back to the car where he made me lean over the trunk while he frisked me for weapons. The car radio coughed gibberish. The officer opened the rear door and pushed me inside. Then he came around front and called in his report to the local dispatcher. Meanwhile, the handcuffs cut into my back. I leaned forward and pressed my face against the front seat cage.

"Get back," he said.

"These cuffs hurt," I protested.

"You want something that hurts?" he said. "Get back."

The car started off and soon another police car was following behind us. We went to a nearby police station where the arresting officer and the one who followed us took me out and walked me inside. They put me in a small room and had me sit on a wooden chair. Again I was told not to lean forward.

A police captain came in and sat on the desk in front of me. He lit a cigarette, eyeing me carefully as he clicked his lighter shut. He offered me a smoke. I refused.

"Do you want to tell me what happened?" he said.

"I ain't talking to no one but my lawyer."

"Your lawyer isn't here," the captain said.

"I know that," I said. "Where's my dime? I wanna make a

phone call."

He laughed and left the room. In the meantime, I heard familiar voices in the hall outside. It was the old couple, the woman sounding hysterical and demanding that they examine the bruises on her arms. "He's a madman," she said. "He nearly killed us both."

"Aw, fuck you!" I yelled. I had enough problems already.

"See? See, what did I tell you?"

The arresting officer came in and pushed me back against the chair. "Boy, are you in a heap of trouble," he said.

"Don't mess with me," I said. "I know my rights."

This went on for quite some time. I wouldn't give them a statement. And they couldn't seem to make up their minds what to do with me. The old couple came through once, just to I.D. the man who had stolen their car. They looked awfully bruised and their clothes were torn and dirty, but I had to laugh when I saw the red vinyl purse. The old woman still held on to it.

"Don't laugh, son. That kind of stuff is gonna get you killed." The captain stood in the doorway. He worked a toothpick between his teeth. "Go ahead," he said to the other policemen, "take this dirtbag to the judge."

I soon learned that I was in a very small town. Going before the judge meant going out to his house. After tossing me in the back of the cruiser, both officers got in the front and we drove out to a nice white mansion with tall wooden pillars supporting the front. They marched me into the judge's den, a cozy room with lots of old photos and a pair of Civil War muskets crossed over a massive stone fireplace.

"Don't you fuckin' go near those," one of the officers said.

"Wouldn't think of it," I replied.

The judge was a thin, white-haired fellow, and we looked at each other but never shared a word between us—until I was ready to leave. Mostly he helped the officers draw up some papers and, when they were through, propped up his feet and talked a little about fishing at some local creek. My shoulders grew sore from having my wrists handcuffed behind me and from being tugged along by having my arms pulled back.

"Well, that'll do it for now, fellows," the judge said, sitting up straight and running his finger behind his collar.

They grabbed me to go. Finally the judge addressed me. "Today isn't your day, is it?" he said.

CHAPTER 36

When I was jailed in Alaska in 1975, I was incarcerated at the State Corrections Center with the drunk tank to myself. My only luxury was a flat plastic mattress that I enjoyed for all of thirty minutes. They took it away from me because an alert corrections officer saw me pulling the little brass breather holes off the sides and they assumed I would try to harm myself with them. For my part I thought they were secret microphones installed by the KGB.

The drunk tank was a big cell with a narrow, steel bench bolted against the wall on three sides. I tried sleeping on the bench the first night but I rolled off, so I spent several days ranting, raving, walking in circles and shivering while I slept on the concrete floor. They turned my toilet off because I abused my water privileges. They warned me about rattling my bars and told me that if I woke up the other convicts, I would not endear myself to the prison population. The worst part of the ordeal, however, was the gurgling drain in the middle of the floor. The Devil lived there. From deep inside his black hole he barked obscenities, tormenting me around the clock. It was pretty much the same scene as seven years later in New York: Nazis and torture and lots of confessions to be made. The correction officers in Alaska wore blue and black uniforms with blue shirts and black ties. Most of them had a silver sword tie tac which I attributed to an Anti-Christ League going back two thousand years. Needless to say, I did not get well in that jail and ended up having to go to the state psychiatric hospital in Anchorage in the middle of the winter, in custody with a pair of transportation officers.

The only good thing about Anchorage was the Northern Lights. One evening when it was about fifteen below zero a few of us patients got to go on an escorted walk around the frozen cinder track. Tiny ice crystals winked in the air and my breath formed little clouds that hung still after each exhale. That's when I saw the Northern Lights for the first time in my life. They looked like a green and yellow curtain wrapped halfway around the city, light streaking down through a rip in the sky. The Lights rolled and undulated like a curtain above a full-blast baseboard heater, only its colors changed as well, seemed to breathe and grow greener, then flash sudden bursts of yellow, white, and even pale blue.

***

The county jail promised to be nothing like Alaska. They took off my cuffs, made me turn my pockets inside out, photographed and fingerprinted me, then, still wiping off the ink with a pair of alcohol swabs, placed me in a large holding bin. It was a giant cage, the same kind of cage that exotic birds live in at the zoo. On the left was a solid row of cells sharing a common steel wall at the back, and outside of them a big, open pacing area with steel tables and two TVs outside the high steel bars, mounted in each corner of the ceiling. The ceiling must have been twenty feet high. Thirty or so inmates milled about the room. A card game involved a few men at one of the tables, and at the other, two guys were advising a third on tattoos. An overweight, gray-haired guard sat at a desk outside the enclosure, dividing his attention between the pages on his clipboard and *Gilligan's Island* on TV.

Of all the things in my environment, I knew the most deadly was the TV. My cellmate could have been a vampire or, at the very least, a maniac with a knife fashioned from the prongs of an extension cord, but I feared that far less than the box on the wall. I watched Ginger in her tight, silver dress as she stood beside the Professor, who was sitting at the table, tinkering with a radio or some other electronic gadget. I estimated that it would take fifteen minutes for the TV to feel my presence. Then it would begin homing in on me like an animal drawn by blood. I had to get out of there fast. There must be a solitary cell somewhere, I thought, a place without TV. I went over to the gray-haired officer.

"Excuse me. I need to get out of here."

The officer looked up and grumbled. He squinted at me, making a shooing motion with his left hand, then went back to staring at his clipboard.

"C'mon, man, I really mean it."

"Get away from the bars, kid."

"Look, you don't understand," I said. "I'm going to go crazy in another minute."

He stood up and came closer. He looked past my shoulder at the other guys in the cage, then spoke to me softly. "You start trouble in there and you're going to wind up on the wrong side of some very mean people. Now go lie down and wait till morning."

I reached through the bars with my hand. "You don't understand," I said, "I'm not going to make it till then."

The officer put his hand on his club. "Get your hands back, I said."

I took two steps back, bent down, and dashed forward, bashing my head into the bars. The guys playing cards stopped talking. I stepped back and repeated the gesture, this time hitting the steel so hard that my head sizzled with pain and my eyes clinched shut, tears forcing through. Again I smashed into the steel. The top of my head throbbed as though some alien were inside, clawing to get out.

"God almighty," the officer said. He called a message into his walkie-talkie. The prisoners formed a half circle behind me, keeping about fifteen feet away.

"The dude's nuts," I heard one of them say.

Two younger officers arrived, and they escorted me out of the holding area. I was dizzy with pain and had to be held under my arms. They took me to the infirmary. A mustached man introduced himself as some kind of doctor, and though I don't remember any conversation, the final outcome was that he accused me of faking a panic attack. Nevertheless he gave me ten milligrams of Valium, a precious little green pill. That finished, I was placed in a cell of my own—with my own guard posted right outside.

I remained confined alone for the next few days. The lack of stimulus calmed me down as I had nothing to do but stare at the walls. My guards, though they discouraged my talking to them, always gave me a rise when they changed shifts and the guy leaving told the new one what kind of weird shit I had been doing or saying that day. Only once did I really freak out, when they de-loused the cell wing and I thought they were killing everyone with poison gas.

During this time I received a visit from Joni and Richard. My guard announced this by banging his stick against my bars. He then escorted me to a long, narrow room with a huge wooden table, a big slab of solid, varnished oak, which formed a barrier across the middle. I sat on one side and they sat on the other, the table so wide that, leaning forward, we could not touch hands. The idea was to keep us far enough apart so that they couldn't pass me things unless they slid them, in full view, across the table.

Richard shook his head when I came in, though he smiled as well. "Guess you didn't like it at New Beginnings," he said.

I laughed. Suddenly I felt less scared. "Am I gonna get out of this one?" I asked.

"Sure," he said. "Sure. But it'll take a little time. I got you a lawyer, the best in the county. He used to be the local D.A."

"We're hoping those people will drop their charges," Joni said.

"People?" I asked. "What people?"

"The people you beat up," she said. "You stole a car,

remember?"

Richard elbowed Joni and told her to lighten up. "It's too complicated to talk about now," he said, "but the thing I want to tell you is to hang loose while you're in here. We can't afford to have anything else go wrong."

"That's right, Mark," Joni said. "Anything that happens in here is out of our control."

"I have a guard right outside my door," I said. "What could go wrong?"

Richard and Joni looked at each other.

"How long till I go to court?"

"Thursday," Richard said. "That's three days away."

"That's why you have to behave yourself," Joni said. "I already found out you've been taking Valium."

"I didn't take it. They gave it to me."

"But you can't do that anymore," Joni said. "It's a drug."

"So?"

"So drugs are the reason you're here in the first place. Drugs are the reason we're all going through hell for you."

"But I was going crazy, Joni. I thought the TV was going to eat me."

Joni pounded the table with her fist. "Can't you see how bad it's gotten? We're going backwards with this. Richard, help me explain it to him."

"I'm not sure he can appreciate your point of—"

"Stop taking his side!" Joni's eyes grew moist with tears and she started wringing her hands. She looked off to the side as her bottom lip began fluttering like a moth on the ground after it bounces off a light.

Richard leaned forward and drew my attention with his finger. "Look, Mark," he said, pointing at my chest, "all you've got to do is go easy. I understand you've got your own cell and someone watching over you. That's great. Nothing'll go wrong. Get a magazine or something. You stay cool and we'll do the rest, okay?"

Joni began bawling, digging in her purse for tissues. I

leaned forward to squeeze her hand but an officer who had been standing in the corner rushed up and grabbed me by the belt loops, pulling me back. "Don't do that again, buddy," he said.

Visiting hours were over about the time Joni stopped crying. Richard looked pretty drained as well. He rose slowly and helped his wife to stand. "We're keeping this from Mom, you know," Joni said, "as long as we can."

"She still thinks you're at New Beginnings," Richard said.

Suddenly Joni laughed—a great, tension-relieving laugh. "I'll tell her you're at 'New' New Beginnings," she said.

"By the way," I asked, "hear anything from Susan?"

On the afternoon of my trial I was told to clean up my cell, gather my possessions, and be ready to leave within the hour. They gave me my shoelaces back. (No dishonor here; when I was in the security wing at Woodside, after my high-school freakout, I had tried to hang myself with my shoelaces, even though I still had one leg and one arm secured to the bed. I had balled up my top sheet and, with my free right hand, knotted it and tossed it like a fishing line at my pair of tennis shoes, which were sitting about twelve feet away on the window ledge. I knocked one down and dragged it across the floor with the knotted end of the sheet. With my teeth I unlaced it, tied one end around my neck, the other to the headboard, and tried to throw myself out of bed, hoping to snap my neck— even though my left arm and right foot were bound by leather collars. When the mental health aide, a young black man, found me on my back with a string around my neck, all he could do was whistle a long, low note and tell me, "Man, you be seriously tryin' to hurt yo'self.")

I ate my final meal (canned carrots and peas, which reminded me of the houses and hotels in a Monopoly game, and a cornmeal muffin next to a flat, dried chicken breast that looked like a wallet). I was turned down when I requested a shower, a razor, and a new set of clothes. Eventually I was led out of my cell to a kid's school desk in the middle of a busy hall. The desk was too small for me but I was told to sit down, and my right wrist was handcuffed to an iron bar attached to the wall. The central office, wrapped in glass, looked like the bridge of a nuclear sub, men tripping switches, checking screens, talking into microphones. I watched the main gate open and slide shut with a clang, the electric locks buzzing.

"Let's go, Dangerous," an officer in a gray uniform said. He reached over me and uncuffed me from the bar. "Stand up," he said. Two officers in blue came up behind him. They took my arms and held them out while a man in white coveralls attached metal shackles to my ankles. Heavy chains looped from foot to foot. Next, my hands were cuffed in front of me and another chain looped between them, then attached around my ankles so that feet and hands were tied together.

"Okay, walk," the gray officer said. All I could manage were short, interrupted steps, and I had to bend forward because the chain connecting my wrists to my ankles didn't allow for my forward strides. This resulted in me yanking at my own shoulders every time I took a step.

The fella in white coveralls stood back and put his hands on his hips. "Looks pretty good," he said.

"Yep," said the gray officer. "He ain't goin' nowhere."

A minute later I was marched into a courtyard and helped into a van. Two officers climbed into the front seat. Two shotguns, locked in brackets, stood upright between them. There were three more seats behind me and on the very last one, near the rear doors, sat two black men in bright orange coveralls. Our eyes met and I knew not to look back again.

It was dusk and the van rolled out from the jail yard. No one had told me where I was going and it wouldn't have mattered if they did. Once more I slipped into a fantasy of torture and execution. So this is how it ends, I thought. Getting driven to some wooded location where they'll kick me blind, finishing the job no doubt with a twelve-gauge to my head.

The sun dropped low over the hills, spreading a fan of

pinkish red flames. The hills grew dark. We drove for a long time and soon all the cars that passed us had their lights on. The western sky darkened until it was no more than a purple strip, and high above it I watched a jet trail glow yellow as it broke into separate dots and dashes. "So," I consoled myself, "this is what a person sees on the last day of his life."

The van left the highway and climbed a small hill. It stopped in front of a white, wooden building that looked to be a small, rural church. There were dozens of cars and a crowd of people standing before the open doors, the yellow light from inside spilling over their shoulders. The officer who drove stepped out and slid back my door. He braced me as I stepped down, my chains rattling as I crossed the dirt lot. I saw Joni in the doorway, standing behind several people who were taking my picture as I came through the door. She had the back of her hand in her mouth and looked to be biting it while wet streaks glistened down from each eye. I was not a pretty sight: my red muscle sweatshirt and blue jeans were still dirty from when I was first arrested. I hadn't shaved, bathed, or brushed my teeth in five days. Just like when I had showed up at her place when the whole ordeal had first begun.

The officers hustled me in, steering me to the left side of the courtroom where I was sandwiched between them on a hard wooden pew. Joni and Richard followed, my sister asking the officer on my left if she could trade places with him. He agreed and she sat next to me, squeezing my hand. She smiled bravely and told me not to worry about a thing. Richard sat at the end of the row, close to where the attorneys sat at their desk.

Our lawyer came over and spoke to Richard. He was a tall, thin man with round, wire-rimmed glasses and a few gray hairs in his trimmed, blond beard. As they talked, the man looked back at me several times. Richard's face at first turned quizzical, then nodded approval. On one occasion, however, when the man pointed my way and seemed on the verge of approaching me, Richard grabbed his arm and made a definite "No!" motion with his head and lips. When the lawyer returned to his desk in the center of the courtroom, Richard came over and put his hands on top ours. "Our attorney doesn't think you need to say anything to the judge," Richard said. "He thinks it's best if he does all the talking for you."

"Did you hear that?" Joni said, locking her fingers in mine. "You don't have to utter a single word, okay?"

The officer on my right grunted sarcastically. When our case number was called I had to stand briefly but after that the entire proceedings went on without me. Once Richard was asked to approach the bench, but other than that it was mostly a conference between the judge and our lawyer. To keep myself from getting scared or saying anything I wasn't supposed to, I stared at the blank wall on the other side of the room. I stared for such a long time that I began to see images come to life as though they were being projected on a movie screen. The most amazing image was that of a typewriter. A big typewriter appeared on the wall, then split in two like an amoeba. Two typewriters hung there for a moment, slowly pulling apart in opposite directions. They reminded me of the two suns I had seen beneath the Brooklyn Bridge. I smiled, knowing everything was going to be all right. The typewriters meant I had two ways to go at all times. I just need to make better choices, I told myself.

CHAPTER 37

1982 . . . and quiet enough to hear a Band-Aid being pulled off in the security wing. It was one in the morning and that particular Band-Aid belonged to George, our only security-status patient, who was attempting a bath in Ronson Lodger's new suicide-proof tub. He had come in off the street a few hours before after being picked up by the police at the King's Rook Club—the same place where I performed my "looney tunes" comedy routine—while trying to get inside the club with a mannequin leg he had stolen from a window display at a downtown department store. That in itself wasn't unusual. It was when the bouncer at the door asked him for his membership card and he produced a dead mouse, placing it on the bouncer's palm, that things got—and forgive the pun—out of hand. A fight ensued, and he was pinned to the sidewalk until the police arrived. He was talking gibberish by then, and they found another six dead mice in his pockets—three of them with their eyes plucked out and two others tied together with dental floss, their fur colored with yellow magic marker. He was obviously crazy. So they brought him to me.

It was Saturday and I was the only male aide on the night shift. George was on suicide precautions so I had to supervise his bath. A handsome, light-complected fellow in his late thirties, he lay motionless in the steamy water, staring vacantly at the drops falling from the heel of his one raised foot. He had a swollen left eye and a cut over the bridge of his nose, the wound exposed because the Band-Aid floated in the water. I kneeled beside the tub, my sleeves rolled up and a soapy washrag in my hand, hoping George would come out of his trance and I could get by without having to wash him myself.

"Do you want to talk about the mice?" I said.

George's eyes rolled my way but his face remained blank. He was a former artist and associate professor at nearby Edinboro State. About four years earlier, in 1976, he had experienced a psychotic episode and had been a client of ours, off and on, ever since.

"You can tell me," I said. "I won't judge you."

George broke into a grin. "So you're the good fairy in this joint," he said. "I'm pleased to meet you." He lifted his hand from the water and held it out to shake.

"I'm Tinkerbell myself," he said, "but please don't tell the doctor. It would hurt his feelings to know he's misdiagnosed me all along."

George sighed and the room returned to silence. In a moment he dipped his foot again, bringing it back out to watch the water dripping from his heel.

"Do you think you can wash yourself?" I said.

"Not tonight. Not without doctor's orders."

"How about if *I* ask you?" I said. "We'll keep it between you and me."

"And will you give me a lollipop? Will you write me up in your report and tell everyone what a good boy I've been?"

I didn't say anything. I liked George and had seen him behave this way on his previous admission. I knew very well how he felt—defeated—totally betrayed by something unpredictable, something inside himself that he couldn't understand yet that wanted to destroy him. And his latest admission to the hospital was proof he'd screwed up again, lost control, and now everyone else could see, too.

"You can make a big deal about the mice," he said. "But I caught every one of them myself. Performing my civic duty. They were rodents infesting my house, spreading disease through my cupboards. Even the cat wouldn't go after them anymore. But of course it will make all the difference in the world as your team of experts sift through the evidence to determine exactly *why* I removed their eyes and put their corpses in my pockets, now won't it? After all, this is psychiatry. We must find the root cause of things. Plucking eyes is not normal. So we must know *why*. That is why it's very important that the good fairy reports what I say accurately."

George slapped the water for emphasis. "Accurately, my friend. You must not prejudice your report with your own superstitions. Your own biased views, you understand?"

"Yes," I said.

George tilted his head back and splashed water on his face, opening his mouth to catch a few drops. "That is, if you really want to know why I did it," he said.

I really didn't care anymore—not when it meant going through a psychological minefield to get the answer.

"You can tell me if you want to," I said. "But I don't need it to file my report."

"Oh good," he said, looking past me to the mirror spyglass on the wall. "I like psychology. Especially the reverse kind. I taught it once in high school. Anyway, here's the secret." He motioned me to lean forward. I did and he reached out and grabbed my head. He caught my ears for a second but his hands were wet and I jerked back and jumped up from the floor.

"Dammit!" he shouted. "I wasn't going to hurt you."

I threw the washrag to the floor. I backed up and pulled out my key, opening the door to the outer chamber.

"What are you doing?" he said. "Calling the police?"

"I'm getting help," I said, "then I'm getting you out of here. You've got two minutes to finish your bath." I still held a picture in my mind of his hands around my neck, holding me underwater.

"But I wasn't going to hurt you, honest. Oh, come on. Let's be friends. We all need playmates, you know."

I fit the key in the lock. George sat up abruptly and water

leapt over the side of the tub. "I wanted to whisper in your ear," he said. "I was giving you the secret, dammit!"

"Keep your secret," I said, signaling the nurse at the desk.

"It was a joke," he said. "Don't you get it? Three blind mice. See how they run."

***

The courtroom adjourned. No one told me what the verdict was. The officers escorted me back outside, this time onto a stretcher and into the back of another ambulance. It was an old-fashioned Cadillac ambulance and I was strapped down on my stomach with my wrists and ankles still in irons, though my arms were now behind my back and the chain between my arms and legs was removed altogether. Three leather belts pinned me behind my knees, waist, and across my shoulders. My head was turned to the side and my face half swallowed by the pillow. I complained once and was told to keep quiet, that there'd be a new home for me somewhere up the road.

The ride seemed to take forever. I grew worried that my neck would lock in place. Already my wrists were numb and my shoulder sockets ached unbearably. We drove on through the night, slowing and gaining speed at the different stops along the way, the green color of the traffic lights bathing my face as we passed under them and the occasional headlights flashing past. It was all very much disjointed and something like a dream. Except my pain, of course. That was very real. After an hour or more we finally stopped. I was slid out the back and helped to a standing position. I drew myself up at the steps of a fortress-like building, a huge brick structure with bars and heavy mesh screens over the first-floor windows. It looked like an old, inner-city school or a National Guard armory. With an officer under each arm, I clopped up the steps, the ankle chains rattling. A nurse and two male orderlies walked ahead of us, the one orderly springing ahead to hold the doors while we passed.

"Hey, buddy," I said as we brushed by him, "ain't it like the St. Patrick's Day Parade?"

On we went down the halls, through some buzzing doors, and eventually into a hospital ward of some kind. At this point two more men in white approached me and the officers unshackled my wrists and legs. It was like being released by a boa constrictor.

To my left, I became aware of low-watt lamps and chairs in a lounge. The police left and the men in white walked me to a desk. It was a nurses' station. On the wall was a calendar with the word "September" below a big red "1."

"Make peace with your God," said a voice from the lounge. It sounded like an old man's voice, and I could see the white top of someone's head against the back of his chair.

My things—a packet of tooth powder and two travel magazines—were placed on the counter and logged by a nurse on the other side. "Raise your arms," said one man and they went through my pockets. "Nothing," said the other.

"Okay, now please take off your shoes."

"Make peace with your God," said the man in the chair. He faced away from me. All I could see was the top of his head and a thin, gray curl rising, most likely, from a cigarette. The lounge was dark and solemn, like a hotel in the off-season, like the mad scientist's library in an old, black-and-white movie.

"Give me your wrist," said the nurse. She snapped a plastic band around it. Printed on it was my name, age, sex, and a series of numbers. Below the numbers was another name, a Dr. Bowman.

"Where am I?" I asked, looking at the wristband.

"You're at Mitchell-Walker Psychiatric Institute."

"Can't be," I said. "I work there. This isn't Manhattan."

"This is Albany. Mitchell-Walker has a separate unit here as well."

The nurse looked at me as though she were tired of explaining the obvious. I looked around, feeling trapped, embarrassed. "And who's this Doctor Bowman?" I asked.

"That's God," said the man in the chair.

PART THREE

WORMWOOD AGAIN

[The] Case of J.H.J. . . . He was born May 25, 1837. On the night of December 31, 1868, in the middle of his thirty-second year, he had the following dream. . . . "I thought," he writes, . . . "I noticed in the sky, in the far southwest, a bright light like a star, about the size of the palm of my hand, and in an instant it seemed to grow larger and larger and nearer and nearer, until it began to light up the darkness. When it got to the size of a man's hat, it divided itself into twelve smaller lights with a larger one in the centre, and then very rapidly it grew much larger, and instantly I knew that this was the coming of Christ. . . ."

TESTIMONY COMPILED BY RICHARD MAURICE BUCKE, M.D.,
COSMIC CONSCIOUSNESS

When you wish upon a star Makes no difference who you are Anything your heart desires will come to you

"WHEN YOU WISH UPON A STAR" FROM PINOCCHIO

CHAPTER 38

June 21, 1992

Dear Jennifer:

Congratulations on your loss of virginity. I knew it was a long time coming—excuse the pun—but now that that awful moment is behind you—perhaps another pun—I assume you are happy to be getting on with the rest of your life. It was nice to meet your boyfriend at the "Big Fifty" family reunion. I can feel pretty good about the choice you made. He seems to be a nice young man, even though a junior in college is hardly a complete mold as far as today's concept of a man is concerned. He's more like a blackboard without any writing on it yet. Or a basketball without any air.

I'm so glad we've been able to keep in touch all these years, Jennifer. How old are you now? Twenty? Twenty-one? You held out longer than most other people (not counting those, of course, who inhabit the low end of the Ugly Curve). However, according to your letters, your reluctance was based on waiting for the "perfect moment." I'm not sure why waiting for the "perfect moment" is such a big deal. That always mystified me. I have a hunch you believed the quality of your first experience would indicate what kind of person you were. You wanted the best, sort of like Christmas based on merit.

Regardless, it sounds like you had a good time—at least

it wasn't in a car—so apparently you're okay. Certainly much better than *my* first time around. By the way, there were many times—especially when you were still in high school—when I wanted to advise you against getting sexually involved. But I had to look at my own life and try not to be hypocritical. You know enough about me to assume I did more than window shop in the premarital sex department. But you're my niece, Jennifer, and I can't help playing Big Brother, Big Uncle, or whatever it is.

That brings me to a related matter. I've spent a lot of time trying to sort out my past. At the fiftieth wedding anniversary, as I observed my mother and father, I realized that my hurt and disappointment with them was fading. I felt more removed from them—removed in a safe, healthy manner—and watched them not as the two people who brought me up and shaped my life, but as two individuals with their own strengths and weaknesses, each of them struggling as you and I do to find value in life and make sense of what goes on.

They never volunteered to be gods, you know, even though I made them gods when I was very young. Nor did they deserve to be the patsies I later blamed all my failures on. Seeing them now made me realize that after all these years they had finally become what they were to begin with—just people, imperfect people stumbling occasionally, as we all do.

Forgiveness is a funny thing. When the forgiving is all over and done, and true acceptance is there, then I don't wish things were different anymore. I wouldn't change them or the past anymore than I'd want to change the color of the sky.

Jennifer, I hope you can remember that parents, uncles, older friends—all of us are human. You're in college now and want answers right away. You're about to inherit what our society can offer you and you want instant justice, you want things to be ironed out evenly, all black and white. College has a way of igniting a young person's rebellion and it's a time when it's very easy for lashing out and finger pointing at what you've just begun to understand. Sometimes you need to balance the urge to change things with a little bit of tolerance. We're all trying to do our best, each changing in the way and at the speed they can best handle.

If there is one lesson I consider more important than all the others, it's this: We need to take full responsibility for ourselves as early as we can. That way we aren't looking for answers from others. Others can let you down. So can governments, religions, philosophies. They trumpet their truth, not necessarily yours.

Our own feelings are our best guides. Believe it or not, inside each of us is a discriminating voice, always available to teach us right from wrong. To activate this voice, try imagining yourself as a good person destined to do good things with your life. (You'd be surprised how few people actually focus on their goodness.) If you're not sure of your goodness, try treating yourself as an ongoing project (a success project, a happiness project, a project of self-respect) and be kind to yourself at those times when you fail. You'll find your voice eventually. It's the voice of intuition. Of feelings. Find it and you'll gain a better idea of which direction you should go. It's both the simplest and hardest thing to do. I don't have anything more to say than that.

Love always,
Mark

***

The last two weeks of September 1983 were a maddening time. I was mad because I was going sane again. I was beginning the process of shedding my past. One day Bowman stopped me as I was about to enter our little office for another session.

"No," she said, "let's try somewhere else." With an orderly as escort, she led me off the floor and into the next building, where we ascended an elevator, going into a large, sunny room with many bookshelves, a pair of couches, and a large, glass-topped desk before a spacious window.

"This is my office," she said. "I thought maybe we could meet here from now on."

The next time we met she brought me over unescorted. She allowed me to examine her things, to ask about her husband and her dark-haired daughter, whose photos leaned against each other on the corner of her desk. She told me where she went to school, how she had taken up scuba diving, and how she took a one-month vacation every year, with her upcoming adventure being planned for France.

I do not know which came first in this process—her opening up to me, or maybe it was the natural by-product of the openness I now felt myself. Our therapy had taken a new turn; I had accepted that the next year of my life might be spent in her company, that she controlled my fate, and I stopped fighting that prospect, stopped seeing her as my enemy.

I fought the Thorazine, however, as best I could. Once or twice I "cheeked" the little brown pill, holding it under my gums as I swallowed my juice. But I felt badly those times, plus realized the odds were that I'd be caught if I did it often enough. I resolved to take my medicine and suffer through it because getting caught and losing the staff's trust in me seemed to be a more damaging situation than the side effects I was feeling.

The drug made me dizzy, lightheaded, gave me yellow, blinding rushes accompanied by tingly skin and a roar in my ears sometimes when I hopped out of bed in the morning or now and then when I bent down to pick up something or tie my shoe. I developed "dry mouth" and the telltale mechanical walk. I waited in dread for my hands to become clawlike again.

My hallucinations lessened dramatically. I wouldn't deny Thorazine played a part, but also responsible was an "exorcism" that came from being around people who were sicker than I was. In mid-September I was placed in a room with three other guys: Robert "Bo" Bradley, Steven Goldberg, and Dead End Freddy. In time I came to realize that each of them represented a fractured part of my own personality, a deformed aspect grown in each of them to an extreme degree.

Bo was a homicidal nut, a hot wire, a young man so embroiled in anger that he was capable of stealing a car—and then some. He was a Brooklyn-born street tough who had moved to Albany where he was last employed as a U.S. Postal worker, until he attacked his superiors in a fit of rage that is sadly very vogue for civil servants these days.

We learn by mirroring each other. What I learned from Bo—by watching him, by seeing where he and I were alike—was the lesson of denial. Bo was the biggest goddam liar I ever met in my life. He slept with six pillows and every night we had the nurse and a couple of orderlies in our room, straightening out the matter of who stole our pillows, Bo denying that he had taken them from our beds. He had Doctor Wu, and by the way he talked about him, one got the impression that sooner or later the staff would find the physician strangled in his office, Bo's fingerprints all over the man's neck—and Bo would insist he was somewhere else at the time. I never believed a single word when he spoke of his past history. He had all this crap about being in a motorcycle gang, of how he knew Roger McGuinn David Crosby and had written songs for them.

The only evidence to support his outrageous tales was an aborted tattoo on his right arm; apparently the artist had intended to draw a skeleton pulling a wheelie on the back of a chopper Harley. Only he had screwed up some detail in the bike—the spokes, Bo said—and ended up coloring the image in, so that what was left looked like a skeleton with two walking canes climbing out of a long, solid box.

Bo always rose to anger whenever his assertions were challenged. It was this I despised in him, and reflecting on my own tendency to be like him, I despised that part of myself as well, vowing to never let myself become the liar and bully he was.

Dead End Freddy, on the other hand, never provided such direct confrontation. A pimply faced, emaciated youth of nineteen with long, greasy hair and clothes that looked and smelled as if he had slept beside a campfire, he was a spaced-out drug gobbler who'd snort the bottom of a birdcage if his peer group asked him. He got the name Dead End from Bo, who misunderstood him when he introduced himself his first day at our lunch table, telling us he was a Dead Head and a veteran of more than thirty concerts. He wore either one or several of those black, heavy metal T-shirts—I couldn't tell because they all looked the same, featuring aging, hairy men dressed like Viking bikers, sneering from behind their heavy metal makeup, clutching their guitars like long-necked penises. Freddy's vocabulary consisted of "cool," "neat," "far out," and other such phrases. His fingertips were orange from smoking marijuana cigarettes.

Like Bo, Freddy became a walking example for me, a parody of my own excess. I saw in him what I still could be—and rejected it. It happened one night in the TV lounge, while I watched him emptying the end tobacco from used cigarettes, transferring the half-burnt shavings to a Bugler paper, which he rolled for his own use. According to his stories, his lifestyle had consisted of partying, partying, then more partying, with an occasional stop for a Slurpee or some potato chips at his neighborhood 7-Eleven. I looked at him and wondered what kind of chemistry his body ran on, what strange elements were coursing through his blood. I thought about Doctor D'Aoust. I thought about John, the junkie my age, who needed help getting in and out of bed. I looked at myself and laughed. What if I were famous, I thought. Would they hire someone like Freddy to play me in the movies?

Watching these guys was like an exorcism by proxy. And by far the greatest impact was done by my third roommate, Steven Goldberg. Steven was the twenty-two-year-old, overweight, obsessive-compulsive son of a Jewish Long

Island tailor and laundromat chain owner. He was cracking up because, only a few months after graduating from a high-class, Ivy League school, he felt that his parents' wishes would never come true, that he would never be the successful businessman they wanted him to be.

He was at Mitchell-Walker long before I arrived, and soon after I moved in with him, he was transferred. But his impact was undeniable. He was the only other person I ever met —even as a mental health worker—who raved about Nazis and death and torture. I feared him at first, thinking he was a double agent, but as the power of my own delusions lessened, I learned to humor the poor fellow, seeing again in him the picture I must have presented to hundreds of people throughout the last two months.

His paranoia came upon him in unexpected surges— sudden bolts from the meal table, accompanied by turning his plate over, or tossing it at the wall. "You're poisoning me!" he'd yell. His pattern was to run to the pay phone and call his mother, demanding that she send a private investigator, switch hospitals for him, or at least fire his current doctor. The last I saw of him he was being carried to a tighter-security ward, writhing and struggling in the arms of his captors, looking like Vince Lombardi being hoisted off the field after winning the big game.

Even the raunchy streak in my sexuality—the lusty part— was exorcised at Mitchell-Walker. One afternoon I was alone, reading in the alcove by the piano. A young woman who had been admitted the night before with much noise and confusion approached me in her threadbare hospital gown. She was about twenty-five, slightly overweight, with that roughened look that comes from substance abuse, hit-and-run relations, and low self-esteem.

"Hi there," she said. "What's your name?"

I looked up from my book. With the light behind her I could see the outline of her body. And through her gown, no thicker than a faded white silk scarf, the enormous brown circles around her nipples poked through like a pair of drink coasters.

I was speechless. She introduced herself as Opal D'Vine —or Opal Design, I'm not sure—and sat provocatively on the arm of my chair. It was immediately clear to me what her intentions were. I could almost smell her heat. As if that wasn't enough, she steered the conversation towards the subject of loneliness and the possible places on the unit where we could be together, alone.

I froze at the opportunity. It was totally bestial. I gathered my book and my papers and made to get up from my chair. "Find someone else," I said, seeing for the first time what sex for sex's sake was all about. A few seconds of relief would never compensate for the feelings I would undoubtedly suffer later. It felt good to say no.

CHAPTER 39

In the latter stages of my therapy I learned that the things that were wrong with me had been wrong with me for quite some time. Bowman asked me to go beyond the stolen car, the suicidal urges. She wanted to know what I felt about life, the future, my parents—long before I ever took my first drink or abused drugs of any kind.

Thus began a process of painful rediscovery. The pain was doubly acute for me because of my experience in the mental health field, reinforced by an attitude of "It doesn't pay to rehash the past; let's get on with it." But there was no moving forward as long as I was operating blind. I had to see clearly where the original damage had been done, where I had started to hate myself, my parents, and those around me. Once again D'Aoust's words revisited me in a haunting enigma: "We are carriers of information." I wondered what he meant by that, wondered if we carried our childhood hurts and misconceptions like an outdated roadmap that could easily mislead us.

My mother was the easier one to understand. Her children's successes, their smiling faces, meant she had done a good job. Anything that didn't measure up to that, even if it was her own standards that were being violated, meant that we had let her down, and in the same sense, that she had failed. She looked to us for her own needs, to bring her the satisfaction that life did not.

My father, on the other hand, was the Invisible Man. He

roamed a limited world, most of his travels revolving around the television and his big, overstuffed easy chair. I called it the Big Green Chair because the living room had green carpeting and every few years or so we'd replace the current chair with a new chair, usually the kind with the handle that you pull to bring up the footrest—all of them green. Each one, after time, would develop a dark oval on the upholstered back, the product of Vitalis on his hair, plus his habit of falling asleep sometime before or after the eleven o'clock news.

My father bowled. My father golfed. I never went with him on these outings. I only knew him as the man in the chair, the king on the throne, the permission machine. It was before his chair where I had to plead my cases: Daddy, can I go with Kelly to the park today? Daddy, can I have a bike like the other boys? Daddy, can I have a quarter?

Since this was the primary place of interaction between us, he milked my requests for all they were worth. When I wanted something he'd tease me, knowing that I was his prisoner, that I had to play along if I was to get what I wanted. "Did you cut the grass today?" he'd ask. "Did you rake the leaves? Clean up the yard?" The worst times were when I was older, when I had to ask him to borrow my own car. (I paid for it; he covered the insurance, the infamous "part-time driver" variety.) It angered and belittled me to have to beg in that way.

All along, though, he had a humor, a detachment for our role-playing games. Basically, he was just looking for stimulation, only he couldn't see that a youngster's needs were so different, so urgent most of the time. He wanted me to laugh at myself, to "play" at being a child, but I interpreted it as disrespect.

There were times, too, when I positively loved the man. Once, when I was down with the flu, after coming out of the doctor's office I complained that my toy soldiers were no fun for me anymore. I felt they were deserting me, declaring mutiny right there in my fingers by not behaving in the same magical way as they had done only months before. Was this part of the flu, I asked.

No, he said. It's called growing up.

We did not take many trips together but there is one image that will never leave me as long as I live. We were in the car at night. He and my mother rode in front; I had the back seat to myself. I curled up on the back dash, under the rear window, looking up at the stars and the black Rorschach blots of trees rolling by. I cuddled with my blanket and stuffed animals. There was something so warm and comforting in that space. I looked over the front seat at my father's dark profile against the low, green lights of the dash. In my heart rose the feeling that he was a captain of a ship, an able-bodied master with his hands upon the wheel. And out there, among the stars and dark shadows of a mysterious world, his guidance was all I required: his watchful eye, his hands steering us straight. I felt safe, secure. I pulled my knees into my chest, drawing my blanket to my chin and closing my eyes in a swoon of love and protection.

During those awful construction work days of '77–'78, on certain weekends when my sister was gone and she let me borrow her car, I occasionally drove the hundred miles or so from Erie to visit my parents in Youngstown, Ohio. I was partly in town to stir up some action with old high school friends, but I also tried to forge a new connection with my parents, staying overnight at their house on most of those trips. My father and I would play gin rummy; my mother and I would launch a conversation, feed it like a fire, only to see it collapse slowly, fizzle out, when her hopes or prejudices became clear and I had to lie or artfully skip over subjects that I feared would turn the exchange into conflict. Things had a way of ending with a sigh, and often the silence opened up like a chasm between us.

(This was after two traumatic hospitalizations. Sometimes it seemed we hardly talked at all. Still, they got to feed me and watch me sleeping safely at night. Mom could buy me socks. They learned from me that I was taking care of myself. They could see I was fed, was still alive. Back then that was all they could hope for.)

It was on one of those trips when I found myself in the basement, looking for something among the tools of my father's workbench, just below the tile ceiling where I used to hide my booze. I opened the drawer where he kept his drill bits. My hands touched the glossy surface of an 8 × 10, black-and-white photograph. I pulled it out and examined it. It was a photograph of my father when he was a young man, maybe in his late twenties. He was among several other young men, and it took me a minute to realize the photo had been taken at Universal Metal and Finishing, the machine shop where he had labored for nearly thirty years, until his heart attack had forced his retirement. He took me there once as a boy and I remembered his machine, a giant lathe, and he and the others in the photo were clustered in front of it, their haircuts and the worn edges of the photo itself dating the image, suggesting these might be the crew of a B-17, all smiling and joshing the way buddies do in-between missions.

I had never seen my father look like that. He was a man, a friend among friends. He was handsome with clear, clever eyes. He had character. He stood tall in the center, the leader's position, his jaw cutting a nice line with his head tossed back, his lips smiling. Honesty and humility shone on his face. He was kind-natured. I thought, why hadn't I ever seen that myself? Was I blind? Did he hide it from me? Where was my father when I needed that friend? And was I somehow to blame?

I stared for the longest time, then put the photo back, knowing I couldn't answer those questions. I only know that I felt terribly cheated, like the image I had owned of him all those years had been a fake. I felt I had missed something important, something which should have been mine.

***

One cool, rainy Sunday Susan came to Albany to see

me. It was early, not yet lunch, and I was back in the day room, staring at the dust collecting under the cushions of the pool table, turning my head occasionally to watch the rain splattering on the slanted concrete window ledge, kicking up little beads that collected on the bottom of the window screen. It was unusually quiet; I sat there alone.

Susan came down the hall, her tall figure and thick, wavy hair cutting an unmistakeable profile as she strode towards me, her calves visible beneath a knee-length, tight black skirt. She wore a black blazer and cradled a stack of envelopes in her arms.

"I've always wanted to see our unit in Albany," she said, stopping in front of me. "Visiting you is the perfect excuse."

I was shocked. I could not stand. Unconsciously I ran my tongue along the front of my teeth, tasting my mouth to see if it were kissable. Susan broke into a gentle smile and handed me my mail. As she did, she leaned forward and kissed me on the lips.

"Well, do you like it more than our floor in Manhattan?" she asked.

"I'm still getting over the embarrassment of being admitted to my own hospital," I said. "Food's better, though." I slid over and patted the other cushion of the couch, Susan sitting down.

I put my arm around her and placed my cheek against her neck. "I thought I'd never see you again," I said.

She brought up a hand and caressed my other cheek. I could hear her heart fluttering, reminding me of times when I had listened dreamily to it slowing down after making love.

"We all have our things to work through," she said. "I'm starting therapy myself. I'm learning how to let go and still love someone. And I'm learning how to forgive, too."

Susan reached down and gathered the rubber-banded stack of mail, placing it once again in my lap. On the top was a pink envelope. In the return address of the left corner I saw the name Catherine Hayes.

"Read it," she said.

Unwillingly, my eyes grew wide. My mouth opened as I held my breath.

"I don't mean out loud," she said, brushing back my hair and kissing my cheek. "But read it in front of me. I don't want there to be any secrets again."

I drew back and slit the envelope with my finger. "By the way," I said, nervously trying to change the subject, "how is the unit doing these days?"

"Well, there's one bad piece of news. They hired a new guy for the night shift. I don't think he'll last, though. I hear he's trying to get on the day shift already."

Inside the envelope was a card with a photograph of a sunset on the desert. As I opened it and began reading, Opal D'Vine and Rebecca, a new admit about Opal's age, strolled down the hall into the day room, where they halted at the pool table, eyes like half dollars, glaring at us. Opal cupped her hand against Rebecca's ear and whispered something, Rebecca pushing her back with an exclamation of, "You're kidding!" Excitedly, they took seats on a couch against the other wall, staring at us in a manner that suggested preteen schoolyard behavior.

"Hope they enjoy the show," Susan said, shaking back her hair. "Tell your friends they'd still look better with popcorn."

I returned to the card. Catherine's opening comments concerned the weather, her good friend, Corrine, and her apprenticeship to a Hopi Indian woman who agreed to help her learn the art of making jewelry. She said some other things about life being better, then devoted the last two paragraphs to questions about why I had never shown up for her mother's wedding. Her attitude showed that she knew nothing about Kelly's party and what had happened to me. She trusted I caught my plane on time. And lastly, she hoped to hear from me soon.

I looked up at Susan. Her smile cued my own. Just beyond her, on the peripheral of my vision, sat Opal and Rebecca, two women that I knew with utter certainty that I had never flirted with either of them. I smiled broadly now, holding Susan's gaze for what seemed to be the longest time.

CHAPTER 40

October 3, 1983
(Afternoon)

No more hard edges. Thorazine has made everything soft.

It is little things now. Little ups and downs. Little frustrations. Yesterday Bo was obnoxious at the dinner table. He made a remark about Susan and if it wasn't for the Thorazine in my blood, I would have hit him on the spot. But all in all it was a minor incident, the kind of thing you expect from him and, coincidentally, the kind of thing that has begun happening with regularity. Twice I went to the front desk and got a pen that ran out of ink. The day before I lost a dollar betting on a football game. It is these kinds of concerns that show me how far I've become "normalized." I surprise myself by complaining that the chocolate milk is warm. I actually care about my coffee mug I am making in ceramics class. I worry when my laundry doesn't come back when it's supposed to.

I'm losing my center. I'm being swallowed by routine. It is like being forced to stare at a horrible view, something you close your eyes against for the longest time. Then, after much resistance you open them—reluctantly—and find yourself not only enjoying the view but wondering about this or that detail. Bowman has a very simple phrase for it: relating to the world around me. Unfortunately, now that I am relating to the world, it resumes control.

Long gone is my chance to get back in school. My play? Completely forgotten. My landlord returned my last rent check, along with a notice that I'm being evicted. Last week my full hospitalization benefits ran out and I am now responsible for 20 percent of my daily room charge bill. Next week it goes up to 40, then 60 percent. But I am handling it well. Those problems are like background music I don't hear anymore.

As of yesterday I have told Doctor Bowman everything. She knows about my dreams, my fears, my anxiety over the end of the world. She knows about the killers and how I'm to blame for Halley's Comet. I told her they should rename it in the same way they came up with Lou Gehrig's disease.

***

October 4, 1983
(Afternoon session)

Today I was paged to the nurses' station and when I got there, Bowman was waiting, wearing a brown woolen coat. She held a blue jacket in her hand.

"Here, I borrowed this from Charley. Would you like to take a walk?"

I was overjoyed to be able to go outdoors. I ran back to my room and pulled on a sweatshirt, joining her as she unlocked the door and stepped outside. It was cool but sunny, the kind of day made for raking leaves, planting bulbs, or one last mowing of the yard. The air smelled like high school football, like ducks flying south.

"I did a lot of thinking last night about what you told me," Bowman said, buttoning her coat and pulling on a pair of brown leather gloves. We strolled past the tennis courts and paused before the trees.

"You mean about the comet?" I said.

She nodded. "Mark, I want you to know that I believe everything you told me. I don't doubt for a moment that you had those dreams. Nor do I doubt that they came true like you said. However . . ."

Her pause was deliberate. I turned my head. For a moment we locked eyes, then my gaze followed hers to the woods ahead of us, the shadows beneath the trees augmented by orange, yellow, and brown splashes of leaves.

"Last night I tried my hardest to put myself in your place," she went on, indicating by looking up that she was searching for the words. "I said to myself, 'If everything's true as he said, then we both face the same problem, don't we?' "

"What do you mean?"

"If your dream about Halley's Comet is true, Mark, then it's not just your life that's threatened. It affects me, my husband David, all my loved ones—the entire planet—isn't that so?"

"Yes." I swallowed hard. She motioned that we should follow a broad path made from bark and wood chips.

"I'm not saying this to make you feel bad," she said. "Believe me, I've never spent so much time putting myself in another's shoes. I'm doing it to help you."

I nodded. "It's okay," I said. "Go on." The path winded gently and climbed the low ridge.

"Anyway, I asked myself how I'm going to live out these next few years," she said, pointing to the golden-leafed maples, the scatterings of leaves on the ground. "That's when it occurred to me that your dream isn't all that unusual. We've all been living with a fear of the end of the world, mainly because of our nuclear bombs. For the past thirty years our world could have been destroyed at any time. Some days it seems an absolute certainty."

I flexed my fingers in the cold, crisp air. We crested the top of the ridge and I could see Mitchell-Walker sprawling below, a campus of old, red-brick buildings, their flat roofs violated by giant air conditioners, their windows made obscene by bars and dark mesh screening. The power plant smoke stack threw a small but steady stream of gray against the sky.

"Do you see my point?" Bowman said. "World disaster

doesn't matter one way or the other. After all, we're all going to die."

At that precise moment a dry brown leaf drifted down and landed in the space between us, underlining the very thing she had said.

"Why is it different for you?" Bowman asked. "We all know the world ends sooner or later. I'm trying real hard to figure out why you've been nurturing this dream, holding onto it the way you have. Is there something in you that wants this disaster?"

I stopped and bent down, picking up a twig. "God knows," I said, still crouching. I placed my palms flat on the ground, feeling the cool, soft earth.

"At one time, like when you were hospitalized in high school, your dream may have been a cause, may have been a part of the problem," she said. "But the real issue, I believe, is what you've chosen to do about it. I wonder if it hasn't been an excuse for self-destructive behavior."

Bowman lead us down the other side of the hill, locking her arm in mine. The feeling was exhilarating. And reassuring. Her breath was barely visible; tiny puffs in the air.

"Mark, a week from today I'm going to schedule your first staffing." As she said those words a jolt went through me. "And though we both know how important this is, I don't want you to worry about it at all. The other doctors are going to ask you questions, but they won't be any different than the ones I've asked you already. No one's going to try to trip you up."

"Will you be there, too?"

"Of course." She gave my arm a squeeze.

"I'm also going to give you outdoor privileges, as of today. And for the upcoming weekend, if you can work it out, you can have an overnight pass."

"A pass? Where will I go?"

"You might try calling your girlfriend."

***

October 8, 1983
(Morning)

I didn't have a reason for it but this morning when I rolled out of bed I got down on the floor and did fifteen pushups. I felt a slight tension in my shoulders, a tightness that used to be familiar and welcome when I had kept myself in shape.

Susan will be here any time now. She rented a car. Yesterday she told me on the phone not to say where we were going since they probably expected us to go back to Brooklyn Heights and sit around and sip coffee, visiting with my family. She said we're really heading for Lake Placid, where we can find a cabin nestled in the autumn scenery. Then she's going to fuck my brains out. "Fuck me into oblivion" is how she put it. Believe me, she *rarely* talks like that.

I've been good to her since her visit. I had missed her so much but just didn't know it. It was when I heard her heart pounding that I realized what she meant to me. Later, when I was having trouble with my Thorazine—it makes my mouth go dry when I'm nervous—she kept getting up and going to the water fountain, where she'd fill a Dixie cup and bring it back to me.

On that visit we talked more about my past, about Catherine, about the mess she found in my apartment. Susan said as far as she was concerned, the incident with the photos never happened. She said it and I believed her. As a consequence, the past few days I've thrown myself entirely on the mercy of this woman. I told her I wanted a second chance. I promised her—and myself—to never tell another lie.

***

Later. Back in the day room. They paged me on the intercom. I stood up and brushed my hand through my hair. I

341

walked past the pool table with the cigarette burns. I walked past Bo, pool cue in hand, the little smirk on his face dropping with his realization of where I was going and who I was going with. I walked past my room, past the showers, past the old console television with the stains from forgotten soda cans, hundreds of rings, interlocked, like the Olympic Games symbol.

I walked up to the nurses' station and there she was. Susan. Like a long, sleek limousine, spinning a set of car keys around her finger. And smiling the way a person does when they give you a gift and can tell you're especially pleased.

***

October 8, 1983

Oblivion.

***

October 11, 1983
(Staffing)

A sunny day. Bowman walked with me to another part of the hospital. Over and over again she assured me that things would go well, as long as I remained honest with the other doctors. At the end of a long hallway of shiny white tile with little green specks in it, we stepped inside a meeting room with a long, narrow table. Coffee mugs sat buoyed on the surface, a steaming ring of them, along with a scattering of pens and papers. Sitting each to a mug were the head nurse, my social worker, the psychologist who administered my personality tests, plus the other three doctors who had patients on our floor.

Once while working at Ronson Lodger—and many times at Mitchell-Walker—I had sat in on a staffing session, which was a question-and-answer process to determine a patient's status relative to his or her capacity to be released. It was part of the law regarding people who had been committed. You could assume that people who had been dragged to institutions might not be telling the whole truth when it came to promising that they'd mend their ways once they got back out. They might very well turn around and kill the person (or persons) who had brought them there. The general hope was that the staffing would uncover such hidden intentions or, no matter what the agenda, indicate to the medical and legal authorities the degree of safety involved in releasing such people.

My mind had been a polluted swamp while working in the hospital. Though I rarely showed up for work under the direct influence, drugs had nevertheless made themselves at home in the organs and tissues of my body. With such anti-establishment chemistry, it was natural that I always took the side of the mental patient. It was my perception that many of the staffings were deliberately structured to induce anxiety in the patient, a baiting game to get him or her to explode. Even the best ones involved a bit of one-upmanship between the doctors as they grilled the patient, seemingly as a means to embarrass their associate by showing how he or she overlooked this or that aspect of their patient's care.

I knew just enough about the mental health system to make myself dangerous. Bowman pointed to my seat. As I sat down and waited for the first question, I told myself to be honest at all costs. I told myself that time didn't matter, nor did it matter if I went to trial. I would pay for my crimes, pay for them willingly. I told myself that there was only one rule in times such as these: If I wanted out in two weeks, I could count on getting two months; if I wanted out tomorrow, I could plan on staying the whole year. Being anxious to leave would guarantee I'd stay there forever. They could smell it on you.

And it magnified their sense of power.

Don't show 'em you want out, is what I said to myself. That's the only way to beat 'em.

Reverse psychology.

CHAPTER 41

In November of 1983 I got out of the hospital. Mitchell-Walker Psychiatric Institute, where I had worked for a year and convalesced for another ten weeks, released me via the judicial system of the State of New York. Upon Doctor Bowman's recommendation, I signed papers that bonded me to the following agreement: One year's probation, during which time I could be hospitalized for any violation or criminal misdemeanor, excluding parking tickets and things like that. If somebody thought I was a little daffy, even if they only suspected it (and this could be family, coworkers, or any bag lady waking up on the wrong side of the street), that person could sign a court order to have me put away faster than cheap beer on Super Bowl Sunday. My word meant nothing. I had no protection, no self-defense.

I was also compelled by court order to see a counselor every week. He, in turn, wanted proof that I was attending Twelve-Step meetings regularly. In addition, he insisted that I maintain myself on two hundred milligrams of Thorazine a day, though I did not have to put each one on my tongue and swallow in his presence. His office was on Eighty-Ninth and Central Park West. During every session he lit up a fat cigar. He had sandy hair and an overly groomed, anal-retentive beard and he looked like Freud's overachieving younger brother. He had a Central Park West heart of gold, discouraging me from calling him after office hours or during office hours on days we didn't meet. That's what my Twelve-Step sponsor was for, he said.

I had nothing to do with the selection of Freud Jr. He was selected for me. To him, our sessions were nothing more than "Story Time from the Astral Plane," and he seemed smug and a little bored as he folded my $55 check in half and stuffed it in his wool sport coat pocket. Just once I wanted to see how he'd react to the feel of a cold pistol up his nose. Just once I wanted eye contact as I stood over him, my trigger finger a quarter inch from separating him from his material things, his eyes big marbles of terror, his lower lip quivering like a slug with a cigarette burn, his bladder weeping on the floor.

By the time I started sessions with the guy I was fed up with the whole system anyway. The last few days at Mitchell-Walker, while I watched my hospitalization benefits dwindle to the point I was paying sixty percent of each day's fee, I actually had to stay an extra day because the outside therapist issue hadn't been solved to everyone's satisfaction. There was some legality over either my working at or being treated at Mitchell-Walker that made it impossible for Bowman to recommend anyone or have me seek outpatient counseling at Mitchell-Walker back in Manhattan. Basically, I was handed a phone book and told to go shopping. When I mentioned my plight to Susan, she had different ideas—ideas based on her personal diagnosis of me. She thought I should see a manic-depressive, that is, a person specializing in the treatment of manic-depressives. She just happened to know one, a fellow she had done research for a few years back. He was the best in the manic-depressive business. He had written several books on the subject and ran a place on Madison Avenue called the Foundation for Manic Depression.

Joni, on the other hand, was big on substance-abuse counseling. She believed my mental illness, no matter what it was called, sprang from my flirtation with mind-altering drugs. In her view LSD was the chicken, manic depression, the egg.

I called the manic experts and I called the drug debuggers. I called several of each. No matter who I talked to, they were immediately put off when they discovered I was taking Thorazine. "That's for schizophrenics," they said. "Go see someone who works with schizophrenics."

"But I'm not a schizophrenic," I said. "At least not anymore." By now manic depression was looking better and better. There'd be lots of blood tests and I'd be on lithium the rest of my life, but I could probably play that up at parties as a writer's badge of honor. Besides, all my mediocre work I could blame on lithium, which was supposed to level you out. Chicks might like it too. On every first date they'd hear about my chemical imbalance, about how dangerous I could be. There'd be a time-bomb feeling in the air, a sense that they were with a werewolf whose Moon-B-Gone prescription might, at any moment, be about to run dry.

Still, no matter who I talked to—manic, schizo, druggie —they were ready to work with me, provided I played their particular game. It was up to me as to what avenue of treatment I strolled along. I was as confused as ever and Bowman's diagnosis didn't help: emotional illness with acute psychotic episode.

Other factors came into play. Insurance benefits, unemployment benefits, all kinds of things depended on the "reason" I went into the hospital. In some cases "drug induced" psychosis was to my advantage, at other times it was not. Drug induced was better for the courts because it translated into temporary insanity. However, drug induced wasn't good for unemployment because it implied I might be irresponsible. As for insurance benefits, that depended on my policy. A big wink from my social worker there. No one at the insurance company would ever see my chart, she said, so we could put on the form whatever we wanted. I'd have let her put "animal necrophiliac with a fetish for frogs" if it would have extended my hospitalization benefits. Without pointing fingers, let's just say that there were lots of gray areas, dark areas, and a Milky Way's worth of little white lies. It was only paperwork. Besides, it still came down to one awful truth: somewhere, sometime I would need another job. And no matter what I had been or what I was now, I could never mention the slightest hint of mental illness at a job interview or on my employment application. As far as work was concerned, last August, September, and October never happened to me. I had been somewhere else.

In the days after discharge, the landscape of my life became a most unusual one. At first, Joni and Richard didn't want me on my own back in Manhattan. They asked me to stay a few weeks with them. That was fine with me; I was scared to walk back into my apartment anyway. I had a strong premonition I wouldn't like what I found. Staying in Brooklyn Heights allowed Joni's kids to get used to me all over again. Courtney would scrutinize me in her angelic fashion, remarking in complete innocence how I should go to the library on Thursdays if being near Rowena was going to bother me again. Or I'd make up a story to tease Jennifer, and she'd remark, unthinkingly, "You're crazy," and her eyes would drop, and it would be obvious she was sensitive on my behalf. I'd catch them both at the dinner table looking at me as if I might do something sudden, or perhaps studying me like I was an imposter, trying to reason how this person they loved could have been the same one to jump off a bridge. Courtney would cry for me and tell her mom how worried she was whenever I stepped out the door. I'd come home and hold her and squeeze her and tell her it was okay to worry like that, that it meant she loved me and that made me feel good. Both her and Jennifer made me promise over and over that I wouldn't hurt myself again.

During those first few weeks after discharge I experienced mild anxiety, an unheard, unseen current of fear, a suppressed but constant companion, like the rustle of blowing leaves you only become aware of once you say goodbye to whom you're walking with and must now walk alone. It wasn't the fear of unnatural things, for they had been replaced by the demons of real life.

As Christmas neared (and I celebrated four months of sobriety), it was becoming more and more apparent that I would never work again at Mitchell-Walker. They said I needed a doctor's clearance before they would even consider hiring me back. My head nurse stalled, then my department head, and pretty soon I got the runaround, being bounced between the personnel and employee health departments. Nobody wanted to get honest with me. Meanwhile, this undetermined status held up my pursuit of unemployment claims. On top of that, my first hospital bills started coming in. The initial one was for $18,000.00, though after my benefits were exhausted, I ended up owing them only four thousand dollars, plus a thousand to D'Aoust, a couple thousand to New Beginnings, a thousand to my attorney, and five hundred each for my last two ambulance rides.

On top of all that, I was getting evicted by my landlord. I borrowed money to pay my back rent but he wouldn't accept the check, preferring instead to challenge me in court. I had to march down to Canal Street and play games with his toadie lawyers, which amounted to the case being dismissed because the lawyers left the courthouse when they saw I couldn't be double talked into giving up my rights. I learned from other people who had been through the same thing that this was a typical procedure and that I shouldn't be surprised if it happened again.

Richard, who had operated mostly behind the scenes throughout my summer ordeal, now stepped into the spotlight and provided an important boost to my morale. My first night in Brooklyn Heights, after we had finished eating, he came into the den, bundled up in winter clothing, and handed me my coat and a new pair of gloves.

"Come on," he said. "I'll show you where the medicine is."

CHAPTER 42

I got dressed and stepped outside, and Richard led me several blocks to a church off Montague Street. He took me to a Twelve-Step meeting.

On the way back, without my asking for it, he proceeded to tell me of his own difficulty with accepting the Twelve-Step program. "It's real humbling to find out you've done it wrong all your life," he said. "The problem with the meetings, as I see it, is that they remind you how badly you once played your cards. But that's where the strength is, too. If you hang in there, pretty soon you'll hear your own story. When you can see you're no different than anybody else, that's when the healing can begin."

Richard and I became meeting buddies. Every evening we'd walk through the Heights, to and from meetings, talking about the new life before us. Richard was like a lot of other alcoholics in that regard; he needed the consolation of philosophy. Talking about God, justice, the meaning to life— this was a trademark of people who attended the meetings.

Richard's pet subject concerned the importance of not being too proud to see when we're wrong. "Pain has been our most effective teacher," he told me one night. "For some of us, our *only* teacher. The problem is that alcoholics have an unnaturally high threshold for pain. We always wait till the river's at the door before we think about getting any flood insurance."

Part of his own insurance was a worn paperback copy of

Alan Watts's *The Wisdom of Insecurity*. He sat in the den and read it all the time. Eventually I picked it up and began reading it, too. The book turned out to be one of the best gifts Richard ever gave me. The other was a line he said over and over, especially when we talked about my bills, my unemployment situation, or the million other obstacles that littered my way. "The future is friendly," he'd say. "You must believe that the future is friendly."

Richard paid off my attorney, the ambulance companies, and advised me that Mitchell-Walker was making it hard on themselves by expecting me to pay them when they wouldn't hire me back. (He stopped short of advising me not to pay them.) He said I should keep pushing them to rehire me, or at least to make a decision, and that possibly the route to take was to ask if they could reassign me to a less controversial, non-patient role.

I called and made them one last proposition. This they agreed to, provided I passed an interview with one of their physicians. A few days before Christmas I walked through the doors of the familiar main wing, down the marble hallway, announced myself to the same receptionist who had handed me my paychecks, and was eventually shown into an office where I sat in front of a vaguely familiar man who asked me no more than a dozen questions. The interview lasted less than an hour.

That evening Susan joined us for dinner. Everyone wanted to know how the interview went. When I mentioned the doctor's name, Susan's eyes lit up like a deer's caught in a poacher's high beams. This doctor who had interviewed me, she explained, was the top-ranking psychiatrist in the world, the current head of the American Academy of Psychiatric Physicians. He was responsible for the most updated and authoritarian books on the subject. He had held every top post on the international psychiatric scene, lectured throughout the world, and was reputed to be a shrewd, cold-hearted grizzly bear when it came to clinical diagnosis.

Susan looked at me as if I had gotten a bad break in a judging contest. She sighed. The kitchen got gloomy.

"No matter," Richard said, raising his sparkling cider glass. "Let's toast to the future. No matter what happens, we know it gets better than this."

The day after New Year's the phone rang at Joni's. I was sprinkling food in the goldfish bowl. Courtney and Jennifer dashed after the phone, Jennifer calling my name as she held it away from her little sister, who was clawing at her after being pushed down in the scramble. I took the phone in the kitchen. It was Mitchell-Walker. They informed me of their decision.

No deal.

***

Susan and I were together the day I reentered my apartment. It was exactly as I had left it on July 27, 1983, the day I had leapt off the Brooklyn Bridge. The place was a monument to psychosis, filled with the kinds of things studied by police psychologists when the serial killer is captured and his abode searched for evidence. Photos, cryptic writings, burnt papers—proofs of a mental massacre.

I was unaware of it then, but the photos of Catherine continued to have their effect on Susan. Though she had been kind and supportive through her visits in Albany, she couldn't shield herself from the terrible news bulletins coming in: Catherine taped to every wall, to the mirror on the floor, to the bathroom door, to the refrigerator behind a Mr. Peanut magnet. The panties, the love letters, the poetry—all signs of infidelity and lack of character on my part.

We cleaned the place and boxed all the old photos. I tried to show lack of reverence for them. I even thought of burning them in a new pile on the floor.

The one thing I *really* wanted to do was to cry. I wanted to break down and ask her forgiveness. Not for the forgiveness itself, but so that I could be sure I was capable of feeling remorse. I wasn't sure if I could feel at all. Standing there in the middle of my psychotic mess, the only way I could absorb the visual trauma of the room itself, the pain, the sickness it represented, was to detach so thoroughly that, in essence, I pretended it had happened to somebody else. Were I to feel anything, I feared it would open a door to my past, and through it would stream not only the recent, painful lessons with Bowman and D'Aoust, but still more unacknowledged memories, of drugs and self-destruction, of casual, faceless sex partners, all the way back to my one-nighter with Lilly, which had always made me feel "cut off" and unredeemable.

I wanted to feel so I could feel for Susan. It was pure selfishness. If I could feel for her, then it would mean that I was a good guy, that I had a heart, that I had a chance to be loved by somebody else, which, frightened and insecure, is what I most wanted.

But I was cold inside, totally incapable of regret or remorse. It was as if Catherine, Susan, the bridge, my entire past was locked up inside some impenetrable wall. And though my mind *knew* I had done wrong, *knew* how I had affected others, my mind would not allow this information into the region of my heart. I looked at myself as through a two-way mirror. I watched, but refused to feel.

We slept that night in the loft. Susan lay on her back, stiff, looking up, her face vacant of emotion. I held her and neither of us talked. I had the feeling that we had just come home from a funeral. We had buried a good friend and were mourning the fact that we would never see him again.

"Did I ever tell you about Robert?" she said, allowing her limp hand to be squeezed by my own.

"You've mentioned him," I said, referring to her former boyfriend. Robert had been popular, a musical genius, outgoing, energetic, and lots of fun to be with. Susan and he were the perfect couple. They had dated five years until one morning, after a party with friends in a Montreal hotel, they found him floating facedown in the swimming pool, victim of an overdose.

On one of our first dates Susan and I went to see *The Big Chill*, when all of a sudden, as those hands dressed the corpse in the beginning of the movie, Susan started crying hysterically, requiring me and an usher to help her out of her seat and into the ladies' room. That's when she first told me about her former boyfriend.

***

December 1983 was my first sober Christmas. Joni threw a party centered around non-alcoholic punch. A giant wreath of fresh spruce greeted Susan and I at the door. Inside, the smell of mulling spices and fresh pine wrapped us in a warm, nostalgic embrace.

Deja Vu: Barry Gordon was there, the man who might have directed my first play. He pulled me aside and spoke some simple pleasantries, then told me how sorry he was about my "bad luck." All I could do was look at him and shrug my shoulders. I felt that we had both lost out. Even *that* emotion was filed for later use.

Can of Worms had come and gone, had missed its only chance—if it ever had one. There was no reason to feel sorry. Barry, no doubt, would be there for the next one. "Everything that rises must converge," the poet once said.

I watched Susan talking with some friends of my sister. She looked lovelier than ever and it hurt all the more to know I was losing her. I could give her no reassurance. After all, I couldn't manufacture feelings that didn't exist. Lately, a part of me—the part most resembling the past voices of my demons —had been advising me to break up with her. Listen, the voice said, you're just throwing good money after bad. There's no way you can ever get back to square one with her. She knows too much. Five years from now, the voice said, when you come home late or forget to take out the garbage, do you want to hear, "I should have never married a schizophrenic!" when she lays into you? She's like an old car that needs new parts all the time. You're better off with a new model.

The voice further convinced me that Susan treated me like a car as well. Perhaps it was true. Our sex life—what still remained of it—was totally mechanical, giving me the feeling that as I climbed upon Susan, she became a hydraulic rack and serviced my needs in a manner no different than a grease monkey changing my oil. There was no more rapture. No more abandonment. She seemed to endure sex rather than relish it.

The next night we went to a Greek restaurant and talked once again about releasing our feelings. She said I was angry and could tell it was hurting me to bottle it inside. I thought she wanted me to stage a demonstration of proper anger, so I picked a fight with her, standing up and yelling at our table. Conversations halted, glasses and forks stopped tinkling, and the entire restaurant staff huddled at the entrance to the kitchen. Red-faced and biting on her lower lip, Susan slapped a twenty-dollar bill on the table and dashed outside into the rain. I came after her and caught her as she was about to climb in a cab.

"How did I do?" I said.

"Marvelous," she said. "You really pissed me off."

"But that's what you wanted, right? You wanted to see me get mad."

"You're mad, all right. Leave me alone. I just want to get out of here."

"But it was a test, right? We're just playing a game."

"Go play with someone else!"

Part of me wanted out of the relationship. But at the same time I was frightened of losing her. I was back in Manhattan but we only spent one or two nights together out of the week. On those nights alone I would wake up with a jolt. The orange face on the clock would say it was three or four in the morning.

I'd lay there, unable to get back to sleep, and imagine she was planning her life without me, perhaps dreaming of the next man who could offer her more.

My fear made me work desperately to please her. We constantly talked about my illness, my delusions. In my efforts to open up and rebuild myself to her specifications, I spilled as much of my past to her as I had been giving my therapist. I wanted her to understand me. I thought if she knew how bad I once had been, she'd be able to see how far I'd come along. She might take pity and forgive me. So I told her about Lilly and Rhonda and Carolyn Dobbs, the student nurses, my days as a whore.

Big mistake.

I found myself pulled by opposite emotions. I would be this passive, compliant thing, telling all, sparing nothing, seeking to prove my loyalty by punishing my own wickedness, by confessing over and over as a way to sever myself from my past. Surely she would see how I loathed the old me.

And then suddenly, I'd hear another voice that told me what a fool I was. It accused me of handing over my secrets and willpower to someone who shouldn't be that close. At these times I'd grow resentful and feel inclined to blame Susan for controlling my life. We fought bitterly then. I believed it was for our own good—at least for a little while—that I push her away.

Meanwhile, the best New York University could do for me was to place me on sick leave until spring term. Because I had missed a term already, there would be no tuition help until the following year. Basically, I would have to start all over, as far as qualifying for scholarships was concerned. Still, I was able to sign up for two classes. I'd attend part-time, and if I could find the money, make up some of my losses when summer came.

More bad news in January: There was a catch-22 at the unemployment office. Somehow (and no doubt it was a matter of one wrong word on one wrong form; one of those little white lies coming back to get me) but my status was such that, in order to receive unemployment benefits, I had to divulge a little more than I was willing to risk about my past hospitalization. With what little they knew about me, they weren't sure if I shouldn't be applying for worker's compensation, or some such thing. I hated the unemployment line anyway, the long wait, the runaround, the whole experience of being treated as a child. Since Mitchell-Walker was a dead-end, I decided it made more sense to start afresh with resume in hand rather than expect the government to come to my aid. "Screw it," I said, and walked out, I also decided against ever working in another hospital again. I'd go out and do my best to get a job in the writing field. I mentioned my plans one night to Richard and Joni. They were delighted.

CHAPTER 43

Strange days in New York City. The air was cold. The streets got icy. January winds pinched between the buildings and caught you broadside when you crossed the street. Gales roared double-force through the intersections. Traffic lights bobbed. Neon signs swayed. Everywhere you looked umbrellas littered the streets, turned inside out like squids about to jettison.

I was penniless. Seven thousand dollars in debt. And still on Thorazine. I went to three, four, sometimes as many as five Twelve-Step meetings a day. I carried a schedule and went from Harlem to the Bowery, looking for the circled triangle on the door, the secret sign that meant somewhere inside was a person or two who might lift their chin off their chest and tell me it was all worthwhile. All I wanted was to get through the day. I only wanted to go home and sleep the good sleep, to lay my head on my pillow with some hope that things would bet better. "The future is friendly, Mark." The meetings were smoky and crowded. The coffee tasted like tarpaper shingles. I'd hunch forward on the hard metal chairs and turn my Styrofoam cup in my hand, carving grooves with my thumbnail—when I had thumbnails, that is.

Richard directed me to the best meetings in Manhattan. He'd come into town and we'd make a meeting together. He started bringing the newspapers, opening them to the "Help Wanted" pages, and circling the jobs we thought I could handle. I'd feel low and tell him how I'd pay him back for the lawyer and the ambulances the minute I got steady money. But he'd tell me to forget it, that all he wanted to see was me stay sober and maybe wear a smile. "The future is friendly, Mark. Very friendly."

Anytime I got squirrelly, his place was mine. Joni and I had some afternoons together where we went for coffee and danish and got to know each other all over again. Through that horrible winter the brightest spot on my horizon was the healing between my sister and me. We talked about Mom and Dad and how all of the brothers and sisters had made their break from the nest. We decided not to look so much at the way our parents had brought us up, but at the way we had forged our independence. We were no different than anyone else in the world. "Everyone," Joni said, "is wounded by the process of growing up."

One afternoon Joni and I held a pow-wow over the issue of my longstanding dependence on her. I wanted to shuck off the old husk of relating to each other as though we were still fourteen and seven, fighting over who washed the dishes and who got to dry. I told her she made me feel that she was substituting for my mother, that her opinions sometimes implied that I couldn't think for myself.

In the way that only Joni could say it, she remarked that my last independent decision had me bobbing for apples beneath the Brooklyn Bridge. I didn't take it critically; I laughed. I told her about my decision to throw my wallet away and she chuckled heartily over that. Then she teased me about the car I stole from New Beginnings. "Most people who steal cars make sure there's nobody in them," she said.

From conversations like these I came to see that for many years Joni had been more than simply worried about me. All the time I had lived with her in Pennsylvania she had watched out for me in ways I never knew. Joni recalled how we had talked about lithium years ago, how she had cooked for me and tried to introduce me to better foods. She used to ask me to go jogging with her on the beach and she had invited me to join her and her friends in tennis. She had even offered to pay for counseling back when she was barely making ends meet herself.

I told her again about my dream of her friend, Patricia, at the swimming pool, then the muddy water. I asked her if she believed in dreams coming true. "Well, it's going to be pretty hard for that one to come true," she said. "Patricia's moving to Los Angeles."

I wasn't surprised. Ever since the new year, a gradual shift had been occurring in the world I had only just gotten used to once again. Patricia and her husband were selling their house and moving out West. Next door to them, Judy and Dave, other familiar faces, had recently divorced and sold their place, too. Around the corner, and still sharing the same backyard, yet another couple moved out, good friends of ours who had seemed like they'd be around forever.

Barry Gordon got a job with Disney Studios in Florida. I started back at NYU but the experience there grew hollow. I knew that my bridge jump was public knowledge and convinced myself that no one would ever take my writing seriously in the same sense that after Chappaquiddick, no one trusted Ted Kennedy anymore. How could I write about life, love, and values after trying to take my own life?

The shift reverberated all the way to Ronson Lodger. I had called Kelly in the early days of August after being seen by Doctor D'Aoust. (Back when I was planning on walking to Pennsylvania.) I was pretty crazy then, but I'm sure I must have told him something about the bridge. For certain he knew I was in the hospital and that I wanted his help. But he made no offer. He never wrote or called.

Then came January and a phone call out of the blue from Pete Sheridan, one of the orderlies—now a nurse—from the old Ronson Lodger gang and a good friend of Kelly's. It was very late at night and I'm pretty sure he was drunk. He was calling me because his wife had just left him. "I've got nobody to talk to," he said, "except you." So I listened. The poor guy had a right to some emotional support. And to let him know he wasn't alone in his troubles, I told him what had happened to me. He couldn't believe the part about the Brooklyn Bridge. He kept asking me to repeat it. He had been at Kelly's party, too, and had gone down the river with me in the very same raft. I told him about the drugs and how I had lost my mind. I figured by then the problem with his wife had seemed no bigger than a rash on his ass. Soon he seemed okay and I sensed there was nothing more I could do for him, so we both hung up.

A few weeks after that, about the middle of February, I got a phone call from Kelly. He practically threatened to kill me. He said an ugly rumor had started around the hospital, a rumor that alleged he slipped me drugs and that I nearly killed myself jumping off some building in Manhattan. The fucking rumor had caused his being passed up for a promotion and he was pretty sure any further advances at Ronson Lodger were blocked for years to come.

Personally, I always felt he was too cool for his own good. He seemed to fool a lot of people and made friends easily, but there would always be those who saw beyond it.

I would have apologized, but never once, not even after he had finished blowing steam, did he ask how I was doing or what had really happened that night at his place. All he cared about was what my near-death experience had cost him. I pulled the phone away from my ear; he sounded like an angry dwarf trapped inside. I laid the phone on the couch and went out into the hallway. I went downstairs and checked my mailbox even though I knew the postman hadn't come. I stopped to stare at some flowers in a pot. I walked back up the steps, listening to my feet echo in the stairwell. When I finally reentered my apartment the phone was where I left it, belly-up with a dial tone sound, the same kind of sound when somebody's heart waves turn to a straight line on the EKG screen.

February: meetings, meetings, meetings. I could have

pulled the petals off a daisy, saying, "The program loves me. The program loves me not." Cold, bitter nights walking to meetings with Richard. He wore one of those flat tweed caps that you see in the movies on British gents motoring through the countryside, like a mushroom resting on his head. All this time the Mafia was leaning on him and making his life miserable. If anybody should have been concerned about danger in the alleys, it should have been him and not me. Richard's hit men were real. My sister—who finally got the story out of him after finding a .32-caliber snub-nose in a shoebox—said he was thinking about closing down the shipyard rather than work with the mob.

At school, my credit load was easy so I concentrated more time on looking for work. I also quit taking my Thorazine. I felt strong enough and didn't owe anything to my jerk-off analyst. My energy picked up, and with it, an occasional hot flash, which I interpreted as a warning of a panic attack. But the flashes never went any further than that, never turned into fears of demons, hallucinations, or anything like that. If I wanted demons, I took a subway.

Sometime in March I qualified as one of three finalists for a position as editor of the employee newsletter at Presbyterian Hospital. The job payed reasonably well, and I used my Ronson Lodger background to my best advantage. But the opportunity fell through, mostly because they gave me a barrage of grammar tests and exercises to see if I could write the typical pyramid-style news release. I didn't do well; being aware of rules is like writing with a professor standing over your shoulder.

There were other jobs, mostly applications or sending in my resume by mail, but none of them came as close as the one at Presbyterian. It was a hard blow to take. But then a few weeks after that, I spied an opening for an editorial assistant for a nursing magazine. It payed shit but that made it all the more attractive; I sensed that it was a real job with a real future.

I sent in my resume and a few days later, the telephone rang. Linda Palmer, who introduced herself as the editor, said she'd like to speak with me in person. Bring your clippings, she said.

***

The office of the *American Nursing Journal* was on Thirtieth and Eighth Avenue, a block south of Madison Square Garden. It was part of a nonprofit nursing organization founded at the start of World War II. They leased the fifth floor of an old building wedged between a parking ramp and warehouse supplying the garment industry. The place was a cluttered, dismal mess. Boxes of computer forms littered the halls, stacked to the ceiling. I stepped into the restroom for a last-minute grooming and couldn't use the sink because stacks of old magazines blocked it like a medieval fortress. The toilet had rust in the bowl, a thick, red scum that broke apart when I urinated on it.

Linda's office was cramped and—in relieving contrast—tidy. The editor's tools were concentrated on a long working surface across from her desk: T-square, photo cropper, typeface sheets, handbooks of style. The little wheel for photo proportioning hung on a nail in the wall. Linda, an attractive brunette about my age in loose-fitting jeans and a baggy red sweater, shook my hand and invited me to sit. I declined a cup of coffee. "Well," she said upon returning with a cup of her own, "let's see what kind of writing you've been doing lately." I handed her some clippings which she gazed at more like photographs, barely scanning them. In between long, deliberate sips she asked about my past, what I was doing at NYU, then proceeded to tell me what the job would entail. Near the end of the interview she took me to the adjoining office and showed me where I would work. An old Underwood electric typewriter stood like the Rock of Gibraltar—the ancient, *ancient* Rock of Gibraltar—among a sea of scattered papers. Pencils, most barely two inches long and some with teethmarks, attested to the lack of materials and attention my position had earned in the past. I turned on the typewriter and it jumped alive, groaning more like a lawn mower than anything belonging in an office building. The fourth letter I hit, the K in my name, stuck on the platen like a spitball on the wall. I looked at Linda and we both knew the jig was up; she wasn't fooling me as to what kind of crap I was getting into. Every window in the place looked like it hadn't been cleaned in three or four years.

We went back to her office. My disappointment showed, but I brightened somewhat when I glanced through her publication. Four color covers. Clean typesetting, nice balance between copy and ads. I realized my name on the masthead would go a long way to furthering my interests in the writing field. I also knew I was desperate for anything—any job was better than starving to death. Anything was better than Twelve-Step meetings and walking in the cold.

Before I left I let her know I was seriously interested. I agreed, the pay was shit. But there's other things than money, I told her. She raised an eyebrow. And with that understanding between us, I had no doubt she had found her man.

CHAPTER 44

Linda called me a few days after my interview. "You got the job," she said.

What I didn't know, however, was that my future employer, the nursing organization, was shipwrecked in a sea of troubles. I should have suspected something when I first digested their name, a name that required memorization skills and a full set of lungs to pronounce it: The National Association and Nonprofit Foundation for Directions in Nursing. Even their acronym, NANFDN, announced that this was an organization that didn't expect to become a household word. They were hundreds of thousands of dollars in debt and hadn't paid for the past four issues of their magazine, which went out to nurses all across the world.

I didn't know any of this, of course, when I showed up for my first day of work. After all, I was only the editorial assistant. Linda and I, that was it. The whole magazine. But I knew waste and clutter when I saw it. There was also something fishy about the organization's staff. Right off the bat I knew something was wrong. They seemed to show up but never do anything. A dozen people came and went, but they never seemed to interact or have anything to do with each other. Linda kept her door closed most of the time.

I shared office space with Gloria, a sassy Costa Rican gal who worked in the records department. Young, outgoing—but married—she was the only person beside myself who didn't spend most of the day counting the spokes in the cobwebs that stretched from her desk to her chair. About a week into the job I told her of my perceptions. She rolled her eyes. "Everybody's dead here," she said. "But don't make any waves about it now. I think Linda is leaving."

After one month of employment, guiding me through one issue, Linda put in her notice and wished me lots of luck. She had a position as associate editor waiting for her at *Vanity Fair*.

"Nice move," I said.

"Thank you," she replied. "You made it all possible. Besides, you're going to do great. Don't sweat it."

"This is probably the fastest promotion I'll ever have," I said.

Linda was kind enough to disclose the salary she had been making. It was much, much more than an editorial assistant made. It was a whole lot more than a psychiatric aide made, too. And knowing that I was the last of the line, that absolutely no one could walk in there and take over my job, I decided to raise the editor's salary a little more, and this was my request submitted to Brenda, the executive director. She agreed.

So I became editor. I started going out to eat. I went out often and ate very well. I put an extra dollar or two in the Twelve-Step basket. I started paying back Richard. I even sent Mitchell-Walker a check.

But one day I opened the files and saw what a rotten, debt-ridden ship I was sailing. I got into the membership files and renewal forms and saw that nothing had been updated for ages. Libraries all across the country were requesting the magazine but no one had answered them; hundreds of uncashed checks filled a manilla folder. There were thousands of dollars in checks that were no good because they were more than six months old. What kind of place throws away money, I wondered. Then came the phone call. It was the printer. He was pretty frank with me. My first issue would be my last if they didn't start receiving what was owed to them.

"And how much is that?" I asked.

"Eighty-six thousand dollars, plus interest."

So, that's the kind of place that throws away money. The kind that doesn't pay who they're supposed to.

Suddenly my hospital bills took on a new perspective. But after a brief consolation, I became doubly worried. I decided to keep NANFDN's financial straits to myself. I didn't want Joni or Richard or anyone else worrying about me again. It seemed like things were going to get tight, like oatmeal through a funnel, but I had a hunch I'd squeeze through all right.

***

Did I mention that I broke up with Susan? Actually, she broke up with me. Over the phone. Right after I told her about my promotion. That probably made it easier for her, believing I was going to be able to take care of myself.

Anyway, I had seen it coming. We hadn't been together in almost two weeks. On the phone we exchanged no undying words of dialogue, no vows of remembrance, no exclamations of how our lives had been changed for the better, enriched because of the time we had spent together. It was more like canceling your cable TV. You knew you might miss it, but you knew life would go on.

The final irony had been that there was only one photo—a snapshot taken of the two of us at Asbury Park by one of my sister's friends. That was all I had to remember her by.

***

Then came the news the staff was going to Seattle for the annual nursing convention late in April. There'd be seminars and workshops and elections to the board of directors. I was to come along and answer questions about the journal.

The convention was held at the Seattle Hilton. We packed boxes and boxes of registration forms, typewriters, all kinds of equipment. We hauled crates filled with journals—my latest "last" issue—and packed ourselves in a 737 and flew to the

West Coast. Once there we rented microphones and overhead projectors. We unpacked boxes of brochures provided by the Seattle Visitors and Convention Bureau, telling our esteemed members of the many restaurants and attractions in and around the city. And no sooner did we get our brochures and typewriters ready, and the purple crepe paper draped over our table in the lobby, than the members began arriving, gathering together like dustballs under a bed. We had dozens of workshops to sign up for. During the busy hours I helped with registration, writing people's names on a round button that they pinned on their chests. When it was less busy, Gloria and I ran a booth selling coffee mugs and T-shirts. Imagine a T-shirt with nothing on it but the letters NANFDN. We sold two.

The second day we were beat. The convention goers treated our staff like indentured servants. They were older women, mostly overweight, equal numbers of whites and minorities. They were plainly hostile to every one of us, especially me, the newest, the youngest, and the only man. The animosity compounded with a nasty rumor going around that the executive director was in trouble. The rumor alleged that others now knew of the organization's financial health.

After dinner I escaped to the top floor to catch a swim and soak in the hot tub. The elevator ride was heaven; for the first time in forty-eight hours I was alone. When I stepped into the pool area Gloria was already there, smiling from the frothy depths of the Jacuzzi. I lowered myself in slowly and let out a sigh.

"This is what I hate about conventions," Gloria said, motioning with her hand. "We get all this luxury and splendor and absolutely no time to enjoy it." She hoisted herself out of the tub and for the first time I saw what a splendid figure she had. I hopped out and stood beside her, becoming instantly aware of the lights of the city sprawling thirty floors below. We stood side by side in front of the pool, and I could turn and view Seattle in every direction. I also took a second look at Gloria, her shapely legs glistening with water, a few fine hairs capped with tiny beads of the stuff.

"Oh my God," I said.

A hot flame shot through my head. The pool and the tile surrounding it seemed to buck with a violent motion, as though the building were swaying from an earthquake. Everything spun wildly and I fell first to my knee, then into the water. My head hit the bottom in the shallow end, further jolting my senses as the memory of the Brooklyn Bridge flashed through my mind. I came to the surface and at the same time, in my mind, I broke through the memory of my suicide attempt, going back behind it to another memory, that of my dream of the woman and me beside the swimming pool. This was the dream. Exactly. Though not New York and not Patricia, this was the very same place and situation that the dream foretold. I then thought about the second half of the dream, about the river with the muddy banks. I saw my mother and father in the car and my sister behind them, the car on a low hill and the giant star in the sky, the huge comet bearing down.

I came out of the water a choking, bug-eyed mess. Gloria couldn't tell if I was playing a joke or had suffered a heart attack. I told her I was fine. I would not describe what had happened.

It was a while before I could towel off and get back to my room. When I got there I called room service and ordered a six pack of beer. It came fifteen minutes later. I grabbed one and opened the tab. I knew without the slightest doubt that the future had caught me once again. Something terrible was about to happen. My dream coming true was a warning sign. Fate was at hand. I had to be ready to see it coming; I'd have to act in an instant if I wanted to grab the reins.

I took a long swig and felt the beer roll down. I held up my other hand and noticed it was shaking. Fate or not, I wasn't going anywhere for a while.

***

The next day was Sunday, the last day of the convention, and the day for electing all the new board officials. Quite unexpectedly I was called before the board in their committee room. I was told that every department had to make a full accounting of themselves. Could I please tell them about the status of their journal?

I could not lie. I told them about the debt, about the awful mismanagement. I told them I couldn't figure out how a magazine with such a fine reputation could have been produced in an office like ours. (The executive director and staff weren't in the room at the time.)

I sensed they appreciated my honesty. So I played my best card. I told them I had been looking over the old issues, the good old issues from the good old days. (The average board member was about eighty years old.) I told them I liked what I saw and that the best thing for their journal was a return to the good old days. I held up a more recent issue and told them how I'd improve it. I told them how I'd boost circulation and ad revenues by 40 percent.

They bought it. They applauded. Then the president of the board said the darnedest thing. An old, red-haired biddy with liver spots on her fat, flaccid arms, she hauled herself into a standing position to address both me and her court. "Mr. Wolyczin," she said, "I don't doubt for one minute that you could sell us the Brooklyn Bridge. However, you must produce results. And produce them, quite possibly, in the most dire of circumstances. The election results are in, and the new board will convene in the closing moments this afternoon. As of this moment you are without an executive director. It is just as likely, once we review our finances thoroughly, that next week or the week after, you may no longer have a job."

She looked about the room. I felt last night's beer gathering at the end of my penis. "We will take into consideration the fine speech you've just made," she continued. "However, our first task is to find a new executive director. It'll be upon her recommendation as to what becomes of you. I am sorry to present you with such unfortunate news. I ask that you mention this to no one, especially other staff members, as we have two more departments that have yet to report. And by the way," she said, picking up my most recent issue, "this looks pretty good to me. I hope you realize how important our magazine is to our members."

"I do," I said. I do, I do, I do.

CHAPTER 45

Back in New York City, the organization got turned over like a raffle box before the drawing. The old executive chief had vanished, and we were under orders not to touch a thing. As if by inverted Newtonian law, you never saw a place get so neat so fast. File cabinets that no one had been in for years were suddenly humming open and closed, open and closed. The same people who, two weeks before, wouldn't have hustled if the building was on fire were now going through their respective departments like frantic treasure hunters looking for a million-dollar prize. Everyone got busy folding, assorting, paper clipping, and alphabetically ordering everything from budget requests to expense reports to the paper towel racks in the washrooms.

It was all for nothing. Three days after we got back, Ilene Hanson, the new executive director, walked through the door. For the next two weeks I don't believe she ever left that place. Tall, with short brown hair and a masculine carriage, she went through everything. She took a permanent seat in front of the old mainframe computer and started printing out documents of all our financial transactions. She scooped up everyone's expense reports and went through them line by line. She walked into each department and demanded a detailed accounting of how things were handled on a daily basis. She went through the mail—every piece by herself. If there were mouse turds under the water cooler, she knew how many, what color, and which mouse they belonged to. I don't think Ilene was thirty-four years old yet, but she handled the association as if she had been training for the job her entire life.

A week after Ilene got there, pay day arrived with solemn perversity, like an invitation to a party where a murder is to take place. Rumor had it we were all getting canned. On the subway that morning I couldn't help feeling that I was the subject of an economically depressing newscast, the kind where the reporter sticks the microphone in the face of some factory worker who tells the camera how the plant is closing down and he and his buddies are shit out of luck. I hadn't had a drink since we returned to Manhattan, but my mind was already mapping out the many bars between work and my apartment, such was my conviction that this was the last day of my brilliant career.

It was a drizzly morning, the sky the color of a blank movie screen. I had just gotten my coat off and was looking over a half dozen used NANFDN coffee mugs cluttering the sink, trying to decide which one would be the easiest to clean, when Ilene postured in the doorway and asked to see me in her office. I poured my coffee and followed behind.

She closed the door. We made some chitchat, but not much. She was a no-nonsense person. Straight suits. Dark, solid colors. Flat shoes. Turned the thermostat down when she left in the evening.

"You know, you could have done a lot worse in Seattle," she said, "a lot worse, believe me." Then she made the comment that I had made a fairly good impression on those-who-would-believe. "An excellent dancer," she said with a slight smile. Then to my surprise, she said my position was secure.

"An outrageous salary," she said, "but that's not the issue. Neither is your talent nor the way you perform your job."

"What's the catch?" I said. "I suppose this means you're phasing out the magazine."

"Heavens no," she said. "It's one of our few visible benefits. Without that we don't have a pipeline to our members. And we sure as hell couldn't ask for dues."

Abruptly, Ilene changed the subject. She wanted to know if I was ready to relocate for the glory of commanding my own nursing journal. I'd be working with a new printer and could redesign the publication from the ground up, provided my changes met with her approval, of course. It was a wonderful idea. But in all the excitement I nearly passed over the operative word.

"Relocate?" I said. "Relocate where?"

"St. Louis, Missouri. I understand you're a Midwest boy."

"That was Ohio," I said.

"Around here," she said, "that's considered a neighboring state."

***

I was the only staff member to remain on board. It wasn't because I was irreplaceable or that all the others had been fired, it was mostly because I was the only unmarried one and the only one willing to move to Missouri.

I was also willing to take the chance that the association might go belly up and I'd never see another paycheck again. Ilene was up front with me on that, though she didn't rake over all the details until June—after I had packed up my world and landed in St. Louis, a total stranger in a town I had only driven through once.

What a shock. There was barely time to pack, let alone say goodbye or think about what I was doing. Joni hated to lose me. And Richard worried that I might abandon the program.

I had a strange feeling as the plane descended over St. Louis before landing. We passed north of downtown and I could see the Gateway Arch like a big, silver wishbone with its ends jammed in the ground. Beside it lolled the Mississippi River, a crooked trough of watery caramel that brooded beside the tall buildings of the downtown area. Memories of my "clear water" dream came back to me, and I wondered if this new place had indeed been foretold way back in my Penn State days, and the decision by the board in Seattle had of course been necessary in order for me to follow through with the second part of that dream—the part about returning to dirty water.

Things seemed on schedule; Halley's Comet was less than two years away. The crazy thought passed through my mind that, if I encountered demons in St. Louis, they might go easier on me than they had in New York. Then I prayed I'd never meet demons.

We set up shop in an office above the freeway, three floors up with an uninspiring view of bone-white concrete hotels, a 7-Eleven, and a dozen fast food restaurants that trailed away to the airport a half mile up the road. Our glass was tinted and specially soundproof. Every other minute a jet angled into the sky, roaring, banking with a glimmer of wings, then disappearing into the gritty summer haze that seemed to hang permanently above the northwest part of town.

Ilene told me what financial straits we were in as we unpacked the entire NANFDN world that had come across country by giant moving van. It was a mountain of furniture: oak secretarial desks, bulky, rusted file cabinets, boxes and boxes of papers and magazines.

"There's a good chance we'll go bankrupt," she said, "and you'll be stuck out here without a leg to stand on. But there's an equal chance we'll both get through this and have lots of great stories to tell, provided anybody wants to hear them."

I was nuts to trust her, but trust her I did. We were hundreds of thousands of dollars in the red and all of Manhattan was looking for us, creditors lined up a mile long with bills in their hands that we couldn't possibly pay. On the day they hooked us up, Ilene hesitated to plug the phone in.

"I'm going to do everything in my power to keep us afloat," she said, digging into her purse for quarters for the Coke machine in the hotel lobby across the road. "It makes me mad as hell to see what a mess this association has gotten into, mostly on account we were too ignorant and trusting to police our own. I feel responsible. If I'd have known how bad things were getting, I'd have shown up in New York five years ago. Left the husband to watch the kids and slept right there in my office. It makes me sick to see a lot of good people getting hurt because our board members—and dammit, I was one of them—because our board was too proud or lazy to figure out something was going wrong."

Ilene and her CPA husband had two boys and lived about thirty miles outside the city. Since she was the only one willing or able to travel to Manhattan to do CPR on the dying association, there was no debating her decision to move NANFDN to St. Louis, bringing it closer to her home. It would also put a little distance between us and the creditors.

That first week we worked eighteen to twenty hours each day, just moving things and separating each department from the other. We grunted and groaned behind moving dollies and we had to tape down the file cabinet drawers because they'd fly open and take our heads off if we weren't careful. Ilene and I moved every desk, every box and item by ourselves. We'd finally quit around two in the morning, pulling up seats by an old radio tuned to a country-western station, her music of choice. By the end of each day we looked like a pair of chimney sweeps. We'd prop our feet on boxes we hadn't opened yet and talk about most anything we could think of, which usually meant we got back on the subject of nursing and the problems she was uncovering with every new stack of files she went through.

In time I grew very fond of Ilene. She loved the association, loved it in the same sense as other people love and cherish their own families. She defended it like a momma bear. And she spoke of and defended many principles as well, she being the first person I had ever encountered—with the possible exception of Dr. D'Aoust—who really lived with a sense of higher purpose. Altogether these qualities compelled one to respect her as a person, to regard her as a natural leader, and to return to her the fierce loyalty and dedication she inspired day to day.

That first month we struck a deal. Next to herself, I would be the last asset to go. As long as there was money in an account and our checks weren't bouncing, she'd keep paying me until the lawyers locked the doors. I lived on that promise for the next six months.

That's how long it took for our next issue to be printed.

CHAPTER 46

St. Louis provided a series of tests. Throughout the summer of '84, I faced a major test in regard to finding my way around a strange and complicated city. In the townships fanning westward from St. Louis—as in no other towns I'm aware of—the names of streets changed for no apparent reason. Kirkwood Road suddenly became Lindbergh Boulevard. Brown Road bent and became Howdershell, which shortly thereafter became Shackelford. Practically in the same neighborhood, Charbonier turned to Aubuchon, then turned into Missouri Bottom Road.

Actually, during those first months in St. Louis problems with street directions would have been a luxury, considering I didn't have a car. I never needed one in New York. And getting one in Missouri was not going to be easy. I had no recent driving record; in fact, the last thing I drove I stole from someone else. Other than that, nothing from New York indicated I had ever operated a car. My old Pennsylvania license was decomposing in the muck of the East River. Even then I had always driven someone else's car; I had never carried my own insurance. I had never owned a credit card. I had no credit history. Yet here I was, a ninety-day-old Missouri resident with no track record or references, trying to pull together a down payment on an automobile while facing thousands of dollars in unpaid medical and legal bills.

Just as the season turned to autumn and the weather turned foul, I managed to get an American Express Card.

Hallelujah. I had to get verification from Pennsylvania, but finally Missouri granted me a new driver's license. Now I could rent a car. I rented one every weekend and drove it to the limit that free mileage would allow.

I spent Thanksgiving and Christmas alone. I had signed a one-year lease on a cramped, bleak apartment that was even closer to the airport than our office. It didn't have tinted or soundproof glass and the Air National Guard fighter jets, ripping the sky with their vertical takeoffs, rattled the tea ball dangling from its chain above the sink and the salt and pepper shakers on the back of the stove.

I would be lying if I didn't admit to missing Susan that first year in St. Louis. Some of it was just plain horniness, "raging hormones," to use one of Susan's phrases. Often I experienced a damp heat that matched the humid weather, a kind of wet, expectant tension that produced days when I'd find myself driving the freeway and having sexual fantasies based on nothing more than the shape of some woman's hair in the car in front of me. Or getting turned on by the girl in the white shorts in the Newport cigarette billboard ad. I stared hungrily at any woman who crossed my path.

Part of it was lust but part of it was genuine longing for a meaningful relationship. Unfortunately, it was just such a meaningful relationship that I had lost with Susan. That realization caused an echo effect, a remembrance of other breakups, and the accompanying thought was that I only missed my water once my well was dry. I found myself missing Catherine in the same way, but with this one difference: that while I shared my doubts and demons with Susan in the hopes it would keep us together, I had no intention of ever telling Catherine what had happened at Kelly's party, nor the bridge or any other aspect of my last hospitalization. I didn't want that part exposed. Pride played a role, too; I still couldn't resolve what I'd tell her in regard to missing her mother's wedding. There seemed to be no way out of it except to admit I had screwed up. These feelings resulted in me sending her only one postcard, just to notify her of my change of address.

There was another difference between Catherine and Susan. While Catherine and I had been accidental lovers, Susan and I had gone into it with a much more serious intensity. We worked hard to make a deeper connection—which made it all the more difficult to let her go. For months I played over our intimate moments, recalling her hundred-thousand-dollar hands, how I sucked those fingers, how they pressed my asshole when I was on top of her, how her nails raked me like the Blue Angels trailing white lines across my back.

Eventually I got reconnected with the Twelve-Step program, driving to weekend meetings and being driven to or walking to nearby meetings during the week. I opened up more than I had in New York. I didn't mind sharing the uncertainties in my life, and as a consequence, people were drawn to me who could help with my loneliness, confusion, and fear. The desire for drink or drugs didn't seem to be there anymore. Even more distant were the old voices that used to inhabit my head. It seemed like the devils and Nazis had belonged to someone else, or that maybe they were part of a play I had written, or just something someone had told me or I had seen on TV.

The biggest single change was that, instead of fighting the Twelve-Step program, I came to see it as a necessary lifeline to sanity. True, there remained a lot of suffering at the meetings. At times I resented people for holding onto their suffering—grafting it to themselves, so to speak. Coincidentally, at the same time I loathed myself for still "needing" the meetings, thinking, "Why am I here, feasting on this pain?" and berating myself for using the program as an emotional crutch. What I failed to see was that many people weren't there because they needed the meetings, rather, they were there to love and guide less fortunate people who came to those meetings in a similar state as mine. They weren't there to get. They were there to give.

I kept in touch with Richard, calling him at least once a week. Now and then I'd complain. He'd tell me it was my problem, whatever it was. We'd argue but that was good. It got my juices flowing. I almost wanted to get healthier to spite him. And that was good, too. Then he'd sign off with his favorite saying, "The future is friendly, Mark," and I'd close my eyes and try to imagine a world where that was true.

In early January I bought a new car. A silver sports car. At the same time Ilene announced that we were out of the woods financially and her weeks and weeks of computer work had finally paid off—we had an updated mailing list by which we could send out dues notices and rescue the association. We celebrated with sparkling cider. Within a month, checks started pouring in. Bags of them. In February she hired two new employees. As soon as funds were available, she said, we could print our next issue.

Print one we did. It was a great issue, a true comeback featuring 1984's Miss Universe, a licensed practical nurse, on the cover. It was sixty-four pages and every line, dot, dash, and comma was mine. Success felt heady. Achievement felt good.

There remained one area in my life, however, where I could find no success of any kind—my relationship with my parents. The last time I had seen them was in 1982, over a year before my suicide attempt. I didn't call or write them throughout my ordeal and they didn't know I was moving to St. Louis until a few days before I left. My sister had told them.

I had no logical reason for feeling so estranged from them. It was an avoidance, a sense that the less they knew the happier we all would be. I didn't want to be vulnerable to my mother because I feared that she'd question my move, fill me with *her* doubts and consequently make me feel that I was doing it against her wishes, hurting her by striking out on my own. A good indicator of where our relationship stood was the Catholic greeting cards she had been mailing me every month or so, the kind with the praying hands and the announcement that sixteen masses were being said in my honor. I realized having priests pray for me was a positive gesture, but I always associated praying with hopeless cases, terminal illnesses, outbreaks of war. Every time I received one of her prayer cards it was like being the quarterback of a football team where, when the coach sends in a new play, the first thing the guy says in the huddle is "Coach wants to remind you we're losing really bad."

I knew she loved me and supported me. I knew she was allowing me to decide what's best. Yet there I was, the little kid in me still uncertain if I was a dirty boy.

Unfortunately, yet is often the case, it took tragedy to finally bring my parents and me together. Late one spring afternoon I came home to a ringing telephone. It was my mother on the other end. "Richard's dead," she said. "He died of a stroke this morning."

As my mind repeated those words and began digesting their meaning, the objects in the room seemed to spin away from me, the walls pulling back. For a second I felt I was on an island in space, just a speck in the void, a little man with a phone in his hand and a cord connecting to nothing. I felt cut off from something that had stood for life itself. Then, as though flying by thought, I was carried across the country back to Brooklyn Heights. As though in some dream where time had stopped I could see Richard in the den in his black leather chair, flipping through his Alan Watts, pausing to tap the bowl of his pipe against the cork knob in the center of the ashtray, the blackened tobacco spilling out like a tiny load of coal. He smiled and asked me if I wanted to read that evening's *New York Times*. He then made a joke about the mayor and asked me if I had a yellow marker so he could highlight a certain paragraph in his book.

For a moment it was as though I were a visitor in a spirit museum, a place where the IS is ALWAYS SO. Richard sat with a smile, preserved in eternity. In simplicity. In the common light of an average day.

CHAPTER 47

At the age of fifty-three, Richard Kerrigan was laid to rest. It was a beautiful April day, a turquoise dome over the jagged New York skyline, a skyline that made a matching backdrop for the marble crosses and headstones of Calvary Cemetery in Queens. Standing in a semicircle around a coffin draped with red roses, I played tricks with my eyes, making the rows of grave markers march backwards and join the Empire State Building, the World Trade Centers, the Chrysler Tower, all of them giant tombstones as well, great, tall mausoleums shouldering the sky.

Joni was devastated, still in shock. Richard had died in her arms in the hallway in the morning. He had just finished his coffee and was going in the bathroom to shave. They called it an embolism, a sudden clot at the base of his brain. He died within minutes, my sister watching the light fade in his eyes, clutching his weakening hand, screaming and weeping and knowing it was already too late to dial 911.

I flew out the following day. At the funeral parlor that evening I passed circles of her friends and overheard the word "shock" being whispered as eyes gazed upon her. I, too, worried about Joni. She seemed encased in some kind of bubble, some underwater diving bell, and I could tell the face she presented was not the real Joni at all. The morning of the funeral I stepped into her bedroom to grab a hairbrush and caught her staring into space. It was then I knew she shouldn't be left alone. Yet at the same time I realized all her support would eventually taper off. I would be gone in a couple of days, after that, my parents would have to go. One by one, her friends would go, too. They'd leave cookies, casseroles. But sooner or later their jobs, their relationships, their lives would call them back. It would be then that she'd feel his loss most deeply.

Perhaps, one night within the shadows of the kitchen, after the kids had gone to bed, she'd catch a glimpse of him on the floor with hand outstretched, his lips silently calling. Or maybe she'd see him in his chair like I had when I got the news over the phone. She'd open a cupboard and there'd be his favorite coffee cup, looking down from the shelf like an icon, like an artifact. For many nights afterward, while the grandfather clock chimed the darkest half hours, she'd have those falling-off-the-edge-of-the-world dreams, with the even worse waking up to a half-empty bed, the aching, half-empty heart, then the thought-filled vigil till dawn. These would be followed by the solemn, still-life mornings after the kids went to school, mornings when it would take all the energy in the world to dust a dresser or boil an egg. Too often she'd catch herself touching his shirts, his ties, going through his cuff link box and smelling his cologne, finally wandering into the den— his den—and make-believing he was back, asleep, perhaps, in his reading chair with his head to one side and his pipe in his hand.

"We're going to stay an extra week," my mother said to me after the funeral as we rode back in the second limo behind Joni and her girls.

"I wish I could do the same," I said, "but I can't."

She took my hand in hers and kissed it. "You're closer to her than any of the other children, you know." Dad nodded in agreement.

"She saved my life, Mom."

Mrs. Margaret Ann Wolyczin, who sat in the middle, started sobbing and put her head on my shoulder. At the same time Dad reached over and patted my other arm. "It's good to see you, son," he said. "I'm proud of the way you're taking care of your sister."

"I'll never repay her, you know."

Mom looked up, her face red and smeary. "It's . . . it's really wonderful to see you taking care of yourself. Every time we get one of your issues or hear from Joni, I just can't believe it's my son. My son, the successful publisher."

She planted a moist peck on my lips. "I'm only sorry we have to get all the good news from Joni. Why don't you write us more often?"

"That's right," Dad said. "If we knew how good you were doing she wouldn't be saying all those masses for you. They cost good money, you know."

Up front the limo driver laughed. "If ya's don't mind my interruptin', I wanna tell ya's this is the biggest damn funeral procession I've ever driven for. Even the mob don't bury 'em like this anymore. And I oughta know. I drove for Joey Gallo's funeral. This Richard Kerrigan guy puts ol' Joey to shame."

That was true. I had never seen so many people come to honor the dead. Half of Brooklyn's Twelve-Step population was there, dozens of neighbors from the Heights, plus a solid stream of workers from the shipyard; grimy, rough-featured men with their hats in their hands, their eyes cast down and some showing tears.

I am fairly certain Richard never gave in to the mob, even after they had threatened his family and his very own life. Unknowingly, the limo driver had paid a high tribute to my brother-in-law; Richard had had the last laugh. I also believe he had been placed on this earth to help me at my most critical time. Without him I might not have ever been delivered to Doctor D'Aoust or Bowman—and certainly wouldn't have come out of jail alive. It was as though, his job completed, God needed Richard to help out somewhere else.

***

The summer of '85 turned out to be a season of

reconciliation. With some encouragement from Joni, I began to call my parents on a regular basis. I took a new apartment on a better side of town. I had money in the bank and one weekend, out of the blue, I drove to Ohio and surprised Mom and Dad, taking them out to dinner Saturday night. The next morning I went to church with them and was shocked and somewhat saddened when I heard the priest announce that Blessed Family's order of nuns was dissolving that very day. School enrollment had tumbled and no new nuns were joining the order anymore. Immediately after mass, the priest said, they were holding a homecoming reception for all the old sisters who had come back to say goodbye.

My mom grabbed my arm. "I hope you'll come with me," she said. "Some people want to speak with you."

I couldn't believe the scene I walked into. There in the cafeteria, only a few feet from the stage with the trap door where we used to skip classes and eat pizza we had stolen from the school kitchen—there stood Sister Mary Ellen, Sister Ann, Sister Cecilia, each wrapped in familiar dark blue, all the characters who had battled with me in the days of my youth.

I stood in shocked silence. It was as if the past had arranged a special atonement, a kind of Appomattox between me and the Catholic Church. My mother, who must have also understood the importance of this truce, ran about and reintroduced me to my former enemies, having me stand close with my arms around them as she snapped photos to commemorate the event.

"Of all the weekends to come home!" she kept saying, flustered with joy. It *was* great. It was as if all the ghosts from an old battlefield were suddenly set free from their sentry posts, finally allowed to rise in victory.

Tiny Sister Ann said it the best of all. "I remember you," she exclaimed, standing back to appraise the man who had tormented her many years before. "I could never manipulate you like the others. Your spirit was too strong."

We both laughed. Her words were kind and true.

On the drive back to St. Louis, cruising the highway in my new car, I flashed on the distant possibility of the world coming to an end. Already it was in the news, the comet coming sometime in February. Life was going well for me now. I didn't want it to end. Not for me or anyone else, for that matter. I supposed that if I would have had children, I'd have never entertained the thought at all. Perhaps I had never cared for the world, I thought, because I had never made an effort to put something at stake.

***

A few weeks later Catherine stopped at the office, having gotten my address from one of our magazines she had discovered at a friend's in New Mexico. She was passing through on her way back to Erie. She had a ring on her finger and she couldn't talk long; someone was waiting in the car.

I shut the door to my office and hugged her, tears racing down both our faces. She was getting married next month, she said, to an archeologist. She'd be going to Mexico and then possibly Iraq.

I stepped back and gazed on her face, our hands still touching until she dropped hers as a signal to depart. We hugged once more and promised to remember each other kindly. As I was about to ask if I could write her, she said she knew where she could find me and that she'd drop a line once she and her husband had finally settled down. We kissed once more and she left. After watching their car exit the parking lot, I dimmed the office and went outdoors, eventually getting in my car and driving nowhere, just through the neighborhoods, looking at nothing, until I ended up at the public pool, where I parked in the shade and watched the little kids play "Dare" off the diving board.

That October I arranged to fly Joni out to St. Louis for the Fall Classic, a recovery convention featuring speakers, a dinner, and a grand ballroom dance. Mom and Dad drove out from Ohio. At this time my little brother Derek was living with me, having moved from Alaska after he confided in me that he, too, was getting involved in drugs. I suspected it for some time but could not break through his denial in any of our phone conversations we had had up to that point. The way I handled it was to write a feature story in my magazine, a piece on self-esteem called "Freedom Within." Ostensibly it was a letter to a young man about to begin nursing school. However, in 36-point bold type, I began the letter with the words "Dear Derek," and left it up to him to read between the lines. It worked. He called me and asked for my help.

The convention was a glorious affair. Mom met a lot of my new, sober friends and Dad danced with all the women. He was smooth and agile and for one blissful moment, I believed I saw a flicker of the young man standing with his buddies in front of his B-17. My heart swelled.

Joni looked better and seemed to be coming out of her six-month depression that had left its mark. Her face, though always beautiful, now carried an imprint of sadness, a deep melancholy around her eyes that made her expressions, rather than duller, seem even more powerful—more connected to her heart. Her face was more sensual, yet at the same time, more spiritual, more sincere. She had a new openness after bearing so much pain.

"You know Richard would be very proud," she said, "to see you doing for Derek what he had done for you. That was the one thing he wanted the most for you, Mark."

I was surprised how easy it was to spend time with my parents. Listening to them chatter I realized their likes and dislikes were no reflections of my own. Occasionally Mom stated her preferences—like when she discovered I had "borrowed" some of her mother's antiques on my last trip back to Ohio—but I learned to respect her and to not take her too seriously. That made the phrase "I'm sorry" a whole lot easier to say. I realized I had it in me to give to her now, but that I could only give her that which was truly mine. It was up to her to respect my individuality, no matter what I gave her, to accept it or reject it, which was her issue, not mine.

Sunday night after the convention was over, I decided to drive them down to the airport to show them the office where I worked. We spent a few minutes looking at proof sheets and T-squares and green words on a computer screen, then I thought we'd wrap up the evening at Lindbergh Boulevard, where there was a parking area for watching the jets as they touched down on Lambert Field.

I parked Dad's car on the service road and helped my mother walk sideways down the embankment to the fence at the edge of the field. Ahead of us stretched the blue landing lights. A Boeing 707 whooshed over our heads. It was so low and loud we ducked in reflex. As the big plane touched down tires screeched, releasing little plumes of smoke. A few moments later another one landed.

"It's getting cool out here," my father said. "I think your mom wants to go."

"Good enough," I said. "Let's go home."

I let the others go ahead of me. I watched one more plane and turned to follow, noticing my brother and sister climbing in the back of the car. As I stepped up the embankment a powerful feeling took hold of me, a sense that I was walking onto the stage of a play, as though I was about to speak lines that had been written for me many years ago. I got to the car and looked inside: Mom and Dad in front, Joni and Derek in the back. There was something about Joni's face at the window. I had the keys in my hand but I stood frozen in place. Over the roof of the car I could see it—a large, glowing light. It came closer and closer. It was the giant star in my dream, but unlike the dream, not quite the size of the flaming fireball. Instead, it broke off into several other lights, each smaller than the original.

My mind snapped back and forth between the dream

and reality. Finally I understood what I was looking at. The lights were jets descending on their landing approaches. For a moment they had been in a line, a golfball-sized cluster, but now there were six, seven, eight separate lights moving towards me.

My sister's face came to the window—exactly as it had in my childhood dream. But this time she wasn't afraid.

"We're waiting," she said.

I continued to stare at the sky in wonder. The lights glistened like snowflakes, the result of tears in my eyes.

"Little brother," Joni said, "I believe you're doing the driving. Come on. You're the one who knows the way home."

THE END

AFTERWORD

Mark went on to business success with taglines always bringing a smile with any marketing task. Headlines with puns. Stories told with words or video with insight and heart. Later, while a columnist for the *Shelton Journal*, his super popular column "On the Trail" infected readers with a contagious love of the wild.

We had 25 adventurous years together as life partners and creators, traveling near and far, visiting springs - hot and cold, camping, foraging. Our business served businesses, government agencies, and non-profits with billboards, print media, and digital and video storytelling.

Now and again, Mark wondered, "Should I publish *Arc of a Diver?* "
"Will it change my place in the community?"
As we encountered suicides among our dear ones, it changed to, "Who cares what others think; this offering may help someone."

"We should do this" went the recurring discussion.
Action slowed by the manuscript being 479 typewritten pages.
No computer files... Who will type it?
No time for this now.
Let's take a hike.

The unthinkable happens.
A heart attack takes Mark in a day.

After the shock, *Arc of a Diver* became mine to do.

Bringing an author's writing to press after death? I sought out his writer buddies, especially those with dead writer relatives to sort out weeds. "Should we edit the story written in 1991 to tastes now?"

Would Mark have edited his words? Likely, yes.

How to know what he would change?

Final decision: Mark's not here, best to leave his words as he wrote them.

Almost two years after his passing, I bring *Arc of a Diver* to you as an act of productive grieving to be released in May, 2024, his 67th birthday.

REFLECTION

Mark Woytowich was, in my estimation, a genius of huge proportions! He was gifted at transforming stories of ordinary people into extraordinary video productions. His love of wilderness, water falls, and wild things guided novices into magnificent outdoor adventures in the beautiful Pacific Northwest. His compassion and raucous humor endeared him to people of all backgrounds. His life had a grounded spirituality that never was locked into dogma, rituals, or institutions.

Where did this all come from? I wondered, and then I read this book. Here he details the arduous journey he made as a young adult through the wilderness of his own psyche. I read it in awe of his mastery of metaphors and similes which help the reader feel, through these practical images, the experiences he was having. His path led him from a suicide attempt off the Brooklyn Bridge to the gamut of mental health therapy and practices. Out of it emerged the person whose life made a difference to all who have come to know him.

Pastor Terry Oliver
March, 2024
Shelton, Washington

ACKNOWLEDGEMENTS

Mark for this creation and for his lingering great spirit keeping my fire alive.

Cindy Sund, who when shown the 479 pile of typewritten pages said, "You should do this." That brought an inward Yikes, but it stuck.

Sean McGrady for his valuable guidance and tough love to grasp the difficulty of the task without killing my spirit. Also, for his practical steps for getting it done, like finding online skill hubs, like Reedsy.

Elizabeth Thorlton my publication midwife for magically transforming 479 typewritten pages to a digital clean file, providing the necessary files to cross this finish line.

Dale Hubbard and Terry Oliver, Mark's man buddies, for occasionally visiting me and sharing truth with irreverent cajolery sessions aided by the healing power of laughter and red wine.

Shelton Mason County Journal, especially Justin Johnson, Gordon Weeks, Shawna Whelan, John Lester, Kirk Ericson and Karen Hranac, for providing Mark a way to reach his choir of wild coyotes by publishing his "On the Trail" column.

TrashMashers! Litter Posse, founded by Mark in 2020 to remove trash from wild places, returning them to pristine beauty. Choosing tarnished locations, Mark would also share his hidden gem as a reward. A reminder: this is what we are fighting for. This weirdly brave group knew the best of Mark, in, as it happened his home stretch. TrashMashers have sustained me during this raw time, continuing his work.

Lastly, our friends, family, and cats.

BOOKS BY THIS AUTHOR

Where Waterfalls And Wild Things Are

Colorful descriptions and pinpoint directions to dozens of waterfalls, swimming holes and breathtaking canyons in the southeastern Olympics

ABOUT THE AUTHOR

Mark Woytowich

May 23, 1956 -- May 6, 2022

A writer, always.

A bold storyteller, skirting the edge of appropriate while finding connection between hearts.

Now free from his body, still travels wild places and whispers to us in rushing waters.

Made in the USA
Columbia, SC
05 July 2024

38166305R00220